Simon Scarrow worked as a lecturer before becoming a full-time writer. THE LEGION is his tenth novel about Macro and Cato, heroes of the Roman army; all the earlier Roman novels, including the No. 1 bestsellers CENTURION and THE GLADIATOR, are available from Headline (see inside for a full list of titles).

Simon Scarrow is also the author of a quartet of novels about the lives of the Duke of Wellington and Napoleon Bonaparte. YOUNG BLOODS, THE GENERALS, FIRE AND SWORD and THE FIELDS OF DEATH have been published to warm acclaim.

To find out more about Simon Scarrow and his novels, visit www.scarrow.co.uk.

THE LEGION

SIMON SCARROW

headline

First published in 2010
by HEADLINE PUBLISHING GROUP

First published in paperback in 2011
by HEADLINE PUBLISHING GROUP

7

Cataloguing in Publication Data is available from the British Library

ISBN 978 0 7553 5376 7

Typeset in Bembo by Avon DataSet Ltd,
Bidford-on-Avon, Warwickshire

Printed and bound in Great Britain by
Clays Ltd, St Ives plc

Headline's policy is to use papers that are natural, renewable and
recyclable products and made from wood grown in sustainable forests.
The logging and manufacturing processes are expected to conform
to the environmental regulations of the country of origin.

HEADLINE PUBLISHING GROUP
An Hachette UK Company
338 Euston Road
London NW1 3BH

www.headline.co.uk
www.hachette.co.uk

As ever, I am grateful to my wife, Carolyn, for checking over the script as I worked through the novel, and for putting up with me while I was thoroughly lost 'in' the book. Thanks also to my father, Tony, for casting another set of eyes over the final draft. Much of the background detail was gleaned from various research trips to Egypt and down the Nile. My thanks to Ahmed and Mustafa for sharing their knowledge of their fascinating country. There are few nations with such a rich and ancient heritage and they are rightly proud of Egypt.

THE ROMAN ARMY
CHAIN OF COMMAND

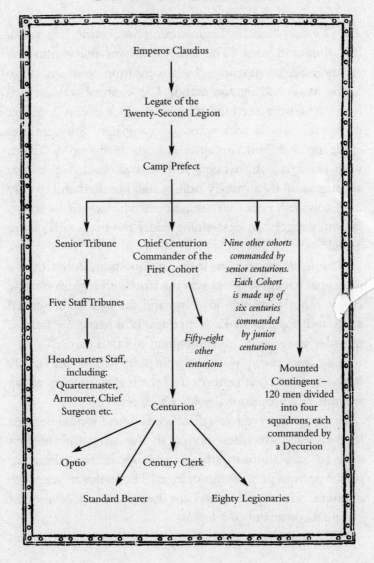

Emperor Claudius

Legate of the
Twenty-Second Legion

Camp Prefect

Senior Tribune

Chief Centurion
Commander of the
First Cohort

*Nine other cohorts
commanded by
senior centurions.
Each Cohort
is made up of
six centuries
commanded by
junior
centurions*

Five Staff Tribunes

Headquarters Staff,
including:
Quartermaster,
Armourer, Chief
Surgeon etc.

*Fifty-eight
other
centurions*

Mounted
Contingent –
120 men divided
into four
squadrons, each
commanded by
a Decurion

Centurion

Optio

Century Clerk

Standard Bearer

Eighty Legionaries

The Organisation of a Roman Legion

The Twenty-Second Legion comprised some five and a half thousand men. The basic unit was the century of eighty men commanded by a centurion with an optio acting as second in command. The century was divided into eight-man sections which shared a room together in barracks and a tent when on campaign. Six centuries made up a cohort, and ten cohorts made up a legion, with the first cohort being double-size. Each legion was accompanied by a cavalry unit of one hundred and twenty men, divided into four squadrons, who served as scouts and messengers. In descending order the main ranks were as follows:

The *legate* was a man from an equestrian rather than a senatorial background, as was the case with legions outside Egypt. The legate would command the legion for several years and hope to make something of a name for himself in order to enhance his subsequent political career.

The *camp prefect* was a veteran who would previously have been the chief centurion of the legion and was at the summit of a professional soldier's career.

Six *tribunes* served as staff officers. These would be men in their early twenties serving in the army for the first time to gain administrative experience before taking up junior posts in civil administration. The senior tribune was different. He was destined for high political office and eventual command of a legion.

Sixty *centurions* provided the disciplinary and training

backbone of the legion. They were hand-picked for their command qualities. The most senior centurion commanded the First Century of the First Cohort.

The four *decurions* of the legion commanded the cavalry squadrons and hoped for promotion to the command of auxiliary cavalry units.

Each centurion was assisted by an *optio* who would act as an orderly, with minor command duties. Optios would be waiting for a vacancy in the centurionate.

Below the optios were the *legionaries*, men who had signed on for twenty-five years. In theory, a man had to be a Roman citizen to qualify for enlistment, but recruits were increasingly drawn from local populations and given Roman citizenship on joining the legions.

Lower in status than the legionaries were the men of the *auxiliary cohorts*. These were recruited from the provinces and provided the Roman Empire with its cavalry, light infantry and other specialist skills. Roman citizenship was awarded on completion of twenty-five years of service.

The Imperial Roman Navy

The Romans came to naval warfare rather late in the day and it was not until the reign of Augustus (27 BC – 14 AD) that they established a standing navy. The main strength was divided into two fleets, based at Misenum and Ravenna, with smaller fleets based in Alexandria and other large ports around the Mediterranean. As well as keeping the peace at sea, the navy was tasked with patrolling the great rivers of the Empire such as the Rhine, the Danube and, of course, the Nile.

Each fleet was commanded by a *prefect*. Previous naval experience was not a requirement and the post was largely administrative in nature.

Below the rank of prefect the huge influence of Greek naval practice on the imperial fleets is evident. The squadron commanders were called *navarchs* and commanded ten ships. Navarchs, like the centurions of the legions, were the senior officers on permanent tenure. If they wished, they could apply for transfer into the legions at the rank of centurion. The senior navarch in the fleet was known as the *Navarchus Princeps*, who functioned like the senior centurion of a legion, offering technical advice to the prefect when required.

The ships were commanded by *trierarchs*. Like the navarchs, they were promoted from the ranks and were responsible for the running of individual ships. However, their role did not correspond to that of a modern sea captain. They were in charge of the sailing of the ship but, in battle, the senior figure was actually the officer in charge of the ship's complement of marines.

As far as the ships go, the most common class of vessel was the small patrol galley, usually termed a liburnian. These were propelled by oars or sails and had a small complement of marines. In the same class was the bireme, somewhat larger and more capable of holding its own in battle. The larger warships, the triremes, quadrimes and quinquiremes, were something of a rarity by the age in which this book is set, relics of a bygone age of naval warfare.

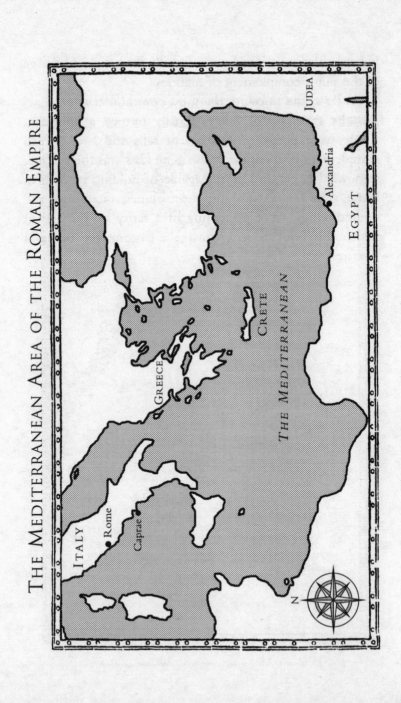

THE MEDITERRANEAN AREA OF THE ROMAN EMPIRE

ITALY
Rome
Caprae

GREECE

CRETE

THE MEDITERRANEAN

JUDEA

Alexandria

EGYPT

N

THE ROMAN PROVINCE OF EGYPT
IN THE FIRST CENTURY

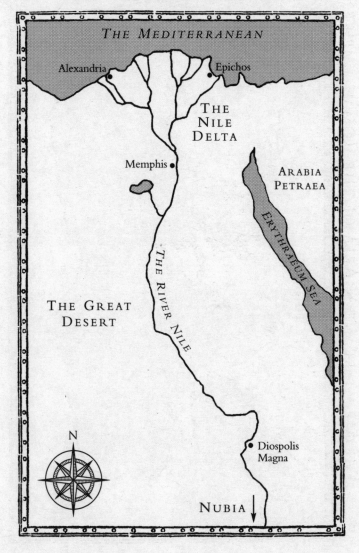

CHAPTER ONE

The commander of the naval supply station at Epichos was having his morning meal when the optio in charge of the dawn watch made his report. A light drizzle – the first rain in months – had been falling since first light and the optio's cloak was covered with droplets that looked like tiny beads of glass.

'What is it, Septimus?' Trierarch Philipus asked tersely, dipping a hunk of bread into a small bowl of garum sauce in front of him. It was his custom to walk his rounds of the small fort and then return to his quarters to have his breakfast, without interruption.

'Beg to report a ship has been sighted, sir. Heading along the coast towards us.'

'A ship, eh? Just happens to be passing along one of the busiest sea lanes in the Empire.' Philipus took a deep breath to cover his impatience. 'And the marine on watch thinks that's unusual?'

'It's a warship, sir. And it's making for the entrance to the bay.' The optio ignored the sarcasm and continued to deliver his report in the same deadpan voice that he had used ever since the trierarch had taken command of the outpost nearly two years ago. At first Philipus had been delighted at the promotion. Before, he had commanded a

1

sleek liburnian warship in the Alexandrian flotilla and had grown heartily sick of the stifling lack of opportunity that went with being a junior officer commanding a small vessel that rarely ventured out of the port's eastern harbour. The appointment to the small naval station at Epichos had given him independence, and at first Philipus had striven to make his supply station a model of efficiency. But, as the months dragged on, there had been no sign of any excitement and the men of the station had little to do beyond provisioning the warships or imperial packets that occasionally entered the small, low-lying harbour as they made their way along the coast of Egypt. The only other duty Philipus had to discharge was to send a regular patrol up the Nile delta to remind the natives that they lived under the watchful gaze of their Roman masters.

And so Philipus eked out his days commanding a half century of marines and as many sailors, together with an old bireme – the *Anubis* – that had once served in the fleet that Cleopatra had taken to support her lover, Mark Antony, in his war against Octavian. After Antony's defeat at Actium, the bireme had been absorbed into the Roman navy and served with the Alexandrian fleet before it was finally sent to end its days at Epichos, beached in front of the small mud-brick fort that overlooked the bay.

It was a dismal posting, Philipus reflected. The coastline of the Nile delta was low and featureless, and much of the bay was taken up by mangroves where crocodiles lurked, lying still like fallen palm logs as they waited for any prey to come close enough to be rushed. The trierarch lived in hope of adventure. However, he mused, the nearest he would ever get to that this day was overseeing the loading of biscuit, water and any supplies of cordage, sail or spars on to the new arrival. Hardly worth disturbing his breakfast for.

'A warship, eh?' Philipus bit off some bread and chewed. 'Well, it's probably on patrol.'

'I don't think so, sir,' said Optio Septimus. 'I've checked the station's log book and no warships are due to put into Epichos for at least a month.'

'Then it's been sent on some detached duty,' Philipus continued dismissively. 'The captain has made a landfall to pick up water and rations.'

'Shall I order the men to arms, sir?'

Philipus looked up sharply. 'Why? What's the point?'

'Standing orders, sir. If an unknown vessel is sighted, the garrison is to be alerted.'

'It's not an unknown vessel, is it? It's a warship. We are the only people who operate warships in the eastern Mediterranean. Therefore it's not unknown, and there's no need to trouble the men, Optio.'

Septimus stood his ground. 'Unless the ship is making a scheduled call, it is unknown, according to the book, sir.'

'The book?' Philipus puffed his cheeks. 'Look here, Optio, if there is any sign of hostility then you can call out the garrison. Meanwhile, inform the quartermaster that we have a visitor and that he and his staff are to be ready to revictual the warship. Now, if I may, I'll finish my breakfast. Dismissed.'

'Yes, sir.' The optio stood to attention, saluted and turned to stride down the short colonnade towards the exit to the commander's quarters. Philipus sighed. He felt guilty about treating the man with disdain. Septimus was a good junior officer, efficient, even if he wasn't terribly imaginative. He had been right to cite standing orders, the same orders that Philipus had carefully penned in the early days of his appointment when the first flush of enthusiasm for his new post had governed his actions.

Philipus finished the last mouthful of bread, drained his watered wine and rose to make his way to his sleeping chamber. He paused by the pegs on the wall, and then reached for his breastplate and helmet. It would be as well to greet the commander of the ship formally, and to ensure that he was efficiently served, so that a favourable impression was conveyed back to the fleet in Alexandria. As long as his record was good, there was always a chance that he might be promoted to a more prestigious command, and could leave Epichos behind him.

Philipus tied his chinstrap and adjusted his helmet, then slipped his sword belt over his shoulder and strode out of his quarters. The fort at Epichos was small, barely fifty paces along each wall. The mud-brick walls were ten feet high and would present little obstacle to any enemy who decided to attack the supply base. In any case, the walls themselves were cracked and crumbling and could be knocked down with ease. In truth, there was no danger of any attack, Philipus mused. The Roman navy commanded the seas, and the nearest threats by land were the kingdom of Nubia, hundreds of miles to the south, and sundry bands of Arab brigands who occasionally raided the more isolated settlements along the upper Nile.

The trierarch's quarters were at one end of the fort, flanked by the granary and the warehouse for ship's stores. Six barrack blocks lined the street running down the middle of the fort towards the gatehouse. A pair of sentries unhurriedly stood to attention at his approach and presented their spears as Philipus passed between them and left the fort. Although the sky above was clear, a thin mist hung across the bay, thickening where it lay over the mangroves so that the tangle of rushes, palms and shrubs assumed a vague spectral form which Philipus had found a little disturbing when he had first arrived. Since then, he had frequently joined the river patrols and had become used to the early-morning mists that often cloaked the Nile delta.

Outside the fort lay a long strip of beach, reaching round the bay towards the mangrove. In the other direction it gave way to a rocky strip of land that curved out towards the sea, creating a fine natural harbour. Directly in front of the fort lay the beached bireme, which came with the command. The chief carpenter had lavished many months of his time on the old warship and he and his men had replaced worn and rotting timbers and applied fresh tar to the hull and re-rigged the mast and spars. The sides had been repainted with an elaborate eye design at the bows. The ship was ready to put to sea, but Philipus doubted that this veteran of Actium would ever see action again. A short distance to one side of the *Anubis* a sturdy wooden jetty projected from the shore forty or so paces out into the bay to allow visiting ships to moor alongside.

Although the sun had not yet risen above the mist, the air was warm and Philipus hoped that he could quickly dispense with any formalities arising from the arrival of the ship and remove his breastplate and helmet. He turned and strode along the dusty track that led towards the look-out post. The small tower was built on a rocky outcrop on the strip of land forming the natural breakwater of the harbour. At the end of the strip another, sturdier, watch-tower guarded the entrance. Four bolt throwers were mounted on the walls, together with a brazier, so that any enemy vessel entering the narrow channel leading into the harbour could be subjected to the torment of incendiary fire.

When he reached the lookout post, Philipus entered the shelter at the bottom and saw three of his marines sitting at a bench, chatting in muted tones as they ate their bread and dried fish. As soon as they saw him they rose and saluted.

'Easy, boys.' Philipus smiled. 'Who reported the approach of the warship?'

'Me, sir,' one of the marines said.

'All right then, Horio, lead the way.'

The marine lowered his bread into his mess tin and crossed the interior of the tower and climbed the ladder leading to the roof. The trierarch followed him and emerged on to the platform, next to the signal brazier, made up and ready to be lit at a moment's notice. A section of the space was sheltered by a roof of thatched palm leaves. The sentry who had replaced Horio stood at the weathered wooden rail, gazing out to sea. Philipus joined him and Horio and stared towards the ship approaching the entrance of the bay. The crew were busy furling the sail, a wine-red spread of goatskin decorated with the broad wings of an eagle. A moment later the sail had been lashed up and oar blades extended from the sides of the vessel and dipped down into the light swell. There was a brief pause before the order to take up the stroke was given and then the oars rose, swept forward and down, cutting into the water and thrusting the bows of the ship forwards.

Philipus turned to Horio. 'Which direction did it come from, before it made towards land?'

'From the west, sir.'

The trierarch nodded to himself. From the direction of Alexandria, then. Which was odd, since no warship was due to pay a visit to the outpost for at least another month, when it would drop off despatches and the quarterly pay chest. Philipus watched as the ship passed by the tower guarding the entrance of the harbour and continued across the calm waters towards the jetty. He could see the sailors and marines lining the sides as they surveyed the bay. In the wooden turret at the front of the vessel a tall figure in a plumed helmet stood erect, hands spread out on the rail in front of him as he stared towards the jetty and the fort beyond.

A movement over by the fort caught Philipus's attention and he saw Septimus and the quartermaster, together with a small escort of sailors, making their way down to the jetty.

'Best join the reception committee,' he mused. Philipus took a last look at the ship crossing the bay, a picture of efficient grace against the tranquil backdrop of distant mangrove. Then he turned to climb down the ladder.

By the time he had returned to the end of the jetty, the warship had slowed and the order to backwater carried clearly to the three officers and the sailors as they advanced down the jetty to greet their visitors. The rowers held their oars in the water and the resistance of the blades quickly killed the forward motion of the vessel.

'Ship oars!'

There was a dull rumble of timber as the oars withdrew through the slots on each side of the ship and it continued to glide round towards the jetty as the men on the tiller steered the liburnian alongside. Philipus could see the officer in the turret clearly now: tall and broadshouldered, younger looking than he expected. He stood impassively as his trierarch bellowed the orders for the sailors to make ready their mooring ropes. As the ship edged towards the jetty, ropes snaked through the air from the men in the bows and Philipus's men caught them and heaved the vessel alongside, until the side creaked up against the bundles of woven reeds that protected the jetty's posts. Another line was tossed to the men waiting near the stern and a moment later the ship was securely moored.

The officer descended from the turret and strode across the deck as his sailors opened the side port and slid a gangway on to the jetty. A squad of marines had formed up nearby and the officer gestured towards them as he stepped across on to the jetty. Philipus strode forward to greet him, extending a hand.

'I'm the commander of the supply station, Trierarch Philipus.'

The officer took his hand in a powerful grip and nodded curtly. 'Centurion Macro, on secondment to the Alexandrian flotilla. We need to talk, in your headquarters.'

Philipus could not help raising his eyebrows in surprise and he was aware of his subordinates exchanging an uneasy look at his side.

'Talk? Has something happened?'

'My orders are to discuss the matter with you in private.' The officer nodded towards the other men on the jetty. 'Not in front of anyone else. Please lead the way.'

Philipus was taken aback by the younger officer's terse manner. The man was no doubt a recent arrival from Rome, and therefore inclined to treat the local military with a haughty arrogance that was typical of his kind. 'Very well, Centurion, this way.'

Philipus turned and began to make his way along the jetty.

'Just a moment,' said Centurion Macro. He turned to the marines waiting on the deck. 'With me!'

They crossed the gangway and formed up behind the centurion, twenty armed marines, all burly men with powerful physiques. Philipus frowned. He had been expecting to exchange a few pleasantries and some news before he gave the order for his quartermaster to see to the ship's needs. Not this brusque encounter. What could the officer have to tell him that was so important that it had to be said in private? With a stab of anxiety Philipus wondered if he had been wrongly implicated in some crime or plot. He gestured to the officer to follow him and the small column made its way towards the shore. Philipus slowed his pace until he was at the side of the centurion and addressed him quietly. 'Can you tell me what this is about?'

'Yes, shortly.' The officer glanced at him and smiled

slightly. 'Nothing that need worry you unduly, Trierarch. I just need to ask you some questions.'

Philipus was not reassured by the reply and kept his silence as they reached the end of the jetty and marched up to the gates of the fort. The sentries stood to as the officers and marines approached.

'I don't imagine you get many ships calling in here,' said Centurion Macro.

'Not many,' Philipus replied, hoping that the other man was revealing a more conversational aspect of his seemingly cold character. 'Occasional naval patrols, and imperial couriers. Other than that, a few ships with storm damage over the winter months, but that's about it. Epichos has become something of a backwater. I wouldn't be surprised if the governor in Alexandria didn't reduce our establishment one day.'

The centurion glanced at him. 'Fishing for information about my being here?'

Philipus looked at him and shrugged. 'Of course.'

They had entered the fort and Centurion Macro stopped and looked around. The place was quiet. Most of the men were in barracks. The night watch was finishing off their morning meal and were preparing to rest. Some of the other men were sitting on stools outside their barracks, playing at dice or talking quietly. Centurion Macro's eyes keenly took in the details.

'A nice quiet posting you have here, Philipus. Quite out of the way. Even so, I imagine you are well provisioned.'

Philipus nodded. 'We have ample grain and ship's stores. Just not much call for it these days.'

'Perfect,' Centurion Macro muttered. He turned and nodded to the optio in command of the party of marines. 'Time to proceed, Karim.'

The optio nodded and turned to his men. 'Take 'em.'

As Philipus watched, four of the marines abruptly drew their swords and moved back towards the sentries on the gate. They just had time to turn at the sound of the men approaching before they were cut down with a savage flurry of blows; they had no chance to even cry out before they were killed. Philipus stared in horror as the bodies slumped to the ground either side of the gateway. He turned, aghast, to Centurion Macro.

The man smiled at him. There was a light rasp, a blur of movement and the trierarch felt a sudden blow in his stomach, as if he had been punched, hard. There was another blow that left him gasping in agony. Philipus looked down and saw the other man's hand clenched round the handle of a knife. An inch of blade showed before it disappeared into the fold of his tunic, just below the bottom of his breastplate. A red stain spread through the cloth even as Philipus stared down at it in numbed incomprehension. The centurion twisted the blade, tearing through vital organs. Philipus gasped for breath and grasped the knife arm in both hands. 'What? What are you doing?'

The centurion withdrew his blade and Philipus felt a quick rush of blood as it poured out of the wound. He released his grip as he felt his legs buckle and he collapsed on to his knees, staring up at the centurion in mute horror. Through the gateway he could see the bodies of the sentries and, beyond, one of the marines striding into clear view in front of the fort and punching his sword up into the air three times. This must have been a prearranged signal, Philipus realised, and a moment later there was a cheer from the liburnian as men who had previously been hidden along the deck swarmed over the side on to the jetty. Philipus saw the quartermaster try to draw his sword, but he was overwhelmed with a glinting series of sword blows, as were the stunned optio and the sailors. They were dead even before they could draw their weapons. Their assailants rushed along the jetty and up towards the entrance to the fort.

Philipus slumped against the wall of the gatehouse and unbuckled his breastplate. He let the armour drop to one side and pressed his hands over the wound with a groan. The officer who had stabbed him stood nearby. He had sheathed his dagger and was shouting orders at his men as they rushed into the fort, cutting down any opponents they could find. Philipus looked on, in agony. His marines and sailors were being butchered in front of his eyes. Those who had been playing dice outside the barracks, and others who had emerged at the first sounds of fighting, now lay dead. Muffled cries and shouts from the barracks told of those who were being killed inside. At the end of the street a handful of men who had snatched up their swords tried to stand their ground but were no match for their skilled opponents who parried their blades aside and struck them down.

The centurion looked round the fort and nodded with satisfaction, then turned and gazed down at Philipus.

The trierarch cleared his throat. 'Who are you?'

'What does it matter?' The man shrugged. 'You will be dead soon. Think on that.'

Philipus shook his head, already he could see spidery dark shadows at the fringes of his vision. He felt giddy, and his hands were now slick with blood as he failed to stem the flow. He licked his lips. 'Who?'

The man untied his chinstrap and removed his helmet before squatting down at Philipus's side. His hair was dark and curly and the light line of a scar marked his brow and cheek. He was powerfully built and well balanced as he sat poised on his haunches. He looked into the trierarch's eyes steadily. 'If it is any comfort to give a name to death, then know that it was Ajax, son of Telemachus, who killed you and your men.'

'Ajax,' Philipus repeated. He swallowed and muttered. 'Why?'

'Because you are my enemy. Rome is my enemy. I will kill Romans until I am killed. That is the way of things. Now, prepare yourself.'

He stood up and drew his sword. Philipus's eyes widened into a frightened stare. He threw up a bloodied hand. 'No!'

Ajax frowned. 'You are already dead. Face it with dignity.'

Philipus was still for a moment and then he lowered his hand and turned his head up and to the side, baring his throat. He clenched his eyes shut. Ajax drew back his arm, aimed the point just above the notch in the trierarch's collarbone, and then drove the blade in with a powerful thrust. He ripped the sword free and a jet of crimson spurted out. Philipus's eyes snapped open, his mouth sagged and he gurgled briefly before he bled out, limbs trembling, then he was still. Ajax used the sleeve of the dead man's tunic to wipe his sword clean and then sheathed it with a metallic snap.

'Karim!'

One of his men, a dark-featured easterner, came trotting forward. 'Sir?'

'Take five men, work through the buildings. Kill the wounded and any others that may have been missed. Have the bodies rowed across the bay and dumped in the mangrove. The crocodiles will make short work of them.'

Karim nodded, then looked above the head of his leader and thrust out his arm. 'Look!'

Ajax turned and saw a thin trail of smoke rising up into the clear sky beyond the wall of the fort. 'That's the watchtower. They've fired their signal beacon.' Ajax looked round quickly and waved over two of his lieutenants. He addressed a tall, muscular Nubian first. 'Hepithus, take your squad to the lookout post at the double. Kill the men and put the fire out quick as you can. Canthus, take the tower at the head of the bay.'

Hepithus nodded and turned to bellow the order to his men to follow him, before running back through the gate. The other man, Canthus, had dark features and had once been an actor in Rome before he was condemned to the arena for seducing the wife of a prominent and vindictive senator. He smiled at Ajax and beckoned the other party to follow him. Ajax stood aside to let them pass, and then strode across to the wooden steps that led up on to the wall of the fort. From there he entered the gatehouse and a moment later emerged on to the tower platform. He surveyed the supply station and took in the fort, the bay, the small river craft drawn up on the sand a short distance from the mangrove where a stretch of river led inland. In the other direction he watched as Hepithus and his men stormed into the lookout post and extinguished the signal fire. The smoke trail that marked the sky began to disperse.

Ajax scratched the stubble on his jaw as he considered his situation. For months he and his men had been on the run from their Roman pursuers. They had been compelled to seek isolated bays on the coast and watch the horizon of the sea for any sign of the enemy. When supplies had run low, the ship had emerged from hiding to snap up lone merchant vessels or raid small coastal settlements. Twice they had seen Roman warships. The first time, the Romans had turned to pursue them and had chased Ajax and his men into the night before the fugitives changed course and then doubled back, losing their pursuers by dawn. The second time, Ajax had watched from a rocky islet as two ships sailed past the hidden cove where his vessel had lain hidden, palm fronds tied to the mast to disguise it.

The strain of being on the run for so long had taken its toll on his followers. They were still loyal to him and followed his orders without complaint, but Ajax knew that some were beginning to lose hope. They could not long endure a life where they lived in daily fear of capture and crucifixion. They needed a new sense of purpose, like they had once enjoyed when they followed him during the slave revolt on Crete. Ajax looked round at the supply base and nodded with satisfaction. He had taken a second ship, together with stockpiles of food and equipment that would last for many months. The outpost would be a perfect base from which to continue his struggle against the Roman Empire. Ajax's expression hardened as he recalled the suffering that Rome had inflicted upon him and his followers. Years of hard slavery and the perils of life as a gladiator. Rome must be made to pay, Ajax resolved. As long as his men were willing to follow him, he would take the war to their enemy.

'This will do for now,' he said softly to himself as he considered the supply base. 'This will do very nicely indeed.'

CHAPTER TWO

Centurion Macro swung his legs over the side of the cot and then stretched his shoulders with a grunt before he carefully rose to his feet. Even though Macro was short and stocky, he still had to bow his head to avoid cracking it on the deck timbers above. The cabin, tucked into the angle at the stern of the warship, was cramped. Just large enough to fit his cot, a small table with a chest beneath it, and the pegs on which hung his tunic, armour, helmet and sword. He scratched his backside through the linen of his loincloth and yawned.

'Bloody warships,' he grumbled. 'Who in their right mind would ever volunteer to join the navy?'

He had been on board for over two months now and was beginning to doubt that the small force despatched to hunt down the fugitive gladiator and his surviving followers would ever find them. The last sighting of Ajax's ship had been over a month before, off the coast of Egypt. The Romans had followed, once catching sight of a sail on the horizon, only to lose contact during the following night. Since then the search for the fugitives had proved fruitless. The two Roman vessels had searched along the African coast as far as Lepcis Magna before turning about and heading east, scouring the coastline for any sign of Ajax and his men. They had passed by Alexandria two days earlier, low on provisions, but Cato – the prefect in charge of the mission – had been determined to push his men on to the limit before breaking off the search to resupply his vessels. Now Centurion Macro was hungry, frustrated and fed up with the whole business.

He pulled his tunic over his head and climbed up the narrow flight of steps on to the deck. He went barefoot as he had quickly discovered the disadvantages of wearing army boots on a warship. The neatly sandstoned decks provided little grip whenever they got wet and Macro and the other soldiers had a hard time keeping on their feet with iron nails on the soles of their boots. Two centuries of legionaries had been assigned to the warships to augment the strength of the marines; a necessary measure since Ajax and his followers, most of whom were former gladiators like their leader, were more than a match for even the finest soldiers in the Roman army.

As soon as the trierarch saw Macro emerge on deck, he approached him and nodded a greeting.

'A fine morning, sir.'

'Is it?' Macro scowled. 'I'm on a small, crowded ship, surrounded by the briny and without even a jar of wine for company. Fine doesn't enter into it.'

The trierarch, Polemo, pursed his lips and looked round. The sky was almost clear, only a handful of brilliant white clouds drifted overhead. A soft breeze filled the sail with a satisfying bulge, like an over-indulged epicurean, and there was a gentle swell on the sea so that the ship rose and fell in a regular, comfortable rhythm. To the right the thin strip of coastline stretched out peacefully. To the left the horizon was clear. A quarter of a mile ahead lay the stern of the other ship, leaving a creamy churn of water in its wake. All in all, as good a day as a sailor could wish for, the trierarch mused.

'Anything to report?' asked Macro.

'Yes, sir. The last barrel of salted mutton was broached this morning. The hard bread will be exhausted tomorrow and I've halved the water ration.' The trierarch refrained from offering any advice on the troubling supply situation. The decision on what to do about it was not his, nor even Macro's. It was up to the prefect to give the orders to put into the nearest port and reprovision the ships.

'Hmmm.' Macro frowned. Both men glanced towards the leading warship, as if trying to read the mind of Prefect Cato. The prefect had conducted the hunt with a hard-driving obsession. One that Macro could understand easily enough. He had served with Cato for some years now, as his superior until very recently. Cato's promotion had been deserved, Macro accepted readily enough, but it still felt peculiar to have their former relationship inverted. Cato was in his early twenties, a slender, sinewy figure that belied his toughness and courage. He also possessed the brains to plot his way through the dangers that had faced them over recent years. If Macro had to choose a man to follow, it would be someone like Cato. Having served for nearly fifteen years in the Roman legions before being promoted to the rank of centurion, Macro had enough experience to spot potential and yet he had been wrong about Cato, he reflected with a rueful smile. When Cato had trudged into the fortress of the Second Legion on the Rhine frontier, Macro had thought that the skinny youth was hardly likely to survive the hard training that lay ahead. Yet Cato had proved him wrong. He had shown determination, intelligence and above all courage and had saved Macro's life in his first skirmish with a German tribe raiding across the great river that marked the boundary of the Empire. Since then, Cato had proved himself to be a first-rate soldier again and again, as well as the closest friend Macro had ever had. Now, Cato had won promotion to the rank of prefect and for the first time he was Macro's superior. It was an arrangement that both men were struggling to get used to.

The prefect's determination to track down Ajax was as much motivated by a desire for revenge as it was by the need to carry out his orders. Even though he had been tasked with taking Ajax alive if possible, and delivering him to Rome in chains, Cato felt little inclination to do so. During the slave rebellion on Crete, Ajax had captured the woman betrothed to Cato. Julia had been kept in a cage, and left to endure in her own filth and in rags while Ajax had tormented her with the prospect of her torture and death. Macro had been captured at the same time and had shared the same cage, and his thirst for vengeance was almost as powerful as that of his superior.

The trierarch cleared his throat. 'Do you think he'll give the order to put in for supplies today, sir?'

'Who knows?' Macro shrugged. 'After yesterday's little incident, I'm not so sure.'

The trierarch nodded. The previous evening the two ships had made towards a small coastal village to anchor for the night. As they had approached the shore the inhabitants of the cluster of mud-brick buildings had fled inland, taking their valuables and as much food as they could carry. A party of legionaries had cautiously searched the village and had come back empty-handed. No one had remained behind and any food had been carefully concealed. The only sign of something out of the ordinary was a number of freshly dug graves and the burned-out remains of a handful of buildings. With no one to interrogate, the legionaries had returned to the ships and during the night they had been attacked with slingshot. Macro had only been able to see a handful of dark figures against the lighter loom of the beach. The rap of stones on the hulls and decks and the plop of the shot landing in the water had continued all night. Two of the marines had been injured before the rest of the men were ordered to keep down. The sporadic attack ended shortly before dawn and the two ships had set sail at first light to continue searching for Ajax.

'Deck there!' the lookout called from the top of the mast. 'The *Sobek* is spilling her wind!'

The trierach and Macro stared forward. The sail of the other ship was billowing as the crew released the main sheets to slow the ship.

'Looks like the prefect wants to confer,' the trierarch suggested.

'We'll know soon enough. Bring us alongside,' ordered Macro. Then he turned and made his way back to the cabin to retrieve his sword and vine cane and put on his boots so that he would be more presentable in front of his superior. By the time he had returned to the deck, his own ship, the *Ibis*, was closing up on the other vessel's quarter. He could see Cato at the stern, cupping his hands together as he called across the swell.

'Centurion Macro! Come aboard!'

'Yes, sir!' Macro shouted back and nodded to the trierarch. 'Polemo, I'll need the tender.'

'Aye, sir.' The officer turned to order his sailors to raise the ship's boat from its cradle on the main deck. While several strained on a pulley rope, others steered the small boat over the side and then it was lowered into the sea. Six men clambered down and took up the oars and then Macro descended the rope ladder and cautiously made his way to the stern seat and sat quickly. A moment later the craft shoved off and the sailors heaved on their oars, propelling the boat towards the *Sobek*. As they approached the side, one of the sailors lowered his oar, took up a boat hook and caught the rope looped either side of the gap in the ship's rail. Macro clambered forward, steadied himself and waited for the boat to rise on the swell, then launched himself at the ladder hanging down the ship's side. He climbed quickly, before the swell passed and dunked him in the sea. Cato was waiting for him.

'Walk with me.'

They made their way to the bows where Cato curtly ordered a couple of sailors aft so that the two officers would not be overheard. Macro felt a pang of concern as he noted his friend's gaunt features. It had been several days since they had last spoken face to face and once again Macro noted the dark patches round the young man's eyes. Cato leaned forward and rested an elbow on the thick timber of the bulwark as he turned to face Macro.

'What is your supply situation?'

'We can last another two days if I put the men on quarter water allowance. After that they won't be good for anything, even if we do find Ajax, sir.'

A flicker of pained irritation crossed Cato's face at Macro's reference to his superior rank. He coughed. 'Look here, Macro, you can drop the "sir" when no one's listening. We know each other well enough for that.'

Macro glanced round at the men further along the deck and turned back. 'You're a prefect now, my lad, and the men will expect me to treat you as such.'

'By all means. But when I need to speak frankly to you, in private, then we speak as friends, all right?'

'Is that an order?' Macro replied sternly and then his lips could not help lifting a little, betraying his real mood. Cato raised his eyes. 'Spare me the aggrieved feelings of a former fellow centurion, eh?'

Macro nodded and smiled. 'All right then. So, what's the plan?'

Cato concentrated his weary mind. 'Ajax's trail has grown cold. The men need a rest.'

'And so do you.'

Cato ignored the comment and continued. 'Both ships are all but out of supplies. We will turn about and make for Alexandria. We're three days out so we'll need to find somewhere to take on water and rations. I just hope we don't meet the same reception we had yesterday.' He frowned and shook his head. 'That was strange.'

'Perhaps they took us for tax collectors.' Macro shrugged. 'Can't say that I'm impressed by the hospitality of the natives. Hope we get better treatment in Alexandria. If all the gypos are as friendly as that lot then I shall be glad when the chase is over and we get back to Rome, eh?'

'That might not be for some time yet, Macro. Our orders are clear. We are to hunt Ajax down, whatever the cost, and however long it takes. And that's what we will do until we are issued new orders. No Roman province, nor even Emperor Claudius, can afford to rest easy while Ajax and his followers are still at large. You've seen at first hand how he inspires his followers. He could raise the standard of rebellion anywhere across the Empire, and the slaves would flock to his side. While Ajax lives he is a grave threat to the Empire. If Rome falls, there will be chaos and everyone who lived under the protection of the legions, free and slave alike, will fall prey to barbarian invaders. That's why we must find and destroy Ajax. Besides, we owe him personally, you and me.'

'Fair enough. But what if he's given us the slip? Ajax could be anywhere. He could be at the other end of the Mediterranean, or up in the Black Sea. He might even have abandoned his ship and headed inland. If that's the case then we've as much chance of finding him as finding a straight lawyer in the Subura quarter of Rome. Speaking of which, you have a pretty good reason to return there as soon as possible.' Macro lowered his voice. 'After all that's happened, Julia's going to need you at her side.'

Cato glanced away, down into the blue depths of the sea. 'Julia has been in my thoughts almost every day, Macro. I think of her, and then I imagine her in that cage Ajax kept the pair of you in. It torments my mind, picturing what she went through.'

'We both went through the same thing,' Macro replied

gently. 'And I'm still here. Still the same Macro as ever was.'

Cato looked up at him sharply, his gaze intense. 'Really? I wonder.'

'What do you mean?'

'I know you well enough to see how bitter you are, Macro.'

'Bitter? And why not? After what that bastard put us through.'

'And what did he put you through? What exactly? You haven't told me much about it. Neither did Julia before we left Crete.'

Macro watched him closely. 'Did you ask her?'

'No . . . I didn't want to remind her of it.'

'Or is it that you didn't want to know?' Macro shook his head sadly. 'You didn't ask, and now you are forced to imagine instead. Is that it?'

Cato stared at him and then nodded. 'Something like that, and the fact that I did nothing to help you.'

'There was nothing you could do. Nothing.' Macro rested his elbows on the bulwark. 'Don't take it out on yourself, Cato. That won't achieve anything. It won't help you catch Ajax. Besides, all you have to know is that Julia is a strong woman. Whatever she went through, give her some time and she'll cope with it.'

'Like you have?'

'I'll deal with it in my own way,' Macro said firmly. 'If the gods see fit to place Ajax in my path, then I'll carve his fucking balls off and ram them down his throat before I finish with him. I swear it by every god that I have ever prayed to.'

Cato raised his eyebrows and gave a dry chuckle. 'Sounds like you've managed to put it all behind you.'

Macro frowned. 'I will, when it's all over.'

'And until then?'

'We don't rest until we've carried out our orders.'

'Good. That's settled.' Cato eased himself up. 'Then I'd better give the orders to turn the ships about and make for Alexandria.'

Macro stood to attention and saluted. 'Yes, sir.'

The moment of companionship was at an end, Cato accepted sadly. They were prefect and centurion once more. He nodded at Macro and raised his voice, as if he was an actor declaiming in front of an audience. 'Very well, Centurion. Return to your ship and take station behind the *Sobek*.'

They turned back towards the main deck and had almost reached the base of the mast when the lookout's voice called from above.

'Sail sighted!'

Cato halted and tipped his head back. 'Where away?'

The lookout thrust his hand out, pointing off the port bow, out to sea. 'Over there, sir. Hull down. Eight, maybe ten miles.'

Cato turned to Macro with an excited gleam in his eye. 'Let's hope it's our man.'

'I doubt it,' Macro replied. 'But he might have seen or heard something of Ajax.'

'That's good enough for me. Now back to your ship and make sail. I'll close on him from the sea, you from the direction of the coast. There'll be nowhere for him to run, whoever it turns out to be.'

CHAPTER THREE

The ship made no attempt to evade the two warships and seemed to wallow, directionless, on the sea. As the crew furled the sail and used oars to manoeuvre closer, Cato could see that the sail was billowing freely. The sheets had been set loose or cut, he decided. The wide beam and high stern were those of a cargo ship and Cato felt briefly disappointed that he had been cheated of finding his prey. There was no sign of life on the deck, and the steering paddle rocked gently from side to side as the waves sloshed against the hull.

To landward, Macro's ship was making the best use of the offshore breeze to close swiftly before using oars, although he would reach the cargo vessel a short time after the *Sobek*.

'Shall I form my lads up, sir?' asked Centurion Proculus, the commander of the legionaries assigned to the prefect's ship.

'No. I'll use the marines. They're trained for boarding actions.'

Proculus breathed in sharply, offended at having to give way to men he considered his inferiors. Cato ignored him, well used to the tensions between the two services. Besides, the decision was his. He turned to the decurion in charge of the ship's complement of thirty marines. 'Diodorus, have your men formed up ready to board.'

'Yes, sir. Shall I deploy the corvus?' He nodded to the contraption lashed to the deck in front of the mast. The corvus was a gangway, which was raised and lowered by a pulley. A wooden pin at one end allowed it to pivot round, over the side of the vessel. At the far end was an iron spike like a crow's beak. When the device was in position above the target vessel's deck, it was released and the spike would slam down, piercing the deck and pinning both ships together while the marines rushed across and into action. Although there was no sign of life, Cato decided to stick to convention in case there was a trap waiting to be sprung.

'Yes. Use the corvus. If you need to be reinforced we can send over the legionaries to settle the issue.'

Proculus puffed up his chest. 'We'll get the marines out of any trouble, sir. You can depend on us.'

'Glad to hear it,' Diodorus muttered sourly as he made off to issue his orders.

As the *Sobek* closed on the cargo ship, the deck teemed with armed men taking up their positions. When all was in readiness, they stood still, awaiting the order to go into action. The warship's trierarch slowed the beat of the sailors manning the oars and cautiously brought his vessel up on the stern quarter of the drifting hulk. When he judged that they were making just enough to carry them down the length of the cargo ship, he shouted the order to ship oars.

Cato had put on his full armour and climbed into the turret on the foredeck to survey the other vessel as the

Sobek glided alongside. There were dark streaks around the scuppers which faded away as they approached the waterline. Blood, he realised. A moment later he saw the first of the bodies, a man slumped over the side rail. Then more corpses scattered across the steering deck.

'Make ready the corvus!' Diodorus bellowed and there was a grating creak as the gangway swung out, round and over the side of the cargo ship.

'Release!'

The gangway dropped, the iron point curving down, gathering speed, and then it slammed into the deck with a splintering crack.

'Forward marines!' Diodorus cried out, raising his sword as he climbed on to the gangway and raced across towards the other ship. His men ran after him, coarse, leather-soled boots pounding the boards of the gangway. In moments the marines were across and warily fanning out across the deck of the cargo ship.

Cato climbed down from the turret and called out to Proculus. 'You and your men wait here. If I call for you, come at once.'

'Yes, sir.'

There was no sound of fighting, no shouts or cries of alarm from the cargo ship, and Cato left his sword in its scabbard as he strode across the gangway, briefly glancing down at the water washing between the two hulls. Despite being aboard for the best part of two months, he still feared and hated the sea; another good reason to pray that his current quest came to a successful conclusion as soon as possible. When he reached the far end of the gangway, Cato jumped down and looked round slowly. There were bodies strewn across the deck and dark patches of dried blood. The cargo hatches had been dragged aside and the freight below was a jumbled mess of goods: shattered amphorae, discarded bales of cloth and split sacks of rice and spices. Diodorus was squatting beside one of the bodies and Cato joined him.

'There's little sign of corruption.' The decurion sniffed and then touched his fingers to the blood on the deck beside the corpse. 'Still tacky. They were killed only a day or so ago. Certainly no more than two days.'

'If this is the work of Ajax, then we're closer to him than I thought,' Cato mused, rising up.

'Maybe, sir. But equally it could be the work of pirates.'

'Really? Then why take so little, if anything, from the hold? There's a fortune in spices down there. That doesn't make any sense if the ship was taken by pirates.'

'Sir!' a voice cried out. 'This one's alive!'

Cato and Diodorus hurried towards the marine standing beside the mast. He stood aside and revealed a thin, sun-burned figure, naked save for a soiled loincloth. At first Cato thought the man had thrown his arms up, but then he saw the broad black head of the iron nail that had been driven through his palms into the wood, pinning him upright, high enough so that he could not fully stand on the deck and had to carry his weight on his toes and the balls of his feet. A faint groan issued from the man's mouth and his breathing was shallow and laboured.

'Get him down!' Cato ordered. He turned towards the *Sobek* and shouted, 'Send the surgeon over!'

While two marines supported the man's weight, a third

grasped the head of the nail and began to work it free. The man gasped and cried out. His eyes, bloodshot and rolling up, flickered open. It seemed to take a long time to get the nail out of the mast and then the man collapsed into the arms of the marines.

'Lay him down.' Cato gestured to the nearest marine. 'Give me your canteen. You and the others, search the ship for any other survivors.'

He leaned over the man as he pulled the stopper from the canteen, wincing as he saw the cracked and bloody lips. Slipping one hand behind the man's head, Cato eased it up and poured a little water over the face. The lips smacked as they felt the water and there was a groan of relief as the liquid trickled inside his parched mouth. Cato fed him some more sips and stopped when he choked and coughed, spluttering as he turned his face aside.

'Thank . . . you,' he croaked weakly.

'What happened here?' asked Cato. 'Who attacked you?'

The man's swollen tongue licked his cracked lips and he winced painfully before he made his reply. 'Romans . . .'

Cato exchanged a glance with Diodorus. 'Romans? Are you certain?'

A shadow passed over the deck and Cato looked up to see the mast of the *Ibis* as Macro's ship drew alongside. An instant later there was a dull thud as the ships nudged against each other. Then the sound of boots landing on the deck. Cato looked up and saw his friend. 'Over here, Macro!'

Macro strode over, glancing round at the deck. 'Looks like they had quite a battle.'

'More of a massacre, I think. But we found this one alive.' Cato gestured towards the torn flesh of the man's hands. 'Nailed to the mast.'

Macro let out a low whistle. 'Nasty. Why would they do that?'

'I can guess. They wanted to leave a witness behind. Someone who might live long enough to report what happened.'

The surgeon from Cato's ship came trotting up with his haversack of dressings and salves. He knelt down beside the survivor and examined him quickly, feeling his pulse. 'He's in a bad way, sir. Doubt I can do much for him.'

'All right. Then I need to find out what I can before it's too late.' Cato leaned forward and spoke gently into the ear of the man. 'Tell me your name, sailor.'

'Mene . . . Menelaus,' the voice rasped softly.

'Listen to me, Menelaus. You are badly injured. You may not live. If you die, then you will want someone to avenge your death. So tell me, who did this? Romans you said. What did you mean? Roman pirates?'

'No . . .' The man whispered, and then muttered something more, a word Cato could not quite catch.

'What's that?'

'Sounded like he said worship,' Macro suggested. 'Doesn't make sense. Worship?'

Cato felt an icy thrill as he grasped what the sailor was trying to say. 'Warship, that's it, isn't it? You were attacked by a warship?'

The sailor nodded and moistened his lips. 'Ordered us to heave to . . . Said they were checking the cargo . . . Started killing us . . . No mercy.' The man's brow wrinkled at the memory. 'He spared me . . . Said I was to remember his name . . . Then they held me against the mast and forced my hands up.' A tear glistened in the corner of the man's eye and then rolled down his skin and dripped from his ear.

'His name?' Cato prompted gently. 'Tell me his name.'

The sailor was silent for a moment before his lips moved again. 'Cent . . . Centurion Macro.'

Cato sat up and looked at his friend. Macro shook his head in astonishment. 'What the fuck is he talking about?'

Cato could only shrug before he turned his attention back to the sailor. 'Are you certain? Are you sure he said his name was Macro?'

The sailor nodded. 'Macro . . . That was the bastard's name . . . Made me repeat it to be sure . . . Centurion Macro,' he murmured, then his face contorted in agony.

'Sir,' the surgeon intervened. 'I have to get him out of the sun. Below deck in the *Sobek*. I'll tend to his injuries there.'

'Very well. Do what you can for him.' Cato eased the sailor's head down and stood up. The surgeon called over four of the marines and ordered them to lift the sailor's body as gently as possible. Cato watched them make their way towards the gangway, and then turned to Macro. 'Odd, don't you think?'

'I have an alibi,' Macro responded with harsh humour. 'Been busy hunting fugitive slaves.' He jabbed his thumb at the sailor being carried across the gangway. 'What's that Centurion Macro business about?'

'It's Ajax. Has to be.'

'Why?'

'Who else would use your name?'

'No idea. But if it is Ajax, why do it?'

'His idea of a joke, perhaps. That, or something else.'

'What?'

Cato shook his head faintly. 'I'm not certain. But there's more to this than there seems.'

'Well, if it is Ajax and his men, then we're back on their trail.'

'Yes, we are.' Cato puffed out his cheeks. 'The timing isn't great, though.'

'What do you mean?'

'We've run out of supplies. Water's almost gone. We can't continue the pursuit until we've replenished our food and water. We'll take what we can find aboard this ship, and then make for Alexandria.'

Macro stared at him. 'You can't be serious . . . sir.'

'Think about it, Macro. If he has a day or more's head start then he could be over a hundred miles away by now. How long do you think it will take us to find him? How many days? If we attempt it then we run the risk of being in no condition to fight him, or being too weak to even make it back to port. I have no choice. We make for Alexandria. Then we take on supplies, and try to get enough reinforcements to search this area thoroughly.'

Macro was about to protest once more when Decurion Diodorus approached to make his report. 'Sir, my men have searched the ship. There are no other survivors.'

'Very well. Tell your men to bring whatever's left of

the food and water up on deck and divide it between our two ships.'

'Yes, sir.' Diodorus saluted and paced back towards the marines milling about the cargo hold. 'Right, you dozy lot! Sheathe your swords and down your shields. There's work to do.'

Macro was staring hard at Cato. He cuffed his nose.

'What is it?' Cato asked wearily.

'I was thinking. You'd better be right about this. If Ajax gives us the slip again while we return to Alexandria, then the gods know how we'll pick up the trail again. It's been over a month since we last heard any news of him.'

'I know.' Cato gestured helplessly with his hands. 'But we have no choice. We have to go back.'

Macro pursed his lips. 'That's your choice, sir. Your order.'

'Yes. Yes it is.'

Three days later the *Sobek* led the way into Alexandria's great harbour. The vast structure of the lighthouse constructed on the rock of Pharos island by order of Ptolemy II towered above the two warships. The men aboard had all been seconded from the Roman forces at Alexandria to help crush the slave rebellion on Crete and so were used to the extraordinary vision of the lighthouse. Cato, too, had seen it before, but nevertheless paused from his pacing up and down the deck to marvel at the scale of Ptolemy's ambition. Besides the lighthouse, there was the vast complex of the Great Library, the tomb of Alexander the Great and the broad avenue of the Canopus which ran across the heart of the city. Everything about the city was designed to impress visitors and foster a sense of superiority in its citizens.

It was close to midday and the noon sun forced Cato to squint as he looked up at the lighthouse. A steady column of smoke rose from the fire that blazed permanently at the very top of the tower, proclaiming the presence of the city to ships far out at sea, or along the coastline of Egypt.

Cato looked down again, clasping his hands behind his back, and resumed his pacing along the main deck of the warship. It had become a habit since the hunt for Ajax had begun. Being cooped up on a small vessel was anathema to Cato's restless spirit and the routine of walking the deck gave a limited amount of the exercise he craved, as well as time to think.

He was deeply frustrated by the enforced delay in pursuing Ajax. However, there was no alternative. Even with the food and water they had gleaned from the cargo ship, the men were starving and their throats were parched. They were in no condition to fight Ajax's desperate gang of fugitives, most of whom were gladiators. Men who had spent years training to do nothing but fight and kill in the arena. The bodies on the cargo ship had been weighted and buried at sea, together with the sailor who had been nailed to the mast and had expired a few hours after he had been taken aboard the *Sobek*. A small prize crew had been put aboard the cargo ship with orders to make best speed to Alexandria. The warships had gone ahead, driven on by the prefect in his desire to return to the hunt as swiftly as possible.

'Furl the sail!' the trierarch, Phermon, ordered from the stern. 'Make ready the oars!'

Moments later the *Sobek* continued towards the naval harbour, lying next to the royal palaces, once the home of pharaohs but now the quarters of the Roman governor of Egypt and his staff. The oars rose, swept forward and fell in a steady rhythm as the ship glided over the calm waters towards the stone jetties where the Alexandrian fleet was moored. Already Cato could see a sentry rushing from the signal tower at the entrance to the naval harbour to report the arrival of the two ships.

Cato made his way aft and descended into the stern cabin. He was a head taller than Macro and was forced to stoop uncomfortably as he put on the cleanest of the two tunics that he had brought with him from Crete. Then he struggled into the vest of scale armour and fastened the harness over the top. The harness was decorated with the silver discs of the medals he had been awarded during his service in the Second Legion. The unit had been part of the army that had invaded Britain a few years earlier when Cato first proved himself as a soldier, and won promotion to the rank of centurion. Now he was a prefect, an officer singled out for senior command.

But only once his rank was confirmed by the Emperor, Cato reflected. And that was not likely to happen if he failed to find and destroy Ajax, the bloodthirsty rebel who had done his best to destroy the province of Crete. He had also managed to capture the Egyptian grain fleet when it had put into Crete on the way to Rome, thereby threatening to starve the people of the capital. For a brief moment Cato felt a grudging admiration for his enemy. Ajax was the kind of man who understood all the forces in play, and made his plans accordingly. Truly, he was as dangerous a foe as Cato had ever faced and he presented the gravest of threats to Rome itself. Such a danger could never be tolerated and if Cato failed to capture or kill Ajax, then the Emperor would not forgive him. A refusal to confirm his promotion to prefect would be the least of Cato's worries. More likely he would be reduced in rank and sent to end his days in some gods forsaken outpost on the furthest fringe of the Empire. That would mean an end to his military career, but there would be a higher price than that. He would be forced to give up Julia.

The daughter of a senator could not be expected to endure the hard life on a frontier post. She would stay in Rome and find a better prospect for a husband. The thought cut deeply into Cato's heart, yet he would not blame Julia if that happened. Despite his feelings for her, Cato was rational enough to know that love had its limits. The idea of having Julia follow him into exile and growing to resent him for it filled him with dread. Better that he should go alone, and have a memory to cherish, than have his failure compounded by gnawing bitterness.

Cato adjusted his harness, then reached for his sword belt and slipped it over his head on to the shoulder. Lastly, he opened the small chest at the foot of his cot and took out the leather scroll case that contained the orders he had been given by Julia's father, Senator Sempronius, to track down Ajax. A separate document stated that he had been promoted to prefect, subject to imperial confirmation. Between the two documents, Cato hoped that he would have sufficient authority to secure the assistance of the governor in carrying out his mission.

He was not looking forward to meeting the governor again. The last time, Cato had sailed from Crete, on Senator Sempronius's behalf, to ask for reinforcements to put down the rebellion. It had been an uneasy confrontation, and only the threat of being co-opted into the ranks of those who would share the blame for the fall of Crete had induced the governor of Egypt to grudgingly provide the necessary men and ships to defeat Ajax.

Cato picked up his helmet, took a deep breath and exhaled slowly, then turned to climb back on to the deck, where he could complete his dress without having to crouch down to avoid crushing the crest of his helmet. As he fastened the straps under his chin, Cato watched the trierarch and his men complete the final stage of their approach to the jetty. Mooring cables were tossed ashore to waiting sailors and the *Sobek* was eased into position, creaking up against the woven mass of reed fenders.

Cato turned to the trierarch. 'I want you to go ashore and find the fleet's quartermaster. I want both ships resupplied as soon as possible. There will be no time for any shore leave for the crews. I intend to put back to sea the moment I have reported to the governor and fresh supplies are on board.'

The trierarch puffed his cheeks and responded in an undertone. 'Sir, the men are exhausted. They've not seen their families for months. A day or two ashore will put heart back into 'em.'

'They are to remain on the ship,' Cato said firmly. 'Any man who attempts to go ashore will be treated as a deserter. Is that understood?'

'Yes, sir.'

'Good.' Cato turned away and saw that the *Ibis* was mooring directly astern. The gangway was already run out and Macro scrambled on to the jetty and made his way alongside the *Sobek* to wait for Cato.

'Remember what I said,' Cato warned the trierarch, and then turned away to go ashore. As soon as he stepped on to the paved surface, it seemed to Cato that the land was shifting unsteadily beneath his boots. He struggled to adjust his sense of balance and Macro winked at him.

'Now that is a strange feeling.'

'Quite,' Cato agreed. 'Come on.'

They set off along the jetty, the heat beating off the stones beneath them. Ahead, at the gate leading from the jetty towards the palace buildings, a party of legionaries stood waiting, a centurion standing in front of them, vine cane held across his thighs as he stood with his feet apart.

'Didn't take long to send out a reception committee,' Macro remarked. 'Someone was quick off the mark in calling out an honour guard.'

'Yes.' Cato frowned. 'But how could they know?'

'Perhaps you're not the only one with good eyesight,' Macro suggested mildly. 'Still, full marks to the officer in charge of the watch.'

They continued, as steadily and with as much dignity as their sea legs allowed, towards the waiting soldiers. As they approached the gate, the centurion stepped forward and raised his right hand in a salute.

'Are you Prefect Quintus Licinius Cato, sir?'

'Yes.'

'And you, Centurion Lucius Cornelius Macro?'

Macro nodded. 'I take it you're here to escort us to your commander?'

The centurion looked mildly surprised.

Cato shook his head. 'There's no time for formalities. I have to see the governor, at once.'

'Formalities?' The centurion gestured to his waiting men. 'I think you misunderstand, sir. We've not been sent to greet you. I've been ordered to place you under arrest. Both of you.'

'Arrest?' Macro glared. 'What the bloody hell are you talking about. Arrest?'

'Wait!' Cato held up his hand. 'Whose order is this?'

'Comes straight from the governor, sir. Soon as he had word that the ships were entering the harbour. You're to be taken to the watchroom and held there until further orders are issued. If you'll follow me, sir?'

'Why?' Cato stood his ground. 'What are the charges?'

The centurion stared at them. 'I should have thought that's obvious, sir. Murder, and piracy.'

CHAPTER FOUR

They were left alone in the watchroom. The door remained open and four sentries stood guard outside. The room itself was well-proportioned with high ceilings and ventilated by large windows high up on the walls. The distant sounds of the city outside the palace merged into a constant low drone.

Cato was sitting at a table, drinking a cup of water, savouring the fact that he no longer had to limit himself to a small ration.

Macro glanced out at the guards and crossed the room and sat on a stool opposite Cato. 'What the hell is going on? Why are we under arrest?'

'You heard him. Murder and piracy.'

'What kind of crap is that?' Macro fumed. 'We're officers of the Roman army. And you, you're a prefect.'

'Glad you've noticed.'

'How dare they treat you like this? By the gods, some fool will pay for this, and pay dearly.'

'Macro, there's obviously been some mistake. It'll be sorted out. There's no use flaring up, you're just wasting your energy.' Cato filled another cup and pushed it across the table towards his friend. 'Here. Have a drink.'

Macro gritted his teeth as he controlled his temper.

Then he took the cup and drained it quickly and set it down with a sharp rap. 'Another.'

This time he drank more slowly then pushed the empty cup away. 'That's better. Bloody tongue was starting to feel like a strip of old boot leather.'

'I know what you mean.' Cato nodded. 'I hope water's been provided for the men on the ships. They're still out there in the sun.'

Macro frowned at him. 'I think you should be concentrating on our predicament rather than theirs.'

'Why? Didn't you always tell me that a good officer thinks of the well-being of his men before his own? You used to be quite adamant about that when I was your optio.'

'Did I?' Macro grumbled. 'What good is that doing you right now, eh?'

'It's taking my mind off being stuck in here with a firebrand who is storming around the place like a caged bull.'

Macro's weathered and scarred face creased into a smile. 'Sorry. I just don't take kindly to being called a murderer and pirate. A killer and plunderer, yes. That goes with the job.'

'To some minds that would seem to be a distinction of degree rather than category, Macro,' Cato replied wryly.

'Really?' Macro raised his eyebrows. 'Then fuck 'em, I say. I'm no murderer.'

Cato had become well used to the rather rough and ready nature of Macro's soldier's sophistry and simply shrugged.

Their conversation was interrupted by the sound of

boots in the corridor outside the watchroom and a moment later the guards stepped aside to admit the centurion in charge of the arresting party, as well as the governor of the province and a scribe. The centurion stood to one side and bowed his head as he announced, 'His Excellency, Gaius Petronius, governor of Alexandria and the province of Egypt, and legate of the Emperor.'

Cato and Macro stood up and bowed their heads as Petronius strode to the centre of the room and stopped, hands on hips, a dark expression on his face. He snapped his fingers and pointed at the corner. The scribe hurried over, sat cross-legged, and took a waxed tablet and stylus from his satchel.

Petronius rounded on Cato. 'I let you take my forces to Crete to quash rebellion, not to spread it about even more widely. You two have a lot to answer for.' Petronius glared at them. 'You've got the entire delta region up in arms and not just them. The merchants' and traders' guilds of the city want your heads. I'm tempted to give due legal process a miss and let the mob tear you to pieces, before their mood boils over into open revolt.' He folded his arms. 'So please, in the name of all the gods, tell me just what the hell you two think you are up to?'

'Up to, sir?' Cato shook his head. 'I don't understand.'

'Bollocks! I've been getting reports for the best part of a month that you have been terrorising the coastal villages. Landing, demanding supplies and killing those who refuse to cooperate. I've even heard that you have been stopping ships, torturing their crews for information and then killing almost everyone on board before you move on.'

Macro and Cato exchanged a quick look.

'Oh, don't deny it!' the governor raged. 'I have reports naming you. And a handful of witnesses that you have been kind enough to spare. More than enough evidence to have you nailed to a cross before the day is out. So,' he forced himself to control his temper before he continued, 'I ask you again, what do you think you have been playing at? According to the last despatch I had from Crete, you had been sent to track down a renegade slave. Not to foment yet another rebellion here in Egypt. I'm not sure who poses the greatest threat to peace in the Empire, a renegade gladiator, or the two moronic thugs sent to track him down. To add insult to injury you are using my men, and my ships, to carry out your dirty work. Don't think that has escaped the notice of the mob either. One of my patrols was stoned as it passed through the streets yesterday. I lost an optio and one of the men. All thanks to you two and the heavy-handed way you have gone about hunting down this character, Ajax.'

'But we've done nothing, sir,' Macro protested. 'None of it's true.'

'Tell that to the witnesses.'

'Then they're lying. Someone's put them up to it.'

'We shall see. My prosecutors have been taking statements, gathering evidence. I shall take every possible step to put you two on trial as soon as I can. Then, a public execution. That might just be enough to satisfy the mob and calm things down here in Egypt.'

Macro snorted with derision. 'You're having me on! It's utter shit, all of it.'

'Trust me, Centurion, that's exactly what is going to happen. What's more, the Emperor, and that snake of his, the imperial secretary, Narcissus, will approve my action without a moment's hesitation.'

Cato had been listening to the heated exchange in silence. Now, as understanding dawned, he smiled without humour.

'What in Hades are you grinning at?' asked the governor. 'I see no cause for amusement.'

'It's Ajax, sir. He's responsible for all of this.'

'Ajax?'

'Of course. He's been covering his tracks. Better than that, he's been stirring up the locals in his wake.'

'What do you mean?'

'We came across a ship, adrift, a few days back. All the crew dead, save one who told us that it was the work of Centurion Macro.'

Macro snorted. 'Which came as something of a bloody surprise to me, as you can imagine.'

'It also explains why those villagers fled when we landed on the coast the day before,' Cato continued. 'He's been a busy lad, our gladiator.'

'I assume you can prove this?' said the governor. 'Can this survivor of yours testify that the man who attacked his ship was not Macro?'

'Unfortunately not, sir. He died soon afterwards.'

'How convenient.'

'Not for us, it seems. Nonetheless, you produce your other witnesses and see if they can identify either of us as their attackers. That should prove our innocence.'

The governor was silent for a moment and then nodded. 'Very well. You have a point.' He paced to the door and clicked his fingers at one of the guards standing outside. 'You, go and fetch that temple priest, Hamedes. He's being held over at the palace barracks. I want him brought here at once. Don't tell him anything about these two officers. Understand?'

The guard saluted and turned to stride off down the corridor. Petronius returned to Macro and Cato. 'I'll know soon enough if you're telling me the truth. One of the temples on the delta was raided ten days ago. The priests were killed and the temple's strongbox was taken. Only one person was spared. He turned up at the gates of the city yesterday, babbling about the Roman soldiers who had attacked the temple. He was taken into custody to have his wounds dressed and to be fed and rested before we took a statement. We'll see what he says when he encounters you two.' He paused and stared at Macro and Cato for a moment before he continued. 'However, if you're being straight with me, and this is all the work of Ajax, then it seems we're dealing with a rather more dangerous and resourceful enemy than I thought.'

Cato nodded. 'Oh, he's all that and more. Utterly ruthless. My guess is that he has ambitions to stir up a fresh revolt here in Egypt. That's the only thing that makes sense.'

'But why?' Macro interrupted. 'Why doesn't he just run and go to ground? Find somewhere to hide until we give up the chase, then he and his followers can live out their lives as free men.'

'No, they'll always be fugitives. Ajax knows that. There can be no peace for him. No matter where he goes, Rome will never give up the hunt. So, all that is left to him is to fight on. It's all he knows. One way or another he will always be our enemy. Until he is found and killed.'

'That can't happen a day too soon,' Petronius added with feeling. 'I already have enough problems containing the situation on the upper Nile without this new trouble along the coast.' He paused and crossed over to the table, pulled up a stool and sat down, gesturing to Cato and Macro to do the same. The scribe remained sitting in the corner, discreetly taking notes. Cato glanced at him, mindful of the need to choose his words with care since Petronius would have a record of what was said.

The governor poured himself a drink before he continued. 'The province seems to be afflicted by a confluence of threats at present, even before this gladiator of yours turned up – assuming that you are not responsible for the actions that have stirred up the locals.'

Macro bristled, and Cato shook his finger slightly to warn his friend not to react. Petronius missed the gesture; he had his cup in both hands and was staring down at the shimmering surface.

'For the last three months the Nubians have been carrying out raids against our southern frontier,' he went on. 'Each time, they have penetrated further along the Nile, but always withdrawing before we could gather sufficient forces to trap and destroy them. It's my belief that they have been testing our defences and reconnoitring the ground in preparation for a larger operation. A few days ago I had that confirmed in a report from the strategos of the nomes on the border with Nubia.'

Macro looked at Cato and cocked an eyebrow. He cleared his throat. 'Excuse me, sir. What do you mean by these, er, nomes?'

Petronius looked at him irritably and shrugged. 'Should have known you weren't familiar with arrangements here. It's a hangover from the time before Rome made Egypt into a province. The nomes are administrative districts. Each one is under the control of a strategos and a local council. They did a good job of collecting the taxes and taking care of local legal matters so Rome saw no need to change things.'

Macro grunted. 'Glad to see the Greeks got something right.'

'Actually, the Greeks adapted the system from the natives.'

'What? The gypos?'

Petronius smiled. 'You really have no idea, do you?'

'About what, sir?'

'This province. Egypt was a great power once. Long before Rome was even a tiny village of farmers scratching a living on the banks of the Tiber.'

'Bollocks.' Macro jerked his thumb towards the heart of the city. 'That lot?'

'It's true, I assure you, though don't ever attempt to get one of the locals to tell you the full story, unless you have a few years to spare.'

Cato coughed. 'Sir? About the Nubians?'

'Oh yes.' Petronius refocused his thoughts. 'The strategos at Syene. Anyway, he sent several spies across the frontier to gather intelligence. Most didn't come back, then at last he heard from one. The man had seen columns of Nubian warriors massing a hundred miles or so beyond the cataract. They were led by Prince Talmis. He's the eldest son of the King of Nubia. He's already extended their kingdom into Aethiopia and has quite a reputation as a general. He means to enhance it by attacking this province, I'm certain of it.'

'But why?' Cato asked. 'Have the Nubians been provoked?'

'In a manner of speaking,' Petronius admitted. 'A year ago, the Emperor ordered me to send a survey to map the Nile to its source. I advised him that such an expedition would cause friction with the Nubians. They're a touchy people.'

'No doubt. I would imagine they suspected this was a prelude to invasion. Why else would Claudius want the area mapped?'

'The imperial secretary gave me his firm assurance that there are no plans to invade Nubia. The purpose of the expedition was purely scientific.'

Macro scratched his cheek. 'And you believed Narcissus, did you, sir?'

'Whether one believes Narcissus or not, once the Emperor gives the order then the thing is done. So I sent the cartographers up the Nile with a small escort, and a message of goodwill.' Petronius paused.

'What happened?' asked Macro.

'Prince Talmis sent their heads back with a message warning us to keep our noses out of Nubian territory.'

Cato leaned forward. 'And, naturally, you sent out a punitive column.'

'Of course. What else could I do? Rome is not prepared to suffer such an insult to her authority. Our men burned several of their settlements, enslaved over a thousand of their people and destroyed whatever irrigation infrastructure they came across. Since then we've had these raids and I've had to send reinforcements south to bolster our defences along the frontier. Under normal circumstances the garrison of Egypt is perfectly capable of defending the province and keeping order. We have two legions, the Third based here in Alexandria, and the Twenty-Second at Heliopolis. There's also nine cohorts of auxiliaries based in forts across the delta and along the Nile. However, as you well know, I had to lend my good friend Senator Sempronius three thousand men from the Third Legion and two auxiliary cohorts to put down the revolt on Crete. He has still to return most of those men. Right now, I have two cohorts of legionaries available to hold Alexandria. A thousand men to control over half a million. Not an easy job at the best of times. But since this business with Ajax began – if you're telling me the truth – the sailors and merchants have been up in arms demanding protection. That's over and above the usual friction we have between the Jews and the Greeks. Then there's the fellahin, the peasants, along the coast, ready to revolt, thanks to these raids on the villages and the sacking of that temple. Oh, and there's one other thing,' he added bitterly. 'The latest readings of the Nilometers suggest that we're in for a poor crop.'

'Too little water?' Cato surmised.

Petronius shook his head. 'Too much. The Nile's going to flood much higher this year, which means it will take longer to recede and the crops will have to be planted late. The fellahin are going to go hungry and the tax take is going to fall. I have the men to deal with the first problem, but as sure as Vulcan made little knuckledusters, I'll get it in the neck once the imperial treasury detects a shortfall in Egypt's tax take.' Petronius raised his hands helplessly. 'So, as you can see, your friend Ajax has arrived on the scene at the very worst of times.'

Macro's eyes narrowed darkly. 'Ajax is no friend of mine, sir.'

'Figure of speech,' Petronius excused himself lightly.

They were interrupted by a rap on the door frame. All three turned as a guard entered the room. 'Sir, got the gypo from the temple you wanted outside.'

Petronius winced. 'Soldier, I really would rather that you and your companions referred to our provincials in less pejorative terms.'

The man blinked. 'Sir?'

'Egyptians, not gypos, eh?'

'Yes, sir.'

'Very well, bring him in.'

Cato looked around at Macro and took a sharp breath as they waited for the survivor from the temple to be brought in to tell his tale.

CHAPTER FIVE

Hamedes was tall and solidly built. His bruised head had been shaved, but several days without any attention had left it with a dark furze. Somewhat younger than Cato, his eyes were deep-set either side of the wide curved nose that was typical of the native race. He wore a plain red military tunic, which Cato guessed must have been lent to him. He stood before them barefoot and unbowed. He spoke in Greek, fluently.

'You sent for me, sir,' he announced, somehow making the last word sound like a condescension.

'Indeed.' The governor nodded. 'I'd like you to tell your story to these two officers.'

'Why? I've already given a statement, which was taken down by your scribe. It's not necessary, a waste of time.'

'There's no need for the high and mighty act,' said Macro with a frown that would have unnerved a less easily subdued man than Hamedes. 'Just be a good lad and give us the details.'

The priest looked Macro up and down. 'And who might I be addressing, if I may ask?'

Macro puffed his chest out. 'Centurion—'

'Enough!' Cato intervened. 'You are here to answer our questions, not ask your own.'

'Really? I thought I was here because I am a witness to Roman aggression against the temple of Isis at Keirkut. The temple is now a ruin, and its servants are carrion meat for the vultures. I am here to see that they have justice, sir.' He paused briefly. 'That is, if those who come from Rome are familiar with the concept. Meanwhile, it seems that I am a prisoner.'

Macro glanced at Cato and spoke quietly. 'Quite full of himself, isn't he? If he wants to play us around then I'm quite happy to take on the role of interrogator.'

'Not yet,' Cato replied quietly. 'Let's see what we can learn by less obtrusive means, eh?'

He turned to Hamedes. 'The governor has asked us to join his investigation into the incident. We could read the report, but I would prefer to hear it directly from your own lips. It would be of considerable assistance to us in seeking the justice you desire.'

The young priest stared back, and then nodded. 'Very well. I am prepared to cooperate on that basis.'

'How good of you,' Macro muttered, and Cato shot him a warning look.

'Tell them what you told me, Hamedes,' said Petronius. 'If you please.'

'Very well.' He closed his eyes briefly to compose his thoughts. 'It was the last hour of the day when they came. The high priest had begun the ceremony of Ra's entry into the underworld. The senior priests were by the altar on the river landing. The rest of us were kneeling on the bank of the river, around the sacred barge. That's when I first noticed the sail. A Roman warship had entered the river from the sea and was making for the eastern bank of the tributary. The high priest seemed to pay it no attention and continued with the ceremony, preparing the bushel of wheat to be burned as an offering to Ra, the most wise and merciful.' Hamedes briefly clasped his hands together and bowed his head. 'The ship continued towards the landing. At the last moment they took in their sail and turned to come alongside the steps leading down into the Nile. At once the Romans threw down a ramp and came ashore.'

'Were they in uniform?' asked Cato. 'Like myself?'

'They wore tunics like yours but they were white. They had swords, shields and helmets like those worn by your auxiliaries.'

'Marines then,' said Macro. 'It fits with what we know.'

Cato nodded. 'Carry on. What happened next?'

'They surrounded us and forced us to gather around the barge of Ra, most wise and merciful.' Hamedes repeated his earlier gesture. 'Except for the high priest. They took him aside, to be questioned by their commander. He came ashore last.'

'Can you describe him to us?' Cato said evenly, ignoring the glance that Petronius shot towards him.

Hamedes frowned. 'Tall, muscular. Brown eyes. More Greek-looking than Roman, but then that's to be expected in Egypt. He wore scale armour, a plumed helmet and a blue cloak. And he had a sword, the same kind that all you Romans carry.'

'You saw him up close, then?'

'Yes, I was near him when he questioned the high priest.'

'So you would recognise his face again, if you were to see him?'

'I am sure of it.'

'Fine.' Cato waved a hand. 'Please continue.'

Hamedes nodded. 'He told the priest that he was acting under the orders of the governor at Alexandria. The officer announced that a new edict had been issued confiscating all the gold and silver held in the temples. He demanded that the high priest show him where our vault is. The high priest refused. He was angry. He told the officer that the temple was sacred ground and that the Romans were defiling it. He ordered the officer to take his men and withdraw. Instead the officer told his men to bring him one of the junior priests. Then he drew his sword and beheaded the man. He asked the high priest where the vault was again, and killed another man when he did not get a reply. He continued killing us, one by one, until finally the high priest spoke. He cursed the Roman, then took him to the vault. The Romans made four of us carry the caskets of gold and silver coin to his ship. Then, when we had finished, he began to kill the rest, starting with the high priest.' Hamedes paused, and when he spoke again there was a tremor in his voice. 'I saw the blood run down the steps and into the Nile . . .'

'Did you try to escape?' asked Cato. 'Did you hide perhaps?'

'No. I was too scared to move. I think we all were. Before I realised it, I was the last one alive. He came close to me, closer than we are now, and stared at me in silence for a while. I was sure that he would kill me, so I turned to the west to offer one final prayer to Ra, most wise and merciful—'

'Yes, thank you,' Macro interrupted. 'I think we can take that as read. Get on with it.'

Hamedes glared briefly at Macro. 'I prayed, then he grabbed my shoulder and pulled me round to face him. He said that Rome had had enough of the insolence of our priests. He said that the Emperor had decreed that it was time for the old religions to be erased. He told me that I had been spared so that I might spread the message. The officer said that I was to remember his name, and that he was acting according to the orders of your Emperor, Claudius.'

'Most wise and merciful,' Macro muttered, and shook his head apologetically as Cato frowned at him.

Cato turned back and fixed the priest with a steady eye. 'And what was the name of this officer?'

'As I told your scribe,' Hamedes said to Petronius and then nodded towards the corner. 'He said he was a prefect. Prefect Quintus Licinius Cato.'

'Are you certain?'

'Yes. He made me repeat it.'

'And then?'

'He struck me on the head with the guard of his sword. I was knocked cold. When I came to I was lying on the bodies of the other priests, my robes soaked in their blood. The Romans had gone. They had set fire to the priest's quarters, and they had filled the temple with wood, palm leaves and oil and set it alight. The paintings on the wall, the sacred records of the temple, all burned away. It blazed right through the night and in the morning all that remained was a scorched hulk.' Hamedes winced at the memory. 'I was alone. The temple was gone. All that was left for me to do was come here and seek justice. That, or revenge. I swear, by all the gods of my people, that I will seek out and kill this Roman, this Prefect Cato.'

'The man who attacked your temple is no Roman,' Cato said firmly. 'He is a slave, a fugitive, masquerading as a Roman. He has been murdering your people along the Egyptian coast for the best part of a month now.'

'He was a Roman,' Hamedes replied vehemently. 'Do you expect me to believe that he isn't? Were his men pretending to be Roman too? Was his ship pretending to be a Roman warship? What kind of fool do you take me for?'

'The warship was real. And those were Roman uniforms he and his men were wearing. The man's name is Ajax. He captured the ship and killed its crew. We have been pursuing him for some months now.'

Hamedes stared at Cato suspiciously. 'I don't believe you.'

Petronius nodded towards Cato. 'Have you ever seen this officer before? Or the man sitting beside him?'

'No.'

'Be certain.'

'I am sure of it. I have never met them until now.'

'Then would it surprise you if I was to say that this man is Prefect Cato, and his companion is Centurion Macro?'

Hamedes shook his head. 'What trickery is this?'

'There's no trickery,' the governor told him. 'Well, none here and now, at least. This man is Prefect Cato and what he says is the truth. The one who attacked your temple and butchered your companions was an imposter. He intends to provoke your people into rebellion. He aims to fill their hearts with a desire for revenge. And he has been succeeding admirably. Now you know the truth. I need you to help us, Hamedes.'

The Egyptian still looked bewildered and Petronius softened his voice. 'You are a priest. Your people respect you and your word carries weight with them. I need you to tell them the truth. And not just them, but the Alexandrians as well.'

'What do you propose, sir?'

'I will summon the leaders of the merchants' and shipowners' guilds. I'll give them an audience in the palace and you can tell them what you have learned here.'

'Why should they believe me? You must know how the Alexandrians look down on us. Why would they take the word of an Egyptian?'

'Because I suspect that the ordinary Egyptians despise the Romans even more than the Egyptians are despised by the Greeks. If you take our side, it will give the Greeks something to think about. Better that the truth about Ajax comes from you than from us.'

Hamedes nodded. 'I understand. I just hope that I am believed.'

The following evening, Governor Petronius sat on an elaborate formal chair on a dais at the end of the audience chamber. He was flanked by Cato and Macro to one side and two scribes sitting on mats on the other side of the dais, one to take down the words of the governor, another the comments from his guests. As was his custom, Petronius ensured that there would be a record of the meeting since it might well become part of his defence at a subsequent trial in Rome should he ever be charged with corruption or incompetence.

The audience chamber was lined with towering

columns with capitals in the characteristic lotus flower design of Egypt. This was the same audience chamber where the Ptolemies had handed out their decrees to their kingdom. The last of their line, Cleopatra, had played host first to Gaius Julius Caesar and then to Mark Antony in this hall, seated on the same dais as the present governor. However, the ceremonial glitter and solemn speeches of amity between two great powers had long since faded into history. In their place stood a crowd of anxious and angry Alexandrians, held in check by a line of stern-faced Roman legionaries. Hamedes had finished relating his experience and confirmed that the man who had claimed to be Prefect Cato was not the same as the man at the governor's side. Further witnesses who had been spared by Ajax were produced to support the governor's claim that the raiders were imposters.

At first only a few voices were raised to denounce the governor, accusing him of concealing renegades within the ranks of the Roman forces occupying Egypt. Petronius listened to the arguments for a moment, until too many voices were calling out for any sense to be made of what was said. He leaned towards Macro.

'Centurion, be so good as to shut them up for me.'

'Yes, sir.' Macro took a deep breath. He cupped his hands to his mouth and roared, 'QUIET!'

The chamber was designed to echo the commands from the throne, and in any case, Macro's parade-ground voice could stop a recruit dead in his tracks a couple of hundred paces away. The tongues of the Alexandrians were swiftly stilled, and when all were silent, Petronius spoke.

'I can assure you that the men who have been raiding the coastal settlements and raiding your ships are not Romans. The whereabouts of the vessels of the Alexandrian fleet are accounted for. The perpetrators are a separate element, and their leader has been identified as the fugitive slave, Ajax.' Petronius paused. 'With that in mind, I trust I can rely on you to return to your communities and help quash the rumours that are sweeping through every quarter of the city. That is the responsible course of action. If anyone here is discovered to have perpetuated the lie that Roman forces have been involved in these raids, I will have no choice but to have them charged with sedition. Those found guilty will face confiscation of their property and exile, or death.'

A handful of the crowd fell to mumbling, before a man stepped to the front and raised a hand. 'Sir, may I speak?'

Petronius nodded.

'It is one thing to discover the truth behind the raids, and quite another to put an end to them. This fugitive and his gang are still at large. What do you propose to do about this threat to our trade? I can tell you that word of our losses is spreading to neighbouring provinces. Ship-owners are already refusing to sail to and from Alexandria, and those that do are charging ruinous fees. I am sure that I speak for every merchant here when I say that I pay my taxes and in return I expect my business to be protected to the fullest extent.'

'Of course!' Petronius responded loudly. 'And I am sure that you are equally concerned to protect the lives of the crewmen of the ships carrying your goods.'

The merchant shifted uncomfortably as he nodded.

'Naturally. It goes without saying that the well-being of our employees and shipping contractors is also close to our hearts.'

'Assuming they actually have hearts,' Macro muttered under his breath.

'That's quite an assumption,' Cato replied softly.

Petronius glanced at them and then turned his attention back to the Alexandrians' spokesman as the latter continued. 'Sir, the question I asked is unanswered. What are you going to do about this renegade?'

'The matter is in hand. Prefect Cato is leading a special task force with orders to find and destroy the renegade slave.'

'Clearly the prefect hasn't had much luck so far!' a voice called from the crowd. There was an angry chorus of agreement before Petronius held up his hands and demanded that they hear him out.

'I have utmost confidence in Prefect Cato. He is the best man for the job and it will only be a matter of days before he completes his mission.'

'How many days?' another merchant asked. 'It's already been more than a month since the trouble started. Another month will kill my business.'

There were more shouts, against a backdrop of bitter disgruntlement.

'Quiet there!' the prefect called out anxiously. 'Quiet, I said! Prefect Cato will have every military resource in Alexandria made available to him in order to facilitate the capture or destruction of Ajax.'

Macro nudged his friend. 'That's news to me.'

'And me.' Cato smiled faintly. 'Most welcome news.'

★

'What else could I say?' Petronius said irritably as he conferred with the two officers in his private quarters after the audience. 'You heard 'em. Their mood was almost rebellious. A number of them have influential contacts in Rome. If that isn't bad enough, the last two emperors have handed out Egyptian estates to their favourites as if they were party snacks. Even Narcissus has a few parcels of land in the delta. The trade in grain and other produce from those estates is being put in jeopardy by Ajax. Narcissus is the kind of man of influence that I'd rather not get on the wrong side of. So it's vital that Narcissus and his friends know that I am doing all that I can to keep a lid on the tensions here in Alexandria.'

'But you're not going to actually give us what we need to do the job, are you, sir?' said Macro.

'No. I can't. I told you, our forces are stretched thinly as it is. I can't afford to send them on some damned wild goose chase.'

'It wouldn't be a wild goose chase if we had more men and more ships,' Macro persisted. 'We could cover the ground more quickly, and be there in overwhelming strength when we eventually find Ajax.'

'If you find him.'

'We'll find him,' Cato said firmly. 'You have my word on it.'

'What if he quits the delta?' Petronius asked. 'What if he sails north, or west? What then? You'll be wasting time chasing shadows.'

'He won't leave the area. Why should he? He's doing a great job of stirring up local feeling against Rome. He'll stay here as long as he thinks he is undermining our interests in Egypt. Give us the fleet and we can find him and trap him in short order.'

'Give you the fleet?' Petronius smiled mockingly. 'I'm already having to use the marines to supplement the city watch. Besides, every available man is needed to counter the Nubians.'

'I need the fleet,' Cato insisted.

Petronius breathed in sharply and briefly considered the demand. 'I'll give you six more ships. But only for one month. That's as long as I can spare them.'

Cato considered the offer. Eight ships in all should be enough to deal with Ajax and his men, but the limited time was a problem. 'One month might not be enough.'

'That's all you have. After that I want you and your men to join the command of the legate of the Twenty-Second at Diospolis Magna. I suggest you get moving, Prefect.'

CHAPTER SIX

'It's like hunting for a grain of sand in a sack of salt,' Macro complained as he followed Cato and Hamedes along the strip of shingle towards a handful of beached fishing boats. 'Bloody Ajax is all but invisible.'

'We will find him,' Cato replied evenly. 'Whatever it takes.'

'It's not whatever that matters, but whenever. The month is almost up, Cato. If we don't find him in the next five days we will have to give up the search.'

'I am well aware of that, Centurion.'

Macro pressed his lips together in a thin line. The failure to find Ajax had tested his friend sorely, and Cato had recently developed a strategy of referring to Macro's rank when he grew weary of discussion or did not want to be contradicted. So they continued in silence walking steadily down the beach towards the fishermen, who were absorbed in the task of plucking the writhing silver fish from their nets and tossing them into baskets. Hamedes went first, ready to speak to the natives in their own tongue and reassure them that the three of them posed no threat. The priest had willingly volunteered to join the hunt when Cato had asked him to act as their guide and translator. The temple at Keirkut had been his life. Recruited to the priesthood when barely a child, it was the only family he had ever known and the desire for revenge burned in his veins.

Cato and Macro wore only their tunics and belts, with the dagger scabbards tucked out of sight behind their backs. Hamedes wore the simple flowing robe of the fellahin. The fishing boats had been sighted by one of the skiffs that Cato had sent in to patrol the Mendesian mouth of the Nile. The rest of the flotilla lay in a shallow cove by the sea. Cato and the others had landed out of sight of the fishermen and removed their armour before approaching them.

Due to the predations of Ajax, it had been difficult to gather any intelligence from the smaller Egyptian settlements along the coast. At the first sight of a Roman sail, or men in Roman uniform, the villagers had simply fled. The only news that Cato had gleaned from the locals had come from chance interceptions of the few vessels that had dared to put to sea, and the handful of times when they had been able to approach people without causing them to run and hide, as now.

'They've seen us,' Macro muttered as one of the fishermen looked up when they had closed to within a hundred paces. At once the man called out to his friends and they dropped their nets and snatched up their clubs and gutting knives. They were torn between abandoning their catch and running, or staying to confront the three men approaching them. There were twelve of them, Macro counted, odds of four to one, if there was any trouble. The fishermen were thin and sinewy and were not professional fighters. Even so, the overwhelming advantage in numbers lent them sufficient courage to stand their ground as they warily watched the three men making their way towards them.

'Tell them we mean no harm,' Cato said to Hamedes. 'We want to buy their catch, and talk.'

Hamedes nodded and called out a light-hearted greeting. The nearest of the fishermen replied sharply, holding out his hand, clearly commanding them to stop. There followed a brief exchange before Hamedes spoke softly to Cato. 'I've told them who we are. The one speaking for them is the headman of their village. He asks if we are alone. I said we are.'

Cato nodded uneasily and hoped that the marines he had left back at the skiff did as they were told and kept out of sight. 'Ask him if he has seen any other Romans recently.'

There was a lengthy exchange in which the headman jabbed his hand downriver. A moment later the priest turned back to Cato. 'A warship entered the mouth of the river several days ago. It stayed for the night and left the next morning.'

'Which direction did it take?'

'West.'

'Towards us?' Macro frowned. 'We never saw it.'

'It must have slipped past us in the dark,' said Cato. 'Or they sighted us first and turned back, or went and hid along the coast. Assuming it was Ajax, that is.' He reflected briefly. 'It has to be him. We're supposed to be the only naval forces operating along the delta.'

Cato gestured towards the fishing boats, small craft

made from bundles of reeds, tied together with ropes. 'Ask him if we can buy some of their catch.'

Hamedes translated and the other man cautiously beckoned them closer. Cato kept his hands out, where they could be seen clearly, and walked towards them. The dark eyes of the fishermen watched him closely and they drew back into a loose semi-circle as Cato and his companions approached the baskets. Scores of fish flipped about inside, and others opened and closed their bony mouths, as if gasping. More fish struggled in the nets. Cato gestured to them.

'Tell him we didn't intend to interrupt their work. They can continue, while we talk.'

With suspicious glances at their visitors, the fishermen went back to expertly plucking the catch from the folds of their nets while the headman conversed with Hamedes.

'He asks how much we wish to buy.'

'One basket will do.' Cato took the purse off his belt and took out some of the silver coins that Petronius had issued to the flotilla to pay for supplies. 'Here, ten obols.'

The headman's eyes momentarily lit up and then his face formed a dismissive expression.

'He says twenty. He has many mouths to feed in his village. If he sells his catch, some will go hungry tonight.'

'Bloody haggling,' Macro growled.

'Twelve,' Cato responded to Hamedes. 'It's a fair price. Tell him.'

The headman shook his head.

'Fifteen. He says he's robbing himself. But he can see

that you are a good man, so he makes this price just for you.'

'Fifteen obols,' Macro puffed irritably. 'Does he think we're complete fools?'

'Shhh,' Cato hissed. 'Fifteen it is.'

He counted out the coins and handed them over. The headman palmed them quickly and shoved them into a dirty linen haversack on the nearest of the boats.

'Tell him there's another five obols for him if he can tell us if he has heard anything about the location of the men who have been raiding the coast. Ask him if he has any idea where they might be hiding.'

The headman thought for a moment before responding.

'He says he will tell you what he knows if you pay him ten obols.'

'Cheeky bloody sod!' Macro chuckled. 'Cato, do you want me to persuade him to offer us a discount?'

'No. We need all the goodwill we can get. Let's not do Ajax's work for him, all right, Centurion?'

'Yes, sir.'

Cato handed over some more coins and waited for Hamedes to interpret.

'He says that a village was attacked on the next tributary to the west two days ago. Most of the villagers managed to escape, and fled to his village. That's why there are many more mouths to feed.'

'We must have missed something,' said Macro. 'Perhaps he didn't slip by us after all. Sir, we should turn back and search to the west.'

Cato was silent for a moment. His ships had scoured the coastline between Alexandria and here at the Mendesian mouth of the Nile. Every bay and inlet had been explored. Aside from the occasional evidence of one of Ajax's earlier raids, there had been no trace of the fugitives. It was possible that they had scuttled their ship and ventured deeper into the delta but Cato felt convinced that his enemy would not risk abandoning the warship, his only means of escape to sea. If the headman's information was accurate, that left two possibilities. Either Ajax had abandoned the delta and sailed north across the Mediterranean, or he had concealed his ship well enough to escape the eyes of Cato's flotilla.

'We'd better get back to the ships. Hamedes, give him my thanks, and tell him that we will not rest until we have destroyed Ajax. Then his people will be free to live in peace.'

The headman shrugged. 'He says that between the danger of Ajax and the burden of Roman taxes, what peace can a man hope for? There is no freedom. Not for the fellahin.'

'Not much we can do about that,' Macro said dismissively. 'Here, give me a hand with this basket.'

Hamedes made their farewells and took up the woven handle on one side of the basket while Macro took the other. Then, with Cato following, deep in thought, they made their way back down the narrow beach towards the point where the skiff and the marines lay out of sight.

'At least we'll have fresh meat on the menu tonight,' Macro mused happily as he glanced at the fish.

'They'll make good eating,' Hamedes grunted as he adjusted his grip.

'They'd better. I'd wager they're about the most expensive fish ever caught in Egypt,' Macro concluded ruefully.

That night, the crew of *Sobek* ate fried Nile carp, while the men of the other ships drawn up on the beach sullenly chewed on their hard tack. Cato and Macro were eating from their mess tins by the light of a cheery blaze of palm logs. Hamedes sat cross-legged on the far side of the fire, reading a prayer scroll he had borrowed from a temple in Alexandria. The fish, roasted over the fire, had been delicious, Macro reflected happily as he lowered his mess tin and licked his fingers. He glanced at Cato, and saw his face in profile, washed in a warm red glow, in deep concentration. Macro patted his chest and burped. 'Excuse me.'

'Hmmm?' Cato looked round absently.

'Ah, so you are still with us.'

'Yes. Of course.' Cato lowered his mess tin, and Macro saw that a good half of the fish remained. He gestured towards it. 'You finished with that?'

Cato nodded.

'Then do you mind if I, er . . .'

'Help yourself.'

Macro nodded his thanks and tucked in.

'Something's not right about what we were told by those fishermen,' Cato announced quietly. 'I'm certain we searched the coast thoroughly, and we didn't find any trace of Ajax, or the ship.'

'Obviously we didn't look hard enough,' said Macro, between mouthfuls.

'It's possible. But if I was in Ajax's position, I would

pick a base as far to the east of Alexandria as possible, away from the fleet.'

'If you were Ajax, surely you would want to be in striking distance of the main shipping lanes?'

'I'd not want to be within striking range of Alexandria. I'd want to be somewhere well off the main routes, away from settlements and with a clear escape route to sea if I needed to get out quickly. Somewhere well to the east of Alexandria. So we're not going back on our tracks tomorrow. We'll continue to the east.'

Macro swallowed quickly and set the mess tin down. 'Why? You heard them today. The most recent attack was to the west, and that's where they saw that ship heading.'

'True, I don't doubt what they say they saw, but I can't convince myself that Ajax is hiding in that direction. It doesn't make sense. Look, Macro, you know the man better than me.'

'Thanks for the reminder.'

'Ajax is as smart as new paint. He's also determined to cause us as much trouble as possible. You and me in particular, given that he blames us for the death of his father. Using our names was a nice touch.'

'You two know him then?' Hamedes interrupted, lowering his prayer scroll. 'You knew his father? How so?'

Macro smiled. 'Our man Ajax wasn't always a gladiator. In his earlier life he was a pirate, like his father, Telemachus. The prefect and I were part of the expedition sent to defeat Telemachus. We did the job. The pirate chief was crucified and his son was sold into slavery along with the rest of the prisoners we took. Only it turns out that he was picked to train as a gladiator before some fool bought him as a bodyguard and took him to Crete. Right now I wish we had nailed the bastard up alongside his father. We could have saved ourselves all this grief, and be back in Rome.'

'But we didn't,' Cato cut in. 'And now we must finish the job we started long ago. As I said, Ajax is clever, and he's consumed by hate. But I doubt he would throw his life away in some reckless act of revenge. So he will have a plan to clear out of the Nile delta if there's a danger he could be trapped here. That's why I think he is further to the east.' Cato unrolled his reed matting and lay down, pulling his cloak over him. 'In the morning, we sail east to Casium and then work our way back towards Alexandria.'

The next day the fleet put out to sea and steered east under full sail. A stiff breeze was blowing and the trierarch of the *Sobek* advised Cato to give the order to take in a reef in order to relieve the strain on the sail, mast and rigging. They were close to the deadline that Petronius had set for abandoning the search and Cato was determined to make the most of the time that remained. He ordered the trierarch to remain at full sail, and signal the rest of the ships to follow suit.

As the sun sank over the horizon, the flotilla reached the small port of Casium and spent the night taking on water and fresh provisions. At dawn, they set sail, heading back towards Alexandria. It was Cato's intention to search the coastline thoroughly. If Ajax was hiding anywhere, it would be along this stretch of the delta. He was sure of it.

The *Sobek* cleared the harbour mole as the sun glinted above the eastern horizon. Hamedes lowered himself on to his knees to face the sun and stretched his arms out, eyes closed as his lips mumbled a prayer. He was not alone. Those of the crew who shared his beliefs followed suit and performed the ritual as quickly as possible before returning to their duties. The sails were set, and the sheets hauled in and cleated. The priest, whose rites were more involved, continued for a while longer before he rose to his feet and stretched his shoulders. He caught Cato's eye and there was the briefest of pauses before he smiled a greeting.

'I have offered prayers to Isis that you find what you seek today.'

'Thank you.' Cato nodded. 'I think I need all the help I can get.'

'Sail in sight!' the lookout's cry interrupted them.

'Where away?' called the trierarch.

'Dead ahead, sir!'

Cato hurried forward and was joined by Macro, the trierarch and Hamedes a moment later. The western horizon was clear. For a while they stared hard, then Cato thrust out his arm and pointed. 'Over there!'

The others followed his direction and, as the *Sobek* lifted on a swell, there was a tiny gleam of white, then it was gone. The trierarch turned and raised his head towards the lookout. 'Can you make her out? Is it a warship?'

There was a long pause before the reply came. 'No, sir. Too small. Looks like some kind of a fast yacht. Yes, sir. I'm sure of it. She's altered course and is making for us.'

'A yacht?' Macro scratched his chin. 'Wonder who's in such a hurry to find us.'

'More to the point, why?' asked Cato. 'Trierarch, alter course towards that vessel.'

'Yes, sir.'

The warship swung towards the yacht and the two vessels closed quickly. Less than an hour later, a young Roman officer, who Cato recognised as one of Petronius's tribunes, climbed on to the deck of the *Sobek* and strode towards Cato.

'Urgent despatch from the governor, sir.' The tribune held out a leather tube with the governor's seal securing the cap. Cato took the tube, broke the seal and took out a small scroll of papyrus. Moving to the side of the ship, he unrolled it and read through it quickly, then again to be quite sure about the contents of the message. He rolled it up and gestured to his friend. 'Macro, on me, please.'

'What is it, sir?' Macro asked in an undertone once he had joined Cato.

'The Nubians have crossed the frontier. They've invaded Egypt. Petronius has ordered the Twenty-Second to advance up the Nile to Diospolis Magna. He aims to mass all his available forces there before moving against the Nubians.'

'Which means he wants us to return to Alexandria at once, I take it.'

'Yes.' Cato clenched his fist round the scroll, crushing it. 'It seems that we are obliged to abandon the hunt for Ajax.'

Macro's heart felt leaden with disappointment and looking at his superior he could see that Cato shared his bitterness. Macro cleared his throat. 'It's just for now, sir. We'll continue the job once the Nubians are dealt with. We'll find the bastard, don't you worry. He'll pay for what he did to me, and to Julia. I swear it, on my life.'

Cato stared at him and nodded. 'As do I.'

Then he took a deep breath and crossed the deck towards the tribune. 'Tell the governor we are making full sail and will return to Alexandria without delay.'

'Yes, sir.' The tribune saluted, and then hesitated. 'Is there anything I should report to him, sir? Any progress you have made in locating the renegade?'

'No. There's nothing,' Cato admitted. 'Now be off.'

The tribune went to the side and climbed down the rope ladder on to the deck of the sleek yacht. At once the crew fended it away from the side of the warship and raised the triangular sail. The wind filled the sail with a dull crack and the yacht heeled as it picked up speed and pulled away from the *Sobek*, heading west.

Cato turned to the trierarch. 'Set course for Alexandria. Signal the other ships to follow us.'

'Aye, sir.'

As the warship got back under way, Cato stood at the side rail, staring towards the coastline. Ajax was out there, somewhere, and free to continue wreaking damage along the delta, unavenged. It was a bitter thing to swallow, but there was nothing that could be done about it.

The wind strengthened during the day and the ships ploughed through a choppy sea, sending clouds of spray exploding into the air as the bronze-capped rams punched through the swell. The rigging, taut under the strain, hummed as it vibrated and the yardarm stretching across the deck bowed under the pressure from the sail, all under the anxious eye of the trierarch. Then, in the middle of the afternoon, there was a faint crack and Cato turned to see that one of his ships, the *Thoth*, had slewed to one side. The yard had shattered and the sail collapsed beneath the splintered ends of the length of timber.

'Heave to!' the trierarch ordered. 'Signal the order to all ships!'

Cato bit back on his frustration as the flotilla rolled gently on the waves. The trierarch hurriedly went below to consult his charts and then came back on deck to report to Cato.

'There's a small naval station only a short distance along the coast, sir, on the Tanitic mouth. The *Thoth* can put in there under oars to pick up a spare yard and then catch up with us tonight. She's the fastest sailer in the flotilla, sir. It shouldn't take her long.'

'Very well, pass the word to the trierarch of the *Thoth*. As soon as it's done, we continue on course.'

The trierarch nodded and hurried to the stern of the warship where he picked up a speaking trumpet and bellowed the instructions back to the *Ibis*, who passed them on to the *Thoth*. Shortly after, the oars emerged from the hull and began to drive the vessel through the waves towards the shore as the crew on deck cut away the shattered yardarm. The rest of the ships braced up their sails and continued to the west.

The flotilla was beached well before sunset in order to

give the *Thoth* a chance to catch up before night set in. The crews set to work building their fires for the night and then cooking some of the fresh rations they had taken on at Casium. The sun crept down towards the horizon and as it touched the palms on the distant headland, Cato came across Hamedes staring out to sea.

'I thought you'd be at prayer.' Cato smiled, jabbing his thumb towards the setting sun.

The priest flashed a guilty smile. 'I'm worried about the other ship. It hasn't arrived yet. It hasn't even been sighted.'

'No. The repairs are probably taking longer than was thought. I don't suppose a small naval station gets many visitors other than . . .' Cato fell silent. A cold tide of dread seeped up through his guts. He turned and hurried down the beach towards his ship, seeking out the trierarch.

'The supply station you sent the ship to. Tell me about it.'

'I've called in there a few times over the years. Not much to say.' The trierarch pursed his lips. 'They carry stores and supplies. They have a small team of carpenters who can make emergency repairs. The garrison covers the Tanitic mouth and mounts patrols into the delta. Used to be a lot busier before it began to silt up and the mangroves made the tributary unusable for shipping.'

'Show me the location on the chart,' Cato ordered.

While the trierarch hurried up the gangway on to the ship, Macro came over. 'You look like you've swallowed a turd. What's happening?'

'I'm not sure,' Cato replied, trying to stifle his anxiety. 'It's just a feeling. A possibility.'

The trierarch returned, clutching a rolled-up map. He knelt in the pool of light cast by the nearest fire and spread the map. His finger traced along the coastline and stopped. 'Here, sir. That's where the supply station is. Epichos.'

CHAPTER SEVEN

The sails had been taken off the ships and the yards lowered to the deck to reduce the chance that they would be spotted from the shore as they approached. The oars were out and the warships were making their way, very slowly, towards the headland. Cato stood in the foredeck turret straining his eyes as he stared towards the distant outline of the watchtower, barely discernible against the night sky. Macro had landed with a handful of legionaries over two hours earlier. Shortly afterwards he had sent a boat back to the *Sobek* to report that there were three ships beached on the shore in front of the supply base, one of which was the *Thoth*. There had been no sign of any movement on the ship. That was proof enough for Cato and he had given the order for the attack he had planned with Macro to go ahead, as soon as the first hint of dawn appeared on the eastern horizon.

Macro would strike first, taking the watchtower on the headland and the lookout post before the sentries could detect the ships approaching from sea and raise the alarm. He had taken Hamedes with him in case they were challenged. Hamedes would claim that he had been forced ashore when his fishing boat had begun to leak. It might buy them a few moments, long enough to spring a surprise.

As soon as the towers were in Macro's hands, he would signal the ships waiting to attack. Cut off from the sea, Ajax and his men would be trapped in the fort. They would have to surrender, or more likely they would choose to fight to the last man. Either way, their end was assured, Cato reflected.

He heard the ladder creaking behind him and a moment later the trierach joined him.

'Too early for Macro to go into action, I suppose.'

'Yes, but not long now.' Cato glanced at the horizon and thought he detected the faintest loom dividing the sea and the sky. 'When we get the signal, I want the ship to enter the bay as swiftly as possible. Ajax must not escape.'

'We'll do it in good time, sir. The *Sobek* will be past the headland long before the enemy can put to sea. You have my word.'

'And I shall hold you to it.'

Neither man spoke for a moment before the trierarch asked, 'Do you think there's a chance that some of the crew of the *Thoth* were taken prisoner, sir?'

'I doubt it. If I am any judge of Ajax's character, he will not have spared their lives. And that might be a good thing.'

'Sir?'

'Those prisoners he took during the rebellion in Crete were often saved for a far worse fate than a quick death.' Cato's tone hardened. 'Your comrades are dead. Set your heart on avenging them.'

'Yes, sir.'

Cato turned and looked round at the dark masses of the other vessels. There was no sound from them, even though hundreds of marines and legionaries stood and waited on their decks, while hundreds more manned the oars. Aside from the faint rush of water along the hulls and the splash of oar blades, the ships were like shadows as they stole towards the coast.

'There, sir,' the trierarch said quickly. 'Dawn's breaking.'

Cato looked. There was a definite glow along the horizon now. He turned towards the watchtower once again. Still nothing. He muttered under his breath, 'Come on, Macro. It all depends on you.'

Macro lay flat on the ground beside an outcrop of rocks. Twenty paces away the squat mass of the tower on the headland loomed against the skyline. Already, there was a thin wash of light that allowed him to pick out some of the detail in the ground around him. His party had disposed of the sentries in the lookout post and had been about to take their second objective when a small group of men had approached from the direction of the fort. There had just been time to take cover, and a moment later several figures strode past. There was an exchange of words with the men in the tower but the sound of the small waves breaking over the rocks on the headland made it impossible to make out what was said.

If the party of men didn't leave soon he would have to risk making his attack against less favourable odds. In addition to Hamedes, he had ten legionaries with him. Ten men against the half dozen who had approached the tower and perhaps another four or five inside. Ten Romans and one priest, Macro corrected himself. Still, Hamedes was solid enough and might be useful in a tight spot. Two tenders and their sailors were waiting in a small cove back along the headland, ready to evacuate them if for any reason they failed to take the towers and had to escape in a hurry.

Macro eased his hand back and drew his sword, wincing at the faint sound of scraping as the tip cleared the scabbard. He held it tightly as he raised his head as much as he dared to get a better view of the tower. Beside him Hamedes took a sharp breath and whispered, 'We should go, Centurion. There's too many of them. They'll kill us.'

'Quiet,' Macro hissed. 'And don't move, or I'll kill you myself.'

He switched his attention back to the tower, clearly visible against the horizon. It would not be long before the sentries caught sight of the approaching ships and raised the alarm, Macro realised. Then, at last, the men from the fort turned away from the tower and began to retrace their steps along the headland. As they passed Macro's hiding place, his heart began to race as he recognised their leader.

'Ajax,' he breathed softly through gritted teeth. He felt his muscles tense like iron and an icy rage gripped his body so that it took all his self-control not to spring from cover and hack the gladiator to bloody pieces. As he lay, trembling with fury, visions, smells and emotions filled his mind with a raw intensity as he recalled the shaming torments that Ajax had subjected him to. Torments that he had tried to forget and suppress. Things he had never confessed to even his closest friend, Cato, and never would. Macro shut his eyes, blanking out the barely discernible figure of Ajax. He breathed deeply, fighting back against the memories that threatened to overwhelm him. When he opened his eyes again, the gladiator and his companions had disappeared down the track that led to the beach on the inside of the headland.

Macro rose into a crouch and turned to the silent shapes lying on the ground behind him. 'On me,' he growled softly.

He moved forward, keeping low, and there was a faint swishing through the dry grass behind him as his men followed. Keeping in the shadow of the rocks, Macro moved stealthily towards the tower. He could see that the heavy door at the base of the tower was open. Above, on the platform, he heard voices muttering and a faint rustle as the morning breeze stirred the tips of the palm leaves of the sunshade. Macro scurried across the open ground in front of the tower, making straight for the door. Then a figure appeared in the frame, and froze. Macro powered forward, lowering the tip of his sword. At the last moment he punched the blade forward and it ripped into the man's midriff an instant before Macro's shoulder struck him in the chest. He slammed the man back through the door, across the interior of the tower until he struck one of the posts holding up the floor above. The man grunted as the breath was driven out of him and warm spittle and blood splattered Macro's face. Clamping his spare hand over the man's mouth, Macro thrust the sword up into the ribcage, ripping through vital organs. His opponent struggled frantically and then abruptly slumped forward on to Macro. He drew back, wrenching his blade free, and eased the body down on to the ground. Around him, his men crowded into the tower.

'What's going on there?' a voice called down the flight of wooden stairs leading up to the platform. 'Portius?'

There was a faint hue of wavering orange light from above, illuminating the topmost stairs.

'Let's go,' Macro growled, running to the stairs and pounding up to the first level of the tower. When he reached the top, he saw a room with several sleeping mats lining the wall, a table and stools and weapons rack. There were two men. One rising up on an elbow, disturbed from his sleep. The other was near the top of the stairs, close to the weapons. He was quicker witted than his companion downstairs and instantly snatched at a spear and lowered the tip towards Macro as he and his men raced into the room. The spear tip thrust forwards and Macro swerved aside, crashing into a stool that sent him sprawling. The legionary behind him did not see the danger until it was too late and the spear thudded into the shoulder of his sword arm, the impact spinning him round against the shaft and knocking it to one side. The next man thrust his way past, and hacked at the spearman's neck, cutting deep. With a sharp cry the renegade collapsed back, on to the floor, the butt of the spear clattering beside him. The man on the mattress made to get up but was cut down before he reached his feet.

'The roof!' Macro called out as he scrambled to his feet. 'Move!'

The first few men ran past, climbing the last flight of stairs. Macro went after them. There was a brief cry of alarm, quickly cut off. As he emerged on to the roof, Macro glanced round. There was a low wall topped off with a wooden rail surrounding the roof. In one corner was the palm-leaf shade. In the opposite corner the signal brazier. There were four bolt throwers. A dull glow came from a small niche where an oil lamp stood ready to light the brazier.

'You two!' Macro pointed at the nearest of his men. 'Get downstairs and seal the door. Barricade it with whatever's to hand.'

He hurried across to the rail and stared towards the fort. A handful of torches glowed by the main gate and by their light he could see a pair of sentries standing on the gatehouse, apparently unconcerned. The dark shapes of three ships lay beached on the shore in front of the fort. There was no sign of alarm.

'Good.' Macro nodded to himself. Then he turned and crossed to the brazier, snatching up some of the kindling. He then carefully picked up the oil lamp and made his way down the stairs and outside. He set the lamp down and made a small pile of the kindling against the side of the tower facing the sea, and presented the flame of the oil lamp to it. The pallid yellow flicker licked the bundle of dry twigs and palm leaves. Then there was a puff of smoke as the flame caught and quickly spread through the rest of the bundle. The wall around the fire lit up with a bright yellow glow and Macro stood back and turned to look out to sea, searching until his eyes fixed on the distant shapes of the warships.

There was a shout from inside the tower and Macro looked up and saw light flickering from a small window halfway up the wall. The light quickly intensified and now the crackle of flames came to his ears.

'What the hell?' He hurried round to the door as the first of his men came stumbling outside.

Macro grabbed the legionary. 'What's going on?'

'There's a fire in the sentry's quarters, sir! The oil lamp must have gone over and set light to one of the bedrolls.'

'Fuck,' Macro gritted his teeth. 'We have to put it out, quick.'

He ran back inside, up the stairs. Already the air was thick with smoke and the flames flared up against the walls, lighting the space in a hellish red light. There were shouts from above as the flames licked up the stairs. Macro looked round desperately, then saw an amphora leaning in the corner. He rushed over and snatched it up, and pulled out the stopper, instantly releasing the sharp tang of wine. Moving towards the fire, and wincing at the heat that struck him like a stinging blow, Macro shook the contents towards the flames. The wine landed in gouts, quenching the flames, but not quickly enough.

'Bugger this,' Macro growled, stepping back. He hefted the amphora, took aim at the wall where the flames were most fierce and hurled the jar. The heavy pottery exploded, wine splattered on the rough plaster and drenched the sleeping mat below. Snatching up a cloak from the table, Macro started beating out the flames.

He looked over his shoulder and saw Hamedes. 'Give me a bloody hand!'

The priest hesitated for an instant, his eyes wide with fear, then he plucked a cloak from a peg on the wall beside him and joined Macro, smothering the remaining flames. When the last of the fire was stamped out, Macro nodded his thanks. He looked round the smoke-filled room. An acrid stench gripped his throat and he coughed. Throwing the cloak down, he stumbled to the stairs, pushing the priest ahead of him, and climbed up on to the roof. He crossed to the wooden rail and breathed deeply to clear his lungs. The dawn was coming up fast; a band of pale light thickened along the horizon. By its glow Macro could already see the full extent of the bay from the shadowy mangroves, across the water to the fort. Several figures had emerged from the gate and were looking directly towards the headland. More appeared on the walls of the fort and then there was a shrill blast of a horn.

'Damn, they've seen the fire.' Macro clenched the rail. A moment later, he watched a strong force of men emerge from the gate. They carried shields and a mix of weapons – swords, spears, axes and a handful of bows. Several of them carried torches that flared brightly as they broke into a trot. They hurried along the path leading to the headland. Macro sucked in a breath. 'Now we're for it.'

Cato had given the order for the *Sobek* to head for the entrance to the bay at full speed and the drum beneath the deck beat the time as the oars swept forward, down and back, powering the warship forward. In the near darkness, Macro's signal had stood out clearly. But then more flames had appeared briefly, licking up out of the tower and illuminating the surrounding rocks.

'What the hell is he playing at?' said the trierarch. 'He's going to give the whole thing away.'

'Something's gone wrong,' Cato responded anxiously. 'How long before we make the entrance to the bay?'

The trierarch squinted at the coastline and estimated

the distance. 'Within the half-hour if we keep up the current speed.'

'So long?' Cato stared at the headland. He forced himself to push his concern for Macro aside and concentrated on the timing. From his experience of the last two months he knew that a well-handled ship could be refloated from a beach in less than a quarter of the time. If Ajax moved quickly he could get his men aboard their ship and make for the open sea before the trap was closed. That could not be allowed to happen, Cato resolved. He turned to the trierarch.

'Can the ship go any faster?'

'Yes, sir. Ramming speed is part of the drill. But we can only keep it up for a short stretch.'

'Then give the order.'

'But sir, it will exhaust the men. They need their strength for when we close to do battle.'

'There won't be any battle unless we reach the bay in time. Your men must row their hearts out. Understand?'

'Yes, sir.'

'Then give the order. Pass it on to the other ships. Go!'

The trierarch dropped down the ladder on to the deck and ran to the midships hatchway to shout the order to his timekeeper. Cato heard the drum increase its pace, and the deck gave a little lurch beneath his boots as the *Sobek* began to speed up. To the east, off the port bow, the sky was turning pink and painting the undersides of a few scattered clouds in a warm delicate hue. Cato willed the ship on. The flames on the tower had died away now and he could not help wondering what had become of Macro and his men. If they still lived, then they were on their own until the warships reached the bay. Even as his thoughts were with this friend, Cato saw a tiny pinprick of light dancing along the headland, then another, and more, and with a sick feeling in his stomach he realised that Ajax and his men were already hunting down Macro and his small band.

CHAPTER EIGHT

'Sir!' a voice called to Macro. 'They're coming!'

He trotted over to the edge of the tower and saw the figures emerging between two rocks, less than a quarter of a mile away. They came on at a run and Macro quickly saw that he and his men were outnumbered at least three to one.

'What are you going to do?' asked Hamedes. 'There's too many of them. We should get out of here while there's still time. Or surrender.'

'Surrender? To that bastard? Never!' Macro snarled.

'Then let's run.'

'Run? Where? We're on a bloody headland. There's nowhere to run to, you idiot. Now shut up and give me a hand.' Macro moved over to one of the bolt throwers and swivelled it round to face the oncoming attackers. 'Open the ammunition box,' he snapped and pointed at a weathered chest beside the wall. While Hamedes fetched a bundle of the heavy bolts, two feet long with heavy iron heads and wooden flights, Macro wound the handle and ratcheted back the thick tarry cord that stretched between the two arms of the weapon. Once it was ready, he took the first bolt from the priest and laid it in the long groove that passed between the boxes containing the torsion ropes. The first of the renegades was little more than two hundred paces from the tower now and Macro pulled out the elevation pin and then grunted as he raised the bed of the weapon, sighted the bolt thrower on the man, then slipped the pin back in. He straightened up.

'Stand clear!'

He glanced round, then grasped the lanyard that released the ratchet. He gave it a quick tug and the throwing arms snapped forward against the leather buffers with a sharp crack. At once Macro looked over the rail and saw the slender shadow slash through the dawn air towards the oncoming men. It flew over the leading man's head even before he was aware it was there. The bolt flew on, past another man before it hit the ground, sent up a spray of grit and ricocheted up and tore through the leg of one of the renegades, lifting him off the ground and sending him spinning into a small group close behind, knocking them down.

'Ha!' Macro growled with satisfaction, and hurriedly prepared the next shot. 'Bolt!' He held out his hand and Hamedes fumbled for the next round. He dropped it and ducked down to retrieve it as Macro cursed him. Looking up, Macro saw that the attackers had spread out and were picking their way forward more cautiously. That suited Macro well enough. All that mattered was to buy enough time to allow Cato's ships to enter the bay. Three of Ajax's men were creeping forward by the rocks where Macro's party had hidden and he swivelled the weapon round and released the catch. There was another crack and the bolt whirred through the air. This time it struck one of the men cleanly in the chest, hurling him back against a boulder where he crumpled in an untidy heap, the end of the shaft projecting from his tunic.

As soon as Macro began to reload, there was a shout and the men sprinted forward in the interval before the next round was loaded. Macro just had time to lower the elevation and fire one last bolt, which flew over their heads.

'That's it.' He stood back from the bolt thrower. 'It's hand-to-hand now.'

The first of the attackers reached the door and pounded on it. To little effect, as the door was secured with a wooden bar and some meal bags had been piled behind it. By the time Macro had climbed down and joined his men, as they snatched up the shields of the renegades they had killed, the first axe blows were thudding into the aged timber. A moment later a long splinter of wood shot back from the inside of the door. More splinters exploded as axes crashed home. Then a long sliver of wood bent down and the dull edge of the axe head protruded, a finger's width, through the door. When the axe was wrenched free, it left a narrow gap through which Macro could see the men outside in the pale dawn light. More blows smashed through the weakened timber and hands wrenched at the shattered lengths of wood.

'Don't worry, lads,' Macro said evenly. 'There's only one way in. All we have to do is keep 'em out until the prefect gets here.'

He glanced round at the men standing poised in the gloom and noted their expressions. Some looked grim but determined, while a handful of others, younger, had an anxious, fearful look in their eyes. It was a centurion's duty to lead from the front, to inspire his men, and Macro eased himself forward towards the door, sword clenched in his right hand. He drew out his dagger and held it in the other hand. With a splintering crack a length of the door was pulled away, then more pieces, until only a shattered fringe remained. Outside, the renegades closed round. The first man stepped up, then kicked the makeshift barrier of meal sacks over. He carried a spear and he lowered the tip and thrust at Macro with a grunt. The leaf-shaped head stabbed towards his midriff and Macro parried it away as he swung to his left. At once he recovered his balance and lunged at the spearman, forcing him back, out of the door.

'Form up around the door!' Macro shouted. 'Take 'em from the side as they come in.'

As the men hurried into place, the spearman thrust again, hands gripping the shaft tightly and legs braced apart. This time he fully concentrated his attention on the centurion, as if they were paired in a duel. He weighed Macro up with an expert eye, and feinted. Macro flinched for an instant and then he grinned.

'I don't fool that easy. Try harder.'

This time the thrust was in earnest and the point shot forward like a ram. Macro slashed down, just above the man's hand, and the point went down towards the floor. Macro's dagger hand darted forward and stabbed into the renegade's forearm. With a gasp, he released the shaft and Macro stamped down on it, forcing the man off balance. He stumbled forward, inside the doorway, as he strove to regain his balance. One of the legionaries stepped up and punched his sword high into the man's back, driving him to one side. He fell on to his knees and slumped down with a groan as the legionary ripped his blade free.

'First blood to us, boys!' Macro cried out, then beckoned to the faces watching him from outside. 'Come on! Who's next?'

There was only the briefest hesitation before a burly swordsman swallowed nervously and made to approach the door. Before he could reach it, a voice called out.

'Stand aside! Let me through!'

Macro felt a cold shiver ripple down his spine as he recognised the voice at once. The men in front of him drew aside, creating a small open space before the door. Into it stepped a tall, powerful man in his early twenties, dark hair falling to his shoulders. He carried a short sword in one hand and a small round shield in the other. His body was protected by a black leather cuirass, decorated with silver whorls. His lips twisted into a cold smile.

'Centurion Macro. Well, what a surprise. I should have guessed you would try to find me.'

'And now that I have, I'm going to kill you,' Macro replied through gritted teeth.

'Really?' Ajax stepped closer, his eyes fixed on Macro. 'Then why not come out here? Let's settle this, man to man.'

Macro felt a burning compulsion to confront the gladiator. The urge coursed through his veins and threatened to cloud his judgement. He clamped his jaw shut and stared back at the man who had tormented him so cruelly barely three months before.

'What's the matter?' Ajax smirked. 'Are you not man enough to face me?'

Macro took half a step forward, almost to the threshold of the tower's entrance, and checked himself.

'Tell you what, Ajax,' he spoke in a flat tone. 'Why don't you come in here to settle things.'

Ajax chuckled coldly. 'A stand-off between us, then. A shame, since I would have liked the chance to humiliate you in front of your men.' Ajax lowered his sword. 'It seems that we'll have to do this the hard way.' He stepped back and turned to his men. 'Shields to the front!'

A half-dozen renegades stepped up. Three stood together and overlapped their shields. The others stepped up to guard the flanks and then Ajax beckoned to some more of his men and they approached the door.

The time for fancy footwork and swordplay was over, Macro realised. This was about to become a contest of brute strength, and Ajax and his men were as powerful and tough as they came.

'Legionaries, on me!' Macro called out, grabbing a shield. 'Quickly, damn it!'

His men scrambled to his side, forming up, shield to shield and swords held level, as they were trained to do for close combat.

'Ready!' Macro barked the order and then called the time as he stepped towards the door. 'One . . . two . . .'

The two sides crunched together just inside the door frame and Macro threw his weight behind his shield as he braced his boots against the grain sacks that had collapsed on the floor. His men pressed in close behind him and Macro could hear the strained breath and grunts of effort all around him as the Romans and the renegades heaved against each other. Those in the front were trapped between the shields and those pushing them from behind. Macro knew that it was a contest between the raw strength of the renegades and the technique of the legions. For a moment both sides pushed with all their strength, and then Macro felt the sacking beneath his right boot begin to give. He tried to adjust his foot, but the sack had split and the loose grain gave little traction. Slowly he was eased back from the door and a gap opened between his shield and that of the man to his left. At once the tip of a sword blade thrust through the gap, mercifully striking nothing but air before it was snatched back.

'Watch it!' Macro warned the others. 'Close up.'

The legionaries heaved forward and pressed the enemy back.

'Come on!' Ajax yelled. 'Push! Sweep them aside, lads. Then kill 'em all.'

Once again the bodies were tightly wedged against each other in the narrow doorway. Macro turned towards one of the men still standing to one side.

'You! Go for their legs, man! Hack 'em!'

The legionary nodded and edged his way round the side of the struggle, then, taking careful aim, he waited until there was a gap and stabbed the point of his sword home, into a calf. The renegade bellowed in pain and instinctively edged back, creating a gap in the shield wall presented to the Romans. Macro pushed forward, driving between two of his enemies and thrusting his own blade out, at an angle, into the side of the man to his right. It was not a lethal blow, just breaking through the skin and catching in the ribs, but the man fell away with a grunt.

Just as the Romans drove the last of their enemies away

from the door, there was a shout from down the track.

'General! General Ajax!'

Ajax, in the third rank of his men, glanced back and saw the figure running down the track towards the skirmish. 'Here!'

He pushed his way out and stood, chest heaving from his exertions. 'What is it?'

'There are warships coming, sir. Several of them. Making straight for the harbour entrance.'

'How far away?'

'A mile, maybe less.'

Ajax turned back, seeking out Macro as he frowned in frustration. 'Damn it! There's no time for this,' he snarled. He stared towards Macro in blind hatred before he recovered his poise. 'Fall back, boys. Fall back. Return to the ships. Fast as you can! We have to get out of here!'

Ajax's men scrambled back and Macro felt the pressure lift from his shield and he had to scramble forward a little in order to retain his balance. He crouched, shield up and sword drawn, breathing heavily. His eyes met those of Ajax, some ten feet away. The gladiator thrust his arm out, pointing directly at Macro. 'It isn't over yet! As Zeus is my witness, I'll cut your head from your body with my own sword.'

Then he turned and joined his men as they warily backed away a short distance from the tower and then turned to run down the track. Macro watched him go with a heavy heart. If Cato and his ships managed to reach the mouth of the harbour in time to prevent Ajax's escape then that reckoning might come soon enough, Macro reflected. He waited until the last of the renegades was a safe distance down the track before he stretched up into a standing position and lowered his shield. Turning towards the sea, he could easily make out the ships from the Alexandrian fleet rowing swiftly towards the shore.

CHAPTER NINE

The sun had crested the horizon as the *Sobek* approached the point of the headland. The coast was bathed in a warm yellow glow which caught the red sails of the warships, intensifying the colour. The trierarch was leaning over the bow and staring down into the water as he tried to pick out any shoals that might threaten his ship. The sea was calm and the lightest of swells brushed up against the rocks on the shore. Cato had dressed in armour and wore his red cloak and plumed helmet in preparation for the coming battle. He climbed up into the turret on the foredeck and surveyed the coastline. For the last half mile of its length the headland was on lower ground and from the turret Cato could see the tops of the palm trees on the far side of the bay. Earlier he had seen the enemy withdraw from the watchtower and had feared that Macro and his men had been overwhelmed. But then his keen eyes had detected the transverse crest of a helmet atop the tower and he knew that his friend still lived.

'Sir!' the lookout cried from his position astride the spar. He pointed across the headland. 'They're on the move!'

Cato turned his head to look, and might have missed it had he not been looking for the enemy ship. A faint sliver of shadow against the haze that lingered across the mainland. The mast of a ship. Then he saw another a short distance behind. Ajax was making a run for it. Looking ahead, Cato saw that the headland bowed out to sea and he realised, with a sick feeling, that Ajax might reach the entrance to the bay before the *Sobek*.

'Increase our speed!' he called down to the trierarch. Phermon looked up and shook his head.

'Sir, the crew have been rowing flat out for the best part of an hour. They're spent.'

'I don't give a damn about that. Order them to row faster.'

'They can't,' the trierarch replied firmly. 'You've exhausted them, sir.'

Cato gritted his teeth in anger. The trierarch was right. He had been desperate to reach the harbour as swiftly as he could, and now the crew had no reserve of strength to draw on at the critical moment. By contrast, Ajax's men were still fresh and as Cato watched the masts of his enemy's ships, he could see that they were gradually pulling ahead. More galling still, they had the advantage of the inside track as they raced across the bay towards the tip of the headland. He thumped a fist on the rail of the turret in frustration. He took a deep breath and spoke as calmly as he could to the trierarch. 'Have your men do the best they can. One last effort is all I ask of them.'

'Yes, sir.' The trierarch saluted and made his way aft to the main hatch and descended below deck to urge his men on.

Cato turned his attention back to the two masts edging ahead of the *Sobek* on the other side of the headland. They would soon be abreast of the watchtower and then reach the open sea and make their escape. The Roman ships would attempt a pursuit, but barring a miracle Ajax and his men would get away, Cato realised bitterly.

A faint movement attracted his attention and he saw a thin dark smudge in the air above the watchtower. There was a brief eddy of smoke and then it settled into a steady trail, climbing into the clear sky. Cato frowned at this new development, but Macro and his men were safe enough now that the enemy was on the run. They could afford to let the tower burn. But even as he was thinking this, Cato realised that the smoke was too localised. A moment later there was a bright flare and a thin trail of smoke arced out from the top of the tower towards the two ships approaching from inside the bay. Another trail quickly followed the first before Cato realised what was happening.

'Bolt throwers.' He smiled to himself. 'Macro's using incendiaries. Clever bastard.'

Macro kept up a steady stream of flaming bolts as the enemy vessels approached, and then there was a dark swirl of smoke from over the headland and Cato saw that the ships had changed course, forced to give the headland a wide berth to avoid the weapons shooting at them from the watchtower. One vessel was already alight. Cato gripped the rail of the turret as he continued to watch. Beneath his feet he detected the faintest of lurches as the men at the oars made one last effort. By the time the trierarch had returned to the bows, the point was in sight and Cato knew that the contest was over. Forced aside by Macro, Ajax and his ships could not reach the open sea in time to make a clear escape.

'We'll have them, sir.' The trierarch grinned.

'So it seems,' Cato replied as calmly as he could manage. 'Have the marines stand to.'

The headland dipped down to a small sandy spit at the edge of the turquoise sea and the *Sobek* continued a short distance beyond before the trierarch ordered the steersman to turn directly into the bay. From the turret Cato had a clear view of the two vessels making towards him, less than quarter of a mile away. To the right was the ship Ajax had seized when he fled from Crete. The other was the *Thoth*, from which smoke billowed from a fire raging amidships. Several men were drawing buckets from the sea and attempting to dowse the flames that threatened the ship. Even so, the crew stuck to their oars and the ship ploughed on, water surging over the ram and down her sides. Cato strained his eyes to see if he could spot Ajax on either ship. There was too much smoke and too many figures dashing around the deck of the *Thoth* to be certain of picking out a single man and he concentrated his attention on the other ship. A handful of archers stood in the turret on the foredeck and more armed men waited on the main deck. Then, as the distance rapidly closed, Cato saw a figure push his way through to the bows, tall and broad and wearing a decorated black cuirass and a brilliantly polished helmet with a black crest of billowing feathers.

'Ajax,' Cato whispered to himself. His heart hardened pitilessly as he beheld the rebel slave who was the cause of so much death and suffering. Cato thought fitfully of Julia and the humiliation she had suffered at the gladiator's hands. His fists clenched hard as he gave his order to Phermon.

'We'll take the ship on the right. Let the other one burn.'

'Aye, sir.' The trierarch cupped a hand to his mouth and turned aft. 'Steersman! Make for the starboard vessel!'

The steersman leaned into his tiller and the ship came round and steadied on a course bow to bow with the oncoming vessel. Cato stared at Ajax, and then slipped his hand down to the pommel of his sword. It was a shame that Macro was not at his side to take his share of the long-awaited revenge, thought Cato. He had little doubt that Ajax and his lieutenants would far sooner go down fighting than be captured and suffer a lingering and humiliating death by crucifixion.

'Excuse me, sir,' a voice called and Cato looked round as a marine climbed into the turret, clutching a bow and a quiver filled with arrows. Two more men joined him and Cato moved to one side to give them room. On the enemy ship he could see Ajax's bowman fitting arrows to their strings before they aimed their bows high as the two ships ploughed towards each other across the tranquil surface of the bay. They loosed off the first volley of arrows and Cato watched impassively as the tiny specks swept up, high into the air, then seemed to pause briefly before plummeting down towards the *Sobek*. Most struck the water, twenty or so paces in front of the bow, disappearing with a faint plop and glittering spout of water. One struck the strake at the front of the ship with a loud crack and the flights trembled for a moment before they were still. The next shots would be in range, Cato knew.

'Shall we shoot back, sir?' asked one of the marines.

'No. Save it for when you can't miss.' Cato leaned

forward and called down to the legionaries crowded together beside the turret. 'Men! Shields up!'

He glanced back over his shoulder. The next Roman ship was rounding the headland and the rest were close behind as they struggled to keep up with Cato's vessel. The crew of the burning enemy vessel saw that escape was impossible and they turned away from the approaching warships, back across the bay in what seemed a futile bid to escape their pursuers.

A series of cracks snapped Cato's attention back to Ajax's ship. The second volley of arrows had struck home, sticking into the foredeck, the bows of the ship and two of the shields held up by the legionaries. Mercifully no one had been killed or injured. The oncoming ship was now no more than a hundred paces away and Cato could see Ajax and his men clearly as they readied their weapons.

'We'll take them on the starboard side!' the trierarch called to the steersman, who made a small adjustment so that the *Sobek* edged fractionally away from the other ship's ram. 'Stand by for collison!'

Cato grasped the rail of the turret and braced his feet on the deck. All around him the other members of the crew hurriedly prepared for the impact. There was a last flurry of arrows from the enemy ship and a cry of pain as a barbed point tore through the neck of one of the archers standing in the turret. Cato spared the man a quick glance and saw him crumple on to the floor of the turret, blood gushing from a severed artery. There was nothing that could be done for him and Cato looked forward again.

'Ship oars!' Phermon bellowed and there was a frantic

clatter and rumble as the crew fed them back into the hull.

The flared tip of the ram caught the enemy ship on the bow and there was a jarring crash as men stumbled forward. Both rams had struck glancing blows and now the ships began to pass alongside each other. The enemy commander had failed to give the order to ship oars and with a series of sharp shattering sounds the oars on the starboard side were smashed to splinters as the *Sobek*'s bow ground along the length of the enemy ship.

'Lower the corvus!' Cato shouted down to the decurion of marines. 'Quickly, man!'

The marines hurriedly recovered their balance and began to swing the boarding device out and over the enemy deck. The archers in the bow were directed towards the danger by their commander and they hurriedly loosed off their arrows at the marines. Unable to defend themselves while they manoeuvred the corvus into position, they were vulnerable to enemy missiles and two were struck down in quick succession as the arrows whirred across the deck. A moment later Cato saw another man cry out as his arm was pierced through.

'Release!' the decurion yelled as soon as the iron point was over the enemy's deck. His men let go of the rope and it shot up towards the pulley as the gangway arced down. The renegades dived aside to avoid being crushed, or impaled, and with a deep thud the spike pierced the deck. There was a jolt and a groan as the stout wooden peg at the base of the corvus took the strain from the remaining momentum of both ships.

'Boarding party away!' the decurion called out as he

drew his sword and scurried across the gangway towards the enemy deck. His men rushed after him, shields raised and swords drawn and ready. The enemy archers loosed more arrows, most of which struck the wooden hoardings that protected the men as they crossed from the *Sobek*. A few arrows overshot, and missed the ship and crew entirely.

Cato turned to the archers in the turret and pointed out their opposite numbers. 'Shoot those men down!'

The marines hastily notched their arrows, drew back the strings as they aimed, paused and then released their fingers, sending their arrows whipping through the air towards Ajax's men. Cato nodded with savage satisfaction as he saw two arrows strike one of the enemy archers and send him sprawling on to his back.

'Good work!' He thumped his fist on the rail. 'Keep it up.'

Leaving them to their business, he jumped down on to the deck and snatched up the oval marine shield he had taken from the *Sobek*'s stores. He turned to the legionaries standing ready on the main deck.

'Follow me. Take prisoners if you can.'

Cato stepped up on to the gangway and strode forward. There were still a few of the marines at the far end, waiting for space to jump down on to the deck of the other ship. The air was filled with the sharp ring and rasp of blade on blade, together with the thuds of blows blocked by shields. A few men, their blood up, shouted their challenges. Cato flinched as an iron arrowhead burst through the hoarding at his side, but he continued forward, head hunched down to provide a minimal target to enemy archers still shooting from the foredeck. He came up against the back of a marine and glanced past to see that there was no one in front of him. Beyond, the deck of the other vessel was packed with men locked in a vicious melee.

'Move on!' Cato ordered. 'Get into the fight!'

The marine glanced back and nodded anxiously before he clambered down from the gangway and pushed his way into the throng. Cato stepped forward and paused briefly to get his bearings. His eyes swept over the seething mass of men, glittering helmets and swords, and splatters of blood. Then he saw the black crest of Ajax's helmet close to the mast as the gladiator hacked at the shield of a marine. The blows drove the man down, then Ajax kicked the shield aside and drove his sword into the marine's face.

An icy tremble of fear gripped Cato's spine but he forced himself forward, on to the deck, and began to push his way towards the mast. 'Legionaries, on me!'

The burly soldiers forced their way to his side as Cato stepped over a body, and then a space opened ahead of him. A swarthy easterner with long hair tied back stood in his path, a bloodied axe in one hand and a curved dagger in the other. As soon as his eyes fixed on Cato he sprang forward with a snarl, raising his axe. Cato raised his shield and took the blow on the upper rim. The impact drove through the metal trim and cut deep into the wood. The shock of the blow jolted Cato's left shoulder. Before he could strike back, the renegade wrenched the axe free and, at the same time, swung his left hand round, towards Cato's unguarded side. The blade punched into the scale armour and glanced downward, ripping through a fold in Cato's tunic.

'My turn,' Cato said through gritted teeth, thrusting his shield forward. The boss caught the man in the ribs, driving the air from his lungs with a gasp. Cato followed it up with a thrust from his sword. Even though he was winded, the renegade nimbly sidestepped the blow and stood, axe raised and knife held ready, as he struggled to breathe. Then one of the other renegades stumbled into his side, and Cato's opponent was knocked off balance. As he tried to regain his footing Cato charged forward, catching him with his shield and driving him back until his heel caught on a body and the renegade fell on to the deck. Cato drove the tip of his sword down into the man's stomach, and then slammed the bottom edge of his shield on to his throat, crushing the windpipe.

Pulling his blade free, he moved on. Cato glanced quickly to both sides and saw that the legionaries were following up on his flanks. Many of Ajax's men were tough but lacked battle training, and were no match for professional soldiers. The attackers had cleared the aft of the ship and now the fight stretched in a rough line across the deck. Step by step Ajax and his men were being driven back towards the bow. Not one of them threw down his weapons and asked for quarter, Cato noted.

He saw the black crest again, no more than ten feet from where he stood, and stepped forward, blocking a thrust with his shield. The man snatched his sword back and tried again, only to have the legionary to Cato's left smash the blade towards the deck with his sword. Then, swinging the point up in a vicious arc, he stabbed the man in the stomach, cutting deep into his vitals.

There was no time to do more than nod his thanks as

Cato thrust a man aside with his shield and then he was face to face with Ajax. The gladiator was wearing a Roman helmet with large cheekguards that obscured much of his face. Dark stubble covered his chin and jowls and his large dark eyes widened as he lunged forward to attack the Roman officer. The edge of his sword swept down towards Cato's head and Cato threw the edge of the shield up to block the blow. Just as the gladiator had expected. The descending sword swept out to the side and cut round, glancing off Cato's shoulder. The change in direction had taken some of the power from the blow, but it still struck Cato hard enough to drive him off balance and numb his arm and fingers so that his grasp of the shield handle loosened.

'Shit . . .' Cato lowered himself and leading with his numbed shoulder he sprang forward into the back of the shield, carrying it against the gladiator. The man was solidly built and rode with the blow as he absorbed the impact. Then he locked his buckler around the edge of the shield and wrenched it aside. Cato just had time to recover and step back as the other man's sword swished past his face. For an instant, Ajax's right arm was carried on by the momentum of the slashing cut and Cato took his chance and thrust his weapon, catching his opponent in the upper arm and opening up a good ten inches of flesh and muscle. Ajax roared with pain and anger and hacked at Cato with the backswing. There was just time to duck and Cato struck again, into the knee this time, splintering bones and cutting through ligaments. Ajax toppled away from Cato on to his side and one of the legionaries sprang forward and thrust down, deep into the gladiator's armpit. Cato heard a rib snap and a loud grunt escaped Ajax's lips as the blade pierced his lungs and heart. His body stiffened for a moment and then slumped forward, face down. The legionary placed his boot on the back of the cuirass and pulled his blade free and moved on to find his next opponent.

Cato stood and stared at the body, unbelieving. His enemy was dead. The hunt was over. But not quite. He shook himself out of his stupor and looked round the deck. Bodies lay sprawled across the planking, and pools and splatters of blood stained the pine timbers. Only a handful of the renegades remained, crammed into the angle of the bow, fighting on like maniacs as they shouted their defiance into the faces of the marines and legionaries.

Cato opened his mouth to speak but it was too dry and his voice caught awkwardly. He swallowed, licked his lips and tried again. 'Fall back! Romans, fall back!'

Most of the marines and legionaries heard the command and obediently stepped away from the enemy. A handful, carried away by their bloodlust, continued until they were pulled back by comrades. The decurion had to whack the flat of his sword on the helmet of the last of his marines to get the man's attention. There was a final thud of a sword striking a shield and then only the sound of rapid breathing, and the moans and cries of the wounded.

'Clear the way!' Cato shouted and the men between him and the survivors of the ship's crew parted. He pointed his sword at the body of Ajax. 'Your leader is dead. Throw down your weapons and surrender!'

There was a brief pause and one of the renegades

laughed, and thrust his sword into the air. 'Long live Ajax! Death to Rome!'

His companions took up the chant. Cato watched them coldly, waiting for them to fall silent. But they continued cheering and he looked towards the decurion. 'Finish them!'

The decurion nodded, adjusted his grip on his shield and sword and then spat on to the deck. 'Marines! Advance!'

They closed ranks again, grim-faced and merciless, and paced towards the last of the renegades on the ship. The latter stopped cheering and braced themselves for their final moments, determined to kill as many Romans as they could before they were wiped out.

It was swiftly over as the marines advanced, shield to shield, swords poised to stab out as they closed with the enemy. There was an uneven rattle of blows against the wall of shields, a clatter of blades and the cries of the wounded, and one last shout of 'Long live Ajax!' and then quiet. The marines, spattered with blood, stood over the tangle of bodies in the bow. Cato sighed wearily as he removed his helmet and mopped his brow. The slave rebellion that had begun in Crete was finally over. There were no loose ends to tie up, save the small matter of taking the other ship that was still ablaze as it made for the mangroves on the far side of the bay. They were cut off from the sea and there would be no escape for them once the other Roman warships cornered them against the mangroves.

His left arm hurt like hell now that the numbness was beginning to wear off and Cato wriggled his fingers painfully as he tried to get some feeling back into the limb. He sheathed his sword and stepped back over the bodies towards Ajax. Kneeling down, Cato grasped the gladiator's shoulder and pulled the body over. The head, still in the helmet, lolled limply and faced away from Cato as the corpse sagged on to its back. He untied the chinstraps with the fingers of his sword hand and then, grasping the black crest, he pulled the helmet off.

'No . . .' He frowned as he stared down at the face, eyes staring blankly back at him and the mouth slightly open. 'No . . . NO!'

Cato glared at the body, then threw the helmet aside as he rose back to his feet. Around him the marines and legionaries stared at the prefect in surprise. Cato raised his hand to his forehead and rubbed it in frustration as he looked down again. The dead man was the same build as Ajax, and had the same dark hair, but that was where the resemblance ended. Cato took a deep breath and turned to stare bitterly at the other ship making for the far side of the bay beneath the swirling haze of smoke. He had been duped. Ajax was still alive.

CHAPTER TEN

Cato ordered the decurion to leave a squad of marines to take charge of the ship and then led the rest of the men back aboard the *Sobek*. As soon as the corvus was levered up from the deck of the other ship, the trierarch gave the order to fend off and unship the oars. The warship got under way and began its pursuit of the *Thoth*. Ajax had almost reached the far side of the bay, but there was no clear route to the open sea. Two of the Roman warships had angled across the bay and blocked his escape. Three more, besides the *Sobek*, were in pursuit and the last ship had hove to on the inshore side of the headland to pick up Macro and his party. Ajax was trapped. His ruse had only delayed his capture, or death, Cato decided as he returned to the turret to follow the chase. A moment later Phermon climbed up beside him.

'He'll not get away, sir.'

'I trust not,' Cato replied flatly. 'That would be difficult medicine to swallow.'

The trierarch squinted into the rising sun, then shaded his eyes as he followed the course of the ship. 'They're still on fire. Why haven't they put it out yet?'

'Perhaps they need every spare man on the oars,' Cato suggested.

'Hmmm.'

They watched in silence for a moment longer before the trierarch shook his head. 'In the name of the gods, what does that fool think he's doing? He's heading towards the mangroves at full speed. They'll run aground for sure.'

Cato nodded. 'Then that's his plan.'

'To escape through the mangrove?' The trierarch shook his head. 'Impossible.'

'Why?' Cato turned to him.

'Sir, I've patrolled the delta ever since I joined the navy. I know it well, and I tell you there is no more difficult terrain than the mangroves. Even if you can fight your way through the reeds and the roots, the mud will suck you down and the air is foul with the stink of decay. If that's not bad enough then the place is alive with insects and leeches, not to mention the crocodiles. It would be suicide to attempt it.'

'If he doesn't, then they face certain death.' Cato looked at the ship, no more than a mile away. 'If I was Ajax, I would take the risk. He has nothing to lose. If he escapes, then he can continue to plague Rome. That's what drives him on.'

As the rowers below deck bent to their oars and the *Sobek* surged across the bay, Cato watched the renegade ship with a growing sense of unease. Despite what Phermon had said, Ajax was determined and resourceful enough to fight his way through the dense tangle of mangrove.

'Look!' The trierarch stuck his hand out.

The mast of the renegade ship shuddered and then

abruptly toppled forward across the port beam, taking the rigging and spar with it. Some of the oars had snapped, others had snagged so that, from afar, the ship looked like a broken insect as it ploughed a short distance into the reeds and low-lying trees of the mangrove before coming to rest. Disturbed birds flitted into the air and the dust and sand that lay like a dull patina on the leaves of the stunted trees stirred into a thin haze about the wreck. The fire flared briefly, then settled into a steady blaze while the smoke swirled into the air. As Cato watched, the tiny figures of the ship's crew picked themselves up off the deck. In moments they had lowered a gangplank into the shallows and the first of them clambered down from the ship, clutching a loose bundle in one hand and a sword in the other.

'They're getting away,' said Cato, his heart dulled by despair at the sight of the crew abandoning the burning ship and disappearing into the tangled gloom of trees and rushes. 'They cannot be permitted to escape, do you understand, Phermon?'

'Yes, sir.' He gestured down towards the deck. 'The lads are doing their best.'

Cato glanced over the side at the oars, sweeping forward and driving through the water, and up and forward again in a swift rhythm. He climbed down on to the deck and turned to face the legionaries clustered on the main deck. 'Listen here!' He waited a moment until they were still and he had their full attention. 'I want fifty men to pursue the enemy making off into the mangrove.' Cato pointed towards the enemy ship. 'You men were with me on Crete. You know what Ajax and his followers have done.

You saw the atrocities with your own eyes. We have to capture or kill him and put an end to his foul work.' He turned to their commander, Centurion Rufus. 'I only want volunteers. Don't pick any wounded men. I don't doubt your men's courage, but it'll be hard going and open wounds will soon fester in those marshes. Those who'll follow me need to leave their armour behind. They're to take only shields and helmets, together with their swords. And rations and water for three days.' He gazed at them for an instant and then nodded. 'That's it. Those who are coming with me, be ready to march as soon as we reach the far side of the bay. Dismissed!'

He turned away and strode forward to the bows to watch as the warships closed up on the burning vessel stuck hard and fast into the twisted roots and silt of the mangrove. The trierarch looked over the side and gave the order to reduce speed, and then backwater, to kill the momentum of the ship as it drew close to the shore. The other warships had also slowed and gave way to the *Sobek* as she edged towards the mangrove, a short distance from the abandoned vessel. The air was filled with the crackle of flames and the sharp reports of bursting timbers. The fire was burning more fiercely than ever and Cato realised that Ajax must have given orders to feed the flames before he and his men had quit the ship.

'Phermon!' Cato had to shout to be heard over the noise of the blaze. 'Get some men over to that ship. See if they can put the fire out.'

'Aye, sir.'

There was the faintest of shudders beneath Cato's boots as the ship ran aground. At once the marines on the foredeck lowered a gangplank into the shallows, muddied by the impact of the ram.

'Here,' Cato called to the nearest of the legionaries. 'Give me a hand with the cuirass.'

While he raised his arms, the soldier eased the armour off Cato's shoulders and laid it on the deck. Cato nodded his thanks and then helped himself to a canteen, one of the waterskins and a haversack, hastily stuffed with hard bread and strips of dried beef. He slipped the strap over his shoulder and picked up a shield, then turned to Centurion Rufus. 'How many men came forward?'

'Fifty, sir. As you requested.'

'All volunteers, I take it?' Cato could not help a slight mocking tone.

'You know how it is, sir. An officer asks for volunteers and woe betide any man who takes him at his word.' Rufus grinned. 'That said, they're all good men. I picked the best.'

'Then let's go.'

As the burly centurion led the first section down the gangplank, Cato turned to the trierarch. 'When Macro and his men get across the bay, tell him to come after us. I should think it'll be easy enough to follow our path.'

'Yes, sir.'

Cato thought for a moment before he continued. 'Then take the fleet back to Alexandria and report to the governor. Inform him that I intend to pursue Ajax until I bring him to bay and finish him for good. Then we'll make our way back to Alexandria. Got that?'

Phermon nodded. 'I'll tell him. And may the gods protect you, sir. I'll pray that Fortuna favours you.'

'I hope so. She's proved to be a fickle bitch from the moment the hunt for Ajax began.' Cato paused and looked at the trierarch gratefully. 'Have a safe voyage home.'

He turned and took his place in the line of soldiers waiting their turn to descend the gangway. The wooden planks bowed under the boots of the men making their way down and Cato had to watch his balance carefully when his turn came. At the bottom of the gangway he stepped into the murky water, which rose up to his thighs, and felt his way towards the shore. Stunted trees sprouted from tangled clumps of roots that disappeared under the water and the stench of rotting vegetation filled the hot air. The legionaries ahead of him swirled through the water towards a small earth bank where reeds grew higher than a man. There was a muttered curse as one caught his boot in some of the roots and pitched forward with a splash. He rose up dripping and grumbling, picked up his kit and continued towards the reeds. Cato probed his way carefully towards the shore and emerged from the cloudy water. Centurion Rufus nodded to him and then bellowed past Cato towards the remaining men.

'Come on, you lazy bastards! Pick it up!' He turned to Cato. 'I sent the first section on ahead, sir. Told 'em to try and keep up with Ajax's men but not to engage them.'

'Good.' Cato approved. 'And have the rearguard section make sure that they mark our progress through the mangrove. Centurion Macro will be following us.' Cato looked round at the dense vegetation and shallow water stretching out ahead of him. 'Besides, we might need to retrace our steps.'

'True, I'd hate to get lost in this place.'

'There's no knowing how far this extends. We have to catch up with Ajax before he finds a path through it and escapes.' Cato settled his waterskin and rations haversack behind his back and then picked up his shield. The air around him was still and hot and insects swirled in shafts of light where the rays of the rising sun pierced the leafy canopy. 'Let's get on with it.'

He gestured to Rufus to join him and strode to the front of the line of legionaries stretching across the small islet. The long grass had been trodden down and ahead a rough trail of hacked reeds indicated the way that Ajax had headed.

He snatched a breath, and caught the odour of rotting plants and stagnant water. 'Column, advance!'

Cato splashed down into the shallows and pushed his way through the reeds that closed in on both sides. Those who had gone before him had crushed some reeds under-foot and hacked away at others so that the passage of the fugitives was clearly marked. Cato hoped that the fact that Ajax was having to cut his way forward would delay and exhaust his men and make it easier for the pursuers to catch up. As the Romans closed on them, the renegades would be forced to turn and fight, or surrender. But there was always the danger that they might try to spring an ambush on the legionaries. Hopefully, Centurion Rufus's leading section would be able to foil any attempt to surprise the main column.

It was tough going and as the sun climbed higher into the sky, its heat blazed down on the line of soldiers struggling through the reeds. The lack of any movement in the air added to their discomfort and perspiration was soon trickling down from Cato's scalp so that he had to brush it away from his eyes as he plodded forward. Eventually Cato could bear the stifling constriction of his helmet no longer, and took it off and tied the straps to his belt. He told Rufus to allow the men to do the same, and pass the word down the line before they continued forward. Behind him, the centurion occasionally tried to swat away the swirling cloud of insects that had been drawn to the men, uttering foul oaths at the mosquitoes.

'Keep it down,' Cato told him softly.

'Sorry, sir. These little bastards are eating me alive. Wonder what they feed on when they can't get Roman?' Rufus swiped at a large mosquito hovering in front of his eyes. 'Hop it, you nasty little cunt.'

Ahead of him, Cato stopped dead and stared down at something a short distance to one side. 'There's your answer, Centurion.'

Rufus waded up to his side to see what Cato had spotted. A body lay in the water, torso collapsed back against the stems of the reeds. The eyes stared blindly at the sun and a trickle of dried blood from the sagging jaw stained the man's chin. There was a steady drone of insects as they fed on the corpse's sweat and blood.

'One of theirs, I think,' said Cato, noting the man's light complexion.

'Good. That means the lads in the leading section have caught up with the stragglers.'

Cato's lips wrinkled as a large mosquito alighted on one of the man's eyes. 'Here, hold my shield.'

He handed it to Rufus and then bent forward to examine the body more closely. The water was dark and brackish, and he could just see a vague outline below the surface. Reaching down into the water, his fingers brushed against a blade and he groped along the metal until he grasped the handle. Straining, he lifted the handle and the body rose up with it, breaking the surface with an oily swirl of ripples. The point of the sword and a good deal of the blade pierced the stomach at an angle close to the ribcage.

Centurion Rufus pursed his lips briefly. 'Suicide?'

'That, or his comrades did this to spare him from capture.'

'Why, sir?'

'Look there.' Cato pointed with his spare hand as he rolled the body over slightly. There was a large wound in the man's side, like a wide thin mouth. The water had washed most of the blood away, and now thin tendrils of red oozed over the exposed wet flesh. 'He was carrying a wound. He would have held them back.'

Cato released his hold on the sword handle and let the body sink back into the water. Rufus returned his shield and the pair of them returned to the narrow passage beaten through the reeds. The rest of the men had halted behind the two officers and stood, knee deep in the stinking water, as they rested on their shields. Rufus thrust his arm out as he saw one of the men raise his canteen and reach for the stopper.

'What the fuck are you doing, Legionary Polonius? Did I give you permission to take a drink?'

'No, sir.'

'Then lower that canteen and don't lay a bloody finger on it until I say so. You drink that, and pretty soon you'll have drained your waterskin as well. Then you'll die of thirst.'

The legionary hurriedly did as he was ordered and thrust the strap of the canteen over his shoulder.

'That's better.' Rufus stared at his men. 'We don't know how long it's going to take to catch the enemy. That water in your canteen is all that you have. You try even a sip of this liquid shit we're wading through and you won't have a dry arse for a month. If you live that long. So, you only drink from your canteen, and only when I say so. Is that clear?'

The men nodded.

'Then pick up your shields and let's move.'

Cato regarded the centurion with approval. Rufus was clearly old school despite a relatively soft posting to Egypt where the legions had not had to participate in a major campaign in living memory. His tone, bearing and the scars on his arms and face marked him out as a professional soldier, much like Macro, Cato decided.

There was a swirl in the rushes close by and a splashing as something large lunged towards Cato. He turned and crouched as he ripped out his sword and raised his shield. A hideous dark shape, water glistening on its knotted hide, burst from between the reeds and a long tooth-lined jaw opened and snapped down on the shoulder of the dead man. Cato froze for an instant, and before he could react the beast lurched back, dragging the corpse with it. There was a last blur of movement, and a leg jerked lifelessly and then the monster and the body were gone. Only the disturbed water, swaying reeds and the rapidly fading sound of splashing remained.

Cato swallowed, and stared at Rufus wide-eyed. 'What the hell was that?' he muttered.

'Crocodile,' the centurion replied, warily watching the spot where the beast had disappeared, as if it might return at any moment.

'Crocodile?' Although Cato had been warned about them this was the first he had seen up close.

Rufus nodded. 'They live on the Nile, and here in the delta.'

'So I've heard.' Cato slowly straightened up. 'Not too thick on the ground, I trust?'

Rufus slapped his cheek. 'Not as thickly as the insects . . . But there are enough of them about to cause a problem. The natives tend to keep away from them.'

'No surprises there.'

'Even so, the crocodiles take the odd peasant, or their mules.'

'They don't hunt them?'

Rufus smiled thinly. 'Who would want to? Besides, they're sacred to the natives.'

'Sacred?'

Rufus looked surprised. 'You've been aboard the *Sobek* for two months and you haven't worked that out, sir?'

'What?' Cato responded irritably.

'Sobek is the name of their crocodile god, sir.'

Cato frowned, cross with himself not to have made the connection. 'Well, if any of them get that close to me again, I may be up for a little sacrilege.'

'I doubt you'd get the chance, sir. They might look cumbersome, but I assure you they can outrun a man on land and outswim him in the water. Best stay clear of them, sir. Them and the snakes.'

'Snakes? Venomous snakes, I take it.'

'Deadly. The cobras particularly, sir. Though they prefer drier ground.'

'That's a small comfort. We have to go.' Cato turned to the other men and saw that several of them were still staring nervously in the direction of the fading rustling and splashing. 'The column will advance!'

He turned, lifted his shield with a grunt and set off again, warily glancing from side to side as he waded through the reeds. The thought of encountering another crocodile unnerved him, but Cato knew that they must press on. Ajax must be caught, whatever the cost. Cato thrust the thought to the forefront of his mind. That was all that mattered. He must lead by example and he forced himself on, pressing forward through the broken reeds, no matter what lurked there.

CHAPTER ELEVEN

The column trudged on through the swamp as the sun rose higher into the sky and caught the soldiers in its full glare. The air, trapped and still, grew hotter by the hour and Cato's mouth began to dry out and then a raging thirst burned in his throat. On his own he would have taken a drink from his canteen by now, but he was waiting for Rufus to give the order to his men first. It would not do to be seen to be weaker than the centurion in the eyes of the other men. So he endured the thirst for a while longer, and then began to wonder if Rufus was refusing to call a halt and allow the men to drink for precisely the same reason. Cato stole a glance back over his shoulder. Rufus was ten feet or so behind him, sweating freely, his lined face gleaming with perspiration, but his expression was fixed and revealed nothing of his thoughts.

At noon the reeds gave way to a small island covered in long grass and Cato took the chance to let the men rest. As they emerged from the water on to solid ground, Cato strode forward a few more paces and lowered his shield, leaning to rest his arms on the rim as he caught his breath. One by one the legionaries emerged from the reeds, staggered up and slumped down in the grass either side of the trail.

'Reckon the men could use some water, sir,' Rufus rasped as he wiped his brow with the back of his forearm. 'I know I could.'

'All right.' Cato nodded. 'Let 'em drink. But mind they take no more than a mouthful.'

'Yes, sir.'

As the men took their meagre refreshment, under the watchful eyes of Rufus, Cato lifted his canteen and allowed himself a small amount, which he swilled slowly around his mouth before swallowing. Then he put the canteen away and paced up to the highest point on the island to search for any sign of life to the south, the direction Ajax seemed to have veered towards during the morning. There was a small clump of date palms nearby, and a handful of fallen trunks amid a tangle of old brown fronds. Cato made his way across to them and stepped up on to one of the trunks. From his vantage point he could see an unbroken sprawl of reeds interspersed with dense clumps of trees and undergrowth stretching out in front of him. But no sign of any movement. The stillness depressed him. He had hoped to have marched quickly enough to have caught up with Ajax and his men. Cato was also worried. There had been no word from the section Rufus had sent forward to stay in contact with the enemy. They might be far ahead, or they could have lost their way. Cato turned round to look back on their tracks. Even though he calculated that they had come no more than five miles over the difficult ground, there was no sign of life. The horizon was clear and nothing moved amid the reeds they had passed through.

After another brief look ahead, Cato returned to the

column and wearily picked up his shield. 'The rest is over, Centurion. Get the men back on their feet.'

A brief look of surprise flitted across Rufus's face before he nodded and faced his men, hands on hips. 'Up you get, ladies!'

There was a chorus of groans and muttered growls of complaint before Rufus cleared his throat and bellowed at them. 'Silence! I gave you a bloody order. Get up. It's time for you to earn your pay. This is what the Emperor's silver is for, and he pays you handsomely. So shut your mouths and pick up your kit, damn you!'

The men rose stiffly and made ready to continue the march. Rufus turned to Cato. 'At your command, sir.'

'Thank you. Forward then.'

Rufus raised his arm and swept it towards the broken trail. 'Column! Forwards!'

With Cato in the lead once more, they trudged through the tall grass to the far side of the island and back into the still, murky waters surrounding the beds of reeds. The afternoon was the hottest part of the day and the heat beat down on the extended line of soldiers and some dipped their felt helmet liners into the water before cramming them over their heads to provide some comfort from the baking temperature. Towards the middle of the afternoon they came across another body, between the twisting roots of a tree. As before, he bore wounds from the morning's fight and had been despatched by a sword thrust. Cato examined him briefly before moving on.

There was still no word from the leading section and there was no longer any doubt in his mind that they had run into trouble or got themselves lost. Cato ordered another brief stop to drink some water and for the men to catch their breath while he talked quietly with the centurion.

'Something's wrong. Your men should have sent back a report long before now.'

'I know, sir.' Rufus untied his neck cloth and dabbed his face. 'Shall I send someone ahead of the column to try and find them?'

Cato considered the suggestion for a moment. 'No. There's no point in risking any more men. If they are still following Ajax, then they'll stop for the night when he does. We'll hear from them then. That's my guess.'

'And if we don't?'

'Then we'll just keep following this path until we run into them, or Ajax and his men. That's all.'

'And what of Centurion Macro, sir?'

'Macro will catch up with us in good time. We can depend on that at least.' Cato smiled. 'He wouldn't miss a good fight.' The smiled faded. 'In this case he wants to be in on the kill more than any other man alive . . . except myself.'

Rufus nodded. He had fought in Crete and knew the tale of Macro's captivity, and that of Julia, the prefect's wife-to-be. 'Then perhaps we should camp early, and give Macro the chance to join forces with us.'

Cato thought it over, then shook his head. 'Each time we stop and rest, the men are slower to continue the march. Best to wait until the full day is done before calling a halt.' He moistened his lips. 'We go on.'

Even though the sun began to descend from its zenith, the stifling heat did not seem to abate as the afternoon crept by. The column struck on, burdened by the cumbersome weight of their shields and tormented by thirst. As the sun slipped into the haze that banded the horizon, the glare mercifully subsided and the reeds began to shade the Roman soldiers, panting from the day's exertions. Cato had never known such exhaustion before. Even when he first joined the legion and endured days of route marches, rising at first light, marching in full kit for sixteen miles before downing packs to construct the camp defences and then putting up tents, making cooking fires and only then being allowed to rest, until his turn came at sentry duty. That had been tiring enough, he recalled, but it had been in the temperate climate of the northern frontier in Germania. Here, the heat, stench, insects and the roots and obstacles under the water that threatened to trip up the unwary all combined intolerably and sapped Cato's strength. Only his will to continue kept him moving forward, step by step.

The shadows lengthened as the column emerged once more from the reeds on to solid ground, and now the broken trail joined an established path, which forked a short distance further on. Cato paused and looked both ways.

'What do you think, sir?' asked Rufus, breathing heavily. 'Left or right?'

Cato wiped the sweat from his eyes and considered the choice. 'Left seems to head to the north, towards the coast. If I were Ajax I would head south, away from the sea, and our warships. We'll go right.'

He lowered his shield and strode across the path to a clump of palm trees and pulled out a handful of dead fronds from the ground beneath them. He took out his dagger and quickly stripped the leaves away and then laid the dry grey stems out in an arrow to indicate the way he had decided to head.

'That's for Macro,' he announced, then picked up his shield and led the column to the right, towards the heart of the delta. Although the path was narrow and the tall grass and palms closed in on it from time to time, it was a welcome change from the murky stench of the swamp. They had marched a mile or so along the track when Cato saw the outline of a handful of buildings above the grass, no more than a quarter of a mile ahead. He turned to Rufus and spoke softly as he pointed them out.

'First sign of life all day.'

'Perhaps the locals will have seen something, sir.'

'I hope so.'

Cato was still concerned over the missing section. If they were not lost in the swamp then it was possible that they had fallen in with Ajax and his men. If that had happened, they would have stood little chance. As they approached the buildings, Cato could see that there was perhaps a score of them, loosely spread along a clear thoroughfare. They should be close enough now to detect signs of life, but there was no sound, save the bleating of a few goats, and no sign of any movement. He felt uneasy as the path turned a corner and opened out a short distance from the nearest buildings. He halted the column. The structures were typical of the region: built from mud bricks and covered with light trestles supporting palm leaves that provided shade yet allowed the air to move freely and keep the interiors from becoming unbearably hot. Cato stared along the length of the small village, then he cleared his throat.

'Helmets on, swords out,' he ordered. 'Tell the men to close ranks. Quietly though.'

'Yes, sir.' Rufus nodded and made his way down the line to pass on the instructions. The tired legionaries hurriedly pulled on their helmets and fastened the chin-straps before drawing their swords and raising their shields. Rufus returned to Cato's side.

'They're ready, sir.'

'Good.' Cato settled his helmet on his head and took a deep breath. 'Come on.'

They paced forward, eyes and ears straining as they moved between the first buildings. There was little sign of life. Only a thin dog stirred, lifting its head to watch them for a moment before raising a leg to scratch its neck and then lying back down and panting. Cato paused to look inside the door of one of the nearest buildings but it was empty. The same was true of the next, and they continued along the route towards the centre of the village. Then Rufus growled. 'There, sir, to the left, by the door.'

Cato looked in the direction indicated and saw the dark stain across the rough bricks. Blood.

'Looks like Ajax passed this way.'

Rufus approached the door and transferred his sword to the other hand as he examined the stain. 'If he did, then it was at least an hour ago. The blood's dry. The question is, where are the bodies?'

'Perhaps most of them ran off when Ajax appeared.'

'I hope so, sir.' Rufus took his sword in hand again and looked round. The village was quiet, except for a loud drone of insects and then Cato realised that it came from a short distance ahead where a shoulder-high mud-brick wall had been built to hold the villagers' livestock. He swallowed nervously as he made his way over to the pen and looked over the wall. The interior lay in gloomy shadows now that the sun was low on the horizon. Heaped inside the pen lay the bodies of the villagers. Old, young, men and women – none had been spared.

'What did they do that for?' asked Rufus as he joined Cato. 'If they needed food then why not just take it and let these people live?'

'Ajax is continuing to make his point,' Cato replied grimly. 'He wants the people of the province to know that we cannot protect them. Word of this will spread and the governor will be facing demands for soldiers to protect every village from Ajax and his renegades.'

Rufus thought a moment and shook his head. 'I'm not so sure, sir. It doesn't feel right. This place is too isolated to serve such a purpose.'

'Then why?'

'To keep them quiet. To stop them giving us any intelligence on the number of Ajax's men, their condition, and the direction they took when they left the village.'

Cato reflected briefly and nodded. 'He would do it for those reasons, sure enough.'

'Sir!' a voice called out and Cato and Rufus turned to see one of the legionaries beckoning to them from between two mule stables on the far side of the thoroughfare. 'Over here!'

They hurried over between the stables where a handful of mules stood staring at their empty mangers, and emerged into an open, dung-covered space. The bodies of the advance party lay sprawled on the ground where they had been dragged and dumped.

'Shit,' Rufus muttered. 'That explains it.'

Cato knelt down and examined the bodies more closely. 'Arrow wounds. Looks like they were ambushed.' As he spoke the words, he felt an icy fist clench round his heart. He looked up at Rufus sharply. 'That's why the villagers were killed.'

Before the centurion could respond, there was a warning shout from the street running the length of the village, then a faint whirring sound and a cry of pain. The two officers rushed back between the stables, shields up as they looked round. One man was down on the ground, propped up on an elbow as he stared at the shaft of an arrow protruding from his breast. Another was staggering around as he tried to grasp the arrow that had struck him in the back, smashing through his shoulder blade. More arrows whirred through the air and Cato saw another man struck in the sword arm, pinning it to his side.

He filled his lungs and bellowed. 'AMBUSH! Shields up. Legionaries! On me!'

CHAPTER TWELVE

As Rufus and his men closed ranks and formed a slender ellipse of shields, Cato saw the enemy. Several figures had run out from cover and stood at the far end of the village, aiming their arrows at the Romans. Glancing back, Cato saw more men blocking the opening through which they had entered the village. Ajax had them caught in a crossfire. Cato saw at once that he and his men could easily cut their way out of the street at either end. Then he noticed more figures flitting between the huts on either side. A moment later a bright flame flared up from a house as the palm thatch was set on fire. More flames flickered into life, clearly illuminating the Romans caught between the buildings. There was a grunt as another man was hit in the shoulder, close to Cato, then a sharp thud and he felt the sting of a splinter on his neck as an arrow tip punched through his shield.

'We have to get out of here!' Rufus gestured back the way they had come.

'No. We've got what we wanted, a chance to tackle Ajax.' Cato thought quickly. 'Take half the men and go back to the entrance of the village. Deal with the archers and then fight your way back along the village, clearing the houses.'

'What about you, sir?'

'I'll take the rest and seize the other end.' Before Rufus could oppose the division of the force, Cato nudged him with his shield and barked, 'Go!'

'Last three sections!' Rufus bellowed above the sharp crackle of the flames. 'On me!'

The centurion backed away carefully, picked up his men and the column split into two as the rear half edged towards the entrance, presenting a wall of shields to their enemy. Cato tightened the grip on his sword handle and called out to the remaining men, 'Follow me.'

A score of men advanced with him, in close formation, into the steady hail of arrows from the end of the street. The shafts cracked against the shields but there was only one more casualty as they advanced towards the bowmen, an arrow smashing into the unprotected shin of a man on the left of the front rank. He stumbled to a halt and groaned as he squatted down behind his shield. One of his comrades moved to help him and Cato shouted.

'Leave him! Stay in formation!'

They were no more than twenty paces from the bowmen now and the flames lit them up against the gathering gloom of the long grass and palms behind them.

'Charge them!' Cato yelled. 'Charge!'

With a dry roar the legionaries burst into a run, keeping low, as they sheltered behind their heavy shields. Ahead of them the bowmen loosed off their final shots and turned to flee.

'They're running!' a legionary shouted. 'After 'em. Cut the bastards down!'

As the Romans surged forward, the archers turned and

ran down the path. Then a movement to the side caught Cato's attention and he glimpsed figures racing out from between the buildings on either side. More of Ajax's men, armed with shields and spears. There was no time to shout a warning before the renegades burst out into the open and took the Roman force in both flanks. They let loose a wild cry as they attacked, thrusting their spears at the unprotected bodies of the legionaries. Three went down at once, skewered on the spear points and thrust across the width of the street under the impetus of the attackers' savage charge. As the renegades burst in amongst them, the Romans turned to fight. There was no time to go into a balanced crouch and size up their opponents. It was a chaotic, frenzied skirmish in the fiery glare of the flames of the burning village.

A snarl close to his side made Cato whirl round and his shield deflected the spear thrust with a dull thud, and an instant later his assailant crashed bodily against Cato's shield, sending him stumbling back, struggling to stay balanced and remain on his feet. Cato braced his boots apart and punched his sword round the side of the shield, and felt it strike home with a yielding tremor as a gasp burst from his assailant's lips. Cato wrenched the blade back and went into a crouch as he looked round at the chaotic melee. His men, and those of Ajax, mingled in a blur of movement as the air rang with the metallic scrape of swords and the dull thuds of spear impacts on shields. Ajax's spearmen had led the charge, and now his swordsmen joined in, well-built men – gladiators – trained for the deadliest combat of all in the arena. But here in the tight press of the village street, the training of legionary and gladiator found little opportunity for expression amid the desperate sword strokes, punches, kicks and head butts.

Cato parried a blow from his side, made a series of hacks at his opponent and then backed away towards the wall of one of the huts as he tried to spot Ajax. The lurid hue of the flames made it hard to tell one man from another and it was only the standard-issue kit of the legionaries that allowed each side to tell friend from foe.

'Ajax!' Cato yelled at the top of his voice. 'Ajax! Face me! Fight me if you dare!'

He heard a laugh to his left and turned towards it, sword raised and ready to strike, but he could not make out the leader of the gladiators. Instead, a burly man in a light tunic and leather cuirass faced him. The man's skin was dark, almost black, and his teeth gleamed as he clenched them and paced towards Cato with a heavy cavalry blade in one hand and a small round shield in the other.

'If you want Ajax, Roman, then you're going to have to kill me first,' the man spat contemptuously and opened his arms to expose his chest and coax Cato into an attack.

'If that's what it takes,' Cato replied coldly.

He feinted towards the man's stomach, forcing him to protect himself. The gladiator was no fool, and blocked the blow with his buckler, before immediately striking back at Cato, aiming straight for his eyes. Instinctively Cato ducked his head and raised his shield, momentarily losing sight of his foe. A mistake, as he realised the moment reason retrieved control from instinct. The rim of the buckler snapped round the edge of his shield and with a roar the gladiator ripped it aside and thrust his blade at Cato's chest. He stumbled back and came up hard against the rough wall behind him. The other man's thrust came to the end of his reach and the point cut through Cato's tunic and pierced the skin and muscle on his chest before being stopped by his ribs. The impact and sharp pain made Cato gasp.

'Hah!' The gladiator's lips spread in a triumphant grin as he advanced a pace, drawing back his sword to strike again, this time a killing blow. As the sword flashed forward, catching a fiery gleam along its polished blade, Cato rolled to one side. He heard the soft crunch of the sword smashing into the mud bricks, and let the momentum of his roll carry him round before he swung his sword in a swift arc angled down so that it cut into the other man's forearm, tearing up flesh and muscle to the bone. The gladiator's teeth snapped shut in a grimace as he pulled his arm back and tried another thrust at Cato. This time the blow was weaker and easily deflected off the curve of the shield and Cato lunged at his opponent's thigh, cutting into the powerful bunched muscles. The other man knew that it was too dangerous to risk continuing the fight, and he backed away, bleeding. Cato watched until he was at a safe distance, then risked another look round to gauge how his men were faring. Two were down on the ground close by, one still and the other screaming as he clutched the stump of his wrist. But the enemy had lost a man too and several were backing away from the fight, into the stark shadows between the buildings that had not yet caught fire.

'They're running!' one of the legionaries shouted in

triumph, and punched his sword into the air.

'Shut your mouth and fight!' Cato snapped, then stepped in amongst the men still engaged in combat. He saw a thin sinewy man with long lank hair standing over a legionary who had been beaten down on to his knees. Even as the renegade's sword cut through the air, Cato thrust out his sword, blocking the blow with a sharp ring, and deflected it aside so that it grazed the legionary's shoulder and caught in a fold of his tunic. As the gladiator tried to pull his blade free, Cato struck the man on the side with his shield, driving the breath from his lungs as he stumbled and fell to the ground. At once the legionary threw himself on the man, locking hands round his neck and crushing the windpipe under his thumbs.

'Fall back!' a voice cried from the end of the village. Cato recognised it at once and turned towards it.

'Gladiators! Fall back!'

At once, the remaining renegades disengaged from their individual combats and backed warily out of range of the Roman swords. There was a brief lull as the legionaries stood and panted. The moment the last of the enemy withdrew between the buildings, there was another whirr of arrows in the fiery glow of the street. This time the archers were shooting from the shadows of the palm trees, almost invisible in the dusk. By contrast the legionaries were clearly visible in the glow of the flames. Two men were hit by the first volley, one in the leg, and another pierced through the neck.

'Shields up!' Cato ordered and his men resumed their earlier formation. 'Keep your eyes on the flanks!'

He quickly looked back over his shoulder. Rufus and

his men appeared to have cleared the far end of the village and chased the enemy bowmen away. For a fleeting moment Cato was tempted to attempt one more charge, to try and run Ajax and his men down, but in the gathering darkness he would quickly lose control of his soldiers and who knew what tricks Ajax had planned for them if the Romans charged after him into the shadows? He had already managed to fool them once with his alternate use of archers and a surprise charge. There was only one sensible course of action, Cato reflected bitterly. He must pull back and plan a fresh attack.

'Fall back!' he ordered. 'Stay in formation and fall back, on me. One . . . two . . .'

The small knot of legionaries paced back, keeping time as the arrows continued to smack against the curved surface of their shields. Some ricocheted inside the formation, striking Cato's men, but their energy was largely spent and they simply bruised the men through their tunics, or caused minor injuries. The wounded men had been gathered up and they clasped an arm around a comrade's shoulder as they limped painfully along in the centre of the formation. Only the dead still lay in the street.

The small group of men steadily made their way back to the edge of the village. On either side fires blazed, hungrily consuming the dry palm roofs and then the wooden supports and meagre furnishings within. The heat was intense in places and Cato could feel it stinging his arms and neck as he and his men tramped past, the arrows lodged in their shields making the formation look like a giant burr. Gradually the enemy archers stopped shooting to conserve their ammunition and Cato's men finally reached the safety of Rufus's position at the entrance to the village. The wounded were helped to the rear, where their comrades dressed their wounds as best they could with linen salvaged from the houses that had escaped the fire. Cato's wound was shallow and he hurriedly tied a band of material around his chest. Dusk gave way to night as Cato and Rufus squatted down in the shadows to consider their options.

'We can't attack frontally, right down the street,' Cato decided. 'We'd make perfect targets for their archers, and they can come up at us from the flanks as we charge.'

Rufus nodded, then suggested, 'I could try to cut round the village and take them in the flank and rear while you distracted them here, sir.'

Cato thought a moment and then nodded. 'That's all we can do. The trouble is that Ajax is sure to be expecting us.'

'Only if he stays where he is, sir. In his place, I'd beat a retreat. He's won as much advantage as he can from the ambush. He knows we'll be forced to try a more indirect approach. Why sit there and wait? The sensible thing to do would be to leave a small rearguard to fool us into thinking he is still there, and then continue to make good his escape, steal as much of a march on us as possible before dawn comes. With good fortune, he might get far enough ahead for us to lose the scent when we continue the pursuit at dawn.'

'You're right,' said Cato. They could not allow Ajax the chance to slip away now that they were closer to him than they had been at any time since he had escaped from Crete. He nodded at Rufus. 'There's too much thick scrub and undergrowth to the right – they'd hear you coming. Take half the men and work round the left of the village through the grass. I saw a dyke on the side of the village before we entered, perhaps a hundred paces from the buildings, so you won't be able to swing out too far that side. Best wait until the flames have died down a bit before the attack, so you aren't spotted.'

'Yes, sir. What will you do when the time comes?'

'Try another charge up the street.' Cato smiled wearily. 'What I lack in imagination I'll make up for in making as much of a racket as possible. Right, then, pass the word on to the men. And let them know they can drink their fill. We'll refill the canteens from the village's water supply when it's all over.'

CHAPTER THIRTEEN

'How many men did we lose?' Ajax asked as he stared at the distant Roman figures at the far end of the village.

Karim, his closest follower, looked up from the wound he was dressing on Hepithus's arm. 'Two dead. One as good as and four wounded. Though all of the wounded can still fight.'

Ajax considered the outcome of the ambush. He had lost two men and had killed or wounded as many as ten of the Romans. A profitable exchange then, though he had hoped to annihilate them completely, or at least scatter them so that they could not continue the pursuit. Some of his men had been in a bad way when they reached the village late in the afternoon. It had taken all his personal authority to get some of them to prepare the ambush. The rest, his fellow gladiators, had been content to make a stand against their pursuers rather than continue to struggle on through the mangrove. The small victory had gone some way towards restoring their belief in him. As he knew it would.

Ajax had a clear understanding of the mentality of the gladiators who followed him, thanks to the years he had lived, and fought, in their ranks. They lived to fight.

Having once been forced to risk their lives at the behest of their masters, they knew the value of freedom and would endure any hardship and any danger rather than submit to being slaves again, or facing execution. It was as well that gladiators respected a hierarchy based on proficiency, Ajax mused, otherwise his leadership would surely have been challenged at some stage since their flight from Crete. But as long as he was unquestionably the best fighter amongst them, they would continue to respect and follow him, and obey his orders. Despite his lapse in judgement. Once again Ajax cursed himself for his complacency. The supply base had been a most useful lair from which to continue their harassment of the Romans. For nearly two months they had eaten well and rested, all the time knowing that they would have to abandon the bay at some point.

They should have quit the place long ago, Ajax realised bitterly. They had made themselves too comfortable. They had done what only the greenest of gladiators ever did – they had lowered their guard. The lookouts had failed to do their duty. He felt a moment's rage course through his veins. The fools had cost their comrades dearly. In the months that the renegades had been at the supply base he had been able to swell their ranks from amongst the slaves on the ships they had preyed on. At the time of the Roman raid, Ajax's original company of thirty of his closest lieutenants and the survivors of his bodyguard had swelled to over three hundred men, enough to crew both ships in the bay, and even the damaged Roman warship that had unwittingly fallen into his hands shortly before the raid.

Ajax frowned as he reproached himself again. It was

inevitable that the warship would be missed, but not nearly so swiftly. As soon as he became aware that the Romans had found his hideout, Ajax marvelled at the speed with which his enemy had guessed the fate of the warship and moved to attack him. The base, all of his ships and all but fifty of his men had been lost in the attack.

Clearly the Romans were being led by an outstanding officer. Now he knew. Ajax had recognised the voice challenging him from the street. The prefect, Cato, who had brought his rebellion on Crete crashing to defeat at the point where Ajax had been certain that he held every advantage. That rebellion had failed. But there would be another, Ajax had resolved. One day, he and his men would be the cadre around which another army of slaves would rise up to challenge their Roman masters. The Egyptian peasants had suffered under the heel of Roman rule, and Ajax's recent masquerade had exacerbated their discontent. Many would be willing enough to support a revolt. Many, but not all, Ajax thought, as he gazed at the burning village.

When Ajax had led his exhausted men out of the swamp and into the village, the headman had greeted them nervously. He had wisely offered water and food to the column of armed men. As Ajax's men had thirstily gulped down the water the villagers brought to them, he had seen the place's potential as an ambush site. Hemmed in by the dyke and reeds on one side, and the tangled mangrove on the other, the village was a natural choke-point. Ajax knew that he was being closely followed by a handful of lightly armed Romans and saw the opportunity to be rid of them. Twenty men were left behind in hiding as the rest pretended to move on. The Romans had followed their trail, past the place of concealment, and then the trap was sprung. Caught between the men who had been hiding and Ajax and the main body who turned about and charged back into the village, the legionaries had been quickly cut down.

The success of the ambush had prompted Ajax to consider repeating it on a larger scale, against the main column of Romans who would be sure to be following up on their scouts. This time the headman ordered them to leave the village, fearful of the reprisals that the Romans would carry out against his village if they found the bodies of their comrades. Ajax had ordered the villagers to be rounded up and held in the goat pen to prevent any of them escaping to warn the Romans. However, the villagers had begun to wail fearfully and were heedless of his demand for them to be silent, even when he had threatened them with violence.

There had been no alternative, Ajax told himself. He had not wished to have the villagers' blood on his hands, but the safety of his men came first. The Romans could not be alerted to the danger. The order was given to his most reliable men and they entered the animal pen and slaughtered the villagers. Years of training in Roman gladiator schools meant they were accustomed to obeying orders immediately, just as they had become hardened to the suffering of others. It was over swiftly and when the last of the dying screams had faded, the village stood still and silent, waiting for the arrival of the Roman column.

Karim finished tying off the dressing round the Nubian's arm and nodded at the man to withdraw from their presence. He wiped the blood off his fingers on the rim of his filthy tunic which stank of sweat and the stagnant odour of the swamp.

'What now, General?'

Ajax glanced at him, wondering if Karim was mocking him. His followers had always referred to him as their general, and in time Ajax had come to insist on the title. Karim used it in front of other men but usually he spoke frankly and without deference when they were alone.

'We wait for them to make another attack.'

'What makes you think they will?'

'What choice have they got?' Ajax replied simply. 'They are here to hunt us down. They must attack, and soon.'

'Why?'

'Because they fear that we may escape them again.'

Karim took a sip of water from his canteen and cleared his throat. 'Then why don't we escape? Now, while they hesitate.'

'Because we are evenly matched. They have no more men than we do. We can kill these Romans and leave their bones to rot in the swamp. Are all the preparations complete?'

Karim nodded. 'Canthus has concealed the stakes in the grass and his men are ready.'

'Then let the Romans attack.' Ajax smiled grimly as he stared at the enemy.

Karim watched him closely for a moment before he spoke again. 'There is another reason why you choose to stand and fight, isn't there?'

Ajax nodded. 'So you heard him too?'

'I did.'

'Then you will know why I must stand my ground and seize the chance to kill that Roman officer. Unfortunately, I did not see the other one with him.'

'Centurion Macro.'

Ajax nodded and clenched his fists. 'To think that I had Macro at my mercy for so many days back on Crete. I could have killed him at any time. I was a fool, Karim. I should have taken justice when it was offered, rather than indulge my desire to torment my enemy.'

Karim shrugged. 'It is always easy to be wise after the event, General.'

Ajax frowned briefly. 'True . . . All the more reason why I cannot endure the thought of losing this chance to have vengeance. For being sold into slavery, and for the death of my father.' Ajax's tone was ice cold. 'As long as Prefect Cato and Centurion Macro still live, I'll not be able to rest, not be able to be content.'

'You shall never have those things while there is still a Rome,' Karim responded wearily. 'What do you think to achieve, my friend? Is your heart set on killing every Roman in the world?'

'If that were possible, then yes.'

'But it is not possible.'

Ajax turned to him and flashed a smile. 'Give me the time to do it and we shall see. Besides, do you think that we are alone in our hatred of Rome? Remember what we got out of that fat captain of the last cargo ship? That the Nubians were poised to invade the south of the province.'

'I remember.'

'Then perhaps we should consider throwing in our lot with the Nubians.'

'Perhaps. But Nubians are an unknown quantity,' Karim reflected. 'It might not be wise to join them, even if they hate Rome as we do. I would not make that decision lightly.'

'Nor would I.'

Karim shook his head pityingly. 'The desire for revenge weighs down on you, my General. The burden blinds you to the responsibility you have to others. To me, and to all those who follow you. And all those who might one day follow you, if you can put aside your personal craving for revenge. You must put reason before feeling. That is what it means to be a true leader.'

Ajax shrugged. 'I am a man, even as I am a leader, Karim. I cannot be untrue to the dictates of my heart. Not for you, or any other who chooses to follow me. I must have my revenge. If the gods are kind I will have it here in this village this night. I will kill those Roman soldiers. I will cut the head off Prefect Cato. But, if I take him alive, then I will do to him what he did to my father and nail him to a cross, and sit and watch as he dies, burning under the sun, begging for water or the deliverance of a quick death. I shall give him neither,' Ajax concluded harshly.

They were both silent for a moment, then Ajax stirred and stared intently down the length of the village to where the legionaries were stirring. As he watched, they formed into a line and presented their shields in the dull glow of the dying flames. At the centre stood a tall, slender figure with a plumed helmet. When the soldiers were ready, he raised his sword and swept it forward and the legionaries began to advance.

Ajax cupped a hand to his mouth and called to his men. 'Here they come! Archers, make ready! Gladiators, on me!'

As the figures of his men rose up from the shadows, Ajax turned to Karim with a grim smile. 'Pray that the gods are generous, my friend, and we end this tonight.'

CHAPTER FOURTEEN

Centurion Rufus and his party had crept away into the long grass beside the dyke shortly before and should be making their way towards the enemy, Cato calculated, glancing down a gap between two of the houses to his left. There was nothing to see there, just the shadows now that night had set in. The fires had quickly consumed the flammable materials of the houses and small flames licked lazily along charred timbers and provided some illumination for the street and the ground immediately to the rear of the houses. Rufus and his men should be able to advance parallel to the street without being seen, Cato decided.

Ahead of him he could see several figures gathering just beyond the far end of the street and he offered a quick prayer to Fortuna that Ajax was amongst them. He could just see more of the dim forms of the renegades spreading out either side of the main body awaiting them and a moment later the first, unmistakable *phut* of an arrow as it passed above his head.

'Incoming arrows!' Cato warned his men. 'Shields up, lads!'

The men in the rear ranks raised their shields overhead to protect the formation from plunging shots. More arrows fell out of the starlit sky and cracked into the shields or pattered off the hard earth as the line, six men wide and four deep, paced forward, behind the sturdy curves and brass bosses of their shields. The archers kept up a steady shower of arrows as the legionaries approached up the street. The knot of gladiators waiting for them stood still and silent, waiting for Ajax's order to attack.

'Watch the flanks!' Cato ordered, anxious to avoid the formation being broken up by another charge of spearmen. The arrows stopped coming as the Romans approached the waiting gladiators and Cato tightened his grip on his sword and shield. When the two sides were no more than ten paces apart, there was a sharp cry of pain from the left, then Centurion Rufus's voice cut through the darkness.

'Forward! Charge 'em! Up the Twenty-Second!'

His men echoed his cry with a roar and a moment later there was another cry, and then a shout and then a deep groan.

'What the fuck is happening over there?' said one of the men behind Cato.

'Silence!' Cato yelled. 'Keep moving!'

Ajax smiled as he heard the cries of pain down beside the dyke. He had been right in his suspicion that the Romans might try to flank him. That was why he had ordered his men to plant sharpened stakes in the long grass soon after they had dealt with the enemy scouts. Now it seemed that the enemy attack had come to grief and, better still, they had charged into the trap. He turned to Karim.

'Take your archers over there and finish them off.' He drew his sword. 'I'll deal with the other party.'

Karim nodded and trotted away to the right, calling on

his men to follow him. Ajax briefly imagined the situation that would confront Karim. The Romans had blundered into the sharpened stakes and several of them were wounded, from the sound of it. As they tried to extricate themselves they would be struck by arrows. If they panicked they were likely to run into another stake. If they held their nerve and groped their way free of the obstacles, they would still make an easy target for the archers. Either way, they were going to pay dearly. He smiled with satisfaction as he strode forward to join his men preparing to take on the Romans still advancing up the street.

'Your shield, General.' One of his bodyguards held it out to Ajax and he slipped his hand through the guard, adjusted his grip, and edged through to the front rank.

'Let's teach these Roman bastards a lesson!' Ajax thrust his sword arm aloft in the salute he had been taught in the gladiator school at Capua. 'Fight or die!'

'Fight or die!' his chosen men chorused, before they settled into a crouch and sized up their enemy as the line of legionaries, boots tramping in unison, came on.

Ajax felt the familiar surge of excitement grip his body, and yet his mind was cool and calculating as he focused his attention on the leader of the small formation, the man who had caused him so much pain in the years since they had fought their first encounter at sea off the coast of Illyria.

'Prefect Cato!' The yell ripped from his throat. 'Tonight you die!'

He charged, his men surging forward on each side, roaring their battle cry as their faces twisted into feral masks of rage and hatred. Years of hard training had turned Ajax's body into a powerful machine and he threw his weight in behind his shield as it smashed into that of the prefect. He saw Cato's plumed helmet jerk back as the Roman line was driven in. Ajax kept his shield in contact with his opponent and thrust forward, sensing the resistance increase as the other man's boots scrambled for purchase on the hard ground. He could hear him grunt with the effort of holding his position. Ajax braced his shoulder and gave a powerful heave, breaking contact as he turned to bring his sword up and forward, pointing the tip towards his foe. The dying flames still provided enough illumination to light the conflict, and Ajax could see the thin face of the prefect, his expression taut and eyes wide as they fixed on him.

Ajax thrust at his face, and the Roman quickly parried the blow aside and thrust back, the blade glancing away as Ajax took it on his shield. The sounds of other duels filled his ears but did not distract him as he directed his mind, body and skill against Cato. He thrust with his shield again, clashing boss to boss with a sharp ring, and then thrusting again, but this time switching the blow into a sweeping cut-over that came down at an angle towards the Roman's shoulder. Cato instantly pivoted back on his right foot so that the sword that would have carved deep through his collarbone swept down through the air instead. At the same time he slashed at Ajax's outstretched arm. There was barely enough time for the gladiator to twist his wrist and take the impact of the blow on the flat of his sword. Sparks flicked into the air, and Ajax stepped back a pace and nodded approvingly.

'You're quick, Roman. But you wouldn't last a heart-beat in the arena.'

'And you talk too much!' Cato spat back and hammered his blade down on the edge of Ajax's shield, driving it low enough to expose his throat as he slid the blade on. It was a desperate attack, Ajax noted coolly, as he dealt with it easily enough, thrusting the shield up, under the extended arm, sending the point skywards. Ajax saw his chance and hooked his shield up, behind the guard of the Roman's sword and jerked it towards him. For an instant the other man's fingers flinched and then the sword handle was snatched from his grasp and it flew back a short distance behind Ajax and landed with a thud.

Ajax laughed cruelly as he lowered his shield and smashed it into the prefect's, and again, driving him back. Then he alternated blows, shield, and then sword, battering at the shield as Cato stumbled away from the onslaught. A figure, one of Ajax's men, fell between them, blood pouring from a deep wound in the skull as he shouted nonsensically at the top of his voice. His fingers spasmed and the long-bladed sword in his hand dropped, point first, and stuck in the ground. Cato snatched at the handle and drew it back behind the shield.

'Out of my way!' Ajax bellowed, slamming the man aside with his shield. He raised his sword to batter Cato again. The prefect rode out the next attack, and then Ajax paused and chuckled. 'By the gods, I could do this all night.'

He raised his sword to strike and Cato lunged forward, clashing shield to shield, as he thrust the blade round in a shallow arc. The point of the sword punched into Ajax's cuirass, slid along the curve at the side and found the gap between the front and back plates where it lodged and the last of the force of the blow carried it into his side, tearing open the flesh. At first Ajax was stunned by the blow, and let out an explosive cry before a brief roar of outrage used up the last of his breath.

'The general's injured!' a voice cried. 'Ajax is hurt!'

At once one of his men thrust his way between Ajax and Cato and launched a savage attack on the Roman, driving him back.

'Get the general out of here!'

'No!' Ajax roared, then grimaced. 'No . . .'

Hands grasped his arms and pulled him away from the fight, back up the street to the far end of the village. He made to protest but had to grit his teeth to fight off the pain in his side. He saw that his men had bested the Romans. More of their bodies lay in the street, and only two of his own men. Yet the gladiators were pulling back, leaving the surviving legionaries staring after them in surprise.

'What are you doing?' Ajax growled. 'Finish them.'

Then Karim was standing in front of him, an anxious expression on his face. 'General, one of our men watching the path says there are more Romans coming. We have to pull back. There are too many of them.'

'No.' Ajax shook his head. 'I had the bastard. I had him at my mercy.'

He felt sick with rage, cheated of his revenge. Then the pain hit him again. He knew that he could bear it well enough. He had been taught to endure worse during his training. 'Let me go back. Let me fight him,' he growled.

Karim shook his head. 'No. I'll not let you die this night, my General.' He turned and nodded at the men clustered about Ajax. 'Get him out of here. Head down the path to the river. You know the place. Go.'

Two men grasped Ajax's arms and placed them over their shoulders and then carried him away from the village, pinned helplessly between them as he gritted his teeth. Once his leader had gone, Karim called the archers to fall back and form up on him. They came from the darkness and formed a loose line across the path, loosing shafts at the enemy and sending them scurrying for cover amid the smouldering ruins of the buildings. At the far end of the village the first of the Roman reinforcements had appeared and Karim called to his men.

'Cease! That's enough. We must go.'

The last of the renegades melted away from the dying glow of the last few houses still alight and disappeared into the darkness engulfing the track that led out of the village. Aside from the occasional crack of a bursting timber in the night and the faint chirrup of some insects in the swamp beyond the dyke, the only other sounds were the agonised groans and cries of the wounded.

CHAPTER FIFTEEN

'What the bloody hell's been going on here?' asked Macro, glancing round at the ruined houses and bodies as he marched up to Cato. 'Looks like you've had quite a fight.'

Cato had retrieved his sword and sheathed it as he nodded a greeting to Macro. He noticed that his hand was trembling, and it took all his self-control to ease the blade back into the scabbard without dropping it. The truth of it was, he was scared, Cato scorned himself. When Ajax had ripped the sword from his hands and driven him back under that powerful rain of sword blows, Cato had been sure that he was a dead man. Nothing could stand between Ajax and his vengeance. The gladiator had been like some wild force of nature, unleashed and implacable. Cato had been only moments away from his death when that mortally wounded renegade had stumbled between himself and Ajax. It had been as close as that, Cato mused in horror. He regarded his friend with an ashen expression and then blinked and nodded.

'Yes . . . Quite a fight.'

'What happened? I saw some men making off as we arrived. Ajax?'

Cato nodded. 'He still lives. I wounded him. His men drew him away when they saw you.'

Macro stared down the street. 'Then what are we waiting for? Let's go after the bastard before he gets away.'

'No,' Cato responded firmly. 'Not now.'

'Why the fuck not?' Macro's brow furrowed. 'We're as close to him as we've been in months.'

'We wait until first light,' Cato said firmly.

'What?'

'That's an order,' Cato snapped. 'I've lost enough men to ambushes already without blundering about in the darkness. I'll not gift Ajax any more Roman lives than I can help. We rest here tonight. Tend to the wounded and let the men slake their thirst. Ajax and his band are just as tired, and have their own wounded to take care of. They'll not go far in this darkness. We can continue the pursuit at dawn.'

'This is madness,' Macro said quietly.

Cato stiffened and drew a calming breath. 'You forget yourself, Centurion.'

'My apologies, sir,' Macro hissed through gritted teeth. 'But we have to go after them.'

'No. I've made my decision. We see to our own first. Have your men gather our wounded. They'll find 'em in the village and over there,' Cato pointed towards the dyke where Rufus and his men had attempted to outflank the renegades. Whatever trouble Rufus had run into, there was no sign of his men, although the wounded were making themselves heard well enough. Cato winced at the sound. 'See to it, at once.'

'Yes, sir. I think our priest friend Hamedes has some

skill with healing. I'll set him to work.' Macro looked searchingly at his friend. 'And you, sir. Are you all right?'

'Fine. I'm fine.' Cato swallowed. 'Just need some water. Now see to the others, please.'

Macro nodded and turned away to shout the orders to his mixed force of marines and legionaries. They were also stripped down to the essentials and, like Cato's force, they were exhausted and parched. But their rest and refreshment would have to wait, Macro grumbled to himself in frustration as he summoned two sections and set up a perimeter of sentries across the path at the end of the village, in case Ajax decided to cause any further mischief. Not that he was likely to. The gladiator was too shrewd. He was a man who knew how to pick his battles, thought Macro. The gladiator struck when he had the advantage, and held back when he did not. When he did give battle he fought with utter ferocity and ruthlessness. Were it not for the irremovable stain of the barbaric way Ajax had treated him, Macro might have found it in his heart to admire his enemy. In another life, Ajax would have made a fine legionary.

'Shame he has only got one life,' Macro muttered to himself. 'And I'll be taking that.'

'Sir?' One of his men looked at him curiously.

'What?'

'Sir, I didn't quite hear the order.'

Macro cleared his dry throat. 'I said keep a good watch, or those bastards will cut your throat before you know it.'

Macro turned and made his way back towards the heart of the village.

★

Cato was sitting on the edge of a stone trough, watching the casualties being brought in from the dyke. Most had run on to the concealed stakes when Rufus had given the order to charge. A number had been struck by arrows as well and Cato realised that the ambush had cost the Romans dearly. Centurion Rufus came limping in, clutching a hand to his thigh. Blood seeped through his fingers. He saw that the wounds of his men were tended to and made his way over to report to the prefect.

Cato stood aside to let Hamedes bend down and examine the centurion's injury. The priest took out his canteen to wash the wound and then reached for a strip of linen from his shoulder bag. 'What happened?' asked Cato.

'The bastards set a line of sharpened stakes from the dyke to the village,' Rufus told his superior. 'They were hidden in the long grass. First we knew about it was when one of the men stumbled on to one. The fool couldn't keep his mouth shut and I wasn't close enough to see what had happened, so I gave the order to charge, while there was still some chance of surprising them.' He winced. 'Before I knew it we had run right into the stakes. I got one in the leg almost at once. By the time the men stopped, most of us had been injured. That's when they hit us with arrows.' Rufus paused briefly and shook his head. 'There was nothing we could do, sir. Some men tried to get out of the way of the arrows, and ran into more stakes. I told the boys to stay put and shelter behind their shields as best they could. I figured our best chance was to wait for the enemy to cease shooting and then work our way out of the stakes.'

Cato frowned, furious with himself for underestimating Ajax. Rufus misinterpreted his expression.

'There was nothing else I could do, sir. I swear it.'

'I understand.' Cato quickly ran a hand through the matted locks of his hair. 'What is the butcher's bill?'

'Eight dead, and sixteen wounded. Three of those won't last the night. Eight are walking wounded. The others will need to be carried out of here.'

Cato looked down at his boots to hide his face. He had led his men into the trap. He had been too keen to get to grips with the enemy. Men were dead because of him and he felt shame at their loss.

'Very well,' he said quietly as he composed himself and looked up. 'Make sure you have that leg wound properly seen to. Then have the village searched for food and water. The men can eat their fill and rest. We'll continue the pursuit at first light.'

'Yes, sir. And what about the wounded? We can't leave them here.'

'I'll detail some of the men to bring them up behind us. Hamedes here can help out. That's all for now, Rufus.'

It was a curt dismissal and Cato sensed the man's resentment as he saluted and turned to limp back to join the rest of his men. Cato looked at Hamedes. 'Ajax killed the people of this village. Are there any rites that you need to perform for the dead?'

Hamedes stared blankly back at Cato. 'Sir?'

'You're a priest. Do what is necessary for them. Once you've finished treating the injured.'

'Yes, sir.' Hamedes bowed his head. 'I'll offer the

prayers. There's no time for the full funeral rites. But we must burn the dead.'

'I thought you people believed in burial.'

Hamedes smiled uncertainly before he replied. 'Depends how much time you have.'

'Very well, tell Macro to lend you a few men to get the job done.'

Hamedes nodded and turned to follow in the footsteps of Rufus, making for the wounded lying in the street.

As he stared at the legionaries, Cato wondered how many of them would realise that he was to blame. How many would resent him and be wary of following him into the next fight?

He turned at the sound of approaching boots and saw the unmistakable stocky bulk of Macro emerging from the darkness.

'Sentries are posted, sir. I've told them to keep a good watch. Don't want anyone catching us unawares. The lads are clapped out so I'll be changing the watch regularly during the night.'

Cato forced a smile. 'So you won't be getting much rest then.'

'I suppose.' Macro shrugged. 'Nothing I'm not used to.'

'And you didn't sleep last night either.'

'True, but I've put up with worse before. Many times.' He gestured towards Cato. 'As have you.'

'I don't think I'll be sleeping much tonight either.'

'You get some rest,' said Macro. 'I'd feel better knowing your mind was fresh when we continue the pursuit tomorrow.'

'Why?' Cato asked bitterly. 'So that I can lead us into another ambush?'

'What is this?' Macro frowned and placed his hands on his hips. 'Do you think to blame yourself?'

Cato looked at him squarely. 'It was my fault, Macro. I should have known that Ajax would anticipate our attempt to flank him . . . I made a bloody mess of it. I was too keen to put an end to him and rushed in.' Cato shook his head at the memory of it. 'Ajax was waiting for us. He had it all worked out.'

'What did you expect? He's no fool.' Macro glanced at his friend and tried to offer a crumb of comfort. 'Still, I expect I would have done the same if I had been in your place.'

'I wonder.'

'Mind if I sit?'

'Be my guest.'

Macro unfastened the straps under his chin and removed the bulky helmet with a sigh of relief. Then he eased himself down on the edge of the trough next to Cato and leaned forward, resting his thick forearms on his knees. He was silent for a moment and then pursed his lips before speaking quietly so that they were not overheard. 'Could you take a little advice? From a friend?'

Cato looked at him. 'From a friend, yes.'

'Right . . . Look here, Cato, you're a bloody prefect now. You can't afford self-pity.'

'Self-pity? No, you have me wrong. This isn't self-pity. It's a question of poor judgement. I led these men badly.'

'And what? You want to take some form of punishment for it?'

'That's what I deserve,' Cato admitted.

'Bullshit. You think you are the first officer to make a mistake?'

'Mistake is hardly the term I'd use for this.' Cato waved a hand towards the casualties. 'Bloodbath, more like.'

'Shedding blood is our stock-in-trade,' Macro responded. 'When there's a fight, soldiers get hurt and killed. That's the way of it.'

'But if men die needlessly, then their commander should be called to account.'

Macro puffed his cheeks in frustration. 'For fuck's sake, Cato, I've seen worse cock-ups. So have you. Sometimes a fight goes your way and sometimes it doesn't. The enemy gets the better of every commander from time to time, even the very best of them. You have to accept that.'

'So you agree that I failed my men.'

'Sure, you screwed up,' Macro said frankly.

'Thanks . . .'

'Cato, I respect you well enough to tell you the truth. If you don't want to hear it then say so.'

'I'm sorry. Speak on.'

'All right.' Macro collected his thoughts. 'The truth is that you are a fine officer. As good as any I have met. I've watched you rise from optio, to centurion and now prefect. I'd wager you'll go further still. You've got the brains for it, and the guts, and though you look like a long streak of piss, you're as tough as old boots. But you lack something.' Macro frowned as he tried to clarify his explanation. 'Not experience – you've had plenty of that, no question about it. No, it's something else . . . Perspective, perhaps. That sense a soldier has once he has served long enough to see generals come and go. Maybe you have been too successful. You've won promotion before you've developed the right temperament for the job, if you see what I mean. You need to learn to accept that making mistakes from time to time – failing – is part of the job. How a soldier copes with failure is every bit as important as how he deals with success.' Macro smiled fondly. 'Do you remember Centurion Bestia?'

Cato nodded as he recalled the scarred veteran in charge of training the recruits when Cato had joined the Second Legion nearly seven years before. Bestia had died during the invasion of Britannia, fatally wounded in an ambush.

'He was a tough one, and he'd served in just about every corner of the Empire. After I was promoted to the centurionate I had a drinking session with him in the mess. He had a right skinful and, as old soldiers will in the company of their own kind, he fell to reminiscing. Anyway, I remember the most impressive story he told me was about some messed-up campaign in Pannonia. Some of the mountain tribes had decided they'd had enough of Roman tax collectors so they rebelled. The Second was sent in to put down the revolt. But the governor had no idea quite how many rebels there were, nor much about the conditions in the mountains during the winter. So the commander of the legion gets caught in a trap, loses a quarter of his men and has to retreat two hundred miles to the nearest fortified town. Took them twenty days and cost nearly half the men. But Bestia reckoned it was the legate's finest hour. He led his men to safety. That's the point, Cato. The real test of a commander is how he deals with adversity.' Macro looked at Cato and nodded earnestly. 'That's the truth of it. So you'd better get a grip on yourself, right?'

'Yes. I understand.' Cato forced a slight smile. 'And thanks.'

'Think nothing of it.' Macro punched him lightly on the shoulder. 'I'd far rather you were in charge and fucked it up than me.'

'Oh, great . . .'

Macro raised his canteen and took a series of swigs before he set it down. 'Ahh! That's better.' He decided to change the subject and glanced quickly round at the ruined village. 'So what's the story here? Where are all the locals?'

'Dead.' Cato pointed towards the pen, a short distance down the street. 'Ajax had them all killed.'

'Why? Why the hell would he do that?'

'Maybe they refused to help him. Or maybe he just wanted to keep on destabilising the province. I don't know the reason.' Cato picked up a pebble and rolled it between his fingers for a moment before flinging it away into the darkness. 'Anyway, they're dead. All of them. And that's why we've got to track that bastard down and kill him.'

'There you go. That's the spirit. Put this day behind you, and concentrate on what you must do on the morrow.'

Cato nodded. Macro rose stiffly to his feet. 'I need to speak to Rufus and the optios about the watch-keeping schedule. You get some rest, sir.'

'I'll try.'

Macro slapped his cheek as a high-pitched whine sounded close to his ear. 'If you can manage it with all these little bastards then you're a better man than me.'

He stooped to pick up his helmet and turned to make his way over to the other centurion, sitting propped up against a mud wall. Cato stared fondly at his friend for a moment, then got up and entered the nearest building. He searched around in the rooms that had suffered least from the fire damage and found a bedroll tucked in a corner. He took it outside, where the stench of burning was less overpowering, unrolled it and lay down on his side, trying to ignore the insects that filled the night. For a while he thought of Ajax, and the moment when his death seemed unavoidable. Then the dreadful exhaustion of the day's march through the mangroves and swamps carried him off into a deep sleep.

Cato woke shortly before dawn, immediately feeling guilty that he had slept while Macro had tended to the watch-keeping. The months aboard the ships had left him in poor condition for a difficult march and his legs ached abominably. Cato rose to his feet with a groan and stretched his back, feeling the joints crack.

'Shit,' he muttered, then rubbed his eyes and looked about. Some of the men had already stirred and a handful were busy constructing litters for the wounded out of wood salvaged from the ruins. The air was delightfully cool and a thin mist lay across the low-lying land around the village. The sight of the mist immediately made Cato uneasy. Here was yet more cover for Ajax, and the men under his own command would not be safe until the morning heat drove the mist away. Cato made his way across to the wounded and stood over Centurion Rufus. He nodded at his bandaged leg.

'How does it feel?'

'It hurts. Not enough to prevent me joining the main column.'

'I want you to take charge of the wounded,' Cato said firmly. 'I need a good man to ensure their safety.'

A brief look of disappointment crossed Rufus's face before he nodded. 'As you wish, sir.'

'You can rejoin us once the wounded are seen to safety.' Cato looked round. 'Where's Macro?'

'He went forward to the picket line a bit earlier, sir.'

Cato nodded and then turned to stride up the street to the far end of the village. As he passed the animal pen he saw that it had burned to the ground during the night and a large tangled pile of charred remains stood within the damaged wall. The air around was still warm and filled with the stench of burned flesh. Cato quickened his pace and strode out of the village. A short distance along the path he saw the first two men keeping watch. At the sound of his footsteps one of them turned to challenge him.

'Who goes there?'

'Prefect Cato. Where's Centurion Macro?'

'Walking the line, sir. He went to the right, should be back any moment.'

'Any sign of the enemy on your watch?'

'No, sir. Nothing. Been as quiet as the grave.'

Cato stared into the mist shrouding the palms that grew alongside the path a short distance off. The long curved fronds of the trees made them look like stooped giants reaching out with their arms. His ears presently heard the sound of boots swishing through the grass beside the path and Macro strode out of the gloom.

'Morning, sir. Rested?'

'Yes, thank you. Anything to report?'

Macro shook his head. 'Nothing. Not a peep out of the renegades. Either they're inhumanly quiet, or they decided to put some distance between us before stopping for the night. I left the optios with orders to rouse the men at first light. Not long now.'

'Very good.'

'Oh, the only other thing is, Hamedes has taken a jar filled with ashes down to the dyke. Seems he had to place the ashes in an irrigation ditch, so they could eventually join the Nile. He said he had your permission.'

'That's right, as long as he doesn't go too far, with Ajax's men about.'

'He said he'd be careful, sir.'

'It's his funeral,' Cato replied and then shook his head. 'Not quite what I meant to say.'

Macro laughed briefly before he responded. 'You don't need to worry about him. He was game for a fight yesterday morning and he kept up with us across that swamp. Pretty good going for a priest. Not like those idle tossers back in Rome, or on the army staffs. He's all right, is Hamedes. I'll make a soldier of him yet.'

'I'm not quite sure that's what he has in mind.'

'You're wrong, sir. After what Ajax did at his temple that lad isn't going to rest easy until he's had his revenge.'

'Revenge?' Cato sighed. 'Seems to be the only thing that motivates us all. Hamedes, Ajax, you and me.'

Macro's eyes narrowed. 'If you're thinking that some-how we're all the same when it comes down to it, then you're wrong. Dead wrong. We executed Ajax's father because he was a bloody pirate. Ajax was condemned to slavery for the same reason. I'm telling you, that bastard deserves everything that's coming to him. The only question is which of us gets the chance to kill him. You, me, or even Hamedes.'

There was a cough and they both turned to see the priest standing a short distance away watching them. Cato was not sure how much Hamedes had heard and cleared his throat awkwardly.

'You've completed your rites, then?'

'Yes, I did what I could under the circumstances. I pray that the gods permit them entry to the afterlife.'

'Hmmm, yes, well, I'm sure you've done your best for them.' Cato looked up and saw that there was a faint loom of pearly grey in the mist. 'It'll be light soon. We'd best get the men ready to march.'

The column continued along the path in the pallid dawn. Cato and Macro went ahead with two sections of legionaries and Hamedes. They stayed close to the head of the main column in case the full force was needed in a hurry. Centurion Rufus followed up with the wounded, and an escort of marines.

A light breeze had picked up and rustled the leaves of the palms growing in clumps along the path. The mangrove soon gave way to swathes of reeds on either side but there was no sign that Ajax and his men had left the path and Cato led his men on, alert for any hint of trouble. As dawn came and the sun rose into the hazy sky, the mist began to lift and an hour or so later the reeds gave way to cleared areas where fields of wheat were fed with water from irrigation ditches. In the distance they caught the gleam of a broad expanse of water.

'That's one of the Nile tributaries,' Hamedes explained. 'We should find a settlement on the bank soon enough.'

'Like that, over there?' Macro pointed and Hamedes and Cato looked ahead to where smoke smudged into the sky. Macro frowned. 'That's not cooking smoke. That's a fire.'

Cato felt his heart sink at the thought of another village laid waste by Ajax and his men. 'Come on, let's pick up the pace,' he ordered, and the advance party lengthened their stride as the path changed direction through the tall grass and date palms and headed straight for the cloud of smoke. As they passed by more fields they could see the roofs of houses ahead, and hear the crackle of flame and then screams and shouts and Cato felt his guts tighten with bitter hatred for the gladiator. The path had broadened into a cart track and they approached the entrance to the village, another huddle of mud-brick buildings, some with additional walls to pen their donkeys, goats, cattle and chickens. A handful of people in the narrow street winding into the village turned at the sound of heavy boots and ran into their houses as soon as they caught sight of the Romans.

'Good spot for another ambush,' Macro commented as he considered the narrow street with alleys leading off it.

'If Ajax was still here, then those people wouldn't be,' Cato pointed out.

They emerged into an open space where a few market stalls stood. Beyond, a stretch of bare earth sloped down to the river. The remains of a handful of reed boats lay smouldering on the shore and a small crowd of natives stood in a cluster, wailing and crying. Cato led his men to the top of the riverbank and halted them, before continuing towards the villagers with Macro and Hamedes. The small crowd nervously parted before him and Cato saw several men sprawled on the ground, lying in their own blood which had poured from gashes in their bodies. Some women, slumped on their knees, leaned over the men, crying inconsolably.

'Looks like Ajax's work,' said Macro.

'Hamedes,' Cato gestured towards the crowd, 'ask them what happened.'

The priest approached them with open hands and there was a short exchange before he turned back to Cato.

'The villagers say that a column of armed men arrived here at dawn and took as many boats as they needed and set fire to the rest. These men tried to stop them, and were killed.'

'Must have been Ajax,' Cato decided. 'Ask them which way he went.'

Hamedes turned and spoke briefly before pointing upriver. 'That way, sir. You can still see them.'

Cato turned quickly to stare upriver. This stretch of the tributary meandered in a fairly gentle manner to the south and there, perhaps two miles away, he could see a handful of tiny fishing boats on the surface of the river, just about to disappear from sight around a bend in the river.

'Ask them if there are any other boats here, or nearby.'

'None,' Hamedes translated.

'What about another village?'

'There is one, half a day's march, downriver.'

'The wrong direction,' Macro growled. 'The bastard's given us the slip again.'

CHAPTER SIXTEEN

This is not a very satisfactory state of affairs, is it, Prefect?' Governor Petronius tapped his finger on the report he had demanded of Cato the moment the small convoy had reached Alexandria. Even though Cato had secured some boats as soon as possible to pursue Ajax further up the Nile delta, he had lost track of him. They stopped at every village to question the locals and although a small group of reed boats had been discovered abandoned some forty miles north of Memphis, that was the last hint of the direction Ajax and his band had taken. Cato had continued to Memphis, whose inhabitants were greatly alarmed by the Nubian advance further up the Nile. Cato had commandeered one of the wide, flat-bottomed sailing vessels that plied the great river and set sail for Alexandria to make his report.

Cato stood in front of the governor's desk and considered how best to respond to such a rhetorical question.

'Sir, the fact is that we discovered Ajax's base of operations and succeeded in putting it out of action. We took his ships and accounted for over two hundred of his men. He has between forty and fifty followers left. However, I fear that he still poses a considerable threat to the Empire. I shall, of course, continue to pursue him but

I will need to have your warrant to ensure the cooperation of the province's officials along the Nile. In addition, I will need men to complete the task. A mounted cohort should suffice.'

Petronius let out a bitter laugh. 'A mounted cohort, you say? A modest request, you might think. But tell me, after having lost one of my warships and its entire crew, as well as thirty of my legionaries, what makes you think I would be prepared to entrust you with any more men? Well?'

'You can't afford not to, sir.'

'Oh, I think I can afford not to. Especially when my forces are thinly stretched as it is. The Nubians have already advanced as far as the first cataract. That fool, Legate Candidus, sent three of his auxiliary cohorts to intercept the Nubian vanguard. They were crushed. I gather barely half of them managed to escape.'

'That is what I heard at Memphis, sir.'

'Then you will appreciate why I seem reticent to lend any more troops to you. Hunting this gladiator down is no longer a priority. I need to concentrate all available forces to strike at the Nubians, and drive them out of the province.'

'I understand, sir, but if we fail to destroy Ajax then you can be sure that he will continue his private war against Rome. He has already nearly cost the Emperor the province of Crete as well as disrupting the sea trade in the eastern Mediterranean. He cannot be permitted to trouble the Empire any longer.'

'Nor will he, once the Nubians have been repulsed. Then, and only then, will I even consider providing you with any more resources to track down this criminal. Do you understand?'

'Yes, sir. I just don't agree with you.'

'Disagreement is not a privilege that a subordinate can exercise, Prefect,' Petronius snapped. 'I am the supreme power here in Egypt. I act in the name of the Emperor and while you are here in my province, you will do as I instruct. That is the end of the matter.' He paused and smiled coldly. 'Well, not quite.'

Cato stood still and silent, waiting for the governor to elaborate.

Petronius rose from his desk and crossed his study to the opposite wall where a long map of the Nile had been painted, from the delta all the way into southern Egypt. Beyond the line marking the frontier, the details were few. He reached up and tapped the map.

'Candidus is concentrating his forces at Diospolis Magna. In addition to the Twenty-Second Legion, he has two infantry cohorts of auxiliaries and two cavalry cohorts. That is all that can be spared. I have scraped together every spare man that I can to join the army. Now it seems that Candidus is short of a number of officers. His senior tribune was the officer commanding the auxiliary force defeated by the Nubians. He was killed in the fight. Candidus is also short of the full complement of centurions. Several of them were on detachment to frontier posts acting as magistrates. They were lost when the Nubians crossed the border.' Petronius turned round to face Cato. 'It is my decision to attach you and Centurion Macro to the Twenty-Second Legion for the duration of the present emergency.'

Cato had seen it coming and had already prepared his answer. 'I'm sorry, sir, but I have my orders from Governor Sempronius. I am to seek and destroy the slave Ajax and his followers. Until that is achieved I am not free to carry out any other duties.'

Petronius's expression hardened. 'How dare you address me so haughtily, you upstart little prig. Who the hell do you think you are? You are an over-promoted junior officer. There is not a drop of noble blood in your veins. You have no family or connections in Rome worth a bent sestertius. You are nothing more than Sempronius's little pet. You would do well to remember that.'

'I hold the commission of prefect, sir.'

'Oh, you may well hold the rank of prefect, for now, but your patron won't be able to save you from cocking up one day soon. Then you'll be broken back down to a rank more suited to your lack of years and experience.'

'Be that as it may, for now I am under the orders of Senator Sempronius.'

'You forget yourself, Prefect.' Petronius smiled. 'In Egypt I act in the name of the Emperor. There is no higher authority. If I give you a command, it is as if Claudius himself gave it. Is that not true?'

Cato pursed his lips. The governor was correct. He had the authority to do as he pleased, until recalled to Rome. He could overrule the orders of Sempronius if he wished and there was nothing Cato could do about it. 'Yes, sir. That's right.'

Petronius nodded his head. 'Then the matter is decided. You, and Centurion Macro, will leave for Diospolis

Magna immediately. My chief of staff has already prepared your letters of appointment. You can collect them as you leave my offices. Any questions?'

'Yes, sir. May I take it that once the campaign against the Nubians is over, you will authorise me to renew the hunt for Ajax?'

'As you wish.' Petronius shrugged. 'However, I suspect that it will be some months before the Nubians have been dealt with. Unless the gladiator is a complete fool he will have fled the province long before then. If not, then I will be sure to consider any request you make. Now, Prefect, you are dismissed.'

'So, how did it go?' Macro asked as he slid a cup across the table to Cato and poured him some wine. He had been waiting in a tavern just outside the palace gates on the Canopic Way, the two hundred foot wide avenue that stretched across the heart of the city. Outside, in the midday sun, tens of thousands of Alexandrians discussed their business or conversed with friends, struggling to make themselves heard above the din of street hawkers and the merchants shouting about their wares to passers-by. Cato had brushed past them, ignoring the endless entreaties to examine their cheap souvenirs and antiques. The traders pursued him with promises that he need only look, without being hassled. Their promises were as cheap as the goods they sold and they only relented when Cato snarled at them to leave him alone.

Cato slumped down on to the stool opposite Macro and Hamedes and quickly drained the cup. He glanced at Hamedes.

'Shouldn't you be trying to find a vacancy in the priesthood of some temple?'

Hamedes snorted with derision. 'Here, in Alexandria?'

'Why not?' Cato gestured along the Canopic Way. 'There's hardly any shortage of temples in the city.'

'The temples here are run by Greek parasites. They filch money from the gullible to line their purses. I am a priest from the true temples of Egypt. I will not defile myself by serving in Alexandria.' Hamedes helped himself to a cup of wine. 'Besides, the Alexandrian priesthoods are a nice little earner and there aren't any vacancies right now.' He shrugged.

'A priest is a priest is a priest,' Macro muttered as he took the handle of the wine jug and eased it back over to his side of the table. 'Anyway, how did it go with the governor?'

'Let's just say that he wasn't too pleased that Ajax got away.'

'So is he going to give us enough men to track the bastard down?'

'Give us men?' Cato laughed drily. 'Far from it. You and I are being sent to join the fight against the Nubians.' Cato pulled the orders he had been given from inside his tunic and tossed them across the table to Macro. 'Read, if you want to.'

Macro gently pushed the papyrus scroll aside. 'What the hell is Petronius playing at? He knows how dangerous Ajax is.'

'It's a matter of priorities, apparently.'

'Priorities?' Macro frowned. 'Since when was letting the leader of a slave rebellion remain at large not a priority?'

'Ah, there you have me.' Cato clicked his tongue. 'That's what I said to the governor. But he was adamant that the Nubians had to be dealt with first. He's probably right,' Cato conceded. 'So, it's back to the army for both of us. Of course, that may yet serve our purpose.' Cato leaned forward and rested his elbows on the table. 'The last we heard of Ajax was that he was heading up the Nile. He's on the run. He doesn't have many men left. The question is, what would you do in his place?'

Macro scratched his neck. 'Look for a new base to operate from. Find new allies . . .' He looked at Cato and cocked an eyebrow. 'The Nubians?'

'That's my thought.'

Macro was not so certain. 'It's a bit of a long shot. Why would he do that? Why not just find a nice quiet route out of the province and bugger off to some far corner of the Empire and cause trouble there?'

'Because the Nubians offer him the best chance of doing more damage to Rome.'

'And why would the Nubians take him on?'

'Wouldn't you? You've seen the handiwork of Ajax and his men. They'd be a useful asset to any army.'

'I suppose,' Macro responded thoughtfully. 'Though I doubt Ajax will take kindly to receiving orders rather than giving them. Trust me, Cato, I've had the chance to watch the man at length. He is determined to serve no master but himself.'

'We all have to swallow our pride sometimes.' Cato eased himself back. 'I could be wrong. He might already be on his way out of the province. But I doubt it. Not while we're here.' A sudden insight struck him. 'In fact,

I wouldn't be surprised if he was hoping that we would be joining the army sent against the Nubians. All the more reason to join forces with them.'

'He hates us that much?'

Cato recalled the insane rage in Ajax's expression the night they had fought in the village and a familiar cold chill rippled down his spine. 'Yes. Yes, he does. I'm certain of it. And that is the only advantage we have right now.'

Hamedes cleared his throat. 'So, sir, when are you leaving for the upper Nile?'

'Tomorrow. There's a military convoy being loaded at the quay on Lake Mareotis. We've been given berths on one of the barges. We leave at dawn.'

'That soon?' Macro thought a moment and shrugged. 'Why not? If Ajax is waiting for us there, the sooner we deal with the bastard the better.' He turned to Hamedes. 'Looks like we'll be parting company. Here's to you.' He raised his cup. 'As gypo guides go, you're all right.'

Hamedes looked at Cato. 'Is that a compliment, sir?'

'From him? Oh yes.' Cato lifted his cup as well. 'Thanks for your help.'

Hamedes seemed troubled. 'The truth is, sir, that I wish to find a place in one of the older temples that still hold to the old faith. Not here, with these con men. I want to return to the upper Nile, where I was raised.' His eyes gleamed. 'And you still need someone who speaks the native tongue, to help you find the gladiator and his followers. I might serve you a while yet, before returning to the priesthood. You know I have as much reason to find him as you do. The blood of my brother priests demands justice.'

'Yes.' Cato could see the intensity of Hamedes' gaze and guess at the feelings that filled his heart and mind and fuelled his desire for revenge. He nodded. 'Very well, you can join us. I'll have you enrolled as a scout. Might as well be paid for your efforts.'

The priest smiled. 'I am in your debt, sir.'

The Nile barges were heavily laden with military supplies for the coming campaign: baskets filled with arrows, the heavier shafts of ammunition for the bolt throwers, newly forged sword blades, shield bosses and trims, tubs of nails and boots. There were scores of legionaries and officers who had been on leave, or detached service, and were returning to their units, along with some fresh recruits. Cato, Macro and Hamedes, laden down with the kit they had retrieved from the Alexandrian fleet, boarded one of the last vessels to leave and were ushered out of the way to the small foredeck while the crew thrust the vessel away from the quay and hoisted the large triangular sail. The hold had been filled and sacks of grain and jars of oil and wine were heaped across the deck.

'It's a wonder the tub stays afloat,' Macro mused as he set his kitbag down and made himself comfortable under the small awning that covered the foredeck.

Cato nodded. There was scarcely more than a foot of freeboard over the side and he wondered what would happen if the barge was caught by a sudden gust of wind. With all the cargo aboard, it would surely sink like a rock and Cato had no desire to be pitched into the Nile. It was not the prospect of swimming to the nearest bank that concerned him so much as the thought of the crocodiles that might be lurking amid the reeds, waiting to snap up some easy prey.

'Rest easy, Centurion.' Hamedes smiled. 'The waters of the Nile are always calm, and the wind constant. There is no cause for alarm. Besides, I have an offering of a jar of oil for the Nile gods.' He patted his kitbag. 'They will protect us.'

'I'm not bloody alarmed,' Macro growled. 'I'm just saying the boat looks overloaded, that's all.'

Hamedes nodded understandingly and then stretched himself out on his back, resting his head carefully on the bulky kitbag he had brought aboard and settled down to get some sleep. The two Romans watched the receding skyline of Alexandria for a while, taking turns to sip from a wineskin that Macro had bought in one of the markets of the Canopic Way. At length, Macro coughed and turned to Cato.

'Do you really think Ajax will be down there, with the Nubians?'

'The more I think about it, the more certain I am,' Cato replied. 'It offers him the best way of continuing his war against Rome.'

'And us?'

'Why not? There's every chance of killing two birds with one stone. Where else would we be when the governor needs every soldier he can scrape together to repel the invasion?'

'I'm not so keen on being considered to be part of the scrapings, if it's all the same to you.' Macro flashed a smile. 'But I take your point. And if you're right, it should make the task of finding Ajax that much easier. But duty first, eh? Defeat the Nubians and then find Ajax.'

'Defeating the Nubians might be a rather harder task than you think.'

'How so?'

'I had a word with one of Petronius's staff officers before I left the palace. I wanted some information on the forces available to Candidus. The two infantry cohorts sound like good formations, but the cavalry is under strength. It's the Twenty-Second I'm not so sure about.'

'They're legionaries. They'll stand up to whatever the Nubians throw at them.'

'I hope so.' Cato rubbed his chin and wished that he had taken the opportunity to have a shave in Alexandria before embarking. 'The fact is that the Twenty-Second is something of an oddity.'

'Oh? What's their story, then?'

'The legion was raised by Mark Antony. He filled the ranks with men from Cleopatra's army. When Antony was defeated by Octavian, the Twenty-Second was integrated into the rest of the army and has been stationed on the Nile since then. They're a mix of Greeks and Egyptians from the Nile cities.'

'You think they might be a bit soft then?'

'Maybe. They have had no part in a major campaign since the civil war. For most of them, this is going to be the first action they've gone into. I just hope they've been trained well enough for the job.'

Macro shook his head. 'Cato, even if the quality of the men is suspect, they're still commanded by centurions, and centurions, my friend, are the same the world over. As hard and demanding a bunch as you will ever find.'

'Not all of them. We've seen our share of bad officers in our time.'

'A few bad eggs, that's all,' Macro replied tersely, not willing to endure too much disparagement of the brother-hood he felt honoured to be a part of. 'The centurionate has a fine tradition. There are always exceptions.'

'Then let's hope we don't find too many of them in the Twenty-Second.'

'I need some rest,' Macro announced suddenly. He removed the armour from his kitbag and punched spare tunics, cloak and boots that remained into a rough pillow and laid his head down, turning his back to his friend. Cato smiled at his touchiness, and then eased himself down on to an elbow as the barge entered the canal that linked the lake to the Nile. On either side the banks were lined with reeds and clumps of palm trees, interspersed with small settlements of the ubiquitous mud-brick houses. Women were busy taking advantage of the cooler morning temperature to wash clothes in the placid waters while children played slightly further out, splashing each other, their shrill cries of joy carrying clearly across the canal. As the barges sailed past, they stopped their games to wave, and Cato smiled as he waved back.

He had grown so used to the demands and the strains of commanding soldiers that he had forgotten some of the simple pleasures of life, he realised sadly. His childhood seemed all too brief to him at that moment. He brushed the sentiment aside, cross with himself for allowing a moment's idleness to sour his mood. He realised that there would be plenty of time for reflection in the next few days, and resolved that he would focus his thoughts on more useful, and pleasing, matters, such as the future he planned to have with Julia when he returned to Rome. And so he spent the rest of the morning watching the landscape of Egypt drift by as the convoy made its way upriver towards Diospolis Magna. Occasionally Macro and Hamedes stirred and exchanged a few words, before closing their eyes again. In the afternoon the convoy left the canal behind and entered the river. The sun beat down on the barges, and a steady hot breeze blew over the deck like the heat from a nearby furnace.

At dusk the barges put into the shore and grounded gently on a grassy stretch of the riverbank. Fires were lit and rations issued and the insects began to swarm round in whining clouds of dark specks against the light of the flames. Hamedes said he would bed down amongst the sailors, once he had drunk his fill of wine.

'Suit yourself,' Macro responded. 'But I'm not going to lie out here and get bitten to death.'

Macro called over several of the legionaries and ordered them to erect the tent he and Cato would be sharing.

'Quick as you can now, lads!' Macro barked as he swatted the mosquitoes away. 'Before these little bastards drain the blood out of me.'

As soon as the tent was up, Macro ducked inside and laid his bedroll out on the ground. Cato joined him a little later, after a last look up at the brilliant display of stars in the heavens. The glow of the fires lit up the linen walls of the tent and occasionally the wavering shadows of men passed along the cloth, like the profiles of the paintings he had seen on the province's temples, Cato decided. No air moved through the tent and it was hot inside. Cato slipped his tunic off and lay sweating in his loincloth. On the other side of the tent, Macro had quickly fallen asleep, even though he had rested most of the day, and his rumbling snores vied with the sounds of chatter and laughter of the men by the fires. Cato smiled and closed his eyes. He might as well make the most of this short, restful interval, he decided.

He woke suddenly, not moving, his eyes wide open, staring up at the roof of the tent. Cato was not sure what had broken his sleep and he was about to stir when he heard the faint sound of movement outside the tent. Then the sound was gone and with a sigh he turned on to his side and closed his eyes again. At once there was a low rush of sound like a long sharp escape of breath. Cato's eyes snapped open as he realised that he and Macro were not alone in the tent. He slowly turned himself back and raised his head to look round. The campfires were still burning and provided a faint rosy light inside the tent. A short distance away, close to the foot of Macro's bedroll, a slender shape rose up from the ground, swaying slightly.

THE UPPER NILE IN THE REGION OF DIOSPOLIS MAGNA

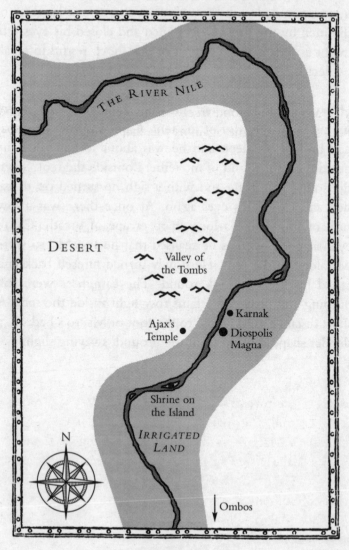

CHAPTER SEVENTEEN

Cato felt his blood freeze in his veins. He sat up, and the noise came again as the shape lurched sideways, moving between the two bedrolls.

'Oh shit,' Cato whispered. He kept as still as he could, eyes fixed on the snake. Behind it he could see the tent pole with his sword and that of Macro's hanging on the peg. His heartbeat increased to a pounding rhythm as he thought frantically. If he moved again he was sure that the serpent would attack. Instead, he licked his lips nervously and whispered as loudly as he dared.

'Macro . . . Macro . . . Wake up.'

The snoring broke up and there was an incoherent muttered grumble from the other side of the tent.

'Macro.'

'Whurgh . . . What the hell is it?' Macro groaned, stirring as he turned to face Cato.

'Keep still!' Cato warned him.

'What?' Macro's head rose. 'What's going on then?'

The snake hissed again, louder, and near the top of its body it began to swell out. The sinewy coils beneath writhed momentarily as it edged forward.

'Shit,' Macro whispered. 'We're in trouble, lad. What do we do?'

Cato stared at the snake. It was close enough now to make out the individual bumps of its scales, and the beady gleam in one of its eyes. A sudden flicker indicated where its mouth was as the cobra's head towered over the two men.

'Just . . . keep . . . still,' Cato whispered.

'Right.'

Cato had seen some snake charmers in the market at Alexandria and knew how fast the serpents could strike. There was no chance of jumping up and dashing past it towards the swords. If either of them tried, they were dead. He reached his left hand slowly towards his tunic, lying rumpled beside the bedroll. His fingers stole across the earth towards the cloth and closed round a fold.

'Macro, I'm going to try and distract it. When I make a move you go for the swords. All right?'

'What kind of distraction?'

'Doesn't matter, just be ready. On three.'

The snake was unsettled by the noises and hissed again, still louder, and the head leaned back, ready to strike.

Cato moistened his lips and spoke softly. 'One . . . two . . . three!'

He whipped up the tunic and jumped to his feet, swinging the tunic waist high through the air towards the snake. The cobra lunged at once, whacking into the cloth before it reversed direction and hissed again. Macro had clambered up and taken a step towards the tent post when the snake slithered round and lunged at him. He jumped back on to his bedroll.

'Fuck, that was close.'

'I'll try again,' said Cato. He wrapped some of the tunic

about his fist and tentatively held the rest out towards the snake. At once it turned its head back towards him, its eyes burning like rubies. Cato moved the tunic to the right and shook it. The snake struck again and at the same time Cato jerked the cloth back. The fangs, caught in the thick strands of wool, came with it and Cato gave a terrified cry as the body of the snake came towards him. He threw the tunic over the cobra's head and with his spare hand he grabbed at the neck, just below the hood. The snake's skin was dry and rough and the coils writhed wildly as Cato struggled to keep his grip and at the same time wrap the tunic about its head with his other hand.

Macro leaped forward, reached the tent post and snatched out his blade. He turned and hacked at the wriggling body and struck the ground instead.

'Macro!' Cato shouted as the head thrashed about inside the tunic. 'Just kill the bastard!'

Macro hacked again, cutting into the middle of the cobra's body. He cut again, this time severing it. Half the coils fell back and flopped about on the ground and Macro hurriedly kicked them to one side. The other half seemed to grow even more wild and Cato hurled it as hard as he could towards the back of the tent where it hit the goatskin with a soft thud and dropped to the ground, writhing frantically, but unable to move from the spot as it bled out.

Cato's heart was beating wildly, his chest felt cold and clammy and he trembled. He turned to Macro and saw that his friend was just as shaken. Macro licked his lips and stared at the dying snake as he spoke in a low, earnest tone. 'I am really beginning to hate this province . . .'

★

'You're the one in charge of the watch, right?' Macro glared at the optio as the latter quickly rose from amongst the men sitting around the fire.

'Yes, sir.' The young soldier nodded.

'Then you're responsible for this getting into our bloody tent.' Macro shook out the tunic and the two lengths of the cobra's body flopped on to the ground. The optio instinctively took a step back and his face wrinkled in nervous disgust. There were surprised murmurs from the other men as they craned their necks and saw the dead snake.

Macro turned and pointed towards the tent. 'The prefect is inside. There is supposed to be a guard patrolling outside the tent to ensure nothing happens to him, right? No enemies, or other threats, get past. I mean that's standard regulation, even here in Egypt.'

'Yes, sir.'

'So where is the sentry?' Macro made a show of looking around and giving up and raising his hands. 'Well?'

'I'm sorry, sir.' The optio swallowed. 'I had a man either end of the camp. I didn't think it would be necessary to post any more than that.'

'Two men?' Macro shook his head. 'The province is in a state of war, and before you say it, I don't care how far away the Nubians are. That's no excuse for sloppy watch-keeping. Let me guess. You're with the Twenty-Second Legion?'

The optio nodded.

'Oh great . . .' Macro took a pace closer and held his finger an inch from the optio's face. 'I want a proper watch posted every night. It is your duty to protect the camp and protect your officers and you have fucked up, my son. The fact is, either the prefect or myself or even both of us could have been killed and the fault would be yours.'

'But sir. Even if there had been a sentry, the snake could have got into the tent.'

'Shut it! You know what your duty is. I suggest you stick to it, or *I'll* be disturbing *your* night by kicking your arse so hard your teeth will fall out.' Macro took a step back, and prodded the snake's body with his boot. 'I'll leave you to get rid of this.'

He was about to return to the tent when the captain of their barge squatted down by the snake and shook his head. 'They don't usually give us any trouble when we camp. Your tent must be pitched near one of their nests.'

'You mean there could be more of them nearby?' Macro fumed.

'No. They're solitary creatures. Unless their young are hatching, of course.'

'Well, thanks for that. I'm bound to get a good night's sleep now, aren't I?' He turned back to the optio. 'Make that two sentries outside the tent.'

'Yes, sir.'

Macro turned and marched back to the tent and pulled the flap shut behind him. He tossed the tunic back to Cato as he crossed to his bedroll and slumped down. 'Bloody optio's from the Twenty-Second. Seems like you were right to be worried about 'em.'

Cato was sitting cross-legged on his bedroll, deep in thought. He shook his head and glanced round. 'Sorry?'

'I said you were right about the Twenty-Second being a bit slack.'

'Oh, yes.'

'Hello, Cato.' Macro waved his hand. 'Still with us?'

'Just thinking.' Cato ran a hand through his hair. 'About the snake. If there's one thing I really can't stand, it's snakes.'

'Why so particular? They're just like everything else in this province: crocodiles, mosquitoes and snakes – never content unless they're sinking their bloody jaws into someone. Fuck 'em. I'm going to try to get back to sleep.' He glanced over at Cato and continued in a more gentle tone. 'So should you. Best get as much rest as you can before we reach Diospolis Magna.'

'Yes, you're right.' Cato eased himself down and lay still, staring up at the roof of the tent. After a while he shut his eyes and lay there listening intently to every sound of the night. Although Macro lay still and silent on his side, he did not snore and Cato realised that his friend's mind was as troubled as his own.

Macro blinked his eyes open and for a moment frowned. The last thing he remembered was being unable to get to sleep, and lying still for what seemed like hours. Well, sleep had come to him in the end, he mused. Dawn was breaking outside and a shaft of light pierced the tent through the open flap. Macro turned over and saw that Cato's bedroll was empty.

He sat up and stretched his arms, yawning widely before smacking his lips. Rising to his feet, Macro saw a dark dry patch in the light-coloured soil in front of the tent post and immediately recalled the scene the previous night when he had cleaved the cobra in two, and pursed his lips sourly. Emerging from the tent, Macro saw his friend sitting on a palm log a short distance away. He was staring out across the misty river, the stopper from an amphora in his hands. A short distance away lay the remains of a broken amphora.

'Up early, or couldn't you sleep?' Macro called out as he strode over to join Cato.

'Not much chance of anyone sleeping when you start snoring.' Cato tossed the stopper aside into the grass. 'At least we weren't troubled by anything else last night. That's something to be thankful for.'

Further along the shore the other passengers and the crews from the boats were rising and rolling up their bedrolls ready to continue the voyage upriver. Hamedes approached them, carrying his kitbag over his shoulder.

'Morning, sirs. I heard there was some excitement last night.'

'You could say that,' Macro replied.

Hamedes tossed his bag down and squatted in front of them. 'The optio told me about the snake just now. Seems you had a close escape. The venom of the Nile cobra can kill a man within the hour. You're very lucky, sir.'

'Funny, I thought I was unlucky that it happened at all.'

The priest tilted his head to one side. 'Perhaps it was an omen. A message from the gods. A warning perhaps.'

'Then again, perhaps it was just a bloody snake which took a wrong turning.' Macro stood up and pointed to two of the legionaries standing by the nearest fire. 'You, and you. Get the tent down and stowed. Make sure the bedrolls are put on the same boat.'

Cato turned to Hamedes and was silent a moment before he spoke. 'A message? I think you might be right.'

'Oh?' A brief look of surprise flashed across the priest's face.

'Yes,' Cato continued. 'We seem to have been dogged by bad luck ever since we began our hunt for Ajax here in Egypt. I'm beginning to wonder if we've offended some of the local gods. You're the man with the expertise here, Hamedes. How do we go about appeasing your gods? Who should we offer prayers to? What sacrifice should we make?'

Macro glanced at his friend. 'Since when did you come over all religious?'

'There's been plenty of times in the last few months when fortune has played us false, Macro. It could be mere coincidence, but I doubt it. On one or two occasions, perhaps, but as often as we have endured it, then a man is right to suspect that the gods, or someone else, are playing their hand.'

Macro puffed his cheeks, not quite sure how to respond. 'You really think an offering is necessary, sir?'

'It would give me some peace of mind,' Cato admitted. 'Will you see to it, Hamedes, on our behalf?'

'Of course, sir.'

'As soon as you can.'

'I will do what I can. The rites associated with good fortune and warding off bad luck were beyond my remit, sir. I was entrusted with more basic offerings. But I will find out for you when we reach Diospolis Magna and I can consult the priests there.'

Cato stared at him and then nodded. 'Very well, that will have to do.' He took a deep breath and stood up. 'Meanwhile, let's get the convoy under way again. The sooner we reach our destination, the better.'

The convoy continued up the river, passing beyond the delta on to the single expanse of water that flowed through the heart of the great desert that stretched west from the Erythraeum Sea across the continent and formed the southernmost boundary of the Empire. From the river Cato could see the rocky scarps that rose up beyond the narrow belt of cultivated land spilling out beyond both banks of the Nile. Between stretches of reeds and palm trees he saw great numbers of fields tended by peasants and tilled by oxen drawing heavy ploughs as they turned over the dark silted soil that was the source of the province's great wealth. Before the time when Rome had coveted the fertile farmlands of Egypt, such wealth had funded the ambitions of the Ptolemies, and before them the ancient lineage of the old Pharaohs dating back to time beyond record.

Though they were forgotten, they had lived in an age of marvels, Cato mused as the convoy passed by the trio of pyramids, guarded by a giant Sphinx, a short distance downriver from Memphis. Though he had seen them several days earlier, on the way to report to Petronius, Cato still viewed them with awe as he stood on the fore-deck shading his eyes as he stared. They were built on the scale of mountains, it seemed, though geometrically perfect in a manner that nature could never achieve. The sides seemed to be glassy smooth for the most part, and patches of what looked like gold leaf reflected the sun's rays in such dazzling splendour that Cato thought they would have been impossible to behold when in their prime.

'Quite a sight,' said Macro as he came forward to stand beside Cato. He stared a moment longer and then shook his head. 'Hard to believe it's the handiwork of the gypos, ain't it?'

'That's hardly a fair comment.' Cato gestured to a village on the shore. 'These people are living in the shadows of their ancestors. They are not the same.' He paused for a moment in reflection. 'Perhaps one day they will say the same of our ancestors when Rome is little more than a curiosity. When our great monuments are crumbling back into the ground.'

'Pfft! You talk utter bollocks sometimes, Cato.' Macro nudged him. 'You know you do.' He cleared his throat and then imitated the same hushed and reverential tones of his friend as he continued. 'Rome is the darling of the gods, brought forth into the world to be a shining beacon of all that is great and best. In the distant future people will stand in front of the gates of Rome and look in wonder on our mighty works and despair . . .'

'Have you quite finished?' Cato asked tersely.

Macro sniffed. 'Give me a moment, I'm sure I might have missed something pretentious I could have said.'

'Fuck off.'

'Now that's spoken like a soldier. Brief, and to the point. Come, forget about all them dusty piles of stone and get into the shade before you start getting even more light-headed, eh?'

Macro slipped back under the awning and sat down. Cato stared at the pyramids for a little longer, but Macro's words had robbed them of some of their mystique and with a sigh he turned and joined Macro and Hamedes in the shade.

Ten days after the convoy left Alexandria the barges sailed round the final bend in the river before Diospolis Magna just after the sun had fallen behind the arid mountains on the western bank. On the opposite bank towered the pylons of the largest temple complex Cato had ever seen. Tall wooden masts rose from brackets on the carved walls and tattered banners of faded red wafted and flickered in the evening breeze. A tall mud-brick wall surrounded the temple, giving it the appearance of a vast fortress. A stone landing stage stood a short distance from the edge of the river, where a more recent quay constructed from wood lined the bank of the Nile.

'Karnak,' Hamedes said with reverence, and then pointed further along the bank to another, far smaller complex. 'And that's the temple of Amun. The city lies beyond.'

The captain of the barge sat at the tiller and gently heaved it away from him as he steered in towards the quay. A number of soldiers were standing guard along the quay and on towers erected behind the walls. As the flotilla approached, a party of soldiers emerged from the ornate landing platform and descended the ramp on to the quay to assist with mooring the barges. The crews tossed ropes across the water to them and one by one the barges were hauled in and the ropes fastened to worn wooden cleats lining the quay.

The two Roman officers and the priest gathered their kitbags and stepped ashore. Cato stopped the optio in charge of the mooring party.

'Where is the army headquarters?'

'Who wants to know?'

Macro stepped forward to tear a strip off the optio for his insubordination but Cato raised a hand to stop him. They were wearing only their standard-issue tunics. Their armour, and insignia, were packed in their kitbags.

'Prefect Quintus Licinius Cato and Centurion Macro reporting for duty with the Twenty-Second,' said Cato and nodded at Hamedes. 'This is our scout.'

'Ah, my apologies, sir.' The optio stiffened to attention. 'You want the priests' quarters, sir.' The optio turned and pointed to the east of the temple complex. 'Over there. I'll have one of my men guide you.'

Cato nodded as he cast an eye over the optio and his men. Most were dark-skinned, like the natives. A few had the lighter skins of the Greeks or Romans. 'Very well.'

Shortly after, they climbed the ramp to the ceremonial landing stage and the vista inside the temple complex opened up. Thousands of men were camped inside the wall, their tents aligned in neat rows stretching out across the compound. In the distance, towards the rear of the complex, lay the stables where the horses of the auxiliary cohorts, and the four squadrons of legionary cavalry, stood sheltered from the sun beneath shades made from palm fronds. A short distance outside the walls, between the temple complex and the city, lay the sprawl of tents belonging to the camp followers. This was where the soldiers could find drink, trinkets and comfort in the arms of women from the numerous companies of prostitutes run by seedy Greek merchants.

'Impressive.' Hamedes nodded. 'I have never seen such a powerful army. The Nubians would tremble at such a sight. I could not guess at the number.'

'The number is less impressive than you might think,' Macro replied. 'A legion has over five thousand men on its roll at full strength. But then, they never are at full strength. The auxiliary units amount to perhaps three thousand men. At best Candidus has eight thousand men to counter the Nubians.'

'But surely, sir, the Roman soldiers are the best in the world? How else could they have won such an empire?'

'There are soldiers and there are soldiers,' Cato responded quietly.

The legionary assigned to escort them to headquarters led them down a short avenue of Sphinxes and through the gates of the first set of pylons, across a courtyard and between two large statues into a hall filled with vast columns. At the far end they turned right towards another set of pylons stretching to the south. The courtyards here were packed with supply carts and thousands of sacks of grain to supply the army once they marched south to do battle with the Nubians. For Hamedes the army's preparations for war were something of a novelty and he kept glancing about him with insatiable curiosity.

'Hey,' Macro called to the legionary. 'You had any word on the enemy?'

The man glanced back and shook his head. 'Nothing for days, sir. Last I heard was that their mounted troops had been seen as far north as Ombos.'

'Where's that?'

'A hundred or so miles upriver.'

Macro turned to Cato. 'Not exactly blazing a path through the underbelly of the province, are they? And Candidus isn't exactly rushing to drive them back either.'

Cato shrugged. 'I'm sure the legate has his reasons.'

'I'd be interested in hearing them.'

They strode down through the last set of pylons, and saw another avenue of Sphinxes heading towards the temple of Amun, over a mile away. A short distance from the avenue was a large low building, surrounded by another mud-brick wall. A section of legionaries stood guard at the gate.

'This way, sir.' Their guide gestured to Cato. The optio in command of the gate raised a hand as they approached.

'Halt! State your business.'

'Officers joining the legion,' the legionary explained and stood aside as Cato reached inside his tunic and took out his orders and handed them over for the optio to inspect. He ran his eyes over the papyrus scroll and then saluted. 'Welcome to the Jackals, sir.'

'Jackals?'

The optio turned and pointed at the standard rising up above the gate leading into the priests' quarters. Above the legion's number, a depiction of a canine head in gold stood out against the red cloth of the fall. Cato and Macro briefly examined the standard and exchanged a knowing glance: there wasn't a single battle honour adorning the staff.

'I expect you'll want to be entered on to the roll, sir.'

Cato nodded. 'But first I wish to see the legate.'

'He's not here, sir. You'll have to see the camp prefect instead. Caius Aurelius.'

'Where is the legate?'

'He left the army several days ago, sir. I heard he was touring the forts along the Nile to make sure they were adequately prepared to hold out against the Nubians.'

'When is he due back?'

'Can't say, sir. Best ask the camp prefect.'

'Where do I find him?'

'Through the gates and straight on, sir. Admin offices are just beyond the pool.'

'Pool?' Macro smiled as they strode through the gates. 'Sounds like a cushy posting.'

In stark contrast to the bland exterior of the wall running round the priests' quarters, the interior afforded comfort in some style at first glance. Palm trees shaded the paved paths that surrounded the buildings. Flower beds were watered by pipes that ran through the gardens. Few plants remained, however, and those that did were sadly neglected and their leaves were covered in a layer of fine dust. The path from the entrance led through a double line of columns and opened out on to a tiled courtyard surrounded by airy cells. A large awning covered the courtyard and in its shade the staff of the headquarters had set up their trestle tables. The clerks were busy cleaning their pens and putting aside their work as they looked forward to the evening meal. On the far side of the court-yard was another line of columns and beyond they could see the mirror gleam of water. The cells of the second courtyard were given over to the senior officers of the army and cots had been set up at the back of each cell while a desk stood at the front. Several officers were still hard at work and Cato asked a passing orderly for the camp prefect.

'Over there, sir. Far end of the pool.' He pointed out a slight man with dark, tightly curled hair, hunched over a large desk as he examined a document. Cato led the small party round the shallow pool. As he approached the cell, the camp prefect glanced up. He looked tired and anxious.

'Yes?'

'Prefect Cato, sir. I've been sent from Alexandria to take up the senior tribune's vacancy. My orders.' He handed the document over. 'This is Centurion Macro, assigned to the legion.'

'And him?' He nodded at Hamedes.

'Our scout, sir.'

Aurelius quickly glanced at the orders and pushed them to one side. 'It's good to have you with us. Even though we had a junior tribune join us yesterday we're still short of the full complement of officers, particularly in the First Cohort. Our best officers can be called on to act as magistrates right across the province. Two of our centurions were serving south of Ombos and we've had no word from them. The same goes for the first spear. He was overseeing the construction of a new fort at Pselchis. Frankly, I fear the worst.'

'Sorry to hear it, sir,' said Macro.

'Well, perhaps no news is good news,' Aurelius replied unconvincingly. 'In the meantime, Prefect Cato, you're acting senior tribune. Centurion Macro gets command of the First Century.' He tapped the scrolls. 'You come highly recommended, and we need experienced officers. As you might know, it's a while since the entire legion saw active service. We've been carrying out policing action most of the time. Still, the opposition's little more than a mob of mounted brigands. That's what we're told, anyway.'

As the man spoke, in his high voice with its sing-song cadence and rhythm, Cato's earlier fears about the combat readiness of the legion seemed to be justified. Aurelius was clearly a man far more at home wielding a stylus than a gladius. Cato could only hope that the legate had wider military experience.

'Sir, if I may, I'd like to present myself to Legate Candidus at the earliest opportunity when he returns. I need to speak to him about the possibility of an additional threat to this region.'

'I'm sure you would like to speak to Candidus,' the camp prefect replied. 'So would I. The fact is, he said he would be back three days ago. I've sent patrols to look for him but there's no sign of him on the road to Ombos. The gods only know where he's got to.'

CHAPTER EIGHTEEN

The Nubian army was in camp twenty miles to the north of Ombos, in a shallow loop of the Nile that watered their horses and camels, as well as the herds of goats that served as mobile rations. There was little sense of the orderly layout that Ajax had seen in the Roman army at Diospolis Magna. The gladiator had halted his column of mounted men on a rocky outcrop a mile away from the camp. Prince Talmis's forces sprawled across the flattened fields of wheat. Ajax estimated that the Nubian army must be at least thirty thousand strong. There were tents dotted around, but most of the men had erected temporary shelters constructed from palm fronds. The majority of the Prince's men seemed to be Nubian warriors, with a smaller contingent of Arabs, swathed in flowing dark robes. At the heart of the camp lay a cluster of larger tents, and Ajax could make out a loose ring of spearmen guarding the cleared perimeter that stretched a short distance around the tents.

'That's where I think we'll find Prince Talmis.'

Karim nodded. 'I hope you're right about this, General.'

'Trust me. He'll welcome us. Especially when we offer him a few tokens of our friendship.' Ajax smiled as he patted the sacks hanging across the back of his horse. 'Relax, Karim, if there's one thing you can be certain of in this world it's that the principle of my enemy's enemy being my friend applies everywhere.'

The flesh wound he had received from Cato was still healing and Ajax twisted round carefully in his saddle to inspect his men. Only twenty-eight of them were still with him. Some had been lost in a skirmish with the Romans five days earlier, and more when they had raided an outpost to seize the horses. Still, most of the gladiators who had formed his bodyguard back during the rebellion in Crete had survived, as had the strongest of the slaves he had liberated from the captured ships. They handled their weapons competently enough, and had plenty of courage and loyalty and in time would prove themselves alongside the cadre of gladiators.

'When we approach their camp, keep your hands away from your weapons. Whatever happens, you do nothing unless I give the order. Is that clear?'

His men nodded.

Ajax gestured to the tall Nubian gladiator mounted astride a horse whose hide was as black as the skin of its rider. 'Hepithus, come forward!'

'Yes, General.' The Nubian clicked his tongue and urged his mount alongside.

'Those are your people. You will act as my translator. Only use the words I speak to you, and you will tell me all that passes between those who address us.'

Hepithus nodded.

Ajax turned back to scan the camp spread out before him. Half a mile from the foot of the outcrop a score of warriors mounted on camels slowly patrolled the northern approaches to the camp. Ajax pointed them out to Karim and Hepithus. 'We'll make for those men. If there's any trouble we'll have plenty of room to make our escape.'

'I thought you said we were guaranteed a warm welcome,' said Karim.

Ajax smiled. 'It is as well to be prepared in case the welcome is too warm, my friend.' He flicked his reins. 'Let's go.'

The small column of horsemen began their descent from the outcrop. A narrow path wound down the slope on to the river plain and the hoofs of the horses immediately kicked up a haze of dust that was bound to be seen by the Nubian patrol. Sure enough, Ajax saw them halt briefly, then one rider turned and urged his camel into a loping gallop as he raced back towards the camp. The rest spread out into a line and turned to approach the horsemen. As they came on, Ajax saw them draw out light javelins from the long quivers hanging from their saddle frames. He turned to call back to his men. 'Remember. Keep your hands away from your weapons unless I say otherwise.'

The gap between the two formations rapidly narrowed and when they were no more than a hundred paces away from the line of camels, Ajax raised his hand and reined in. 'Halt!'

The column clopped to a standstill and the men sat in their saddles, both hands holding on to their reins. The camels approached steadily and then, when they were within javelin range, their leader called out an order and they slowed and stopped. The riders wore dark robes and headdresses and held their weapons in an overhand grip, ready to hurl them the instant they received the order.

Ajax cleared his throat and raised a hand in greeting. 'We come as friends. I wish to speak with Prince Talmis.' He nodded to Hepithus and the Nubian spoke with the leader of the patrol, then turned to Ajax.

'He asks who you are.'

'Then tell him that I am Ajax, the gladiator, leader of the rebellion against Rome on the island of Crete, and I have come to offer my services to Prince Talmis, against our common enemy.'

Hepithus translated and there was a short pause before the leader of the patrol spoke again.

'He wants us to hand our weapons over to his men. Then he will escort us into their camp.'

Karim edged his mount forward and spoke quietly. 'General, it would not be wise to venture any further without the means to defend ourselves.'

Ajax took a deep breath and shook his head. 'We will do as he says. Swords out!'

There was a chorus of steely rasps as his men drew their weapons and held them ready. The Nubians stirred uneasily and several raised their javelins.

'Throw them down!' Ajax ordered and tossed his sword to one side. His men followed suit, save Karim who watched the Nubians warily.

'Do as I say,' Ajax hissed angrily. 'Now.'

Karim swung his arm down and the sword stuck into the ground close by the heel of his boot. The leader of the patrol shouted an order and four of his men made their camels kneel before they slid from the saddles and ran across to the column of horsemen to gather up the weapons. They hurried back and placed them in their saddle buckets before remounting and urging their camels back on to their feet. There was a brief series of throaty grunts from the camels before all was still again. The patrol leader gestured to Ajax to follow him and turned his camel towards the camp. Half his men followed him, and the rest waited for the horsemen to pass by before taking up the rear.

As they entered the camp, the nearest Nubians stood up and watched curiously as they passed by. The odour of manure and woodsmoke filled the air and Ajax cast a professional fighter's eye over the warriors of Prince Talmis's army. Those on the outer fringes of the camp were lightly armed, barely more than simple tribesmen armed with hunting spears and hide shields. Some had bows, or javelins. What they may have lacked in equipment they made up for in numbers. Ajax estimated there must be at least fifteen thousand of them. The next section of the camp was given over to men with swords and armour. Many wore breastplates over long robes and bronze helmets rimmed with linen to shade their faces and necks. There were several thousand of these armoured warriors and Ajax felt his heart lighten at the prospect of the odds facing the far smaller Roman army camped downriver.

Ahead lay the open patch of ground surrounding the complex of tents belonging to Prince Talmis and his generals, Ajax surmised. To their right, in the bend of the river, thousands of horses and camels grazed on the crops of the Egyptian peasants, or drank from the river.

The leader of the patrol halted as he was approached by several of the spearmen guarding the perimeter around the tents. A few words were exchanged and the commander of the spearmen stared suspiciously for a moment before he waved the riders through and pointed to a line of tethering posts a short distance from the tents. Ajax's men were escorted by the camel riders and the spearmen and when they reached the posts, Ajax gave the command for his men to dismount and stand by their horses. One of the spearmen trotted off to the nearest tent and a moment later an officer, in ornate flowing robes and a gleaming vest of scale armour, emerged. He strode up to Ajax and looked him over with dark, deep-set eyes.

'I am told you wish to speak to my Prince.' He spoke in fluent Greek.

'I do.' Ajax nodded. 'I intend to offer him the services of myself and my warriors.'

The officer turned his gaze on Ajax's men, noting their powerful physiques and the scars that many bore on their faces and limbs.

'Are you deserters?'

'We are gladiators.'

'Slaves then,' the officer sneered.

'No longer. We took our freedom with our own hands and have been fighting Rome ever since. Rome is our enemy, as it is yours. That is why we offer our service to your Prince.'

'And what can you offer him that his own men can't, I wonder?'

'This.' Ajax smiled and reached for the sacks tied across the back of his horse. He hauled them down and dropped them heavily on the ground at the feet of the officer. The spearmen tensed and lowered the tips of their spears a fraction, ready to strike. Ajax bent down to untie the tops of the sacks and then reached into the first. He drew out a bundle of red cloth and tossed it to the officer. The latter did not flinch as he caught it and unravelled the material to expose a red standard, cut from its jack. It carried the legend 'Legatus' in gold letters, and beneath, smeared with dried blood, 'Candidus'.

The officer smiled. 'So, slave, you stole the personal banner of the Roman general? Impressive, but my Prince needs warriors, not common thieves.'

'We did more than steal his banner, my friend.' Ajax reached further into the sack with both hands and drew out a severed head. He raised it by the hair and held it aloft. The skin was mottled and the eyelids half open over dull eyes. The jaw was slack and the teeth gleamed behind blackened lips. The warm air was filled with the stink of decaying flesh and the officer's nose wrinkled. He took a step back.

'May I introduce Legate Caius Candidus, lately commander of the Roman army camped at Diospolis Magna. I have his ring hand in the bag as further proof of his identity. The other sack contains the heads of the officers who were riding with him when my men and I attacked the legate and his escort five days ago.'

The interior of the Prince's tent was spacious and the ground covered with rugs and cushions. Light entered through slits in the roof held up by several stout posts. Ajax was standing in the middle of the tent, lit from above so that his body was framed with a faint halo as he faced the Prince. Talmis lay on a couch to the rear of the tent.

He wore a white robe and bejewelled gold rings adorned his dark fingers. Like Ajax he was powerfully built and the outline of his muscled limbs was evident beneath the light folds of his robes. The Nubian Prince's face was broad and a finely trimmed beard ran neatly round his jaw.

On a large brass platter between the two men lay the heads of the Roman officers and the ring hand of Candidus. Talmis regarded them for a moment before his gaze moved up to the gladiator standing before him, flanked by two watchful spearmen from the Prince's bodyguard.

'It is customary for visitors to kneel before me.' Talmis spoke Greek, like many of the more educated members of his father's court. His tone was neutral but Ajax was well aware of the veiled threat implied by the words. Nonetheless, he remained standing and put the onus on the Prince to continue speaking.

'Why do you not kneel to me, gladiator? I can hardly believe that your Roman masters did not teach you the deference demanded of a slave.'

'I am no longer a slave, Your Highness,' Ajax replied firmly. 'Neither are my followers. We are free men, by right of arms. We acknowledge no master and have no loyalty to any kingdom. Therefore we kneel to no man.'

'I see,' Talmis replied slowly, and his lips framed a faint smile. 'Such hubris is a bold approach when you stand unarmed in the middle of my army's camp. If I wished, I could have you cut down to size, should you refuse to kneel to me. And what is a man without his legs?'

'If you harmed me, you would have to kill my men

215

also. And that would deprive you of a useful ally in your fight against Rome. Not to mention those of your men we would kill before you destroyed us.'

'I think you underestimate my bodyguards, gladiator.'

'Really?' Ajax smiled. Then, before the men either side of him could react, he turned and snatched the spear from the man to his right, thrust the shaft between the man's legs and flipped the shaft up so that the guard's leg shot up, and he toppled heavily on to his back. Ajax spun round, spear held in both fists, and blocked the thrust aimed at his chest by the other man, then slammed the butt into his face. Dazed, the man's fingers released his spear and it slipped to the ground. Ajax hooked his foot behind the guard's boot and thrust again with the butt of the spear, sending him thudding to the ground. He spun the spear round and stood over the guard, holding the tip of the spear an inch from his throat. He paused, then lowered the spear and grasped the man's hand and hauled him up before thrusting the spear back into the hands of the first guard who had only just scrambled back on to his feet.

'And I think you underestimate gladiators, Highness.' Ajax resumed his position between the two dazed guards who eyed him warily.

Talmis had sat up quickly as Ajax disarmed his guards and his hand was resting on the handle of an ornate dagger handle. He released his grip and chuckled. 'I should not have doubted you. I had heard rumours that Rome's slave warriors were men to be reckoned with. Now I see the rumours are true.'

'We are not slaves of Rome any longer, Your Highness,'

Ajax replied with quiet intensity. 'And we choose who we offer our service to. For now, we would serve you, as Nubia wages war on Rome.'

Talmis regarded him silently for a moment, and then nodded. 'Then you, and your men, are welcome. There is always a place for fine warriors at my side.' He gestured towards the heads on the platter. 'Now tell me how you came by such a . . . gift. I cannot believe it was a chance encounter.'

'Nor was it,' Ajax replied. 'My men and I had been obliged to flee down the Nile after our last camp was surprised. Word of our presence spread and we had to keep on the move. One of my men is a Nubian, and knows the lands of the upper Nile well. He advised me that Roman settlements were scarce and that we might have a better chance of evading our pursuers if we moved further to the south. As we passed Diospolis Magna in the hills to the east, I saw the Roman army gathering there. I had heard that war was brewing between Rome and Nubia and I thought that I might be welcomed as an ally if I brought useful intelligence to you, Highness. So we observed the Roman camp for some days, noting their numbers and equipment. Then, fortune smiled on us. We saw the Roman commander and two aides ride out of his camp, with a squadron of legionary cavalry as escort. They took the Nile road to the south, and we followed them. When they camped for the night, my gladiators attacked. I slew the legate with my own hand.'

'You did not think to take him hostage and demand a ransom?'

'No. I had an unfortunate experience with my last two

Roman hostages. They escaped me, so I resolved not to take any more.'

'Candidus did not even give you the opportunity to take him prisoner, then?'

'I did not give him the opportunity to ask it.'

'I see.' Talmis stroked his heavy jaw for a moment as he regarded the man standing before him. Ajax returned his gaze with unwavering eyes, without displaying any sign of nervousness or uncertainty. At length the Prince stopped stroking his chin and opened his hand. 'Before I make any alliance with another man, I make a point of understanding precisely what it is that impels them to seek an alliance in the first place.'

'A wise precaution, Highness.'

'Just so.' Talmis nodded. 'The question I ask you is why you so evidently hate the Romans with every fibre of your being?'

'Is it not enough that I do hate them?'

'No. I must know all.' Talmis smiled thinly. 'Indulge me.'

Ajax was silent for a moment before he replied. 'I was forced into slavery and sold to a gladiator school. I was treated as a common brute, and trained to kill men at the behest of my master, for the entertainment of the mob. It is not a condition with which I was comfortable, Highness. I was born free and I will die free and I will never again be a slave.'

'So, you would make slavery your enemy? Then you would make an enemy of me, for I have slaves by the thousand.'

'My enemy is not slavery,' Ajax countered. 'My enemy is Rome.'

'Then you are an ambitious man indeed.' Talmis smiled. 'Your ambitions exceed your means, gladiator. You cannot afford such an enemy as Rome. That is the privilege of kings and princes – not slaves, gladiators or common free men.'

'Yet I choose to make Rome my enemy, Highness. If a man is not free to choose his enemies then he is not free at all.'

Talmis raised his eyebrows. 'That is a peculiarly extreme definition of liberty . . . I suspect that there is a less abstract motive for your hatred of Rome, or perhaps your hatred for specific Romans. Am I not right?'

Ajax was still for a moment and then nodded.

'Then tell me what really drives your hatred.'

'I would rather not, Highness,' Ajax replied quietly. 'The wounds are deep. Is it not sufficient that I swear to serve you loyally, whatever the ultimate reason?'

'It is not sufficient for me,' the Prince replied firmly. 'In exchange for accepting you into my service I demand that you keep no secrets from me, and if you ever deceive me I will have your heart cut out.' He paused briefly to let the threat sink in. 'So tell me, gladiator, what has driven you to offer your services?'

Ajax drew a deep breath and sighed. 'Very well. Then know that before I was a slave, I was a pirate. An ignoble and parasitical pursuit, some might argue.'

'And well they might.'

Ajax pursed his lips and continued. 'The truth is that we were a brotherhood, loyal to each other and motivated by lust for booty. Many of us had women and children. We were bound to each other in the same way that other people are. Life was good. We took what we needed and perhaps more than we needed on occasion. Then came the day when the Romans decided to hunt us down and exterminate us, like vermin.'

'As I would have done, if you had preyed on my kingdom.'

Ajax looked pained. 'I know that, and accept it. But whatever you may make of me and my brothers, it is still the case that they were family and friends and they were all that I had ever had. The Romans destroyed it all. They burned our ships, sacked our settlement, massacred our men, women and children.' Ajax swallowed bitterly. 'My own father they nailed to a cross and left to die. They enslaved me and the other survivors.'

'And you blame Rome for this?'

'Rome in general, and those Roman officers who killed my father in particular – Macro and Cato. I had years to nurse my grievance, and then fate thrust us together during the recent slave rebellion on Crete.' Ajax clenched his teeth. 'Again they frustrated me. They broke the rebellion and since then they have been hunting for me and the handful of men who are all that remain of the army of slaves that I led against Rome.'

'And this is why you come here? You wish me to provide you with a haven, safe from those who hunt you?' Prince Talmis's lips rose in a faint sneer. 'Far from offering me the benefit of your service, it is my protection that you seek.'

'No, Highness. All I seek is revenge. I do not care how I attain that, only that I live to see it happen, or die a free man in the pursuit of revenge.'

'Then it seems to me that you are better off hunting down those two Roman officers of yours rather than supporting my cause. I need soldiers, not grudge bearers who use my army for shelter.'

'I do not seek shelter, Highness. I will serve you and do all that I can to further your cause. For now, I ask that you give me a column of your men to command and I will visit death and destruction upon our common enemy. I know how to fight and I know how to lead men. Trust me, and I will prove my words. Besides, I have more to offer you than myself and my men here in your camp. Something that may well provide you with an advantage in the war with Rome.'

'And what would that be?' Talmis asked with an amused smile. He leaned forward. 'What advantage could a fugitive slave offer me?'

Ajax resisted the urge to smile. He had a most useful bargaining counter and once Prince Talmis knew of it, Ajax was certain the Prince would accept the alliance.

'I have a spy in the Roman army. I have infiltrated one of my men, and he will tell us all that we need to know about the strength of the Roman army, and its dispositions.'

Prince Talmis nodded slowly. 'That is good. Very good. Well then, Ajax, it seems that we might be of use to each other after all. I will appoint you as one of my officers and give you men to command. I already had it in mind to teach the Romans an early lesson, and you will be the man to deliver it.'

CHAPTER NINETEEN

'Hmmm.' Macro shook his head. 'Not the prettiest of sights.'

The headless bodies of the legate and two of the tribunes lay in the back of the cart. A cloud of insects buzzed over the bloated corpses and gorged on the blackened tendrils of gristle and bone on the stumps of their necks, and the right wrist of Candidus. A decurion held back the goatskin cover and stood to one side as his superiors gazed into the back of the cart. Cato and Macro had been discussing their appointments with Aurelius when a clerk had intervened to tell them that the patrol sent to look for the legate had found his body, and those of his escort.

Cato clenched his nostrils tightly and edged away from the back of the cart. 'Where did they find them?'

The decurion nodded vaguely towards the south. 'A ravine, some thirty miles up the road towards Ombos, sir. The men of the escort were all dead, save one, but they hadn't been mutilated. Just the senior officers. The survivor's been taken to the surgeon. He's in a bad way. Hamstrings cut and been with almost no water for three days.'

'Did he say who carried out the attack?' asked Macro.

The decurion shook his head. 'He was babbling like a baby, sir. Hardly a coherent word. But it is likely that the attackers were Arabs. They raid from the desert from time to time. Make the most of it while we gather together a column to drive them off. That said, it's unlike them to choose a target like the legate and his escort. Not much in the way of rich pickings after a hard fight.'

'I take it that you didn't find any bodies besides those of our men?'

'No, sir. But then the Arabs never leave their dead behind if they can help it. Makes the natives nervous if they think the Arabs are like some kind of evil spirits who can strike and disappear at will.'

'Then could it be the Nubians?' asked Cato.

'It's possible, sir. But the last report I heard was that they were still camped close to the cataract. But they could have stolen a march on us, or sent a raiding column forward to gather intelligence and harass our outposts. I still think the Arabs are the most likely culprits.' He paused a moment. 'They might have taken the heads and the ring hand to the Nubians to prove their deed and gain some reward. Or it's possible that Prince Talmis has recruited Arab mercenaries to serve in his army.'

'The Arabs then,' Aurelius intervened. 'Once the Nubians are dealt with we shall send a punitive expedition to deal with them. Harshly.' He gestured to the decurion. 'Cover them up. Take them to the legate's quarters. Have their personal effects removed for return to their families and then tell the surgeon's staff to prepare the bodies for cremation.'

'Yes, sir.' The decurion pulled the goatskin back over

the corpses and climbed up on to the driver's bench. With a click of his tongue and a flick of the reins, he urged the mule team into a walk and the wagon rumbled out of the gate of the priests' quarters.

Aurelius watched the cart leave. The fingers of his left hand twitched momentarily before he turned to Cato and Macro with an anxious expression. 'That explains the legate's disappearance.'

It was an asinine thing to say and he winced at himself immediately. Cato could readily understand the shock that the death of the legate might cause his close subordinate.

'Did you know the legate well?'

Aurelius nodded. 'We have served together for the last eight years.'

'So long?' Macro looked surprised. 'Sorry, sir, it's just that I've never known a legate serve so long with one legion.'

'Yes, well, it's different here in Egypt,' the camp prefect responded tersely. 'Candidus was appointed by Emperor Tiberius at the end of his reign. The commanders of the Egyptian legions and the governor are appointed from the equestrian class. The senators are not permitted to hold high office here. For that matter, they're not even allowed to enter the province without the express permission of the Emperor. So the appointments tend to last much longer in Egypt.'

'What about you, sir? You can't have been camp prefect all that time.'

'No indeed. I've held the rank for the last three years. First spear centurion before that.'

Macro glanced at Cato, unable to conceal his shock.

The senior centurion of the legion was traditionally its toughest, bravest and most experienced officer. The thin, dapper figure of Aurelius was adorned with a finely spun tunic and his cuirass was inlaid with swirls of gold and silver. But, unlike Macro and Cato, he did not have a leather harness to carry the medallions they had been awarded for displays of courage and battles won. In every other legion Macro had served in, the camp prefect and the first spear were seasoned fighters with swathes of awards on their chests. '*You* were a first spear, sir?'

'I was.' Aurelius frowned. 'I have served my time, you know.'

Macro was about to say something when Cato coughed loudly, warning his friend off. Before Macro could intervene any further, Cato spoke. 'What are your intentions now, sir?'

'My intentions?'

'Yes, sir. You are the next in the chain of command. Now that Candidus is dead, you are the commander of the forces gathered at Diospolis Magna.'

'Of course I am,' Aurelius replied shortly. 'I know that.'

He stood still for a moment, looking down at his boots, and then nodded to himself. 'I'll summon my senior officers. They have to be informed about Candidus's death. And then we shall set about dealing with the Nubians.' He looked up, straightened his back and cleared his throat. 'We shall meet here at headquarters at noon, gentlemen.' With that he turned and marched back into the entrance of the priest's quarters.

Cato watched him go and then spoke softly. 'What do you make of our new legate?'

Macro dabbed at the sweat on his brow. 'Have to say that I'm not encouraged. It seems that the man's been a professional stylus-pusher throughout his career. I've never seen the like of the Twenty-Second. Must be the cushiest posting in the entire army. Swanning around the Nile while their officers have nothing better to do than wait until it's their turn to take the job of first spear centurion or camp prefect. Gods!' He shook his head in frustration. 'I just hope the other senior officers aren't the same. Or their men. I tell you, Cato, I don't fancy going into battle against the Nubians with a bunch of time-serving bureaucrats at my side.'

Cato nodded as he stared into the mid-distance and Macro sighed wearily. 'All right then, what's on your mind?'

'Sorry?' Cato stirred and looked at his friend vaguely.

'I know that look on your face. The body's there but the mind is off with the muses. So, what are you thinking?'

'We should go and see the survivor of the ambush.'

'Why?'

'There's something not quite right about it.' Cato chewed his lip. 'The decurion seemed to know his business and I could see he wasn't convinced that either the Arabs or the Nubians were responsible for killing the legate. Come on, Macro.'

The hospital had been set up in a large airy pavilion to the rear of the temple complex. The legion's surgeon was doing the rounds of the men on the army's sick list when Cato and Macro located him. Like most of those who served in the same capacity in legions across the Empire, the surgeon was an easterner. His dark face was rimmed with silvery hair, cropped short over his scalp and along his jawline. The creases in his skin told of the long years he had served in the profession. He regarded the two Roman officers coolly as he heard Cato's request to see the wounded man who had been brought into the hospital shortly before.

'He's resting. The man is exhausted and cannot be questioned.'

'It won't take long. I just need to find out one thing. Then he can rest.'

'No,' the surgeon replied firmly. 'I will send word to you when he is in a fit state to talk.' He paused to look at them. 'I do not know your faces. You must be new appointments to the Jackals.'

Cato nodded. 'Senior Tribune Cato and First Spear Centurion Macro.'

'Senior tribune?' The surgeon looked surprised, then bowed his head. 'My apologies, sir. I took you for a more junior officer.'

Macro stifled a smile.

Cato ignored him as he confronted the surgeon. 'And you are?'

'Chief Surgeon Archaelus, sir.'

'Look here, Archaelus, I must speak with your patient. Urgently.'

'I appreciate that, sir, but it is my professional view that it would be detrimental to his recovery, his survival even, if he is put under any further distress.'

Cato had exhausted his cordiality, and hardened his tone. 'I have no time for this. I order you to let me see the patient. At once.'

As chief surgeon, Archaelus carried the notional rank of centurion and was outranked by the legion's senior tribune. An order had been given and there was little he could do but obey. He bowed his head reluctantly. 'If you'd follow me, sir.'

He turned and led them through the pavilion's colonnade and into the more sheltered part of the structure where the priests had held their banquets in the years when Karnak was at the height of its influence. Unlike much of the rest of the temple complex, the walls were covered with painted symbols. Overhead the ceiling was dark blue and covered with five-pointed representations of stars in yellow. Linen screens had been erected around the most severe cases in the hospital, and they kept out the worst of the hot wind and dust.

'Here is your man.' Archaelus indicated a man laying naked, except for his loincloth, on a low cot in the middle of the pavilion's banquet hall. One of the orderlies sat beside the patient, gently daubing an ointment on to the sunburned flesh. Cato could see the blisters on the legionary's face. He had lighter skin than most of the other men and Cato guessed that he must be Alexandrian. As well as the burns on his face and limbs, the man's thighs were bandaged and there was a dressing on the side of his chest. Beneath the blisters and ointment on his face, it was clear that the soldier was strikingly handsome with fine bones beneath his skin.

'What's his name?' asked Cato.

'Optio Carausius.'

Cato looked round, saw a stool, and drew it across to the side of the cot. He sat down and leaned closer to the optio. The man's breathing was light and ragged and his brow was creased. Perspiration pricked out in the hairline and his dark hair was plastered to his scalp in thick dark ringlets.

'He has a fever,' Cato observed.

'Yes, sir. His wounds were not cleaned until he reached the hospital. I fear they are poisoned. However, he may recover.'

'Is that likely?' asked Macro.

The surgeon shrugged. 'We have done what we can. His life is in the hands of the gods now. I have made a brief offering to Serapis on his behalf. If it is accepted then he may recover. But even if he does, he will be a cripple for the rest of his life.' Archaelus indicated the bandaged thighs. 'The attackers severed his hamstrings so that he could not leave the site of the ambush. It would seem that they intended him to survive and remain to be found.'

Cato glanced at Macro. 'Something we've encountered before.'

Macro frowned. Then his expression altered and he stared at Cato. 'Are you saying it's him, Ajax? He did this?'

'It could be. We pursued him upriver as far as Memphis before the trail went cold. He could have continued along the Nile as far as here. And he's certainly bold enough to attack the legate and his party, and good enough to come off best. He's even left someone to tell the tale.'

'Only this time, he won't be able to pin it on us,' Macro sneered. 'But why take the heads? He's a mad, cruel bastard, I know, but he's not done that before.'

'Perhaps the decurion was on the right track with

regard to the Arabs. It's possible that Ajax took the heads as proof of the dead, to offer them to the Nubians.'

Cato turned back to the optio and leaned closer to him. He spoke softly. 'Carausius . . . Can you hear me?'

The soldier did not stir, so Cato gently laid a hand on his shoulder and spoke again. 'Carausius . . . You must tell me who attacked you.'

With a faint groan the man turned his head away from Cato and mumbled.

'What's that?' Macro moved round to the other side of the cot and leaned over. 'What did you say? Speak again.'

Archaelus intervened. 'Centurion, go easy on him.'

Cato ignored the surgeon and shook the optio's shoulder gently. 'Tell us. Who attacked you?'

The optio's eyes flickered open, clenched shut and then opened again, darting around as he tried to speak through cracked lips.

'We didn't have a . . . chance,' he whispered. 'They . . . fought like . . . demons. Came at us out of the dusk.' His voice fell away into an incoherent mumble.

Cato waited briefly and then tried again. 'Who?'

The legionary slowly rolled his head towards Cato and licked his lips. 'No name. Just said he was a gladiator.' He paused, wincing at a sudden wave of pain. Then, as it passed, his eyes focused again. 'A gladiator . . .'

'What else?' asked Cato. 'Come on, tell us.'

'Told me to be sure that . . . Cato and Macro knew it was . . . him.'

'Thank you, Carausius. Rest now.' Cato leaned back and looked across at Macro. 'Now we know.'

Macro nodded. 'And he sends us a direct challenge.

Whatever we may think of Ajax, you have to admit that he has balls of steel.'

Archaelus cleared his throat. 'It seems you have what you need. Would you mind continuing your discussion elsewhere now?'

Cato stood up and beckoned to Macro and the two left the banqueting hall and stepped out of the pavilion into the bright glare of the sun. The harsh light forced them to squint until their eyes began to adjust.

'On the upside, at least we know Ajax is nearby,' said Macro.

'True, but not very comforting. And if he does join the Nubians then I fear our situation has taken a turn for the worse.'

The prefects of the four auxiliary cohorts, together with the centurions of the Twenty-Second Legion and the remaining tribunes, sat on benches at one end of the colonnaded pool at the army's headquarters. Word of Candidus's death had got round the camp and the men were conversing in low, anxious tones. Cato and Macro sat slightly apart, and the latter regarded the other officers with a critical eye.

'Too many old men and too many who look unfit.'

Cato said nothing, but he knew that his friend was right. The long years of untroubled garrison duty had made the men of the Twenty-Second soft. A large number of the officers were running to fat – there were clear gaps between the front and back plates of their cuirasses, which could not accommodate their heavy torsos. Their fleshy jowls and veined noses betrayed their fondness for drink.

There were others who looked more like the centurions Cato was familiar with from the other legions he had served with since he had joined the army. Powerfully built men who shared the steady, unflappable demeanour of the centurionate. They at least looked as if they would serve well enough when the campaign got under way. However, Macro was right that rather too many of them looked as if they were nearing the end of their careers. It was sad to see how a legion's combat readiness could be so badly eroded by the benefits of a prolonged peace.

There was a loud stamp of boots as the sentries at the entrance to the colonnade stood to attention and an optio barked out. 'Commanding officer present!'

The officers rose and stood stiffly as Aurelius strode down the length of the pool, his reflection wavering in its surface as a light gust of hot air wafted over the water. He took up his position behind a campaign table and stared round at his officers in a theatrical manner, as if seeing them for the first time.

'Be seated, gentlemen.'

The officers eased themselves back down and sat quietly, waiting for his address to begin. Aurelius carried a slate tablet in his hand and he laid it down on the table before him and glanced at the notes he had made in the wax surface. Macro watched with a twinge of unease. He preferred commanders who addressed their men without notes, as if their words came from their hearts. Aurelius had revealed himself as one of those officers who lacked belief in their own authority and needed prompts to carry them through such occasions. It was not a good sign, Macro decided.

Aurelius looked up and cleared his throat. 'As all of you no doubt have heard, the legate is dead. He and his escort were wiped out a few days ago as they were on the road to Ombos. Whether this was at the hands of Arab brigands or a Nubian patrol we do not yet know.' He paused and swallowed. 'As camp prefect of the Twenty-Second Legion, and therefore the senior officer present, command of the army falls to me. It is my duty to lead our forces against the Nubians and complete the task started by Legate Candidus, namely to drive the enemy out of our province as swiftly and decisively as possible.'

Cato noticed that while some of the officers nodded approvingly at their new commander's intentions, most did not. Some looked apprehensive and a few muttered quietly with their neighbours.

'To that end,' Aurelius continued, 'I will be finalising our campaign plans with my staff officers after this meeting. Orders will be sent to my senior officers at first light tomorrow. And speaking of officers, I am pleased to introduce the two latest to join the legion. Firstly, my new senior tribune.' He gestured to Cato to rise. 'Cato is newly arrived from Alexandria where the governor has appointed him to the Twenty-Second Legion for the duration of hostilities. Despite his young years, the governor assures me that the new tribune has a fine military record. As does my new first spear centurion. Stand up, Macro.'

'I'm not a bloody performing monkey,' Macro growled as he stood up and stared round at the other officers, straight-lipped.

'You may sit,' Aurelius said graciously. Once Macro and Cato were back in place, the new commander looked over his officers once again and then nodded. 'We have been set a great challenge, gentlemen. It has been a long time since the legion and the auxiliary cohorts of the province have been called upon to prove their mettle. There are some who doubtless say that we have grown soft, that the soldiers of this province compare poorly with those of the rest of the Empire.' He paused to consult his waxed tablet briefly. 'To them I say you are wrong. Our day has come and we will show the rest of the Empire what the soldiers of the province of Egypt can do. I have heard that the enemy outnumber us. So much the better. We shall win even greater glory.' He had a quick glance at the wax tablet again and smiled. 'The eyes of the Emperor are upon us, my friends. The Roman Empire looks to us with bated breath. When we have won our great victory, the Empire will never forget us and every man here will walk in honour until his dying day!'

Aurelius thrust his fist in the air. A handful of officers followed suit, then a few more, anxious to win the favour of their new commander. Some of the more experienced and professional officers merely nodded or applauded politely. Others, Cato noted, sat in stony silence. Once Aurelius realised that he had won all the acclaim that he was going to get, he raised his hands and gestured for quiet. 'That's all for now, gentlemen. You are dismissed.'

There was a low hubbub of conversation as the men rose and edged away around the pool and filtered out through the columns at the far end. Macro turned to Cato. 'Quite the orator, our camp prefect,' he said wryly. 'There wasn't a dry eye in the house, though for my part it was due to embarrassment. What a pillock.'

234

'I think he meant it. Every word of it.'

'You're not serious?'

'Oh yes. He knows he is never going to make his mark as a competent staff officer. This is his one chance to win some fame. This has potential to become a dangerous situation, Macro.'

'Really? I thought the fact that we are outnumbered, the soldiers are of questionable quality and now it's possible that Ajax has thrown in his lot with the Nubians meant that things were already dangerous.'

Cato frowned at him. 'All right then, it could be even more dangerous. Happy now? Come on, we have to speak to Aurelius.'

'What about?'

'We have to persuade him to rein in his thirst for glory.' Cato made his way round the end of the pool towards the table where Aurelius was talking to a handful of other officers, some of whom Cato had seen at headquarters since he and Macro had arrived. Aurelius turned towards them as they approached and smiled warmly.

'What did you think of my small oration?'

'Inspiring,' Cato responded warily.

'I know. I have been waiting for the chance to make such a speech,' Aurelius continued in a pleased tone. 'I confess that I was much influenced by a book I read in the Great Library some months back. Battle addresses of history's great commanders. A minor work by Livius, but beautifully written. Just the stuff to stir a man's blood, eh?' He tapped Cato on the chest.

'I haven't had the chance to read it, sir,' Cato replied evenly. 'Perhaps I will once the campaign is over. Speaking of which, I would welcome the opportunity to discuss your plans for the campaign. I assume you will be following normal practice and therefore include both myself and the first spear centurion in drawing up the army's orders, sir.'

A brief look of irritation clouded Aurelius's expression. 'There is no need, Tribune Cato. The plans were drawn up by the legate and his closest advisers. Now they are dead. Only I remain from the ranks of those he trusted with his scheme for defeating the Nubians.' Aurelius paused briefly. 'Of course, I may see fit to amend some details, but I have my own advisers.' He indicated the four men standing to his other side. 'So I will not need to trouble you for any advice.'

'It's no trouble, sir. We would be glad to offer you the benefit of our considerable experience.'

'Your considerable experience?' Aurelius smiled faintly. 'Tribune, these men and I were, in all likelihood, serving the Emperor when you were but an infant suckling at your mother's tit. We can manage with the experience we already have between us. But I thank you for your offer all the same.' His eyes brightened as another thought struck him. 'However, I have every wish to put your abilities, and those of good Centurion Macro, to use. I would be obliged if you would take charge of the training regime of the legion. The men are already fine soldiers, but a little exercise and some sword practice will hone their spirits to the appropriate edge, I should think. Macro here has the stern look of a drill instructor, and the voice of one too, I should imagine. Let your experience be of use to the Twenty-Second Legion in that manner, eh?

Leave the operational planning to those who have served in Egypt and know the ground well.'

'It ain't as simple as that, sir,' Macro responded. 'We have good reason to believe that the Nubians have been joined by the fugitive slave that Prefect – Tribune Cato and I had been hunting before we were reassigned to the legion.'

'Oh? And how did you come by this snippet of intelligence?'

'We questioned the survivor of the ambush, sir. He told us that a gladiator led the attack and left a survivor to tell the tale.'

'Nonsense,' Aurelius said firmly. 'The man is delirious. You heard the decurion say so earlier this morning.'

'He seemed lucid enough when we spoke to him, sir,' said Cato. 'If Ajax serves with the Nubians then I think it is vital that we, who have faced Ajax before, and know his methods, should be involved in any plans that are made for the coming campaign.'

Aurelius shook his head. 'I think the fact that you have failed to track down and capture this man is eloquent testimony of your failure to comprehend his methods, Tribune. Perhaps it is time a fresh mind was set to the task. Meanwhile I would like you, and Centurion Macro, to take care of the training. I want a full report on your training scheme, and an accurate projection of the number of men who will be fit to serve once the campaign begins. I would like that report on my desk as soon as possible.' He offered them a brief smile. 'I think you will soon see that we have the measure of our enemy, without the help of any advice you might care to offer. That is all, gentlemen.'

'Yes, sir.' Cato saluted, and after a brief hesitation Macro followed suit. They turned about and strode swiftly away from Aurelius and his staff.

'Why the hell didn't you say something, sir?' asked Macro in an undertone.

'I did, in case you missed it.'

'How dare he dismiss us in such a fashion!' Macro fumed. 'You in particular. No commander of a legion ever ignores the advice of his senior tribune and his first spear centurion. Not if he's any good.'

'It is only common practice, Macro. He is under no obligation to consult us.'

Macro was silent, then he glanced at Cato. 'Fuck, you were right, sir.'

'I was? What about?'

'The situation just got more dangerous.'

CHAPTER TWENTY

Five days later Cato and Macro were standing to one side of the makeshift parade ground outside the temple complex. It was late in the afternoon and the regular breeze that swept in from the desert was swirling the dust kicked up by the First Cohort of the legion as it tramped round the circuit, laden with full kit and marching yokes. A number of men had already collapsed from exhaustion and had been hauled aside to recover in the shade of Karnak's outer wall. The stragglers were being driven on by the centurions and optios Macro had selected to act as his drill instructors. Some of them had served in other legions and still clung to the hard-won values that had been instilled before they were posted to Egypt. They shouted abuse and threats at the legionaries, and used their sticks freely to spur the men on.

Macro regarded the scene fondly. 'Like old times. Nothing I like better than getting the men ready for battle.'

'Nothing?' asked Cato with an amused expression.

'All right, there's wine and there's women too. I'm not that picky. Find me a boozy, belligerent Amazon and I'll die a happy man.'

Cato laughed and then turned his attention back to the

exhausted men as they paced past the two officers. 'What is the condition of the First Cohort?'

Macro rubbed his chin. 'Most of the men are sound enough. They struggled on the first two days, but they've rediscovered their marching boots. They're ready for the campaign. Battle drill is another matter.'

'Oh?'

'The sword skills are there. They've had regular weapons practice at least. The trouble is that some of the formations are shaky. When I tried each century on forming a testudo there were gaps wide enough to drive a battering ram through. Looked more like an upended colander than a bloody tortoise. They're getting better though, now that I've turned my best officers on them.'

'What about the others?' asked Cato. 'Are some of the officers still claiming to be excused duties?'

Macro nodded sourly. 'When I told 'em to join the men this morning, they refused. I gave them the order, and at once that fat git, Aescher, went straight to Aurelius and asked that he and the others be excused.' Macro discreetly pointed out the officers sitting in the shade of a small shrine at the far end of the parade ground. 'They came straight back with their permission in writing.'

A slave stood to one side cooling them with a large fan made from woven palm leaves while some women from the camp followers sat on their laps and laughed playfully as the officers fondled them. Macro sniffed. 'Smug bastards.'

'Quite,' Cato agreed. 'It does the men no good to see their officers sitting it out. And that includes us. I think we need to set an example, Macro.'

'What did you have in mind, sir?'

'Have all the officers issued marching kit tomorrow morning, whether they are excused from drilling or not. You and me included. And also, find Hamedes and have him join us.'

'Hamedes?' Macro smiled. 'I haven't seen him for days. Bloody little drill dodger.'

'He asked me for permission to visit the local temples. He says he knows some of the priests here and is looking for a position once the campaign is over.'

'And he's doing this while on the payroll as a scout, I take it.'

'Naturally.'

'Then he'll have to earn his pay. I'll march him on to the parade ground myself tomorrow morning.' Macro rubbed his hands at the prospect. 'What kind of drill did you have in mind?'

'A route march down the Nile for the First Cohort. We'll have the legion's senior officers, and Hamedes, at the head of the column where the men can see us, and be sure to let the drill instructors know that the officers are not to be given any slack.'

Macro stared at him with an amused expression. 'What do you hope to achieve?'

'Think of it as an experiment in winnowing. Let's see if we can separate the chaff from the men.' Cato folded his arms and turned his attention back to the men of the cohort again. 'What about the other cohorts?'

'A similar picture. The cohorts led by good officers will be ready as soon as they've had a few more days of hard drilling. The problem units are the Seventh and Ninth

Cohorts. They're commanded by cronies of Aurelius.'

'Then add them to tomorrow's route march. The other cohorts can be exercised over the following days.'

'Yes, sir.' Macro grinned briefly. 'What about the auxiliary units?'

While Macro had been put in charge of drilling the legion, Aurelius had ordered him to leave the drilling of the auxiliary cohorts to their prefects. Cato still had oversight of the process. He took a weary breath.

'Both of the infantry cohorts are in fair shape. Their prefects are looking for a chance to prove themselves and win advancement. So they've kept their men on their toes. The Syrian mounted cohort is first class. They know how to look after their horses and they manoeuvre well. The Alexandrian mounted cohort is a different matter. They have something of a superior attitude and their prefect seems to think they are the direct descendants of Alexander's Companion Cavalry. They drink hard and the discipline is a little sloppy. No question of their elan though. I just hope that they last the distance when the army marches. Then they'll have a chance to live up to their self-regard.'

'Or they'll discover that they're a bunch of gutless worms and bolt from the battlefield.'

Cato shrugged uncomfortably. Both men were silent for a moment before Macro continued. 'Any luck with the new legate on the planning front?'

'No. He still refuses to consult me. I've asked him when he intends to lead the army out of Diospolis Magna and he just says we will take the field when the situation is propitious.'

'Propitious?' Macro mused.

'He refused to clarify when I asked him. The thing is, he had better give the order soon, or the enemy will have free run of all the province between here and the cataract. They've already advanced on Ombos. The last report from the garrison there was that the Nubians were about to place them under siege. Even then, Aurelius refused to move.'

'Sounds like our glory-hunting commander is developing cold feet.'

'Perhaps.' Cato did not feel comfortable criticising his commander. In truth he had begun to discover the vulnerability of his position over the last few days. His promotion had elevated him to a position where he should share some responsibility in determining the course of a campaign. Before the suppression of the revolt on Crete, he and Macro had been junior enough simply to be told where to go and who to fight. The strategy was largely determined by other men of higher rank, and officers like Macro and Cato were left to execute their orders. Now, Cato had both rank and experience of command, yet he was still regarded as too fresh-faced or, worse, regarded as too ambitious. How else could someone of his years have advanced to his rank without being ruthless in his ambition? It was a question that those who perceived him as a rival would ask in order to justify their lack of cooperation. It was a double-edged burden, Cato decided, especially as he had never actively pursued elevation to his present rank. It had been conferred on him by those who had valued his achievements in the past. The envy of men like Aurelius would prevent him from providing the best service he could to Rome, and at the same time they would willingly do him down to maintain their own prestige.

With the death of Candidus, Aurelius was the most powerful man along the Nile south of Memphis. If Aurelius was against him then the only course through which he might pursue a complaint was through Governor Petronius in Alexandria. Cato had no patrons in the province. His nearest friend with any influence was Senator Sempronius in Crete – assuming Sempronius had not already relinquished his temporary control of the island and was on his way back to Rome. Cato was on his own, he realised. If he was to have any influence over the direction of the campaign, then he must find a way of working round Aurelius's prejudices towards him. Maybe this was the real test of those promoted to high rank. No longer was he being judged purely on the basis of his talent as an instrument of war. The time had come when political skills were every bit as vital.

'Ah, my chief training officer!' Aurelius greeted Cato as the latter approached his desk at the end of the pool. Torches flickered in brackets attached to the columns and lit up the space with a golden hue. Outside, the sun had just set and the red sky reflected on the surface of the water. Cato hoped that it was not an ill omen for the campaign as he stood erect in front of the legate's desk.

'What can I do for you, Tribune?' Aurelius leaned back in his chair.

'It concerns a training matter, sir. If you recall, you said that I would have complete authority in matters relating to preparing the men for the coming campaign.'

244

'Yes, I did,' Aurelius replied warily. 'Subject to my ultimate approval, naturally.'

'Of course, sir.'

'Well? How are things proceeding?'

'The soldiers are steadily improving and given time they will be in good shape once the campaign begins. It would help to know when you intend the army to march, sir.'

'Of course.' Aurelius nodded, and gestured towards the sheets of papyrus on his desk. 'As you can see, the need to prepare the men is not the only consideration affecting my decision. There are conflicting reports on the location of the enemy. Rumours are rife. Some say that Prince Talmis is no more than fifty miles away. Others say that he is still camped outside Ombos, besieging the garrison there. The overall picture is very uncertain, Tribune.'

Cato was not surprised. Since the ambush of the previous legate's column, Aurelius had restricted the range of his patrols to within half a day's march of the army's base at Diospolis Magna. Any intelligence of the enemy's movements beyond that margin depended upon questioning travellers or those fleeing the Nubians, and the truth had to be filtered out from rumours and wild speculation.

'It appears that the enemy have rather greater numbers than I thought,' Aurelius continued. 'So I have sent a request to the governor for reinforcements before we proceed.'

'Reinforcements?' Cato raised his eyebrows. 'Sir, when I last spoke with the governor he was adamant that every man that could be spared had been sent here.'

'There is always a way to find more men,' Aurelius

responded dismissively. 'In any case, I do not ask for a vast host with which to overwhelm my enemy, merely enough to ensure the job is done well. Until then, it would be imprudent to proceed, even though I am straining at the leash to get to grips with those Nubians.'

Cato briefly wondered if he had ever met so supine a hunting dog. He thrust the thought aside and cleared his throat. 'Sir, it is possible that the enemy are also using this time to call on reinforcements. In any case, the longer they remain on Roman soil the greater the damage they do to the province. The natives are bound to feel resentment that they have been left to the mercy of the invader.'

'All part of the exigencies of war, alas.'

Cato could see that this line of argument would not be productive, and so switched his tactics. He nodded thoughtfully before he continued. 'Something occurs to me, sir.'

'Oh?'

'While I understand your prudence in delaying the opening of the campaign, other men far removed from this theatre of war will wonder at the delay.'

'Only because they lack full understanding of the circumstances,' Aurelius countered.

'Yes, sir. But that will not stop them muttering. My chief fear is that Governor Petronius will anticipate the musings of such men and be concerned lest he be thought to have sanctioned your inaction, as he might see it. When your request for reinforcements arrives, I fear that it may spur the governor's anxiety that the campaign is not being fought to a swift conclusion. Anxiety was ever the enemy of sound judgement, sir. What if the governor felt impelled to replace you with a commander less inclined to prudence? Some hothead who would lead the army in a wild dash straight at the enemy, with little thought.'

Aurelius stared directly at Cato. 'That could lead to disaster. I see what you mean. And there's no shortage of ambitious men in Alexandria who will regard me with envy now that the fates have elevated me to command of the army.' He nodded. 'Men like that thug Decius Fulvius. He's always looked down on me. The thought of that fool being placed in charge of the campaign is frightening.'

'Yes, sir. It is your duty to make sure that the governor has no excuse to send such a man to take command of the army.' Cato did not mention that it was more than likely that Fulvius was still attached to the force in Crete.

'Yes . . . Yes, it is my duty,' Aurelius nodded. 'Damn, I should never have sent that request. It's too late now.' He closed his eyes and made a quick calculation. 'It will take at least another two days for the message to arrive. Perhaps a day for the governor to react and then five days to send a reply.' He blinked. 'I must move fast. The army must be on the march before any reply can reach Diospolis Magna. Within the next seven days. I must consult my staff.' Aurelius paused, and then looked again at Cato. 'I must apologise. You were here to discuss a training matter, I believe.'

'Yes, sir. It concerns the officers of some of the cohorts. They have been avoiding the unit exercises and drills.'

'That's right. They have other duties to attend to. I gave them permission.'

'So they said. However, once the campaign begins,

every legionary and every officer must be able to keep up with the column. We cannot afford to have any men slowing us down, sir. Officers included. As you just pointed out, the legion must march soon, and strike decisively. You cannot permit those officers who are infirm or unfit to hold you back.'

'You're right,' Aurelius agreed quietly. 'They must be made ready for the campaign. They must join their men in the training. I will not allow them to be excused from now on. Is that clear, Tribune? All officers will take part.'

Cato nodded.

'Was there anything else?'

'No, sir. That's all.'

Aurelius regarded him for a moment before he continued. 'Thank you, Tribune Cato. You are a most useful sounding board. It seems there's something more to you than meets the eye.'

It was clear that he had concluded their interview and Cato bowed his head and turned to leave the legate's presence. Only once he had passed through the entrance and entered the colonnade where some of the clerks still laboured at their desks did he permit himself a small smile of satisfaction.

CHAPTER TWENTY-ONE

The pale light of dawn bled out across the hazy sky as the dim figures of the legionaries and their officers made their way out of the temple complex and fell in. A small column of carts stood at the rear to pick up those who failed to complete the march. Macro and Cato had drawn full legionary kit from the legion's stores and retained only their crested helmets to signify their rank. It had been a while since either man had last taken part in a formal route march. Cato recalled the tips given to him when he had been a fresh recruit and placed pads of wool beneath his feet inside his boots. He also folded his cloak across his shoulder to provide a rest for the shaft of the marching yoke. His shield, mess tins and kitbag hung from the fork at the end of the yoke and a javelin rested on the other shoulder. A full canteen and a waterskin completed his load and he shuffled slightly to adjust it to a more comfortable position as he stood beside Macro at the head of the column.

A number of the officers were already in place. The more rotund or elderly men regarded Macro sourly, while their more professional comrades tried not to reveal their amusement over their discomfort.

'Happy-looking bunch, aren't they?' Macro grinned.

'Let's see how they look after the first five miles.'

'Forget them,' Cato muttered. 'Worry about me. If I don't get through it then the whole point of the exercise is lost.'

'You'll do. Tough as old boots, that's what you are, thanks to everything I've taught you.'

'I'd hate to disappoint you.'

'And I'd hate to have to use my vine cane on your back if you begin to falter.' Macro looked down at the short, knotted staff he carried instead of a javelin, the same as the rest of the drill instructors who would be marching with the column. 'Those were your orders, sir. No special treatment for officers.'

Cato nodded. 'Though you might consider taking the sting out of the blow if you can, in my case.'

'Ah, if I did it for you then I'd feel obliged to do it for some of those fat fucks standing over there as well.' Macro gestured to the officers taking up their positions. 'And speaking of slackers, where's Hamedes got to?'

Cato turned and looked towards the temple. 'There he is.'

The priest walked quickly towards them and stopped close by with a nervous grin. 'Do you Romans always march loaded down like mules, sir?'

'You'll be silent, unless spoken to,' Macro replied harshly. 'You're in the army now, lad. Until this is over you can forget being a priest.'

Hamedes had also been issued with full kit and Macro looked him over to ensure that everything was in place and correctly fastened. 'Not bad,' he mused. 'The armour fits well. Did you get some help putting it on?'

Hamedes hesitated before he nodded. 'One of the supply clerks showed me, sir.'

'Very well. Fall in with the officers, where I can keep an eye on you.'

'Yes, sir.' Hamedes smiled, then thought better of it, and turned and strode off, taking up position a respectful distance behind the rest of the officers.

Cato nodded at him. 'For a priest he has a pleasing disposition towards soldiering.'

'That he does,' Macro agreed. 'And he'll be tested to the full in the days to come.'

The last of the legionaries came trotting across to join their centuries and when they were in place Macro hefted his yoke on to his shoulder and strode down the column. He breathed in deeply and began to address the column.

'Today's jaunt will take us eight miles down the Nile and back. Nothing that should present a challenge to real soldiers. I am delighted to see my brother officers joining us today.'

A few men laughed in the ranks and there was a brief catcall before one of the optios standing beside the column turned to try and spot the perpetrator. Failing, he roared out, 'Keep your fucking mouths shut, or I'll 'ave you on a charge.'

Macro waited until there was complete silence again. 'Officers and men of the legions are all expected to complete route marches. It is a minimum standard and applies to all, regardless of rank. There is no excuse for any man here failing to finish the march.' He paused and then strode back to the front of the column, a short distance ahead of Cato and the other officers. 'Column! Prepare to march . . . March!'

Macro paced forward, followed by the rest, four ranks abreast. He led them across the training ground and down the rough track that joined the Nile road. Even this early in the morning the farmers and merchants who were making their way into Diospolis Magna to sell their wares were on the road and they hurriedly pulled aside as the legionaries turned right and began to head north, along the road that followed the course of the Nile.

A few boats were already out, the skiffs of fishermen rowing across the current to inspect their nets, and the larger broad-beamed vessels that carried goods up and down the great river. On the far bank was a thin strip of green vegetation and then the rocky mass of the lifeless mountains rising above the desert.

An hour after the column had set off, the sun had risen over the horizon and the pale yellow disc hung in the haze like an eye surveying the ribbon of water and crops that threaded its way across the great desert of northern Africa. Cato had settled into an easy rhythm; and an early ache that had started at the bottom of his back had faded away and he was starting to feel confident about completing the march. Sweat pricked out from his scalp, saturating his felt helmet liner, and every so often a trickle escaped, coursing down his brow, and he blinked it away rather than transferring the javelin to his shield hand so that he could mop his brow.

Glancing round he saw that some of the officers were already struggling to keep up with the pace. The nearest, a centurion from the First Cohort, was puffing out his full cheeks as he laboured under his kit. One of Macro's training optios fell into step beside him.

'Come on, sir. Put some bloody effort in! I've seen old men march better than that.'

The centurion clamped his lips together and struggled on. Cato turned back, feeling slightly guilty over his plan to break men like that centurion. However, if the man made it through the day then there was obviously more to him than met the eye – though given his girth, Cato thought wryly, that would be something of a challenge. Up ahead, Macro led the way, striding steadily down the road without the slightest sign of tiring.

The heat from the rising sun began to burn the haze and light mist away from the banks of the Nile and the marching men were exposed to its direct rays. The temperature began to rise swiftly and added to the discomfort of the dust kicked up by the passage of thousands of iron-nailed army boots. Every so often the road passed through small villages and little gangs of children would work their way along the column, begging for money in their chirping voices, hurriedly moving on from those soldiers who spat curses or swung a boot at them. Cato just ignored them, concentrating on placing one boot in front of the other as he followed in Macro's tracks. As the sun rose higher, the heat became intense, searing the landscape in its harsh glare. Cato felt the sweat on his back soak through his tunic and plaster it to his skin. Occasionally a cold trickle dribbled down from his armpits and traced its way over his ribs until it caught in a fold of his tunic. His mouth was dry and it was hard to resist the impulse to call ahead to Macro and suggest that he permit the men a short rest to take some water.

After the second hour there was a groan and a clatter and Cato looked back to see that one of the officers had collapsed on the road. A companion stopped and leaned down to help his friend, before an optio pounced, cracking his staff down on the officer's shield.

'What the fuck are you doing? Don't stop, sir! Keep moving!'

'You can't leave him there,' the centurion protested.

'Move!' the optio bellowed into his face, and raised his staff.

The centurion hurriedly straightened up and moved on. The optio remained by the fallen officer and gestured for the legionaries to march round the fallen man. 'Keep moving! Don't stop and gawp! What, you've never seen an officer fall on his face before? Move!'

The column rippled round the prone man and continued its advance without breaking its step. Macro had slowed so that he was just ahead of Cato and muttered with satisfaction. 'There goes the first one. Won't be long before we lose others. Wonder how many more will fall out.'

Cato licked his lips. 'Just as long as I don't.'

'Don't worry. Like I said, I won't let you.'

'Thanks, friend.'

'No need to get sarky, sir. This was your idea, remember?'

'Next time I have a good idea, tell me to mind my own business, eh?'

Macro smiled, but growled, 'Shut up and save your breath.'

Late in the morning, the column passed through a long

grove of tall date palms and Macro called a halt and ordered the men to down packs. Cato stepped to the side of the road and let the yoke drop into the grass. He leaned forward, hands resting on his knees, and panted for breath. Macro, sweating and breathing heavily but otherwise himself, shook his head pityingly. 'You're going soft. That's what promotion does to a man.'

'Bollocks.' Cato reached for his canteen, pulled out the stopper and raised it to his lips.

'Two mouthfuls.' Macro pointed a finger at him as he strode past to have a word with his instructors. 'Not a drop more.'

Cato nodded, and drank what he was allowed, letting the second mouthful swill round his parched mouth before he swallowed. He looked back along the column. Scores of men lay stretched on their backs, gasping. Amongst the officers he noticed a few absences, the faces of men he had hoped would fail to complete the march. The rest looked grim and determined.

As Macro returned to the front of the column, he stopped beside Cato and took a sip from his canteen. 'Four officers and eighteen of the men have dropped out so far. Not at all bad considering the heat. But then these men are used to it. Eight miles done, I make it. Time for a short rest and then we'll turn back towards the camp.' Macro was silent for a moment before he raised a hand to shield his eyes and squinted briefly up at the sun before he took his second sip and capped his canteen. 'That will be the real test of the men. The heat in the afternoon will be crushing. Can't say I'm relishing the prospect. How are you holding up, sir?'

'I'm managing.' In truth Cato's feet were throbbing with pain from the prolonged march on a hard surface and he felt slightly dizzy from his exertions and the heat. But he forced himself to stand upright and look Macro squarely in the eye.

'And you?'

'No problems,' Macro replied as he took in his friend's blanched face. 'If I were you, I'd sit down and rest your legs while you have the chance.'

'Not before you do.'

Macro shook his head. 'Suit yourself.'

He paced slowly along the column, looking down at the officers and men of the First Cohort. They were mostly the product of a blending of the Greek and Egyptian races, darkly featured yet not quite as dark as the natives of the upper Nile. In general they had a somewhat smaller build than the legionaries of the northern frontier of the Empire where Macro had served most of his time. However, they looked tough enough, and they had stayed the distance, so far. But then they should, Macro reflected. The First Cohort was supposed to be the best in every legion. Twice the size of other cohorts, it was entrusted with the defence of the right flank when the legion went into battle. Still, it would be interesting to see how many remained in the column when it returned to camp. The men of the Seventh and Ninth Cohorts had fared as well as their comrades and only a handful had dropped out. Cato had been right to make a point of including the officers, Macro accepted. It had certainly perked the men up – a useful bonus over and above the opportunity to weed out those who were not fit enough for active commands.

As he made his way back down the line to the small group of officers resting beside the road, Macro saw Hamedes sitting to one side. Macro had always assumed that priests were a soft bunch of wasters and was surprised that Hamedes had kept up with the column.

'How are your feet coping?'

The priest stood up as he was addressed and smiled infectiously. 'A most welcome excursion, sir. Though I have to wonder that men who have to carry so much on their backs have any strength left to conquer and hold an empire.'

Macro smiled back and tapped him on the chest. 'That's the secret of our success,' he responded conspiratorially. 'It's *because* we have the strength left that we win.' Macro took a step back and glanced over the priest. 'You've done well, lad. I'll make a legionary of you yet.'

The young man's face was still for a moment before his smile returned. 'An honour, to be sure. Yet I am a man with spiritual, rather than martial, ambitions. When the campaign is over I fully intend to return to the priesthood.'

'We'll see. My instinct is that you are getting something of a taste for this life. Why else would you stick with us, eh?' Macro clapped him on the shoulder and returned to the head of the column. He picked up his yoke and heaved it up on to his shoulder with a grunt before turning to face back along the column.

'The rest break's over! On your feet!'

There was a chorus of groans and swearing that made Macro smile, then the men stood up and raised their yokes as the optios strode down the line bawling out those who responded too slowly to the order. Each century formed up and stood ready, waiting for the order to resume the march. Macro waited until they were still and silent, then bellowed down the line, 'Column! Advance!'

They shuffled forward, gradually picking up the pace. Macro led them a short distance beyond the belt of palms before leaving the road to march round a shrine and then turning back towards the camp, passing down the tail of the column and the covered carts carrying those who had collapsed on the outward leg. Midday passed and the afternoon breeze picked up, bringing with it the lightest of dust from the desert. The grit caught in the men's mouths and their eyes, adding to the discomfort of the scorching heat that beat down on them. Worse still, the glare made the road ahead shimmer as if a perpetually receding sheet of water lay before them, tormenting them with the prospect of assuaging their growing thirst.

More men fell out of line, and this time fewer of them could be coaxed back into place by the blows of the optios and were left for the carts to pick up. Cato had slowed a little so that he was now marching amid the other officers, a short distance behind Macro. Most of the centurions were coping with the strain of the march well enough, some struggled, and the last of those officers who had been avoiding the drills soon gave in and slumped to the side of the road to await the carts.

Cato had never known such heat, not even when he and Macro had crossed the Syrian desert to Palmyra. His tunic, encased in armour, felt tight against him, constricting his breath as he laboured under the weight of the yoke and the broad shield hanging from it. His feet and legs felt leaden and each step became an effort of will. They passed back through the villages near Diospolis Magna and out came the noisy clusters of children again. This time they were met with silence as the soldiers ignored them, unwilling to waste any breath telling the children to go away.

In the middle of the afternoon Cato looked up to see the pylons and standards of Karnak wavering in the distance. His heart lifted at the sight, and he gritted his teeth and looked down again, concentrating on each step in turn, not wanting to look up and see the temples seeming as far off as ever.

'Step up the pace, lads!' Macro called out cheerfully. 'We're almost home. Let's show the other cohorts how real soldiers march!'

His words were met with silence and Macro paused and turned back to face them. 'What's the matter with you? Are we happy?'

Those centurions who had served in the northern legions, and Cato, answered him in a chorus. 'Are we fuck!'

Macro laughed, and turned to lead them the final mile back to the training ground outside the temple complex. The optios hurriedly ordered the men to dress their ranks and raise their chins as they turned off the road and the column trudged on to the open ground, back to the positions they had occupied before they had set off at daybreak.

'Column! Stand to attention!' Macro's bellow echoed back off the mud-brick wall. He set his pack down, reached for his canteen and took a long swig before stoppering it. Then he slowly paced along the lines of sweating, panting legionaries, inspecting their ranks. One more man collapsed as he stood waiting for the column to be dismissed. Macro ignored him. He put his hands on his hips and addressed the exhausted men.

'That is but a taste of what is expected of you once the campaign begins. I know that the Jackals are keen to test themselves in battle with the Nubians. You have the spirit of true soldiers, but you must also have the body. It is the army that marches hardest that also fights hardest, and wins.'

Macro's words died away with the late afternoon breeze. He stared at them a moment longer and then shouted the order. 'Column! . . . Fall out!'

As soon as the order was given the men seemed to sag under the weight of their yokes and then in ones and twos they began to stagger across the training ground towards the north gate of Karnak. Macro watched them for a moment before he caught sight of Hamedes and nodded a greeting to him.

'Well done, lad! Seems you're as fit as any man here.'

Hamedes puffed his cheeks. 'I think I may not take you up on that offer of a place in the legion, sir.'

'Hah!' Macro jerked his thumb towards the gate. 'Get in there and have a good night's rest. When the morning comes you'll wonder what you were complaining about. And then you'll try and get up and feel like a complete cripple.'

'Thank you, sir,' Hamedes said flatly, and walked stiffly away.

Cato was draining the last drops of his canteen when

Macro approached him. 'You went the distance after all.'

'Did I?' Cato's feet burned so much it was an effort to stand up. 'So this is what being dead on your feet feels like . . .'

'Ah, don't make such a fuss.' He nodded towards the carts trundling across the training ground. 'At least you did it. Some didn't. I've had one of the optios draw up a list of those who dropped out.' Macro reached into the sling hanging round his neck and fished out a small waxed slate. 'Here you are.'

'Thanks.' Cato glanced down at his yoke. 'I suppose it would be bad form to call over one of the sentries to carry this back to the supplies officer for me.'

'Very bad form.'

'Shit . . . Well, in for a sestertius, in for a denarius.' Cato reached down and heaved the ponderous weight back on to his shoulder and walked with Macro towards the gate. 'I'll drop this off and eat, drink and have a rest. Then there's one final matter to attend to this evening before I'm done for the day.'

Aurelius looked down at the list by the light of his oil lamp and shook his head. 'These are all good men. I've known them for years. You can't have them removed from their posts.'

'Sir, they failed to complete the route march. They're out of condition. Some of them are so overweight they can't fit properly into their armour any more. They are a liability to the men under their command. When you lead the army against the enemy, those officers will fail to keep up with the army, as they failed to keep up with today's marching column. Who will command their men then? They will lack an officer when they most need one.' He paused. 'They have to be removed from the battle line.'

The legate let out a long sigh. 'It may be true that they are not in peak form but they have other qualities.'

'Such as?'

'Well, er, experience. They spent many years working their way up through the ranks, as I did. There's not much that they don't know about soldiering.'

'How much campaign experience have they had, sir?'

Aurelius frowned and lowered the list. He stared up at Cato. 'You're not going to let this pass, are you?'

'No, sir. You appointed me and Centurion Macro to take charge of the men's training. It is my professional assessment that these men are unfit for active duty. Of course, it would be a shame to humiliate them through demotion or dismissal from the legion. So why not redeploy them to your headquarters, or leave them here to command the garrison? That way they won't hinder their men, and you can make use of their experience.'

'And who will replace these men?'

'Centurion Macro has already identified a number of optios who are good enough to promote to the centurionate.'

'I see.' Aurelius fixed Cato with a cold expression. 'You have it all worked out, don't you?'

'I do my duty and serve Rome to the best of my ability, sir. That's all,' Cato replied evenly. 'In any case, you wanted the legion to be ready to march as soon as possible. The sooner these men are replaced, the sooner you will be able to wage war on the Nubians.'

'Yes. I suppose you are right.' Auelius picked up the waxed tablet. 'I'll have these officers reassigned immediately. Let me know who you and Macro have nominated to replace them as soon as you can.'

Cato nodded.

'Will that be all?' Aurelius asked.

The tone of the question caught Cato by surprise. It was almost as if their positions had been reversed and the legate was asking him for permission to end their meeting. For a brief moment Cato felt pity for the man. His responsibilities exceeded his capabilities and yet he was proud and determined enough to insist on retaining command of the legion and the auxiliary cohorts that made up his modest army. That might well become something of a problem, Cato decided. Aurelius would have to be handled carefully if the Nubians were going to be defeated. He had to be treated with a careful balance between deference and direction.

'Yes, sir. If I may have your permission to be dismissed?'

'Of course.' Aurelius waved his hand towards the far end of the pool. 'You may go.'

Cato bowed his head and turned to walk stiffly away. He had just passed through the colonnade into the adjacent courtyard when one of the junior tribunes came running through the entrance, breathing hard. The legion was Caius Junius's first appointment and he had arrived only a day before Cato and Macro. A sturdy youth, he had the lighter complexion typical of a Roman. Junius was excitable and anxious to please. He hurried towards Cato as soon as he saw him.

'What is it, Junius?' asked Cato.

The officer struggled to catch his breath.

'Speak up, man!' Cato frowned impatiently.

'It's the enemy, sir . . . They're here.'

Cato felt a cold stab of anxiety. 'What do you mean?'

'On the far bank, sir.' Junius gulped down some more breath. 'They've attacked one of our outposts, sir.'

Cato glanced towards the inner courtyard. 'Tell the legate. Then summon the senior officers to headquarters at once. Except you. You're the duty officer at present?'

'Yes, sir.'

'Then once you've told the legate, and sent for the officers, have the assembly sounded. Every legionary and auxiliary is to be ready for action as soon as possible. Now go.'

As the tribune's boots clattered across the flagstones of the courtyard, Cato tensed his jaw. How the hell had the Nubians managed to move so fast?

CHAPTER TWENTY-TWO

'As good a fortification as any,' Ajax decided as he slapped the stone parapet at the top of the pylon. 'This will serve us well.'

Karim looked down at the thick walls of the temple, and the tall outer walls of mud brick. He had a good eye for a defensive position, nurtured during the years he had served his Parthian lord long before he had been captured, sold into slavery and encountered the gladiator. The temple was compact enough to be held by Ajax's men and the small column of Arab warriors that Prince Talmis had placed under his command. It was also unusual by the standards of most other temples in that there was only one entrance in the outer wall, and that was protected by a strong gatehouse. It was almost as if the place had been designed with a military purpose in mind, he thought. Just as well then that only a handful of priests had been inhabiting the temple when the column had arrived at dusk. Their bodies had been thrown into one of the offering rooms.

'Indeed, my General. The site was well chosen by our spy, Canthus. The Roman dogs will have a hard time taking it from us. Or driving us out.'

Ajax noted the wary tone in his companion's voice and

smiled. 'Rest easy, Karim. We are here to act as a diversion for the Prince. It is not my intention to make a last stand. When the time comes, we will make good our escape. In the meantime, our orders are to tie the Romans down for as long as possible.'

Karim was quiet for a moment before he asked, 'Do you trust him?'

'Prince Talmis? About as far as I could spit him. However, it serves our purpose to aid him for now.'

'And his purpose to sacrifice us, perhaps?'

Ajax turned and smiled at his companion. 'Do you have so little faith in me? Do you think that I am blind to the possible dangers of serving the Nubians?'

Karim bowed his head. 'My apologies, General. I did not doubt you. Only the word of the Prince.'

'What is there to doubt? He has promised us nothing but the chance to wage war on Rome, and what spoils of war we may choose to take. I care little for the latter, though I am sure most of the men will be pleased to help themselves to gold and any trinkets they take a fancy to. No doubt Talmis considers that we were cheaply bought, but the chance to strike a heavy blow against Rome is all the treasure I seek. Before, we were twenty fugitives. Now the Prince has given me these five hundred men.' Ajax gestured down into the outer court of the temple where the black-robed warriors were tethering their camels in the twilight. The nasal groans of the beasts carried up to the top of the pylon, almost drowning out the shouts of a couple of men fighting over the ornate robes of a priest looted from the temple.

Karim stared at them for a moment. 'Let us hope they

show more discipline when the time comes to face the enemy.'

'That test comes tonight,' said Ajax. He turned and stared towards the Nile. The distant outline of a small fort and signal tower was visible on a mound a little over two miles away. There had been no sign that the garrison had spotted Ajax and his column as they had approached from the west, out of the desert. On the far bank, a short distance downriver, the Roman army would still be ignorant of their presence, and even when the alarm was sounded, it would be some hours before they could land a strong force on this side of the Nile. Ajax smiled. His spy inside the Roman camp had already proved his worth. Ajax had details of the strength of the Roman army and, even better, information about its senior officers. It was good to know that the two Roman officers he hated with all his heart were close at hand. He had only made one demand of his Nubian ally, that if Macro and Cato were taken alive, they would be delivered into his hands. Ajax resolved to have them crucified – just as they had crucified his father. The prospect filled his heart with satisfaction. He indulged the feeling for a moment before pushing the thought from his mind. Thoughts of revenge must give way to the need for swift action, Ajax reminded himself.

'Karim, I will leave you with three hundred men. I want you to complete the fortification of the temple, and post some patrols out towards the river.' He pointed to a small village that was within long arrow shot of the temple. 'Destroy that, once you have searched it for any food.'

The Parthian nodded.

'You have your orders. I should be back with the other

men some time after the third or fourth hour of the night. Be sure that your sentries and the patrols know that. I would not be killed by an arrow shot by my own men.'

'That would be regrettable,' Karim replied, deadpan.

Ajax laughed and slapped him on the arm. 'Until later, my friend.'

Night had fallen and the warm air was filled with the shrill cry of cicadas, rising and falling as the whim took them. The last of the evening breeze stirred the leaves of the palm trees, making a constant rustle that served to disguise the sound of footsteps as Ajax and his men cautiously approached the fort. The walls rose above them, black against the velvet indigo of the starry night. He had decided to lead the attack with the men of his bodyguard. They would enter the fort and then open the gates for the rest of the assault force, hidden amid small fields of wheat and irrigation ditches that stretched out around the mound. The inhabitants of the houses closest to the fort had already been silenced so that none lived to raise the alarm.

Ajax felt the familiar swift flow of blood in his veins as he braced himself for action. He quietly drew his sword and turned to his men to whisper, 'Let's go.'

He rose into a crouch and began to make his way up the gentle slope towards the fort. Near the crest he could see the small outcrop of rock that supported a section of the wall. Here the wall was no more than ten feet high, just as Ajax had been promised by his spy. Staying low, he and his men moved closer. Then Ajax saw a movement on the wall as a sentry, with a faint sheen of starlight on the curve of his helmet and the blade of his spear, paced slowly by on his round. The gladiator went to ground, waving his men down. Staring up intently, he waited until the sentry had disappeared beyond the corner of the fort, and then he continued forward. When he reached the wall, Ajax waited for his men to catch up and then crept along until he came to the edge of the rocks. Feeling his way carefully, he climbed over them until he reached the point where a large flat boulder stood below the wall. One by one the rest of his men climbed up and spread out on either side. When they were all present, Ajax indicated to the tallest and broadest of his men, a Celt named Ortorix who had once fought as a heavily armoured Mirmillion in the arenas of the eastern Empire. Ortorix stood with his back to the wall and his knees bent, and then cupped his hands together. Ajax placed his boot in the Celt's hands, stretched his arms up the wall and whispered, 'Ready.'

With a light grunt, Ortorix heaved him up and as Ajax's boot came level with his shoulder, he gritted his teeth to edge him up still further. Keeping his weight as close to the rough surface of the mud-brick wall, Ajax groped towards the parapet. Then, as his fingers found it and curled over the edge, he let Ortorix raise him a bit further before locking an arm over the wall. He felt some of it crumble away and prayed that it would hold long enough for him to get a decent purchase on it. Then he swung his leg up, scrambling over the rim and rolled on to the walkway.

At once he rose to a crouch and looked around the interior of the fort. It was constructed in a rough square. A signal tower stood opposite the gatehouse. There were several small accommodation blocks built against the walls. Like the houses of the peasants, they had simple roofs of palm fronds to provide shade while allowing the air to circulate. A cooking fire burned in one hut and the smell of roasting meat wafted on the night air as a handful of soldiers talked in the easy way that men do when danger is furthest from their minds. There were voices coming from the other blocks, and the deep regular drone of snoring close by. The sentry patrolling along the wall had just passed through the gatehouse and was moving away from Ajax. The outline of another sentry stood at the top of the tower gazing out towards the Nile.

Satisfied that he had not been detected, Ajax leaned over the wall and gestured to the men below. Ortorix heaved the first one up and Ajax caught his hands and pulled him over the wall.

'Get over to the gatehouse. Stay out of sight.'

The man nodded and hunched down as he made his way along the walkway. Ajax turned to help the other men up and he had ten over the parapet by the time the sentry approached the corner to turn on to the same length of wall.

'Wait,' Ajax whispered. 'Stay down until I come back.'

He glanced down below the parapet and saw that there was a pile of straw and a mule tethered to a post. Resting in the straw was a fat auxiliary soldier, hands folded together across his bulging tunic. The dark shape of a wine jar lay next to him. Glancing up, Ajax saw the soldier reach the corner. There was no time to look for another place of concealment and he eased himself over the side of the walkway and dropped down into the straw. It rustled briefly and the mule started with a low bray.

'Hrrrmmm . . .' The auxiliary stirred and smacked his lips. 'Whatsmatter?'

He began to struggle up on his elbow and Ajax drew his sword and threw himself on top of the man, clamping his left hand over the auxiliary's mouth. He rammed his sword into the man's stomach, point angled up under the ribs. There was a muffled cry and the man arched his back, nearly throwing Ajax off. As he worked the blade ferociously from side to side, Ajax smashed his forehead down on to the crown of the auxiliary. The man abruptly went limp and slumped back into the straw. Ajax thrust up towards the heart once more to make certain and then wrenched his blade free. He could hear the footsteps of the sentry approaching. Ajax hurriedly eased the body back into a reposed position and threw some straw over the bloodstain on the tunic. Then he buried himself beside the man and lay still. The sentry came closer and then the sound of his steady pace stopped.

'What, Minimus, no longer sleeping?'

Ajax, heart beating wildly against his chest, drew a breath and grumbled, before making a guttural snore as near to the sound of the fat man as possible. The sentry laughed and continued on his way and Ajax carried on snoring until he could no longer hear the footsteps. Then, easing himself up from the straw, he climbed back on to the wall and resumed hauling his men over the rampart. Ortorix came last, heaved up by Ajax and two more of his men, gritting their teeth as they tried not to groan with the effort. With the Celt and the others, Ajax hurried along the walkway towards the gatehouse. The sentry had not emerged from his last circuit and they discovered his body slumped to one side as soon as they entered the low tower.

'Once we get the gate open, get stuck in and make as much noise as you can,' Ajax ordered. 'Understood?'

They nodded to him in the gloom and then he made his way over to the narrow stairs leading down into the fort. Emerging from the tower gatehouse, Ajax gestured to Ortorix to help him and they tried to ease the locking bar into its receiver without making any noise. The sentry in the tower straightened up from the rail and turned away from the Nile to gaze down into the fort. He seemed to be staring directly towards the gatehouse and Ajax realised that he was looking for the other man on duty. He cursed himself for not ordering one of his men to take the sentry's place and continue his beat. Too late for that now, he thought bitterly.

'They'll be on to us any moment,' he said softly to the Celt. 'Let's get this bastard opened up.'

They heaved the bar back and grasped the heavy iron rings and pulled the doors inwards. There was a deep groan from the hinges and the sentry in the tower leaned towards them briefly before cupping a hand to his mouth.

'To arms! To arms!' His voice echoed down inside the fort. 'We're under attack!'

Ajax thrust his sword up, angled towards the barrack blocks. 'Get in there! Kill them! Kill them all!'

With a deafening shout the gladiator and his bodyguards charged forward. Behind them in the darkness another cry went up and hundreds of shadows leaped from cover and ran up the slope towards the open gates.

Ajax raced ahead of his men, making for the line of small buildings to the right. Already the defenders were stumbling out into the night, clutching the first weapon that came to hand, a mixture of swords and spears. None wore any armour or helmets, he noted, giving them no edge over their attackers. A shape rushed out of a door directly in front of Ajax so that he cannoned into him. Instinctively he stabbed his blade high into the man's chest as they collided and the soldier fell away with a pained cry as Ajax stumbled over him. He regained his balance just in time to parry the spear thrust aimed at his throat by another auxiliary who had turned at the sound of his comrade's cry. The auxiliary swung the butt of his spear round and punched it towards Ajax, glancing off the side of his head and grazing his scalp. The pain enraged the gladiator and he charged forward, inside the reach of the spear, and caught him by the throat with his left hand, crushing his fingers into the soldier's windpipe. The auxiliary dropped his spear and clawed at Ajax's hand and then he spasmed as the sword blade punched into his guts repeatedly. Thrusting him aside, Ajax glanced round and saw that his bodyguards were cutting down the defenders across the interior of the fort. Caught by surprise, and assaulted by men who were the best trained killers in the Empire, they stood little chance. Then there was a rush of sandalled feet as the Arabs burst into the fort and joined the unequal struggle.

'We yield!' a figure cried out a short distance ahead of Ajax. 'We surrender! Drop your weapons, men!'

Those outside the fight, and just emerging from their quarters, began to throw down their weapons. There was a last ring of blades and a groan and then a pause in the fighting.

'No quarter!' Ajax bellowed. He lurched forward, cutting down a stick-thin veteran. As the mortally wounded auxiliary tumbled to the ground, Ajax lunged at the fort's commander, a squarely built man with thinning hair. The centurion ducked to avoid the strike and snatched up his blade, twisting to strike Ajax as he rushed past. The blow missed and Ajax spun round, braced his feet apart and faced the Roman.

'Die!' he bellowed, and then launched a savage sequence of blows. The centurion parried desperately and then threw up his sword as Ajax made a cut towards his head. At the last moment Ajax switched his angle and the edge of his well-honed blade cut right through the centurion's wrist and on down into his shoulder. The sword clattered to the ground, still in the grip of the hand, and the centurion fell back with a howl of agony. Ajax stood over him, grinning in triumph, then leaned down and slashed open his throat, leaving the man to shake as his blood pumped out of the severed arteries and pattered across the ground beside him.

Ajax looked up and saw that the fort was in their hands. Not one of the Romans was still on his feet and his men stood over the bodies, breathing heavily as the battle rage began to ebb away. Ortorix laughed nervously. 'We did it, lads.' He punched his sword into the night sky and bellowed the war cry of his Gallic forefathers. The others followed suit and then one of them called out Ajax's name and his companions took up the chant. Around them the Arabs bent over the corpses of the Romans, and hurried inside the barrack blocks, searching for loot.

Ajax nodded at his men with satisfaction. 'Good work! Now let's finish the job. Torch the place!'

As the column headed away from the fort, back towards the temple, Ajax paused to view his handiwork. Bright flames licked up from inside the walls, illuminating the small knoll upon which the fort stood, and casting a wavering glow over the fields and palms for a short distance around. The timbers of the signal tower were consumed by a tracery of flames and then there was a soft burst of crackles as the thatched roof caught fire and went up in a fierce but short-lived explosion of light. Moments later one of the tower legs gave way and the structure lurched to one side, then slowly toppled into the heart of the fort with a burst of sparks. The sound of its crash reached Ajax's ears an instant later.

'A fine sight,' Ortorix muttered happily at his side. 'Warms the heart, so it does.'

Ajax could not help smiling at the comment and patted the giant on his shoulder.

'That'll be hard to miss from the other side of the Nile,' said Ortorix.

'Yes. I think we can safely say that we have announced our arrival. Now let's see what the Romans do about it.'

CHAPTER TWENTY-THREE

The legate and his senior officers made their way through the camp to the landing stage in front of the temple complex by the light of the torches held by the legate's escort. All around them the men of the Twenty-Second and the cohorts attached to the legion were emerging from their tents, armour and weapons in hand. Those who were the first to dress and fasten their straps hurried to their stations as each unit formed up and waited for orders.

As they made their way up the ramp between the line of Sphinxes, Cato could clearly see the flames leaping up from a distant site, hovering a small distance above the rippling sparkles of the reflection in the Nile.

'Is that the outpost?' he asked Tribune Junius.

'Yes, sir.'

'Tell me what you know about it,' Cato snapped.

Junius looked at him in surprise.

'Look, I've only been here a few days,' Cato explained. 'I haven't had a chance to familiarise myself with the area.'

'Sorry, sir. I don't know much. It's little more than a fort. Garrisoned by a half century of auxiliary troops. It's there to keep an eye on the trade route running along the far bank. Or it was, before the Nubians got here.'

Macro stood on the landing stage and strained his eyes towards the distant fire. 'And how do you know that's the work of the enemy, eh? Could be desert raiders, or perhaps some fool's set the granary alight. Has there been any word from the garrison commander?'

'No, sir.'

'Hmmm.' Macro stroked his lip. 'Still, we can't be sure. If you're wrong, Tribune, then you've sounded the alarm and called the entire army out for nothing. You're not going to be a popular man. Oh, and by the way, you don't call me "sir", even if I am the first spear centurion.'

'Sorry.' Junius looked abashed and Cato decided to come to his rescue.

'You did the right thing. It's possible that it's an accident. However, we're on a war footing and it could be the result of enemy action. It's hard to say now that we're not sending patrols out any further than ten miles.'

Aurelius overheard the remark and stirred but he did not say anything, continuing to stare across the river. At length he turned to his chief of staff. 'Geminus, any other reports of enemy movement?'

'None, sir. Nothing from the lookouts, and none of the day's patrols reported anything out of the ordinary.'

'Well, something's up now. It could be an accident. If we've had no report from the fort within the hour then send someone across the river to investigate.'

'Yes, sir.' Geminus cleared his throat. 'And the men, sir?'

'What?' Aurelius turned towards him.

'Shall I stand them down, sir?'

Aurelius looked back towards the fire and was silent for a moment before he replied, 'No. Not until we know for certain what is going on over there.'

Macro glanced at Cato and cocked an eyebrow. Cato ignored him and stared at the fire. It was clearly growing in intensity and looked as if it threatened to consume the entire fort. He made up his mind and approached Aurelius.

'Sir, I don't think we should wait for a report. We should send someone across the river to investigate at once. If it is the work of the enemy then we need to know immediately. Even if it is just an accident we need to know if the garrison requires any assistance.'

'Are you volunteering to cross the river and reconnoitre, Tribune?' asked Aurelius wryly. 'Or are you not too subtly volunteering a more junior officer?'

'I'll go, sir,' Cato replied. He was infuriated by his superior's insinuation. 'Better to send someone with experience.'

'In that case,' Macro intervened, 'I'd better go too, sir.'

Cato turned to him. 'It's not necessary. I can do the job by myself.'

Macro was about to speak, and then remembered that the days of fatherly advice had passed. He kept his mouth closed but looked at Cato imploringly. Cato shook his head.

'Not this time.'

'Why not?' asked Aurelius. 'Surely two sets of eyes are better than one? I'm sure the legion can spare you both for a few hours. Take Macro.' He looked at Cato and forced a solicitous expression. 'For my peace of mind, eh? Oh, and you can take Junius too, as he was so keen to sound the alarm. If it turns out to be a minor incident then perhaps spending a night grubbing around in the darkness might teach him to think twice before reacting so precipitately in future.'

'Is that an order, sir?' Cato asked flatly.

'It is. Report to me the moment you return.' Aurelius raised an arm to gather the attention of the other officers. 'I've seen enough. Come, back to headquarters. Geminus, pass the word to all formations that they are to stand to until further notice.'

'Yes, sir.'

With that, the legate turned away and led his entourage back towards the entrance to the temple complex. Cato shook his head.

'I'm sorry, sir,' said Junius. 'I didn't mean to cause unnecessary trouble. Will the men really hold it against me? Will they resent me?'

'Lad,' Macro smiled at him, 'you're a tribune, doubtless by virtue of family connections, like most who hold your rank. You have no prior military experience and once you have served your time in the legion, you'll be returning to some cushy job in Rome. Take it from me, the common soldiery will always resent you.'

'Oh, dear.' Junius looked crestfallen. 'I had hoped to win their respect at least.'

'You can still do that,' Macro nodded, 'when the time comes to face the Nubians.'

Cato gestured towards the fire. 'That may well happen rather sooner than you think.'

'Or not. Why would the enemy strike there?' asked Macro. 'It doesn't make sense. If they wanted to surprise us then why not go directly for the camp? Why take out an outpost and alert us to their presence? I tell you, it's a false alarm, and when I get my hands on the fool who caused that fire, I'll be sure to give *him* a roasting.'

A figure emerged from the ramp and hurried towards Cato. It was Hamedes.

'Sir, I overheard the exchange with the legate,' the priest said apologetically. 'I wish to go with you. If there is any trouble I will fight at your side. If you give me the chance.'

'No. I don't need you. I have enough men already. Go back to the camp and wait for us there.'

Hamedes looked hurt. 'Sir, I have sworn an oath to Osiris to serve at your side until you are victorious.'

'I'm sure Osiris will understand,' Cato replied placatingly. 'Now return to camp. That's an order.'

Hamedes frowned and then turned away and disappeared into the darkness.

'No question of it, the lad's keen,' Macro said in an amused tone. 'Even after a day's hard marching.'

'I have no quarrel with his attitude, as long as it doesn't start becoming irritating.' Cato strode over to the steps leading down to the wooden quay. 'Come on. Let's get on with it.'

'Well,' Macro shrugged, 'there's no pleasing some people.'

Cato pulled a section of legionaries from the First Cohort and boarded the nearest of the barges, shaking the crew out of their slumber as they lay on deck. The captain gave the order for his two crewmen to fend the barge off and into the current. He was about to raise the sail, but Cato stopped him.

'No. There's a chance that the sail might be seen. Use the oars.'

'It'll take longer,' the captain protested. 'And it'll be tiring work.'

'You'll use the oars,' Cato insisted, and went forward to sit just in front of the mast. Macro and Junius joined him and the legionaries sat on the deck, keeping clear of the two sailors who unshipped the long oars and began to stroke the barge out into the black water of the Nile. They rowed across the current and slowed down to creep forward once they approached the far bank. Ahead, the fire was starting to die down and an odd glow outlined the walls of the fort, dark and gaunt against the wavering light.

Cato turned and called softly back to the captain. 'Get your boat as close to it as you can. If we have to leave in a hurry, I don't want to run any further than I have to.'

The captain grumbled a sour reply and steered the barge along the riverbank. They passed a few small houses whose dwellers slept on, unaware. Once the barge was as near to level with the fort as Cato could judge in the darkness, he ordered the captain to steer in, aiming for a narrow stretch of earthen bank. Having seen one crocodile strike from the concealment of reeds, Cato was fearful of repeating the experience. The barge grounded softly and gently jolted the soldiers. Cato stood up, took off his sword belt and removed his helmet and scale vest.

Macro stared at him. 'And what do you think you're doing, sir?'

'We're not going into a fight, just scouting.' Cato picked up his sword belt and slipped the strap over his head. 'What are you waiting for?'

With a sigh Macro followed suit, and a moment later so did Junius. Cato turned to him. 'Not you.'

Junius paused. 'Sir?'

'You're staying here.'

'I was told to come with you, sir.'

'And I'm ordering you to remain here. I'm leaving you in charge of the boat. Make sure that the captain doesn't get cold feet. If we come running, I want the men ready to hold the bank until we reach the boat. Is that clear?'

'Yes, sir.'

Cato slipped over the side of the barge and splashed into the calf-deep water. He made his way ashore and up the bank to the edge of the long grass that grew there. Macro joined him a moment later and then they set off towards the fort, no more than half a mile away. They reached the edge of a wheat field and picked their way through the crop and then encountered a wide irrigation ditch, with reeds growing along each side. Cato paused, listening.

'What is it?' Macro whispered.

'I . . . nothing. Let's go.' Cato was about to climb down into the reeds when there was loud splash and something large rustled through the reeds a short distance to his left. At once Macro drew his sword. They both froze for a moment.

'What was that?' Macro asked.

'Without seeing it, I'd guess it was a crocodile. I think we should find a way round the ditch.'

'Crocodile?' Macro quietly put his sword away and muttered, 'Good idea.'

They followed the ditch for a quarter of a mile without finding its end, or any means of crossing it. Cato fumed at the time they had wasted and decided to double back. Perspiring freely in the warm air, they retraced their steps until they came across a narrow footbridge supported by a crude wooden trestle.

'After you, sir,' said Macro.

'Thanks.' Cato tested his weight on the narrow plank and found that it bowed slightly. Taking each step carefully, he crossed over and waited for Macro before continuing towards the fort. They were close enough now to hear the crackle of the dying flames. Cato paused.

'I can't hear any voices.'

Macro strained his ears. 'No. Nothing. Looks like I was wrong about it being an accident.'

'If the enemy took the place, then why aren't they still here?'

'Maybe it was a hit and run raid,' Macro suggested.

Cato nodded. 'Perhaps. Let's get a closer look.'

They reached the bottom of the knoll and began to climb towards the fort. The acrid smell of burning filled the air and as they neared the gate, a new odour was added to the stench: burnt flesh. The gatehouse had collapsed and the two officers cautiously poked their heads round the side of the ruined arch. Cato winced as the heat struck his face, forcing him to squint. The interior of the fort had been destroyed by the blaze and by the light of the small fires that still burned he saw the blackened, twisted shapes of bodies.

'That's proof enough for me,' said Macro. 'They were attacked. And no raiding party would have dared take on a fort like this. It might be small, but even so it would present too much of a challenge.'

'I agree. We'd better report back to the legate.'

At that instant a voice cried out in the distance. A rising ululation. It continued for a moment and then stopped.

'That came from the direction of the boat,' said Cato. 'Let's go.'

They hurried down the slope and entered the field they had crossed a moment earlier, following their trail back through the trampled wheat. Then another cry rose up in the darkness, behind them now, some distance beyond the fort.

'Shit,' Macro hissed. 'Whoever that is, there's more than one of 'em.'

They reached the far side of the field and then entered some long grass. This time it was impossible to determine which direction they had come from. Looking at the dull mass of the distant hills to their left, Cato estimated the direction they should take and they set off again. Another cry came from ahead, closer, and was quickly answered by another some distance behind, and then another, away to their left.

'Right, now I'm starting to worry.' Macro spoke in an undertone. 'We'd better get a move on, before any more turn up.'

But Cato was still. 'They can't be hunting us.'

'Why not?'

'How would they know we're here?'

'Maybe they saw us by the fort. Let's think it through later on, eh?' Macro nudged his arm.

Cato nodded and they set off again, moving more quickly, ears and eyes strained to detect any sign of the enemy, or whoever might be making the strange noises. They crossed back to the other side of the irrigation ditch and were heading across the fields towards the grass and the river beyond when Cato heard a harsh grunt to their left, and the soft padding of feet. A voice called out, 'Huthut!'

'Camels?' Macro guessed.

Cato increased his pace to a trot and they both hurried across the last stretch of the field and entered the grass. Almost at once they blundered into a crouching figure. Macro wrenched his blade out and leaped forward, knocking the man down. He was about to strike when a familiar voice gasped, 'Sir! It's me, Junius!'

'Junius . . .' Macro rose up, lowering his blade a fraction. 'Shit. I almost killed you.'

Cato was furious the moment he recovered from his surprise. 'What the bloody hell are you doing here? I told you to stay with the boat.'

'Sorry, sir. I heard someone calling out a while back. I thought it best to investigate.'

'You don't think. You do as you are ordered.'

The sound of camels grew louder and now they could hear voices as their riders talked to each other.

'They're almost on us,' Macro growled. He thrust Junius forward. 'Move. Back to the boat.'

The three officers ran on through the long grass, making

for the river, Junius stumbling in the lead, Macro next, holding his sword ready, and then Cato, constantly glancing over his shoulders for signs of the camel riders searching for them. Then they emerged from the grass and the broad black expanse of the Nile lay before them. Macro glanced both ways and then thrust his arm to the left. 'There's the boat. Come on!'

Cato came out of the grass and saw it, no more than two hundred paces away. As they broke into a run along the riverbank, the swish of grass sounded and their pursuers closed in. They had run half the distance when Junius stumbled and sprawled forward with a loud cry of alarm.

Macro bent down, grasped the scruff of his tunic and yanked the large youth back on to his feet.

'Just give us away, why don't you? Idiot.'

'Sorry.'

Macro kept his fist bunched in the man's tunic and hurried him on. Cato brought up the rear. The tribune's cry had alerted the men and they let out a shout as they spotted their prey running along the riverbank. Glancing to his left, Cato could see several of them riding through the grass, as they made to run down the Romans.

Cato realised there was nothing to be gained from trying to be quiet any more and he yelled out towards the boat, 'Legionaries! On me!'

The soldiers snatched up their shields and clambered over the side and began to struggle up the bank, just as Junius and Macro reached the top and half ran, half slid down towards the water. Cato was a short distance behind them when a camel lurched out in front of him. He dodged round, ducked beneath the long curve of its neck and ran on. The rider shouted in alarm and drew his sword with a dry rasp. But he had reacted too late and Cato was already stumbling down towards the boat, the legionaries falling back with him as they presented their shields to the other riders who had appeared on top of the bank. One of them leaped down from his saddle, landed heavily and then rushed down the slope, crashing into the shield of a legionary. He gave a sharp grunt as the Roman thrust his sword into the rider's gut and then wrenched it free. Beyond, Macro heaved Junius aboard and then rolled over the side on to the deck. Cato clambered aboard and bellowed to the legionaries to follow him. The barge captain and his men were already easing the barge away from the riverbank with one of the long oars. The legionaries turned and splashed into the shallows and scrambled aboard.

There was a crack on the deck close by Cato and he instinctively ducked before he had the presence of mind to shout out a warning. 'Watch out!'

Another arrow whirred through the air close overhead. The barge lurched free of the silty river bed and was caught by the flow of the water and started to drift downriver. The crew hurriedly placed the oars into the rowlocks and strained to get the craft away from the bank. An arrow splashed into the water close by, then another struck the deck. Moments later there was a soft whack and one of the legionaries gave a cry as he collapsed on to the deck, while his shield landed awkwardly and tumbled over the side. Cato saw an arrow shaft projecting from just below the man's neck. The soldier reached for it with both hands, making a ghastly gurgling noise. His boot scraped across the deck for a moment before his struggles eased and stopped and he lay in a slowly expanding pool of his own blood. More arrows splashed into the water behind them before the enemy realised their target was out of range and ceased shooting.

Macro let out a sigh of relief, then turned on Junius. 'Next time the senior tribune gives you an order, you obey it to the letter. Do you understand, you fuckwit?'

'Y-yes. I'll do as you say.'

'Good.' Macro turned to Cato. 'You all right?'

'I'm fine.' Cato turned to look back to the western bank. 'No doubt about it now. Looks like the legate has been saved a job. The Nubians have decided to bring the war to us.'

CHAPTER TWENTY-FOUR

'This is going to be tricky,' said Macro as he stood on the foredeck of the felucca with Cato and surveyed the west bank of the Nile the following morning. The enemy had several patrols watching the movements of the Romans on the opposite side of the river. 'They'll see us coming and be ready to give us some grief wherever we land.'

Cato nodded. The enemy would be able to head off any attempt to cross the river. The problem was made worse by the lack of boats with which to make the crossing. The moment that the people of Diospolis Magna had heard of the enemy's presence so close to the city, many of them had fled. The wealthier inhabitants had hired every available boat and had set off downriver with as much of their portable wealth as possible. By the time Aurelius took action to stop the flight, there were only a handful of barges and feluccas left. Enough to carry five hundred men at a time. The Roman officers on the felucca had already seen at least that number of men waiting for them on the west bank. Any attempt at a landing would be in the face of superior numbers. The first men over the river were going to have to hold their ground while the boats returned with reinforcements. It would be tricky indeed, Cato agreed, with a wry smile at Macro's understatement.

'Tricky or not, it has to be done,' Aurelius announced from the main deck where he sat on a padded stool. One of the headquarters slaves stood behind him, holding a sunshade over the legate. A handful of other officers stood on the deck in the open sun, sweating profusely in the heat. Although there was a strong breeze blowing, the hot air it carried across the river merely added to the discomfort. Aurelius pondered a moment before continuing. 'Before the army can advance, we have to remove the threat posed by this enemy column.'

Macro stared at the nearest of the Arab patrols: six men on camels keeping level with the boat as it sailed slowly upriver, safely beyond bowshot. He was frustrated by the legate's failure to get stuck into the enemy. His patience, limited at the best of times, was being sorely tested by the vacillation of his superior. 'Sir, we don't know how many of them there are over there. It could be a relatively small force. We should focus our attention on dealing with the main army. In my view, it is dangerous to keep handing the initiative over to the Nubians. We should press on and deal with Prince Talmis, sir.'

Cato glanced quickly at Aurelius, but the legate did not take issue with this challenge to his authority. He leaned forward and rested his elbows on his knees, staring at the deck in thought. 'I am not so sure that is wise. It would be dangerous to leave our base in Diaspolis Magna while the enemy is lurking nearby. What if they cross the Nile and attack? They could take the city, destroy our stores and then march on our rear. We would be trapped between the two enemy forces. If we are defeated, then there will be nothing standing between the Nubians and the delta. Governor Petronius will not be able to stop their advance.' Aurelius looked up at Macro. 'If we lose control of the Nile then the wheat supply will be cut off. Alexandria would starve, not to mention the mob in Rome who depend on the grain from Egypt. No, the risk is too great. We must deal with the enemy forces one at a time.' He nodded towards the Arabs. 'Starting with them.'

Macro stirred, about to protest, but Cato addressed him in an undertone. 'He's right. We have to take care of our flank first.'

Macro pressed his lips together for a moment before he replied. 'At this rate the campaign will drag on for months. What about Ajax? Why give him time to escape us again? Is that what you want?'

'Of course not. But we must deal with one threat at a time.'

Macro was silent for a moment before he growled, 'Then we'd better get on with it, hadn't we?'

The legate cleared his throat. 'If you two have finished?'

Cato and Macro faced him and Aurelius glared at them briefly before he continued. 'We must get sufficient men across the Nile to deal with the enemy. Clearly the best course of action is to cross the Nile further downriver and march back along the bank to engage them. The First Cohort should be sufficient to cope with the task.' He nodded towards Macro. 'It is the strongest unit in the legion and should easily defeat the enemy column. Once Centurion Macro has driven the enemy off, I shall send the Syrian cavalry cohort across to screen our flank as the main column marches on Prince Talmis.' He paused. 'Any questions?'

The officers surrounding him remained silent. Cato looked at the Arab patrol keeping pace with the boat, then turned back to face the legate and responded as diplomatically as he could.

'Sir, while I agree with your plan, there is one aspect of it that causes me some disquiet.'

Macro frowned. 'Disquiet?'

'Oh?' Aurelius raised an eyebrow. 'And what aspect would that be, Tribune?'

Cato pointed to the patrol. 'They are following us and watching our every move. The enemy will be ready to contest the landing wherever Centurion Macro and his men attempt to cross the Nile.'

'I can handle that,' Macro said firmly, looking steadily at the legate. 'You have my word on it, sir.'

Aurelius smiled thinly and turned his gaze back to Cato. 'Your friend seems unconcerned by the prospect of a fight. So your sense of disquiet is misplaced. Of course I understand that an officer of your years might be unnerved by the prospect of a river crossing.'

Cato stared at his superior as he struggled to keep his face clear of any expression that might betray his anger at the legate's accusation. He swallowed and spoke in a flat tone when he replied. 'I can assure you, sir, I understand the risks entailed in making an opposed landing across a river as wide as the Nile. Indeed, I took part in such an action during the invasion of Britannia.' Images of the landing briefly flitted through Cato's mind – the languid flow of the Tamesis as he stood in the crowded barge with the men of his century, staring at the roaring horde of Celt warriors waiting for them on the far bank. Yes, he knew the danger that the First Cohort would face, Cato reflected. He cleared his throat and continued addressing the legate.

'That was not my point though, sir. What occurs to me is that since the enemy will be able to oppose the First Cohort wherever they attempt to cross, Centurion Macro might as well cross the Nile here as anywhere else. It would save time, if nothing else.'

'I see.' Aurelius stroked his chin as he looked across the water at the enemy-held bank where the Arab patrol returned his gaze. 'You are right, Tribune. But I wonder,' he turned back to Cato, 'if you would make such a proposal if it entailed putting your own life at risk.'

'Of course, sir. I would be honoured to join the First Cohort when they assault the far bank.'

Aurelius's lips lifted in a thin smile. 'Then you shall have your wish.'

Macro stared round at the rest of the centurions of the First Cohort. Most of them were good men, according to their records and his assessment of them in the days since he had assumed command. Two were newly promoted, former optios replacing officers who had failed to complete the route march. They might well be new to the rank but they were tough veterans keen to prove themselves worthy members of the legion's centurionate.

'I know this kind of action is new to you,' Macro began. 'You may have served along the Nile, or on the delta, since you joined up, but let me tell you, an amphibious operation is a difficult beast at the best of times. It's not standard procedure for the legions, and the tribune and I have only had to take part in a handful of actions of this kind.'

That was something of an overstatement, Cato mused. Macro looked at him and Cato nodded reassuringly for the benefit of the other officers before the commander of the First Cohort continued.

'We will not be going into action as a cohort. Nor indeed as centuries. It'll be every man for himself until we gain a foothold on the far bank. Once we are ashore, it's vital that your men form up on the standards as quickly as they can. Make sure your section leaders know that. They're to look out for their men and try and keep them together. The sooner we can form up each century, and then the cohort, the better our chances of surviving until the follow-up wave can cross the river.' Macro paused and then pointed across to the narrow island, little more than a strip of silt surrounded by reeds, that stood two hundred paces from the far bank. 'I've chosen to cross over there, close to the island.'

The men of one of the other cohorts were already on the island, together with ten of the legion's bolt throwers.

'We'll land the follow-up wave there before the first three centuries cross the final stretch of river. That way we shall have more boots on the ground as quickly as possible. The bolt throwers will be able to cover our flanks once they have finished harassing the enemy before the first wave goes in.'

It was as good a plan as any, Cato reflected. Macro had

done all he could to give his men the best chance. Even so, the first wave across would have a bitter struggle ahead of them. Once they jumped over the side of the boats carrying them to the far bank, there would be nowhere for them to retreat to. They must fight their way ashore, or die in the shallows. Those were the only options and the men knew it. The dice would be cast the moment they stepped aboard and began to cross the Nile.

Macro looked round at his officers and took a deep breath. 'I'm not going to pretend to you that this is going to be anything other than a tough fight. Our losses are likely to be heavy, but this is what we train for, and what we get paid for.'

Some of the men smiled at the last remark and Macro pressed on to make the most of the light-hearted moment. 'Just tell your men to go in hard and cut the bastards to pieces. They're not to stop for anything until they reach the top of the riverbank. Only then are they to look for their standards. Is that clear? Now then, any questions?'

He waited a moment but his officers remained silent, and Macro nodded. 'That's all, then. Return to your units and brief your men. Have them formed up and ready to board the boats the moment the legate gives the signal to proceed. Good luck.'

The officers murmured a reply in kind and then made their way out of the shade beneath the date palms and returned to their centuries, clustered along the riverbank in whatever shade they could find. Macro watched them briefly before he turned to Cato.

'What do you think?'

'They seem up for it,' Cato replied. 'In any case, once

the attack begins, it's do or die. That tends to have a powerful motivating effect on the men.'

'True enough.' Macro looked at Cato. 'What about you? Are you ready for this?'

'As ready as I ever was.'

'You didn't have to volunteer for it.'

'No. But then why would I let you snatch all the glory?'

Macro shook his head. 'Since when did you ever do anything for the glory of it? You always have to have some damn practical reason or other for volunteering.'

'Is that so?' Cato pursed his lips. 'Then let's say that it'll do the men good to see one of the senior officers fighting alongside them. That, and I have to make sure that no harm comes to you. I'm not going to be the man who has to take back the sad news to your mother. That would take someone of extraordinary courage, and foolhardiness. Not me.'

Macro laughed and slapped Cato on the shoulder. 'For your sake then I'll try to stay alive, eh?'

The sun had declined from its zenith as the fleet of small craft set off from the east bank of the Nile. Half the men of the First Cohort sat or stood in the boats, nervously watching as the crews raised the sails and got under way. Watching them, Cato could understand their mood. Weighed down by their armour, the men would sink to the bottom of the river if they fell over the side. The thought of drowning momentarily filled Cato with terror as he vividly imagined his helplessness, encumbered by heavy kit, struggling to free himself as his breath ran out and his lungs burned, and then the final gasp that would fill his throat with choking water and the last desperate flailing of his limbs before he died. He shook the image off and looked at Hamedes sitting on the central thwart opposite him. It was hard to believe that he had ever been a priest, thought Cato. The Egyptian wore a scale armour vest, bronze helmet, and rested a large shield against his knees. His face was set in a determined expression as he stared down. He looked every inch a fighter and Cato wondered if the young man would consider enlisting once the campaign was over. Because he lacked Roman citizenship the legate had refused to take him on to the official roll of the legion and he had been entered as an irregular scout and issued his kit on a temporary basis.

Hamedes suddenly looked up and met Cato's gaze and smiled uncertainly. 'Is it always this way, sir? The sick feeling in your guts before you go into battle?'

'Always,' Cato replied. 'Trust me, it's the same for every man, except Macro. He just enjoys it.'

'It's what the job is about.' Macro shrugged. 'And I happen to be good at it and take pride in that.'

Hamedes examined the centurion for a moment before he spoke again. 'And you never feel fear, sir?'

'I didn't say that. The trick of it is not to let your imagination have free rein. If you can do that and keep your eye on the job then you'll get through it without surrendering to fear. Of course it ain't going to make you invulnerable. A sword thrust is every bit as likely to kill a hero as a coward.' Macro winked. 'So, kick your imagination in the guts and pray like hell to every god out there who owes you a favour. That's my advice, lad.'

Hamedes did not appear to be reassured and shot a questioning look at Cato, who simply smiled and then sat up as straight as possible as the boat began to pass along the island. The crews of the bolt throwers were standing by their weapons, the launch beds angled up in the direction of the far bank. A short distance behind the artillery stood the men of the three cohorts waiting to follow the first wave of the assault. As the boats passed by, the centurion of the Fourth Century punched his fist into the air and called out. 'Stick it to 'em, Jackals!'

The other men echoed his cry as they urged their comrades on. Some of the men on the boats shouted back but most sat in sombre silence as the boats passed out from behind the island and turned towards the bank. The felucca carrying Macro and Cato was a short distance behind the first two craft and Macro stood up and cupped a hand to his mouth.

'You there! Remember your bloody orders! We go in at the same time! Slow down!'

The officers in charge of the two boats hurriedly ordered their crews to spill some of the wind from the sails and gradually Macro's vessel caught up with them. The rest of the flotilla took up their positions on the flanks as the unwieldy line made for the riverbank. Directly ahead of them Cato could see the waiting enemy. Hundreds of them. Half had dismounted and stood in small bands armed with round shields and curved swords that glinted as they caught the afternoon sunshine. In between the men on foot were more Arabs mounted on camels. They carried bows and began to notch their first arrows as the boats approached.

A blast from a bucina sounded and an instant later the arms of the bolt throwers sprang forward and cracked against their padded restraints as they discharged the long heavy shafts, tipped with iron, arcing across the water ahead of the flotilla. Macro clambered up on to the foredeck of the felucca to watch the fall of shot and made a fist as he saw a bolt cut through one of the groups of Arabs with a swirl as three men went down. Another slammed into the flank of a camel and there was a sharp, terrified grunt, before the animal collapsed, sending its rider sprawling into the long grass. A man on horseback rode down the riverbank waving his arm and shouting orders and the Arabs quickly dispersed to present less of a target to the bolt throwers.

'Bloody hell,' Macro muttered as he stared at the man. He squinted and then felt a cold tremor as he recognised the rider. 'It's him . . . Cato! Sir! It's him, Ajax.'

CHAPTER TWENTY-FIVE

Cato stood up and climbed on to the foredeck. He shaded his eyes as he squinted across the glinting surface of the river at the rider. There was no mistaking the powerful physique and the undeniable aura of command that the gladiator wore like a second skin. 'You're right.'

'What I'd give to be in command of the bolt throwers now,' Macro growled. 'I'd have every one of them trained on that bastard.'

Cato nodded vaguely as he continued to stare at Ajax. Some of the crews on the island had realised the significance of the mounted figure and the first of the slender missiles whipped across the river towards him in a shallow arc. It missed, as did the second, and the third struck one of the small group of horsemen reined in behind their leader. Another flew on a true trajectory towards him, but Ajax flicked his reins and moved along the bank and the bolt disappeared into the long grass a short distance beyond where he had been just a moment before.

Macro had been noting the fall of shot. 'That man has a charmed life.'

'Not in the round,' Cato replied. 'He's had his share of suffering.'

Macro looked at his friend sharply. 'What? You pity him?'

'Nothing so undignified. It's just that had his fate been different, Ajax is a man we might have been pleased to call a friend, and proud to have fight at our side.'

Macro snorted. 'And I might have been the fucking Emperor. There's only one course through life, Cato. We are what we are, never what we might have been. As for what we will be, well,' Macro spat over the side into the river, 'that bastard will die. He has the blood of thousands on his hands. I only hope that it's my blade that does the deed when his time comes. I defy the gods to try and stop me.'

For a man who was disposed towards superstition, this was strong stuff and Cato glanced at Macro in surprise. But before he could respond, there was another blast from the bucina and the sharp cracks of the bolt throwers died away as the artillery battery ceased shooting and trained their weapons round towards the flanks. At once the Arabs closed up and Ajax and his men took their shields up from their saddle horns and drew their swords.

'Steer towards those men!' Macro bellowed at the crewman on the tiller. 'There!' He thrust his arm towards the riverbank.

The crewman glanced round at the other boats on the left-hand side and shook his head. 'I can't, sir. We'd have to cut across their bows. We'd risk a collision.'

'Just do it!'

'No!' Cato intervened. 'Macro, we have to hold our course. If we hit another boat we're going to lose men.'

Macro clenched his teeth and nodded, seething with frustration.

The boats moved in towards the bank, cutting ripples through the calm surface of the Nile. On the bank the Arabs gathered and stood ready to resist the landing. Hundreds had dismounted and stood in bands, armed with round shields and curved swords. Some wore an assortment of conical helmets and scaled vests. Behind them, others sat atop their camels and prepared to shoot their bows, or hurl light javelins.

'Prepare to receive arrows!' Macro shouted across to the other boats.

The legionaries presented their shields towards the riverbank and hunched down behind them. Cato and Macro climbed down from the foredeck and took up their own shields and crouched down, peering over the rims as the boats drew closer to the riverbank.

'Here they come!' a voice cried out as the first volley of arrows slashed into the air, rising briefly before they seemed to slow fractionally at the top of their arc, then plunge down swiftly towards the line of boats sailing towards the bank. The enemy had held back until the boats were well within range and so none of the arrows fell short. There was a brief whirr before the splintering thud of an arrow striking the foredeck, the clatter as more ricocheted off the curved surface of the legionaries' shields and the plink of those shafts that missed their targets and plunged into the river. Cato glanced round at the men in the boat. There were no casualties amongst the soldiers. The two crewmen, however, looked terrified. As well they might, Cato thought. They wore simple tunics and lengths of cloth wrapped round their heads, and had no protection from the arrows.

The second wave of missiles shot out across the Nile in a more ragged volley as the more proficient archers notched, aimed and loosed their arrows ahead of their comrades. Then the rain of missiles merged into a continuous stream and the air around Cato was thick with the sound of the lethal iron heads splintering wood and punching into the shields. Some inevitably found their way through the shields, or were deflected by them and struck the men. The cohort's standard bearer, squatting down in the centre of the boat behind Cato and Macro, let out a sharp cry as a shaft pierced his bicep and he lost his grip of the standard. It began to topple towards the side of the felucca and one of the legionaries, fearful of the shame that would fall upon the cohort if the standard was lost, dropped his shield and grabbed the shaft of the standard just in time to stop it falling over the side.

'Good lad!' Macro called out to him. 'Take over from the signifer.'

'Yes, sir.' The legionary raised the standard and then passed his shield across to the wounded signifer before turning his attention back to the enemy.

'Watch it!' The man beside Cato pointed towards the bank. 'Javelins!'

Cato followed the direction indicated and saw that some of the camel riders had dismounted and were now preparing to hurl their weapons. The first ran forward a few paces and threw his javelin. It rose up into the sky at a more languid pace than the earlier arrows. More followed as the first dipped down towards the boat to the right of Cato. It slammed into a shield, piercing the cross laminated strips of wood and bursting through the forearm of the man behind. He let out a cry, then held the rim of his shield and wrenched his arm free of the head of the javelin with a roar of pain and anger. A loud thud wrenched Cato's attention back and he saw the shaft of a javelin quivering in the foredeck.

'Close,' Macro muttered.

There was a groan from the rear of the felucca and Cato glanced over his shoulder and saw that the helmsman had been struck in the midriff by an arrow. He stared down in shock until the blood began to blossom in the dirty cloth around the shaft. He let go of the tiller and grasped the arrow, pulling at it, and then screaming in agony as he blacked out. At once the boat began to come up into the wind, angling round towards the vessel to their left.

'Shit . . .' Cato muttered, seeing the danger at once. He turned swiftly to Macro. 'Hold my shield!'

His friend grasped the handle with his spare hand and Cato thrust his way back through the legionaries crowded into the boat, trying to ignore the continuing barrage of arrows and javelins. Above him the leech of the triangular sail began to flutter. The other crewman sat on the floor of the boat, pressing into the side of a legionary, his face a mask of frozen terror as he clutched the mainsheet in his hands as if it was a lifeline. Cato ignored him and pressed on. He reached for the end of the tiller and forced it round so that the craft began to turn away from the nearest boat. For a moment Cato thought the collision might be avoided, but the felucca was turning too slowly. On the deck of the other boat, faces turned towards the looming menace and then the beam of the felucca struck the side of the other boat. Both sails shimmered violently and the shock of the impact threw the men against each other. On the other boat an optio had been crouching on the foredeck, ready to lead his men ashore the moment his boat grounded. Instead, he lost his balance, tumbled to the side and slid overboard with a splash and did not resurface. More men were sent sprawling in a confusion of limbs and shouted curses.

The felucca rebounded from the impact and a fresh gust filled the sail, easing it round towards the shore as Cato centred the tiller. There was no chance to help the men of the other boat, nor spare them more than a moment's thought. No more than thirty feet from the riverbank the crewman released the mainsheet and the triangular sail billowed freely for a moment before it flapped in the light breeze. The momentum of the felucca carried it on and the craft had only lost a little speed when the boat lurched to an abrupt halt in the silt where a strip of reeds ran along the bank. Most of the legionaries had braced themselves but even so a number tumbled into their comrades and a chorus of grunts and curses broke out until Macro bellowed angrily at them.

'Shut your mouths! Shields up, swords out and follow me!'

He stepped up on to the foredeck, crouching slightly behind his shield, and took a running jump towards the riverbank. He landed with a splash and a brief rustle of trampled reeds. The water came up to his thighs and the silt on the river bed sucked at his boots. Gritting his teeth Macro pressed on, surging through the churned-up water, his shield brushing the reeds aside. He heard more men splashing down behind him, and a quick glance to either side revealed that the rest of the first wave of boats was edging into the reeds to disgorge their legionaries. The air was sweltering in amongst the reeds and Macro's ears filled with the rush of water and the grunts of his men as they struggled to gain firm ground. Over the rim of his shield he could see the nearest band of Arabs bearing down on them, giving vent to their battle cries as they raised their curved blades and charged down the short, grassy slope towards the Romans.

Macro emerged from the silt and checked his pace. More men rustled free of the reeds on either side, and then a moment later Cato was at his side, breathing heavily and eyes wide beneath the rim of his helmet as he braced his boots and raised the tip of his sword towards the oncoming enemy. The Romans were strung out in a ragged battle line along the riverbank and a moment later the dark-robed Arabs plunged in amongst the legionaries and the air was filled with the clatter and thud of shields striking and the sharp clash of metal as blade met blade.

Keeping his shield up, Macro took the first blows without striking back as he readied his sword, holding the handle tightly and drawing it back, ready to thrust. He heard the growl of an enemy on the other side of the shield and could smell the sour odour of camels that had impregnated the man's robes. He waited for the next blow, a cut down on to the metal trim of the shield, and then punched forwards, following up with a quick pace and another thrust which slammed into the body of the Arab. The man grunted as the breath was driven from his lungs. At once Macro swung his shield aside and stabbed with his sword. The Arab wore no armour and the point cut through the man's robes and lost none of its impetus before it struck his ribs. As Macro made to withdraw the blade, the Arab twisted to one side, snagging the sword and almost wresting it from Macro's hand.

'No you don't!' Macro snarled, wrenching the handle. 'Bloody rags these people dress in. Ain't bloody fair.'

With a ripping noise the blade came free and the Arab stumbled back, winded and bleeding. He glared at Macro, raised his shield and sword and fought to recover his breath. Then he attacked again. Macro deflected the blow with his shield, cut down on the man's wrist and then stabbed him in the throat. His foe collapsed on to his knees, dropping his sword as he clasped his neck, vainly trying to stem the blood pumping from the fatal wound. Macro stepped back a pace to quickly take stock of the situation.

To his right Cato was duelling a large Arab in a gleaming scale cuirass. A heavy curved blade, wider at the tip, slashed away at Cato's shield, driving him back until one of the legionaries struck at the Arab's leg, cutting through muscles and tendons. The man's leg gave way under him, he fell back, and Cato stepped up and struck a savage blow to the man's helmet, knocking him cold.

Along the bank of the Nile Macro could see that his men were steadily fighting their way up from the reeds. Above them, fifty paces to his left, Ajax sat on his horse, urging his men on as he punched his sword into the air. Macro turned towards a group of men who had landed from the same boat. 'On me! Form up on me!'

The legionaries hurried into a wedge behind their

centurion, and Cato, seeing them, joined the small formation.

'Let's go!' Macro called out, pacing diagonally across the bank towards Ajax. Only a handful of the enemy stood before them, and some of these hurried away from the cluster of Romans to find easier opponents still floundering at the water's edge. Others, braver, threw themselves on Macro's small band and paid the price for their single-handed pursuit of glory. Then, as the wedge neared the top of the bank, the gladiator turned and saw the danger.

He bellowed an order to the nearest group of camel archers who stood waiting, weapons poised, as they could not shoot for fear of hitting their comrades. Ajax thrust his sword towards Macro and the others and shouted his command in Greek. 'Shoot 'em down! Kill them!'

His meaning was clear and needed no translation. The archers raised their bows, aimed down the bank, and loosed the arrows at close range. Cato winced as a barbed head burst through the inside of his shield, close to his face. To his right a man cried out as a shaft pierced his leg, chipping bone and cutting through muscle just below the knee. He staggered to a halt and crouched helplessly, unable to either continue the advance or shelter behind his shield and deal with the injury.

'Cut it out, man!' Cato yelled at him. 'Cut it out and move on, or stay here and die.'

The small formation closed up and continued forward into the storm of arrows, leaving their comrade behind. The shattering cracks and splitting of wood filled Cato's ears in a deafening cacophony as he paced forward at Macro's shoulder, hunched down behind his shield to protect his legs as best as he could. But being tall, his helmet and crest projected a little above the rim of the shield and an arrow tore through the crest, wrenching the helmet, and then another shot glanced off the top of it, knocking his head slightly to one side and making him briefly dizzy. Cato shook his head and staggered on, fearing that he might stumble and fall, and be at the mercy of the enemy archers. But the dizziness cleared and he clenched his jaw and followed Macro up and on to the bank.

The enemy loosed their last arrows before dropping their bows across their saddle horns and drawing their swords. They snatched up their reins and urged their camels towards the Romans. The beasts let out raw, throaty grunts as they charged with a loping gait.

'Hold!' Macro yelled, bracing his feet apart and pushing his shield out, ready to absorb the impact of the charge. Cato and the others followed suit and crouched, swords ready, sweating under the weight of their armour and the exertion of scrambling ashore and up the bank. The leading camel's neck stretched out above the rim of Macro's shield an instant before its heavy chest struck it a glancing blow. The rider reached out and forward, slashing down with his curved blade, which split the rim of the shield, leaving the tip a few inches from Macro's head. The Arab was at the limit of his reach and Macro rose up and hacked into the neck of the camel instead. The beast's jaw fell open and the tongue shot out as it gave a deep bleat of agony, then swerved aside, away from the small knot of Roman soldiers and straight across the path of the other riders. The camel staggered and collapsed on to its knees.

Another animal stumbled into its flank, nearly unseating its rider. The rest stopped abruptly or tried to swerve aside. Their riders shouted angrily, struggling to regain control of their mounts, as dust swirled about the long spindly legs of the camels.

Macro instantly sized up the situation. 'Jackals! At 'em!'

He ran round the stricken camel as its rider tried to recover his balance and threw himself into the confusion of the riders and beasts beyond. Keeping his shield up, Macro hacked at the dark skin of a bare leg that appeared in front of him. Then, as the rider yelled and steered his mount away, Macro turned and saw another man above him, black against the glaring sun. Squinting, he could not see the blade he knew was slashing down towards him and could only throw up his sword arm to try and block the blow. There was a resounding clang of metal on metal and then the shock of the impact driving down Macro's arm, wrenching his strong wrists and the powerful muscles bunched around his elbow and shoulder joints. The Arab's blade struck the transverse crest of his helmet, breaking through the bronze strip and finally striking the iron reinforcement ridge that crossed his helmet from side to side. The blow would have killed him outright had he failed to block it, but the impact dazed him, blinding his vision with white sparks. He staggered, weaving from side to side, still holding his shield up while his sword arm hung limply at his side. A wave of nausea seized him and Macro feared that he might pass out.

'The fuck I will,' he growled to himself.

He shook his head and his vision began to clear. A fresh blow glanced off his shield, and then he heard a shocked gasp. Glancing to his side, he saw that Cato was between himself and the camel and had punched his sword up into its rider's guts. The Arab wheeled his camel away and clasped a hand to his wound as he rode out of the small cluster of men locked in combat. One of the legionaries was down, a long slash in his sword arm that had opened up flesh and muscle to reveal the bone beneath. But the enemy had lost two men, lying still in the dust, and more were wounded, and now they fell back, away from the heavily armoured infantrymen. Two men started after the enemy but Macro called them back angrily and then turned his attention back to Ajax.

The gladiator was trying to rally the camel archers but they were losing the fight along the riverbank. The legionaries were pushing their way up the slope and spilling out into the fields of wheat beyond. Ajax unleashed his rage at his men, bellowing at them to stand and fight. Though they shared no common tongue there was no mistaking his will, yet his men avoided his eye as they flowed back across the fields.

'Let's go at him,' Cato breathed heavily. 'While we have the chance.'

Macro turned to the other men. 'Come on!'

The two officers led the small party of legionaries towards the gladiator and the handful of mounted men who remained with him. Ajax was staring bitterly after his fleeing allies and was only alerted to the danger when one of his men called out to him and pointed towards the Romans quickly closing in on them. Ajax turned in his saddle and glared for a moment before his expression changed to one of a man in a torment of frustration. He reached for his sword handle and his hand hovered there briefly before he took up his reins and urged his horse away from the riverbank.

Cato felt a leaden pain in his heart at the prospect of Ajax evading them and he yelled out towards the horsemen, 'Stand and fight, cowards! Fight us!'

Ajax's horse high-stepped as his master locked eyes with Cato, then Ajax kicked his heels in and he and his men galloped away across the field, amid the fleeing forms of their Arab allies. Cato ran as hard as he could after them, crunching over the trampled wheat, but they made good their escape and he drew up, gasping for breath as he watched them head for the pale walls of a distant temple.

'Bastard,' Macro panted as he stopped beside Cato. 'Bastard didn't have the balls to stand . . . and face us.'

Cato licked his dry lips and fought for breath. His armour felt like a vice around his body, crushing him under the burden of its weight and the heat which prickled like that from an open oven. He took a deep breath and swallowed. Closing his eyes, Cato spoke through clenched teeth. 'He tasks us . . . tasks us to the limit of our endurance.'

Cato's eyes flickered open. He drew himself up, looked along the riverbank to see the legionaries wearily forming up around their standards. He let out an impatient breath. 'We'd better send word to the legate. Tell him we have secured the bank.'

'I'll see to it,' said Macro.

'And have the rest of your men and the artillery landed as quickly as possible.' Cato gestured towards the temple and continued harshly, 'If they think that they'll be safe in there, they're in for a surprise. They'll be caught. Trapped. This time there'll be no escape.'

CHAPTER TWENTY-SIX

There was a dull thud as another ballista bolt tore into the mud bricks of the outer wall and a small cloud of dust shivered into the air. Ajax squinted down from the top of the pylon and by the failing light he saw that the interior of the wall was cracked and crumbling from top to bottom. The sun had already set and the sky was a deep violet, pricked by the steely glitter of the early evening stars. The Romans were already building fires around the perimeter of the temple wall to ensure that there would be some light to detect any attempt by the defenders to escape. After they had forced a way across the Nile they had brought up three more cohorts of legionaries and some cavalry as well as the battery of bolt throwers from the island.

Ajax had been surprised by the speed with which the Romans had moved to surround the temple complex, and the first of the bolt throwers had begun to shoot the moment it had been set up opposite the curtain wall. Then, as the rest of the weapons were hauled forward by cart, the bombardment had intensified late into the afternoon and early evening.

Two more bolts slammed into the mud bricks.

'They'll have a breach in the outer wall before the first

hour of the night is over,' Karim muttered. 'Then all that stands before them will be the barricades we've put together across the entrances to the temple.'

'Not quite the fortress I had hoped it might be,' said Ajax.

The heavy tall timber doors of the main gate between the first pair of pylons had been reinforced with palm logs cut from the trees that grew a short distance away. The narrow side entrances had also been blocked up with makeshift palisades and parties of Arab warriors armed with swords and spears stood behind the defences, grimly determined to keep the Romans out for as long as possible. After all, Ajax reflected, that was the purpose of the raid down the western bank of the Nile. To delay the enemy advance and give Prince Talmis a free hand to devastate the Roman province along the upper Nile. Ajax and his column were supposed to tie the Romans down for several days but the enemy had reacted far more swiftly and resolutely than Ajax expected. As things stood, his position was looking decidedly perilous.

There was another impact on the wall, near the breach, and this time the shaft burst through before clattering against the solid stone of the temple.

'Perhaps we should try to break out before it's too late, General,' Karim suggested cautiously.

Ajax smiled. 'You think it was a bad decision to make a stand here, my friend.'

Karim pursed his lips. 'It is not for me to say. You command, I follow.'

'That's right. I have my reasons for remaining here.' Ajax pointed towards a cluster of Roman officers standing on a small mound. 'They are there, the two men in this world that I most want to kill.'

'You are certain it was them?'

'I saw them with my own eyes. I heard them call for me.' Ajax gritted his teeth. 'I would have charged them down in an instant had there been a chance to face them individually.' He stared at the distant figures of the enemy officers, their helmet crests and polished breastplates gleaming in the light of a nearby fire as the flames fiercely consumed the dried palm leaves that served as kindling.

'You can be sure that when the Romans attack, those two will be leading their men. And I shall be waiting for them.' He turned to Karim. 'Perhaps it is as well that we are trapped here in the temple. There is no retreat for us now. We hold out as long as we can, and the chance to face my enemies will come. They will die on my sword. Both of them.'

'And we shall die with them,' Karim added quietly. 'You, me, those who have followed you since the first days of the revolt, and our Arab allies. Is that the best way to defy Rome, General?'

Ajax slowly ran a hand through his thick curls. His hair had grown longer than he liked. He preferred a short crop, enough to absorb the sweat on his scalp so that it did not course down his brow when he was fighting. He sighed. 'I begin to grow weary of defying Rome. Of being forced to run and always looking back for sign of my pursuers. There comes a time when the prey must turn and face the hunter. Then there is a last chance to die with purpose, with dignity. Perhaps that time has come. If so, then I shall kill as many Romans as I can while I still breathe. If

the gods are kind, then I shall kill Macro and Cato as well.'
Ajax looked at his friend and clasped his arm. 'Is that such
a bad end? To die on your feet, sword in your hand, with
your comrades – your friends – at your side?'

Karim nodded solemnly. 'Better than to live as a slave,
my General.'

'That is not living,' Ajax replied. 'Merely existing.'

There was another series of thuds as the enemy bolt
throwers continued to break down the mud-brick wall,
then a rumble as a large section gave way and collapsed
into the temple compound in a swirl of dust. There was a
short pause before a brassy note sounded from the Roman
lines. The bolt throwers ceased shooting and then the
signal blew again and a column of legionaries quickly
formed up just out of bowshot from the temple. Eight
men abreast and twenty or so ranks deep. This would be
the legion's First Cohort, Ajax knew. The most powerful
unit at the disposal of the commander of the Roman army.
A handful of officers broke away from the group who had
been surveying the temple's defences and joined the
column. Thanks to his spy in the Roman army, Ajax knew
that Macro was the commander of the First Cohort, and
he found himself praying fervently that Cato would be
joining him in the attack on the temple.

Ajax turned to Karim. 'Pass the word. The breach is
made and the Romans are coming. Have the archers make
ready to give our friends a warm welcome.'

Karim nodded. 'Yes, my General.'

As Karim hurried down the steps leading from the top
of the pylon, Ajax beckoned the Arabs standing a
deferential distance from their commander at the far end

of the platform. They came over and he pointed out the Roman column. Their leader nodded his understanding, his lips parting to reveal gleaming teeth. A moment later Karim's voice carried up to Ajax, and then there were more shouts as his orders were conveyed to the Arabs by the Nubian officers versed in Greek and Arab tongues as well as their own. As the enemy's bucinas sounded again and the column tramped out of the gloom towards the breach, Ajax looked down to see his men scaling the makeshift ladders to bring them up on to the roof of the temple. On the other pylons he could see a small flicker of fire as they lit their bundles of brushwood and dried palm leaves. The flames quickly took hold and illuminated the archers standing by, the first of their arrows drawn from their quivers. Strips of cloth impregnated with oil and pitch had been wound around the shafts, just behind the arrow heads, ready to be ignited the moment the order was given. Karim came running back up the stairs, breathing heavily. He swallowed and made his report.

'The men are ready, General.'

Ajax nodded and then the two men turned to watch the legionaries tramping towards the breach. Behind them, the archers struck some sparks into a tinder box. A moment later the tiny flame was applied to the kindling in the iron brazier and the flames quickly took hold.

'They're in range,' Karim announced. 'Shall I give the order?'

'Not yet.' Ajax strained his eyes as he scrutinised the head of the column. There were two crested helmets there. Officers. 'We'll wait until they reach the wall. I want the first volley to strike them as hard as possible.'

Karim nodded, and they stood in silence and watched as the Romans crossed the stony sand towards the breach, a long black line that seemed like a giant armoured centipede in the gathering darkness. As they approached, an order was shouted and the leading ranks turned their shields to the front to present an unbroken line, sheltering the men behind. They slowed as they reached the rubble below the breach and began to climb up the pile of crumbling mud bricks. As the first men entered the gap in the curtain wall, Ajax cleared his throat.

'Now.'

Karim cupped both hands to his mouth and cried out, 'Archers! Ignite arrows!'

The order was instantly relayed to the Arabs who crowded round the flames of the braziers, offering up the rags at the end of the arrow shafts. Karim drew a deep breath. 'Shoot at will!'

The first arrow rose up in a shallow blazing arc from the far end of the temple and then plunged down into the breach. At once more followed, cutting through the darkness as they converged on the breach, as if the gap in the wall was drawing them in upon itself. The fire arrows rained down onto the head of the Roman column. Some fell harmlessly to the ground, their flames dying away to a flicker as they stuck in the soil. Others burst into sparks as they clattered against the wall, or glanced off the shields and armour of the legionaries. A few found their way through the shields and punched into exposed flesh.

The fiery flow continued, illuminating the breach in an uneven flickering light. Ajax heard the same voice bark out another order and the leading century of the Roman column halted and formed a tortoise. The shields rose up above the legionaries' heads to provide an overlapping roof to protect them from the barrage of fire arrows that rattled down.

There was a sharp crack just below the top of the platform and Ajax glanced over the edge to see a long shaft clattering down. The Roman bolt throwers had begun to shoot again in an attempt to disrupt the aim of the archers. More shots clattered off the sides of the pylons, but some struck home, snatching men off the platforms to send them tumbling down the sides of the pylons, past the vast carved depictions of Egypt's ancient gods.

The Romans pressed on through the breach, leaving several of their men dead and injured in their wake. Closing up their ranks, the men at the head of the column tramped across the narrow strip of open ground. They made for the barricade across the opening through the temple wall into the first of the colonnaded courtyards inside. Ajax stared hard at the leading century but could not see any sign of the two Roman officers.

'Keep shooting,' he ordered the Arab officer in command of the archers. Then he turned towards the stairs leading down into the interior of the pylon. 'Come, Karim.'

They hurried down the steep flight of steps lit at each level by the wan glow of an oil lamp. The first sounds of fighting echoed up the walls from outside and Ajax quickened his pace. As he emerged from the base of the pylon he saw his men crowded between the columns to his left. Ajax drew his sword and ran across towards them.

'Make way!' he called out. 'Move!'

The Arabs glanced round and stepped aside to clear a path towards the barricaded entrance. The gap between the curtain wall and the temple was no more than eight feet wide and had been filled with blocks of stone removed from the small courtyard in front of the main pylons to form a slim fighting ledge. Some of Ajax's gladiators stood there, ready to cut down any Roman that tried to get over. On either side, on top of the temple wall, the Arab archers continued to draw their bows and loose arrows at the Roman column stretching back towards the breach. The legionaries presented a clear target in the flickering glare of the fire arrows and were forced to hunch down behind their shields as they waited for the vanguard to break through into the heart of the temple.

Ajax and Karim heaved themselves up on to the ledge and stood alongside the handful of men defending the wall. A few bodies littered the open ground and the head of the Roman column stood off, twenty feet away, shields protecting the soldiers from the missiles angling in from each side as well as from above. Every so often one of the Romans would bob up to hurl a javelin at the defenders. They had little time to take careful aim before they quickly ducked back behind their shields.

'What are they waiting for?' Ajax muttered to himself.

He had barely spoken when he saw a slow ripple passing down the centre of the Roman column. Then, over at the breach, he saw more men spilling out into the gap between the curtain wall and the temple. They wore the conical helmets and scale armour of auxiliary archers and carried wooden screens with them. The screens were quickly set down and the supports kicked back and then the archers set to work targeting the Arabs on the pylons and the walls of the temple. Ajax paid them little regard, he was more concerned by the activity within the column of legionaries. The shield wall at the front of the formation abruptly parted and a small party of men ran forward with a ramp made from lengths of palm logs tied to a ladder. Another party carrying a second ramp rushed out behind them and they made straight for the barricade.

'Shoot them down!' Ajax shouted, thrusting his arm out. The nearest archers on the roof of the temple turned at once, aimed down and loosed their shafts. Two men fell, one clutching at the arrow that had passed through his thigh, the other shot through the neck. But the ramp carriers ran on. When they reached the wall, the leading pair heaved the end of the ladder up and the poles clattered down on the top of the barricade. At once the nearest Roman soldiers broke ranks and surged forward, boots thudding down on the ramp before the defenders could push it away. Ajax thrust at the poles of the second ramp before the first of the legionaries reached it and the ramp grated back and then toppled to one side. The iron nails of the boots of the leading legionary scraped on the palm logs as he charged up towards the defenders. Ajax glimpsed the shield above him, and the sword blade rising up, gleaming as it caught the light from one of the archers' braziers. He hacked horizontally, beneath the rim of the shield, and the edge of his blade bit into the Roman's shin, just above his ankle, cutting through flesh and muscle before shattering bone. The man let up a shrill cry as his leg gave way and he fell back on the legionary behind him. The second man was knocked off balance and fell off the ramp, together with his wounded comrade, and both landed with a heavy clatter as their armour and shields struck the ground.

The next men rushed up the ramp. This time the leading soldier was more wary, keeping his shield low as he reached the top of the wall. Ajax held his sword hand back as he grasped the edge of the shield and gave it a quick wrench. He managed to pull it at an angle, exposing the thigh and side of the legionary. The gladiator to Ajax's left was armed with a spear and instantly took advantage of the opening to thrust into the Roman's leg. The strike was quickly made and lacked the force to make a crippling wound. Even so, the legionary groaned and drew back momentarily. Then, realising that there was no retreat for him, as his comrades pressed from behind, he came on again, punching his shield out and striking Ajax on the chest. There was nothing Ajax could do to avoid the shield and he rode back with it and fell off the wall, crashing down on to the Arabs waiting beneath. Two of them broke his fall and they collapsed under the bulky weight of the gladiator. The landing drove the wind out of his lungs and for a brief moment Ajax lay stunned on top of the squirming Arabs. Then he struggled back on to his feet and looked up to see that the spearman had struck again, this time into the legionary's groin, and the Roman doubled up, dropping his shield. Karim had climbed up into Ajax's place and now finished the man with a deep cut into his exposed neck. The Roman collapsed on to the ramp and slid back a short distance into the next man.

The end of the second ramp appeared on top of the

wall again and Ajax shouted up to his men, 'Push it back! Keep 'em off the barricade!'

The head and shoulders of the first legionary to make a run up the second ramp appeared as the only other man on the wall hacked at the end of the ramp with a heavy falcata. The wood splintered and Karim struck again as the legionary loomed over him. The strut gave way with a loud crack and pitched the Roman over on to the other ramp, right in the path of one of his comrades who stumbled to a halt just in time to stop himself tripping.

'Don't bloody stop! Go! Go forward!' Macro's voice bellowed from the other side of the wall. Ajax felt his heart harden and grasped the edge of the platform. Heaving himself up, he thrust one of his gladiators aside. 'Get off.'

As the man jumped down, Ajax stared into the enemy soldiers milling around below him until he caught sight of the transverse crest of Macro's helmet. The Roman was standing to one side of his men, and there beside him was the taller form of another officer – his friend, the prefect. Ajax sheathed his sword and turned to wrench the spear out of the next man's hands. It would have been gratifying to save his enemy for a more lingering death, but Ajax knew that he must seize the chance to strike before it passed. At his side Karim clashed with another legionary attempting to cross the barricade. Ajax ignored the thud of Karim's sword on the Roman's shield and hefted the spear into an overhand grip. He raised it up above his head and drew his arm back as he took aim at the two officers. A grim feeling of satisfaction filled his mind as he recalled a similar situation back on Crete when it was Macro who was defending a wall and had hurled the spear that had killed one of Ajax's closest companions.

He breathed deeply and then exhaled in a long, calm breath and threw his arm forward, releasing the shaft of the spear. It flew down from the wall, straight towards the two men.

'Macro! Look out!' The prefect shoved his friend aside an instant before the spear would have caught him squarely in the chest. Instead it struck the prefect, high on the left shoulder, the impact sending him sprawling into the sand and grit of the open ground before the temple wall.

'Ha!' Ajax snarled though gritted teeth, his face fixed in an expression of savage triumph. He just had time to spare the two officers one last look, as Macro stooped over his friend, and then Ajax snatched out his sword and turned back to the fight alongside him. Karim was still duelling with the same Roman, exchanging sword blows that rang sharply. But the legionary was one against two and even as he parried another thrust, Ajax hooked his blade around the edge of the shield and ran it through his enemy's arm, severing muscles. The shield slipped from the Roman's grasp and he instinctively recoiled a pace, out of range of their swords. At once two arrows slammed into him from above, piercing his sword arm in two places. The Roman howled in agony and staggered to the side and fell off the ramp, tumbling on to the bodies of those below.

The attackers at the bottom of the ramp hesitated, then one was struck in the face by another arrow and jerked up to his full height and trembled wildly for an instant before he dropped to the ground. There were more bodies on either side of the leading century as well as a handful of Arabs who had been shot down from the wall of the temple.

'Fall back!' a voice cried out. 'Fall back!'

There was a brief hesitation, then Ajax saw the legion-aries begin to shuffle away from the end of the surviving ramp. More of them took up the cry and the leading century began to break up as it fell back towards the breach.

'Stop!' Macro bellowed at them. 'Stand your ground! Damn you! Cowards!'

Ajax saw him half rise as he cursed his men, then Macro looked down at the still figure at his feet. For a moment the centurion seemed torn, then he bent down and heaved his superior on to his shoulder and began to pace after his men under the awkward burden. Ajax felt sick to the core at the thought of his enemies escaping, then a handful of arrows landed in the sand close to Macro.

'Shoot at the officers!' Ajax shouted, stabbing his sword towards them. 'Shoot them down!'

In the frenzied excitement of the attack only those men nearest to him heard the order and had the presence of mind to pick out the two Roman officers. Ajax watched intently as more shafts whirled through the wavering light of the fire arrows still burning where they had landed. Macro picked up his pace, scrambling away as fast as he could, jinking from side to side to put off the archers' aim. An arrow glanced off the prefect's armour and another flew past Macro's helmet as he made a last dash towards a cluster of the screens that had been erected by the auxiliary archers. Macro unceremoniously dumped Cato down in their shelter and stumbled to his knees beside the prefect.

'Shit,' Ajax muttered furiously, clenching his spare fist. He continued to glare at the archers' screens as Macro dragged his friend in to make him as safe as possible from the Arab archers, whose arrows struck the screen or buried their iron heads into the dusty ground instead. Most of the men from the First Century had already reached the safety of the breach, or were also taking shelter behind the screens. As Ajax watched, the Romans continued to withdraw, the prefect protected by several archers holding their screens up as Macro and some of his men carried Cato to safety. As the last of the Romans fell back through the breach, Ajax ground his teeth.

'We should save our arrows, sir,' said Karim.

Ajax cleared his mind of rage and nodded. 'Give the order.'

'Cease shooting!' Karim called out to each side. 'Cease shooting!'

The Arabs stopped loosing their arrows and climbed down from the temple wall, leaving a handful to keep watch on the enemy. The last of the auxiliary archers pulled back to the other side of the breach and shortly afterwards the bolt throwers fell silent. The night air was disturbed only by a gentle breeze and the cries of the wounded, Roman and Arab blended in a chorus of agony. A handful of the fire arrows still burned, as did the braziers on the pylons and walls of the temple, casting a thin orange light across the scene of the Romans' first assault. They had lost over twenty men, Ajax estimated. But more than that, they had suffered a blow to their morale. The next time they came forward, they would know that they faced a storm of arrows and the same determined defence of the barricade. They would have to advance past the bodies of their comrades and ignore the pitiful cries for help from the wounded. The Roman commander would think twice before making a second frontal assault.

'What now?' Karim mused quietly. 'Do you think they'll make another attempt tonight?'

Ajax pondered for a moment. 'I would, if I was in their place. Every hour they are delayed here is an hour gained for Prince Talmis . . . They'll attack again.'

'Then what should we do, General?'

'Do?' Ajax smiled thinly. 'Nothing. I doubt that even our spy can help us now.'

CHAPTER TWENTY-SEVEN

'How is he?' Macro stood over his friend as the legion's surgeon carefully inspected Cato's shoulder by the light of an oil lamp held by his assistant.

The surgeon sucked in an impatient breath. Without looking up he spoke. 'I might be able to tell you, sir, if you would be kind enough not to stand between the light and my patient.'

Macro stood back a pace.

'Thank you.' The surgeon bent towards Cato and examined the prefect's shoulder. As soon as Macro had withdrawn from the temple compound, he had two of his men carry Cato back as far as the bolt throwers and then sent for the surgeon at once. Cato had struck his head on the ground as the impact of the spear knocked him off his feet. He had blacked out and came round as Macro and Hamedes had carried him away from the curtain wall. He was still dazed, but aware enough of the pain in his shoulder to curse and mumble incoherently. Macro had removed Cato's helmet, harness and scaled armour before the surgeon arrived and now Cato lay on a pile of straw in the corner of a small stable where the air was rich with the aroma of dung. Macro had ordered Hamedes to wait outside rather than crowd the space unnecessarily.

The surgeon eased the tunic off Cato's shoulder and looked closely at the discoloured flesh. 'No open wound. That's good. He was hit by a spear, you say?'

'Yes. Seemed to catch him square on.'

'Hmmm.' The surgeon touched the flesh as lightly as he could and traced his fingers along the collarbone. 'No breaks there. I'll have to probe the shoulder joint. It's going to hurt. I'll need you to hold him down.'

Macro knelt down and firmly grasped Cato's uninjured arm with one hand and pressed his chest back with the other. 'Ready.'

The surgeon leaned forward and gently took hold of Cato's shoulder in both hands. He felt softly for any sign of broken bones or the slackness of torn muscle tissue. Cato's eyes rolled up and he groaned in agony. Satisfied with his superficial examination the surgeon probed more deeply into the shoulder.

'Fuck!' Cato yelled, attempting to sit bolt upright. His eyes were wide open and he glared at the surgeon. 'Bastard!' He head-butted the other man on the cheek.

Macro thrust him back down. 'Easy, lad! He's just tending your injury.'

Cato turned his gaze to Macro with a dazed expression. He nodded and gritted his teeth. 'All right. Go on, then.'

The surgeon rubbed his cheek and then turned his attention back to Cato's shoulder. He pressed his fingers into the discoloured flesh and Macro felt his friend go as tense as a length of timber as he stared straight up, focusing on fighting the agony of his examination. The surgeon thoroughly examined the shoulder and then eased himself back with a satisfied nod.

'Some bad bruising but no broken bones. It'll hurt like hell for some days and you'll need to keep it strapped up, but there should be no lasting effects. I understand you took a blow to the head as well.'

Cato frowned, trying to remember.

'It's common not to recall the incident. How do you feel?'

'Not good.' Cato swallowed and winced. 'Head hurts. Still feel a bit dazed . . . I can recall the attack. Then a spear in the air. Then nothing.'

'Well, that's fine,' the surgeon concluded with a reassuring pat of Cato's hand. 'At least your brain's not been scrambled.'

Macro shrugged. 'Can't say that I'd notice much difference . . .'

The surgeon stood up. 'I want you to rest. Until the dizziness has passed. Then you can get back on your feet. The shoulder's going to be painful for several days, and stiff. Better keep it in a sling. Other than that, I'd say you have had a lucky escape, sir. Just try to stay out of the path of spears, javelins and arrows from now on, eh?'

Macro gave him a droll look and then turned his attention back to Cato as the surgeon left the stable. For a moment neither man spoke, then Macro cleared his throat self-consciously. 'I suppose I should thank you.'

'Thank me?'

Macro frowned. 'Of course. You saved me from that spear.'

'I did?'

'You don't remember it then?'

Cato closed his eyes briefly and then shook his head.

'All right,' said Macro eagerly. 'Forget about it. I'd better go. The legate will want to know what to do next. You stay here and rest, eh?'

He turned and strode across to the entrance to the stable.

'Macro . . .' Cato called weakly.

The centurion turned and looked back.

'Whatever I did, you'd have done the same for me,' Cato said. 'If you'd been standing in my place.'

'True, but I wouldn't have ended up here.' Macro chuckled. 'I'm not lanky like you. If I'd pushed you aside, the bloody spear would have missed me by a mile. Now do as the surgeon said and get some rest.' He left the stable and gestured to Hamedes to follow him.

The legate was sitting on a crude table outside the ruins of a peasant's hut when Macro found him. His staff officers and the centurions from Macro's cohort and the auxiliaries were gathered about him in the loom cast by an oil lamp, waiting. Another of the legion's surgeons had just finished suturing a small gash on the legate's forearm and began to apply a dressing as Aurelius addressed Macro over the surgeon's shoulder.

'Good of you to finally join us.'

'I was seeing to the senior tribune, sir,' Macro replied with a hint of bitterness. 'He was struck by a spear during the attack.'

'How bad is the wound?' Aurelius asked with a trace of anxiety.

'He was lucky, sir. The tribune's a bit battered but he'll recover.'

'Good, we need every man.' Aurelius nodded down towards the dressing being tied round his arm. 'I took a wound myself. An arrow tore open my arm.'

The surgeon glanced up with a surprised expression and shook his head as he finished tying off the ends of the dressing. He straightened up and stood off a respectful distance. 'It's only a flesh wound, sir. But I'd advise you to keep it clean all the same.'

Aurelius nodded and waved the surgeon away. He smiled warmly at Macro. 'A bloody business that first attack, eh? I came forward to watch your progress from the breach. That's when I was wounded.'

He gestured proudly at the dressing with his other hand. Macro did not miss the tone of elation in his voice – the elation of a man who has finally received his first wound after many years of peaceful service without the least chance to prove himself as a soldier.

'Still,' the legate went on, 'it's only a brief setback. We'll take the place with the next attack. I'm certain of it.'

Macro regarded his superior thoughtfully. Aurelius was in a dangerously cheerful mood. Macro had served in the legions long enough to know the symptoms. Having survived an injury, even one as slight as being grazed by an arrow, Aurelius felt invulnerable. He had nothing to prove to his men. He had bled on the battlefield and had earned his right to order them to continue the fight, whatever the cost. The effect would wear off in a few hours, Macro knew. That was the usual experience of having survived a near miss. Cold rationality would soon moderate the legate's sudden zeal for battle. The trick of it would be restraining the man's urge to fight until the proper measures could be taken for the next assault on the temple.

'We'll take it all right, sir,' Macro agreed. 'The moment we've made our preparations.'

'Preparations?'

'Of course, sir. We need to bring forward the bolt throwers to cover the assault at close range. If we knock some loopholes through the curtain wall, the bolt throwers can easily pick off the enemy archers without exposing our crews. Also, we should make sure that any escape routes from the temple are covered.' Macro nodded towards Hamedes. 'The lad here used to be a priest. He knows the layout of the temple. He visited it only recently. Isn't that right?'

Hamedes nodded nervously in front of the legion's senior officers. 'Yes, sir.'

'So tell us what you know,' Macro continued. 'How many exits does the place have?'

Hamedes collected his thoughts as best he could before he replied. 'There's the main entrance between the largest pair of pylons. The doors there are huge, sir. Several inches thick. Even then, there's a small courtyard in front of that with another gate. Besides the main entrance, there are two entrances on either side of the main temple. The one we attacked earlier, and another on the opposite side. They are bound to have fortified that as well, sir.'

'Well, there is only one way to be certain,' Aurelius responded testily. 'I want you to go and see. Report back to Centurion Macro the moment you return.'

Hamedes glanced at Macro who nodded subtly. Hamedes

swallowed and bowed his head. 'As you command, sir.'

He walked hesitantly towards the temple and was soon swallowed up in the darkness. Aurelius turned back to Macro. 'While Cato is out of action you are my second-in-command. You're an experienced soldier, so we'll do as you suggest. Get the bolt throwers forward. Do whatever else you have to to make sure the next attack succeeds. Is that clear?'

'Yes, sir.' Macro nodded.

'And make certain there is no way for the enemy to escape. I want them all killed or captured.' Aurelius reached a hand up to touch his brow. 'Now, I must rest. My wound has weakened me. Wake me the instant we are ready to launch the second assault.'

As the night wore on and a hunter's moon rose low on the horizon, the sound of the Romans' preparations carried clearly to the defenders of the temple: the steady pounding of the outer wall as the legionaries gouged holes out of the mud bricks, and the sawing of wood and hammering of nails as they laboured by the light of some fires out of sight behind a mound two hundred yards back from the curtain wall. From the top of the pylon Ajax could just glimpse some of the legionaries at work and guessed that they would be making new assault ramps and, in all probability, a ram as well. If the first failed, then the latter would surely smash down the roughly constructed barricade. Once that happened, nothing could stop the Romans forcing their way into the temple and crushing the defenders.

Ajax had already considered making an attempt to

break out, but he had seen the legionaries patrolling round the temple earlier in the night, as well as the small parties of men methodically laying a barrier of obstacles on the ground. Caltrops, Ajax guessed. Four vicious iron prongs forged in such a way that however they were cast on to the ground, one spike always pointed up, ready to impale the hoof or foot of anyone attempting to charge over it. Beyond the foot patrols he had also heard the sound of cavalry; hoofs and occasional neighs as they patrolled further out beyond the temple walls.

Midnight came and went and the low moon drifted across the sky, casting a glimmering trail of reflections across the water of the Nile before passing out of sight behind the hills on the far bank. Ajax knew that he was trapped. The remainder of the men who had survived the rebellion on Crete, and the Arab warriors entrusted to him by Prince Talmis, all of them were doomed. The sentiment that filled his heart was not fear, nor failure, only a profound sense of frustration that he had not caused more damage to Roman interests in his brief life. He hoped that his spear had fatally wounded the prefect, and raged that Macro still lived, and might well outlive the final assault on the temple. The thought of dying with his thirst for revenge only half satisfied sickened Ajax. Not that his men would know it; his expression was impassive as he stared towards the Roman lines. To his fighters he was as fearless and resolute as ever and they were readily inspired by his example.

An hour after midnight there was a hurried slap of sandals on the steps inside the pylon and a moment later the dark form of Karim stood panting at his side.

'What is it?'

'General, please come with me. Now.'

Ajax caught the urgency in the other man's voice and turned to face him. 'What is it?'

'It's simpler if you follow me, sir.' Karim looked meaningfully at the other men on the pylon. Some of the Arabs and their officer were in earshot.

'Very well.' Ajax nodded and followed his companion down the stairs. Once they had descended the first three flights, he spoke softly. 'What's happened?'

Karim glanced back over his shoulder. 'It's our man, General. He's here in the temple.'

'Canthus?' Ajax was surprised. He could not think why the spy had taken such a risk to enter the temple, and stifled a surge of anger. The spy had provided useful information about the Roman army and its senior officers, passed on to Prince Talmis's scouts waiting outside Diospolis Magna. His identity had to be kept safe. Whatever the spy's reason for crossing the lines, it had better be good.

Karim nodded. 'Came over the northern barricade. He said he must speak with you.'

'Where is he?'

'I took him to one of the offering rooms, to keep him out of sight.'

'Good.' Ajax approved. Even if the temple fell, Canthus might yet provide some advantage to Prince Talmis, if his identity remained a secret.

They crossed the courtyard and entered the colonnaded hall leading to the shrine. It was dark inside and only the flame burning in the shrine at the far end lit their way.

Two small chambers stood each side of the shrine holding the sacred barge. It had been a very long time since the priests of the temple had received the kind of rich offerings to the gods that had once been commonplace. Now the hall and the chambers smelled musky and abandoned.

A dark shape appeared in the doorway of the offering chamber to the left of the shrine.

'General?' a voice whispered.

'Canthus.' Ajax approached him, his expression hard. 'What are you doing here?'

'General, you have to get out of this trap while there is still the chance. If you stay here, you will die.'

'If that is what the gods will then I will show those Romans how a real man dies, with dignity and honour.'

There was a brief silence before Karim spoke. 'They will not allow that. They will kill you only once you are a broken man, when you can be disposed of in the most humiliating manner possible. That will be the legacy you leave behind for the Empire's slaves, General.'

Ajax knew it was the truth and he nodded wearily. 'Then I must not be taken alive. I shall die here, if not by a Roman sword, then by my own hand, or by yours, my friend.'

'No,' Karim interrupted. 'While there is a chance of you continuing our fight against Rome, you must live. With Ajax at large, no Roman can sleep easily. That is what matters. That is all that can give hope to those who are still in chains, General. You must live. You must escape.'

'He's right,' said Canthus. 'And I'm the only one who can get you out through the Roman lines. There is a way, and if we are challenged they will recognise me.'

'Escape?' Ajax shook his head. 'You would have me shame myself.'

'There is more at stake than your pride,' Karim insisted. 'Sometimes a man becomes more than himself. He becomes an inspiration. His name is a weapon in the hearts of those who follow him, and a threat to his enemies.'

'This is true even if he dies,' Ajax countered.

'If you die, then all that you might still achieve, all your name might yet stand for, is lost.'

Ajax lowered his head and thought for a moment. Earlier that evening he had set his mind to meeting his death here in this obscure temple on the fringe of trackless wasteland. He was tired of running from Rome. Yet, as Karim said, there was more to be wrung out of the situation. He looked up at the dark figure of Canthus. 'What is your plan?'

There was still an hour or so before first light when the small party of men flitted across the gap between the temple and the curtain wall. On the far side of the temple they could hear the uproar as Hepithus led a strong force of the defenders in an attack on the Romans guarding the breach and the bolt throwers and their crews beyond. The Nubian had volunteered to remain behind and cover his leader's escape and Ajax silently pledged to honour his companion's memory with the lives of ten Romans as swiftly as possible.

The ropes that Canthus had used to scale the wall were still in place and one by one the handful of gladiators and the best of the Arab warriors that Ajax had chosen to come with them climbed carefully up the mud-brick wall, keeping flat as they heaved themselves over the top of the wall and then quietly descended to the ground outside. As the last man dropped into the shadows, Ajax tugged the sleeve of Canthus's Roman tunic.

'What now?'

'There's a dry irrigation ditch in that field.' Canthus pointed to a vaguely delineated area of wheat a short distance from the wall. 'You follow me and stay as low as you can. There are two Roman outposts about a hundred paces either side of the ditch. Once we get past them then the ditch joins a wider irrigation channel. There's water in it, so we'll have to go slowly. A quarter of a mile further on there's a cavalry picquet. They were bedded down for the night when I passed them on the way into the temple. The horse line is a short distance from the channel and there are three sentries. If we are challenged, I'll answer. I have the password for tonight. We'll be on them before they realise what's up. Then you take the horses and go, sir.'

'You're not coming?'

Canthus shook his head. 'Provided I get back to the right side of the temple before I'm missed, I should be all right. My cover story's worked well enough up to now. No reason to suppose they'll discover who I really am. I may be of more service to you and our allies for a while yet.' There was a dull gleam as the man grinned. 'Best performance of my life, this. If only the other actors in Rome could see me now and give me due recognition.'

'Recognition? Be glad they aren't here.' Ajax smiled back, then punched the spy's shoulder lightly. 'Let's go.'

Canthus led the way as the string of dark figures crouched low to the ground and crept towards the edge of the field. Behind them the sounds of fighting from the far side of the temple began to die away as Hepithus recalled his men and retreated inside the temple. Entering the field, Ajax moved as stealthily as possible to avoid rustling through the stalks of wheat. They moved forward with painful slowness and all the time Ajax feared that dawn would be upon them before they were safely away from the enemy lines. At last Canthus edged down into the empty ditch and they began to make better progress. The sound of voices caused Ajax to stop, but then someone laughed and the conversation dropped into a low unconcerned tone and Ajax moved on. The ditch gradually deepened and then sloped down into a channel of water that stretched away before them. Canthus went first, easing himself into the water and then wading forward, taking care not to splash. The others followed his lead, staying close to the reeds that grew along the edge of the channel.

Abruptly, Canthus held up his hand to signal the others to stop. The faint rush of ripples washing into the reeds faded away and then all was quiet, except the faint scrape of a horse's hoof and a brief whinny. Ajax turned and beckoned to Karim and the two of them edged up alongside Canthus.

'This is it,' said the spy.

'All right then.' Ajax drew his sword. 'We'll deal with the sentries. Once they're down, the men can take care of the rest while they sleep. Clear?'

The others nodded and drew their weapons and then

Ajax led the way out of the water, up through the screen of reeds. He stopped to look over the ground. The horse line was away to the right, the animals tethered to a rope tied between two palms. Two of the sentries were talking together beside the mounts while the dark shapes of their comrades were scattered a short distance away. Some of the men were snoring. Beyond them a solitary figure strolled slowly up and down. Ajax indicated him.

'That one's yours, Karim. Work your way round there and silence him. I'll count to a hundred before we move on the other two.'

Karim nodded, and then went down into a crouch and moved slowly past the sleeping Romans as he crept into the shadows of a handful of date palms and disappeared from view. Ajax counted off at a measured pace and then nudged Canthus. 'Come on.'

They eased themselves up and out of the reeds, emerging on to a rough track that ran alongside the channel. Ajax rose to his full height and started to make his way towards the sentries by the horse line. They were still talking and did not detect the new arrivals until almost the last moment. Then the first of them spun round and lowered his spear at the two figures emerging from the darkness.

'Halt! Who goes there?'

'Friends!' Canthus called back.

'Then give me the password!'

'Up the blues,' Canthus called back and strode on, hand clenched round his sword handle.

'Pass, friend!' the Roman responded.

Ajax kept up with Canthus as the two of them continued along the track. They were close now and while the cut of Canthus's tunic was unmistakably military, Ajax did not look like a Roman soldier. The two continued to stride forward. At the last moment one of the sentries craned his neck and squinted into the shadows. 'Who are you?'

Ajax did not break his stride as he approached the Roman. At the last moment he sprang forward, lunging with his sword. The point plunged into the sentry's torso and the man folded up with a groan. His companion was stunned into stillness for an instant, then as he began to lower his spear, Canthus parried it aside and thrust his sword into the man's throat. He collapsed to his knees and bled out quickly before toppling aside. Ajax hurriedly finished his man off and turned towards the last sentry. He had heard something and stood on the other side of the small encampment, spear grasped in both hands. Before he could call out, a shadow sprang up from the ground behind him and there was a brief grunt as Karim brought him down. Ajax stared, poised to dash across to Karim's aid, but then the Parthian rose and lifted his sword.

'All done.' Canthus breathed deeply with relief. He turned back towards the channel and let out a low whistle. At once a score of shadows emerged from the reeds and padded towards them. When they had gathered round Ajax, he gestured towards the shapes of the men sleeping but on the ground a sufficient distance from the date palms to avoid any scorpions or snakes dropping on them during the night. 'Kill them, and kill them quietly,' Ajax ordered. 'Go.'

His men crept amongst the sleeping Romans, kneeling down to smother their mouths with one hand while using the other to cut their throats. Here and there a victim struggled briefly and one managed to let out a gurgling cry before being swiftly silenced. When the last of the Romans was dealt with, Ajax led his men to the horse line. The saddles were arranged neatly to one side and took little time to fit on to the horses. A short time after the killing had begun, Ajax and his men were mounted and only Canthus remained on foot.

'You're certain that you wish to remain behind?' asked Ajax.

'Yes, General.'

'If they discover that you're a spy, and they are bound to sooner or later, then you can expect no mercy.'

'I shall be careful. Besides, I am enjoying the deception. I have never played a role like this before.' Canthus's smile faded and he nodded towards the east where the first glimmer of the coming day was rising into the haze above the Nile. 'You'd better go.' He reached up and clasped Ajax's hand. 'May Fortuna ride with you, my General.'

Ajax nodded his gratitude, then released the man's hand, took up his reins and set his mount towards the hills to the west, intending to ride out into the wilderness, away from the Roman forces surrounding the temple. After that they would head up the Nile and find somewhere to cross the river and rejoin Prince Talmis and his army.

He had done as the Prince wished. The column had distracted the enemy's attention and inflicted heavy casualties. With luck the Romans would be anxious about a threat from either bank and divide their already weak forces. Even so, the column had been lost and Ajax was anticipating a frosty reception from his ally.

Nudging his heels in he urged his horse into a trot as they left the spy behind them, surrounded by the bodies of the Roman cavalry squadron. Canthus watched them briefly, then turned and hurried back towards the temple, to rejoin the Roman force before he was missed.

CHAPTER TWENTY-EIGHT

The small column of horsemen had only travelled half a mile or so across cultivated fields before they abruptly gave out on to a sandy wasteland where the peasants' irrigation system stopped. There was no cover here and Ajax reined in as he examined the open ground stretching out before him. To his right the sandstone cliffs and mountains rose up into a barrier that stretched out into the desert in one direction and bordered a stretch of the Nile in the other. The highest rocks were already aglow as they caught the first rays of the rising sun and a thin light spread across the landscape still embraced by the shadows of the failing night.

Ajax clicked his tongue and beckoned his men to follow him as his horse walked out into the desert. At once he felt exposed. There was no place to hide out here and it was vital that they made best use of what little darkness was left. He increased the horse's pace into a gentle canter and his men followed suit, kicking up a small cloud of dust as they headed out across the sand.

'I don't like this, General,' said Karim as he glanced towards the mass of the temple rising up above the grey smears of fields and the spectral forms of clumps of palm trees. 'They must surely see us at any moment.'

'And if they do, they'll assume that we are one of their cavalry patrols.'

'What if they don't?'

Ajax shrugged. 'Then we'll see just how good these horses are.'

The light strengthened and spread its warm loom across the arid wilderness. To their left a Roman trumpet sounded and there was a brief delay before a distant series of cracks announced the opening of the second assault on the temple. Ajax felt a heavy sense of guilt that he had left Hepithus and the rest of his men behind to defend the temple, even though their sacrifice would buy him time to continue the struggle against Rome. With luck, they would sell their lives dearly. He would avenge them in time.

Karim pulled in his reins and pointed ahead. A quarter of a mile away, three mounted men appeared from behind a low dune, heading straight for Ajax and his column. 'What do we do?'

'Nothing,' Ajax replied calmly. 'There's every chance they will take us for their own.'

Karim glanced at the black robes of the eight Arabs who were riding with them. 'Only at a distance.'

Ajax gently steered his horse to one side so that they would not pass close by, but soon saw that the enemy horsemen were making directly for them. 'Shit.'

'We have to do something,' Karim urged. 'We have to stop them raising the alarm.'

Ajax thought quickly and turned to issue his orders. 'Have the Arabs make their bows ready. If we get the chance we'll take them down before they can react.'

Karim nodded and reined his horse in, falling back alongside the Arabs to convey the command to their officer.

As the two parties closed on each other, Ajax tried to calculate their chances of escaping. There was still at least a mile to go before the cliffs opened out on to the desert. If the Romans reacted swiftly enough they could cut him off from the upper Nile. The three horsemen approached without any sign of wariness. Their leader raised his hand in greeting when he was no more than fifty paces away in the half light, and then harshly reined his horse in and called out.

'Who are you?'

'Auxiliary horse!' Ajax called back, nudging his mount to continue advancing. He could sense the Roman's hesitation and the hurried exchange with the other two men. Any moment they would guess the truth.

'Karim!' Ajax shouted. 'Now!'

A word of command was barked and a faint hiss cut through the air as the arrows shot towards the three Romans in a shallow arc. The leader was struck in the chest, and his horse took an arrow in the neck, causing it to rear up and throw its rider. Another arrow struck one of the riders in the thigh and the other shafts went wide. The third Roman turned and instantly kicked his heels in, galloping towards the temple a few hundred paces away. His surviving comrade struggled to pull out the arrow, giving the archers time to string a second volley. This time he was struck in the chest and face and toppled from his saddle into the sand, sending up a small cloud of dust.

'Get that one!' Karim bellowed, pointing to the man

leaning low over the neck of his mount as it galloped to safety. More arrows flew after him but the target was moving swiftly and the range lengthening. Karim drew his sword and spurred his horse forward to give chase.

'Leave him!' Ajax ordered. 'It's too late for that. We must ride!'

Reluctantly sheathing his sword, Karim ordered the archers to cease shooting and then the column broke into a gallop, making for the gap between the mountains and the farmland. As they rode, Ajax cast frequent glances towards the temple and saw that the enemy horseman had reached an outpost. He gesticulated anxiously as he made his report. The shrill note of a horn carried on the cool morning air, and then another. There was still a quarter of a mile to go before the desert opened out when Karim called to him and pointed towards the Nile. Two squadrons of enemy cavalry were racing out from the Roman lines, one heading towards Ajax and his men while the other angled out across the strip of desert, aiming to cut them off.

It took Ajax only an instant to see that they would not reach the gap in time and he raised his arm to halt his men. They stopped their beasts in a swirl of dust. Ajax glanced round. There was only one direction left to them now: north.

'Follow me!' He pulled savagely on the reins and wheeled his mount round before spurring it away from the trap being set for them by the two Roman squadrons. The rest of the gladiators and Arabs turned and raced after him, thundering across the sand, the sunlit cliffs to their left and the orange haze to their right, through which peered the gleaming gold curve of the sun, low on the horizon. Ajax leaned forward, feeling the mane of the horse whip his chin as it galloped, head extended. He felt a bitterness poison his heart at the prospect of being chased down and forced to fight or surrender. His Roman enemies would be sure to relate how he had abandoned his men and run for his life. The only way to avoid such an outcome was to escape and fight on. That was all that mattered now.

The second Roman squadron abandoned the bid to cut them off and turned to join the chase; sixty men against Ajax's twenty. There was no question of turning to fight, he realised. That would doom them to certain defeat. As they pounded along the arid ground beside the cliffs, Ajax saw a defile winding up into the hills to his left. If it led to the top of the rocky plateau, there was still a chance of cutting round the Romans and rejoining Prince Talmis. If not, then at least it would give him and his men a chance to fight on a narrow front and face their pursuers on more even terms.

He indicated the head of the defile and yelled to Karim, 'Over there!'

The party of horsemen headed towards the rising ground. A dusty track lay ahead and Ajax took this as a good sign. All tracks led somewhere and there was a good chance that there was a route out of the defile. Looking back over his shoulder he saw that the closer of the two enemy squadrons was no more than a third of a mile behind them, closer than it had been a moment earlier, he calculated grimly. The track wound up into the rocky ground and the sounds of hoofbeats echoed off the parched stone. Soon the bends in the route hid their pursuers from view and Ajax wondered if there might be a chance to branch off the track and lose them. However, there proved to be little opportunity for such a ruse as the only paths leading away were too narrow and steep for the horses.

Then, just over a mile into what had become a gorge, the track widened out into an open space, surrounded by towering cliffs and jumbles of boulders. Here and there Ajax could see small openings in the rock, like caves. The track seemed to end abruptly at the foot of a tall cliff. There was no sign of life. Nothing moved about them and a profound sense of stillness and foreboding seemed to fill the hot air trapped in the large natural arena.

'What is this place?' asked Karim. 'Those caves, they're not natural. Someone has cut them out of the rock. Look there.'

He pointed towards a larger entrance, half hidden behind a giant boulder. The shaded interior was framed by square-cut masonry, which was covered with small carved symbols, like the ones Ajax had seen cut into the temple. He edged his horse closer and peered into the tunnel. The walls had been painted and they stretched off into the shadows, out of sight. Before he could examine the cave any further, one of his men called out and pointed back down the track. Ajax and his party strained their ears and then they heard it, the clattering echo of hoofbeats.

'Karim! Take the archers and get up on that cliff!' He indicated a jumble of rocks that formed the last bend in the track. 'Wait until they draw level with you before you shoot.'

Karim nodded and hurriedly dismounted to take

Simon Scarrow

command of the Arabs. Ajax faced the rest of his men, all that remained of his followers from Crete. 'The track just beyond the cliff is narrow. We can hold it well enough. Every one of us is worth three good Romans any day, and it seems there are plenty of tombs to go round.' He gestured at the openings in the surrounding rocks and his comrades laughed. 'Let's make sure we fill 'em up with dead Romans.'

Ajax took up position in the middle of the track and his men formed up on either side in a close line of men and horses. They drew their swords and raised the shields they had taken from the men they had killed earlier. The sound of hoofbeats echoed off the jagged and tumbling faces of the rocks in a disorientating clatter and then Karim's voice added to the rising din.

'Here they come! Make ready!'

Ajax tightened the grip on his sword and clenched his thighs against the flanks of his mount. Then the first of the Romans appeared around the base of the cliff, the decurion commanding the squadron and the signifer. As soon as he caught sight of the waiting horsemen, less than a hundred paces away, he threw up his arm and reined in. The rest of the squadron drew up and then the decurion walked them forward as he shouted his commands for his men to make ready to charge. They readied their lances and hefted their shields up from their saddle horns, slipping their hands into the straps before taking the reins back into their left hands. Meanwhile, Ajax was watching Karim and his small party of archers as they notched their first arrows, extended their bow arms and then drew back the arrows, took aim and waited for the order to shoot. Karim was staring down from the cliff intently, marking the approach of the enemy, and as they drew abreast of his position he raised his arm, held it there for a moment, and then swept it down.

'Loose arrows!'

A handful of the Romans looked up and round at the sound of his voice, then the arrows struck home amid their ranks, plunging into horseflesh, glancing off shields and armour with loud raps, with one thudding home into the signifier's thigh, pinning it to his saddle. The Arabs immediately fitted more arrows to unleash on the Romans and the walls of rock echoed with the shrill whinnies of terrified horses, the cries of their riders and the impact of arrows. Ajax watched as several of the Romans writhed on the ground and the rest milled in confusion, trying to shelter themselves and their mounts from the arrows. It was time to strike, he decided, taking a deep breath.

'Forwards!' He nudged his horse in the flanks and it obediently advanced. The other men rippled into motion on either side, and then Ajax increased the pace to a trot. There was no point in charging the Romans. He wanted his men to arrive in one wave, to maximise their effect. The arrows continued to plunge down, creating more havoc in the enemy ranks, and for a moment Ajax feared that the Arabs might become too carried away with the effect of their handiwork and keeping shooting even as he and his comrades entered the fray. However, at the last moment, Karim shouted to his men and they obediently lowered their bows.

The mounted gladiators swept into the disordered Romans, getting up close where their shields could be used to strike their opponents and their swords would be more effective than the unwieldy lances. Ajax slashed at the shoulder of the first man who stood in his path. The edge of the blade failed to cut through his chain mail, but the force of the impact still broke bones beneath and the horseman cried out as he swayed in his saddle. Ajax urged his mount on, striking at the man's neck with a backhanded blow. He did not have time to swing with any force but the blade still found a way under his guard and cut through skin and the spine. As the rider slumped forward, Ajax recovered his sword and steered his mount towards the decurion who sat in his saddle, close to the wounded signifer, protecting the standard. The air about Ajax was filled with dust and the clash and thud as men cursed each other or cried out in pain. A quick glance was enough to tell him that his men were having the better of the fight. Only one of the gladiators had been injured, run through his side with a lance, but it only seemed to have enraged him as he hacked and slashed at the Romans around him with savage fury.

A flicker of light and shadow alerted Ajax to the danger from his side and he threw up his shield in time to block the head of a lance as a Roman made an overhead thrust. The point flicked up, just missing the top of his head. At the same time Ajax swivelled in his saddle and swung his sword in a wide arc with ferocious force. The blade cut right through the Roman's wrist and the lance clattered to the ground, the severed hand flopping into the dust alongside.

'Fall back!' the decurion shouted. 'Back!'

One by one the Romans who were not engaged turned their mounts and galloped down the defile. The rest did their best to free themselves and flee. The decurion thrust the signifer away and stood his ground to cover the retreat of his men. It was a brave gesture, Ajax conceded, but a costly one. Two of the gladiators came up on either side of his horse. The decurion blocked the first attack with his shield and then hurriedly parried a thrust from the other side. As he turned back in his saddle to face the first threat, the gladiator raised his sword high and level and plunged it into the decurion's face. Blood spurted from inside the helmet and the officer flung both arms out before his torso flopped back against the saddle horns.

Karim's archers shot several more arrows at the fleeing Romans, until they had passed out of sight around the next bend in the gorge. Ajax breathed hard as he looked round. Half the squadron had been killed or wounded, mostly by arrows. One of the gladiators lay dead amongst them, the end of a broken lance piercing his chest. Two men had been wounded, the first had been run through. The battle rage was slowly draining from the man's face and now he looked down and saw the ragged tear in his leather cuirass and the blood spreading quickly through the folds of the tunic beneath. It was clear to Ajax that the wound was fatal as soon as he saw it. The other casualty had been injured in the leg, a long gash in the back of his thigh that had ripped apart his hamstrings, crippling him.

'Help them down,' Ajax ordered the nearest of his men. 'Get them to some shade, inside the entrance to the tomb there. The rest of you, finish off their wounded.'

Karim came slithering down the steep slope beside the cliff and dropped amid a fall of shingle on to the floor of the gorge. He smiled brilliantly at Ajax. 'That put paid to their pursuit!'

'For now.' Ajax sheathed his sword and lowered the strap of the shield on to his saddle horn before dismounting. 'The survivors won't be charging up here blindly again. We can be sure of that. No, they'll keep watch on us while they send for reinforcements.'

'Then we'd better find a way out of here.'

Ajax gestured towards the rocks towering on all sides. 'Be my guest. The only way out is a steep climb on foot. We'd have to abandon the horses. Without them we have no hope of escape.' He looked round at the openings in the rocks and smiled grimly. 'If we die here, then we die in the company of kings, my friend. Think on that.'

Karim pursed his lips. 'That is a slender source of comfort, General. Frankly, I'd rather die somewhere a little less barren. If I have to die at all.'

Ajax ignored him. He glanced at the entrances to the tombs. 'When they come for us, we can still give them a good fight. Come, let's have a closer look.'

He strode towards the mouth of the tomb he had seen earlier, and after a brief hesitation Karim followed him, not relishing the dark depths that stretched back into the cliffs. It seemed an ill omen to be trapped amid a valley of the dead.

CHAPTER TWENTY-NINE

'They put up quite a fight,' said Macro as they stood in the larger of the two courtyards in the temple. Cato, his left arm in a sling, nodded as he surveyed the bodies littering the ground. It was late in the morning and the air was already stifling. The cloying odour of blood added to the discomfort of the setting. Several legionaries were picking their way across the courtyard looking for wounded comrades to carry into the columned hall where the chief surgeon had set up his field hospital. Any of the enemy wounded were quickly despatched to put an end to their suffering.

'Quite a fight,' Macro repeated, arms on hips. 'Now comes the fun part. Finding the body of Ajax. I haven't seen him anywhere yet. I'll have to order a more thorough search.'

'Assuming he stayed to fight to the end.'

'You still think he had something to do with those horsemen that were seen earlier?'

'It's possible.'

Macro shook his head. 'I think we would have noticed if he had ridden out of here, right through our patrols. It's not his style. Not from what I recall of him.' Macro's expression darkened as he briefly recalled his period of

357

captivity. 'Ajax would rather make a stand than run off and leave his men to die. Trust me, he's here. We just have to find him.' Macro nudged a severed forearm with the toe of his boot. 'Or what's left of him.'

He looked round the courtyard again and shook his head. 'Have to hand it to them, this lot fought to the last. Not one prisoner. If the rest of the Nubian army is anything like this then we'll have quite a fight on our hands when we finally meet.'

Cato pursed his lips. Despite what Macro said, the legionaries had had no difficulty in driving off the sortie that the enemy had made in the hour before dawn. They had made it as far as the breach and been held there while reinforcements were rushed forward to drive them back into the temple. None of the bolt throwers had been damaged. At dawn the legate launched the second attack in person. He stood in the breach, in full armour, sheltering behind a shield, as he bellowed the order for the bolt throwers and archers to commence bombarding the walls of the temple. This time the missiles were loosed at close range and the legionaries made short work of any Arabs who showed themselves on the walls of the temple and on top of the pylons.

Safe from the danger of arrows, Macro led the First Century forward again. A section of auxiliary archers advanced with them, ready to shoot any defender who risked rising up behind the barricade to try and dislodge the assault ramps. The legionaries trotted up the ramp and fell on the defenders behind, cutting a path through their ranks until they emerged into the courtyard. After that it had merely been a question of finding and cutting down the small groups of survivors who made their last stand in the temple's more easily defended chambers. The last group, led by one of Ajax's gladiators, an African, held out for over an hour in the main pylon, gradually being forced back up the narrow staircase and on to the platform. The gladiator, mortally wounded, had thrown himself off the top of the pylon rather than be taken alive.

'Shame you missed it.' Macro looked at his friend closely. Cato had been too dazed to join the attack and Macro had found Hamedes and told him to take care of the prefect in his absence. The priest helped Cato prop himself up against the trunk of a palm tree to watch the assault. Once the nausea passed and a surgeon's assistant strapped up his arm, Cato had dismissed Hamedes and made his way inside the temple to find Macro. The latter continued in as sensitive a tone as he could manage. 'I know you wanted to be there when we finished off that mad dog, Ajax.' He paused. 'It's funny, I always imagined that it would end in a straight fight between him and either you or me. I didn't think he would be cut down in some bloody skirmish like this. Just one of the faceless dead.'

'We haven't found his body yet,' Cato replied quietly. 'Until we do, it's tempting fate to assume it's all over.'

Macro snorted. 'You always have to see the dour side of events.'

They were interrupted by a blast of notes echoing down into the courtyard and both officers turned and craned their necks to squint up towards the top of the main pair of pylons. Three bucinas were sounding off. Behind them the standard of the Twenty-Second Legion, with its gold-embroidered head of a jackal, was fluttering over the temple. To one side four men were struggling to erect a trophy made up from the weapons and equipment taken from the enemy dead. Aurelius stood, proudly looking on.

'Well,' Macro scratched his bristling cheek, 'at least he's happy. Now he has a great victory to go along with his battle wound. Nothing can stop him. The man thinks he's a modern Alexander the Great.'

Cato stared silently at the legate for a moment. 'Let's hope the mood passes quickly, then. Taking the temple is one thing. Defeating Prince Talmis is quite another. The last thing we need is a commander who underestimates his enemy.'

Macro nodded.

The bucinas sounded again and the legate approached the edge of the platform and raised his arms up to draw the attention of the men below. There was a brief, expectant pause before he spoke, straining his voice to make sure that his words carried the length of the temple. 'Men of the Twenty-Second! My fellow Jackals! Comrades! Today we have won the first of our battles against the Nubian Prince who dares to defile the Roman province of Egypt with his presence! His men lie dead at our feet and their arms are now our trophies.' Aurelius made an extravagant gesture towards the arrangement rising up above the pylon. 'This is but a poor token of the riches and glory that will be ours once we have crushed the main enemy army. As long as there are Roman soldiers in Egypt, the men of the Twenty-Second, and the name of their commander, will be remembered with pride and honour. Think on that, and keep it in your hearts as we march from this place to do battle with the invader!' He punched the air and there was a silence before one of the tribunes on the platform drew his sword and thrust it into the air and chanted. 'Aurelius! . . . Aurelius! . . . Aurelius!'

The other officers joined in and then the cry was picked up by the men down in the courtyards of the temple.

Macro turned to Cato. 'Not the best orator I've heard, but he has the timeless gift of keeping it mercifully brief.'

Cato smiled. 'A pity the same can't be said for most politicians I've seen in Rome.' His smile faded. 'We'll have to make sure he doesn't fall prey to putting posterity before common sense.'

'I'll leave that to you then, sir,' Macro replied. 'It would be better that such advice came from his acting senior tribune than from his acting first spear centurion.'

Cato shot him a sour look. 'Thanks.'

'Goes with the rank.' Macro shrugged. 'Besides, you're a smooth talker. I'd lay good money that you could talk an Aventine whore into giving you a free shag and then handing you a tip for the fine service.'

Cato frowned. 'I'm not certain I have ambitions to be quite that rhetorically effective.'

'It's early days . . . However, we have work to do.' Macro turned to a section of his men who had just finished cheering the legate. 'You lot! Over here at the double!'

They trotted over and Macro gave them as detailed a description of Ajax as he could before sending them to search for his body. He promised a jar of wine to the man who found the gladiator and then dismissed them. As the men hurried away, suitably motivated to work through the growing stench of the bodies scattered through the temple, one of the orderlies from the headquarters staff approached Cato and saluted.

'The legate sends his respects, sir, and requests that you and Centurion Macro attend him in the priest's quarters at the front of the temple.'

Cato exchanged a brief look of surprise with Macro. 'Did he say why?'

'No, sir. Just that he wants all his senior officers summoned. As soon as possible,' he added pointedly, then saluted and trotted off.

Macro lowered his head and kicked a small stone away. 'What now?'

The accommodation built for the priests of the temple had once been a fairly elaborate affair but centuries of neglect had left only a faint reminder of its riches. The heavens painted on the ceiling still retained their lustre but the chambers built around the courtyard were bare and sandblown. The shallow pool that stood in the centre had once reflected its surroundings but the water had long since drained away and a layer of silt almost covered the decorative tiles at the bottom. As Macro and Cato joined the other officers, the legate was standing at the far end of the pool, sketching a diagram in the silt with the point of his sword. His subordinates waited in silence until the legate had finished. Aurelius straightened up and sheathed his sword as he looked round at his officers with a broad smile.

'There's no time to waste on platitudes and niceties, gentlemen, so I will come straight to the point. The enemy is on the run. Today's victory has given the legion heart, and will dismay our foes when they hear of it. Now is the time to press home our advantage, in a way that the enemy will least expect.' He glanced at the nearest of his centurions and clicked his fingers. 'Give me your vine cane.'

The officer hurriedly passed it to his commander and Aurelius pointed the end at his diagram. The officers pressed forward for a better view.

'This is the Nile, from Diospolis Magna to the first cataract. The Nubians' plan is now obvious. They divided their force to allow them to send this column round and take my army from both front and rear. We have put a stop to that scheme, and now we have an opportunity to pay them back in kind.' Aurelius pointed towards Diospolis Magna. 'I will lead the main force up the Nile to confront Prince Talmis. Since he outnumbers me I am certain that he will stand his ground, especially if we can close on him before he becomes aware that we have crushed the column entrusted to the rebel gladiator. The enemy will think that we are walking into their trap.' The legate paused, and then smiled cunningly as he sketched out the movements on his diagram. 'However, it is we who will be springing a trap. As I lead the main advance down the eastern bank, Tribune Cato will take the auxiliary units and march swiftly down the western bank, cross over behind the Nubians and attack their rear. Caught between the two forces, they will be annihilated.' He looked up, his eyes wide with excitement. 'It is as elegant a plan as it is simple. I am sure you all grasp that.'

He paused, as if he was ready to entertain comments, or perhaps he was daring any of his officers to defy him, Cato mused. He eased himself forward, wincing as his bruised arm brushed past Junius. 'Sir, permission to speak.'

'Of course, Tribune.'

Cato looked down at the sand map as he framed his thoughts. The legate's enthusiasm for his plan was evident. He would need careful handling. Cato looked up and met the legate's gaze directly. 'Your plan has the virtue of turning the tables on the enemy, sir. That much is clear. Under different circumstances, it would undoubtedly produce the result you desire. However, the enemy outnumber us by more than three to one. I respectfully suggest that we keep the army concentrated in one column if we are to have the best chance of gaining a decisive victory. If you divide our forces, each column will be weaker than the subtraction of the parts, as it were.' Cato stepped forward and pointed at the diagram of the Nile. 'Besides, where would you have my column cross the river back to the eastern bank, sir? We have barely enough boats to get five hundred men across at a time. You saw how much trouble we faced landing against a far weaker force than I will have to overcome next time. We have too few men to risk dividing the army. Our best chance is a bold strike up the eastern bank of the Nile. Find the Nubian army and force a battle. The quality of our troops should give us the advantage. We can break the enemies' spirit before they have a chance to make their superior numbers felt,' Cato concluded. There was a tense silence and Cato swallowed. 'That's my advice, sir.'

'Duly noted,' the legate said flatly. He stared at Cato for a moment before he continued. 'I am pleased that you share my confidence in our men. The Jackals and the auxiliaries have proved they are up to standard. Their mettle is beyond doubt. That is precisely why we can afford to divide the army. Each column will be more than able to look after itself. Moreover, the enemy will not think for a moment that we would dare to divide our army. They know they have the advantage in numbers, and they expect us to go on the defensive and hand the initiative to them.' Aurelius paused as a thought struck him. He smiled faintly as he resumed. 'Which is exactly what I have been encouraging them to think. Prince Talmis has fallen into my trap. That is why he foolishly sent his column down this bank of the river. He never expected us to respond so swiftly, or so effectively.'

Cato coughed. 'Then perhaps we should learn from his mistake, sir.'

Aurelius shook his head. 'I don't think you grasp the . . . subtleties of the situation, Tribune.'

Cato raised his eyebrows. 'Subtleties, sir?'

'I am always ready to let my subordinates learn from my experience,' Aurelius replied graciously. 'Our enemy has been induced into thinking that we are too cautious to act decisively. He thinks that he can dictate when and where he will give battle. Therefore he has become complacent. It is that complacency which we will exploit. The very last thing he expects us to do now is for us to attack him from two directions. Surprise will be on our side, and it will enhance the advantage we already have in terms of the quality and morale of our men.' Aurelius paused and smiled at Cato. '*Now* do you grasp my strategy, Tribune?'

Cato stared back at him, his mind reeling with the

myriad risks that the legate was prepared to take. The auxilary column would surely be detected long before it ever crossed back to the eastern bank. Prince Talmis would have all the time he needed to choose which Roman column he crushed first. The Nubians also had lighter forces and could march more swiftly than their opponents. Either column could be defeated long before they closed the trap. There was a further issue, Cato reflected. Less than a quarter of the army had taken part in the assault on the temple. The rest were still in camp on the far bank. They had missed out on the attack and therefore would still be as green as grass when it came to facing the enemy for the first time. Cato well knew that it was hard to predict the behaviour of men facing battle for the first time. Some would fight like heroes. Most would anxiously follow their training and obey orders but be disposed to follow the example of others. Other men would stand in line, hearts pounding in terror, and then their nerve would break and they would run. If enough of them did that, the contagion would spread through their comrades like wildfire and the army would be doomed. He took a deep breath.

'Sir, it is my considered opinion that the risks outweigh the advantages. It might be different with a battle-hardened army. I strongly suggest that you reconsider your plan.'

The legate regarded him curiously. 'Tribune Cato, you have fought in a number of campaigns, haven't you?'

'Yes, sir.'

'I will not ask you to bore us with the details, but you have faced Celts, Germans, pirates, Parthians and rebel gladiators. True?'

'Yes, sir.'

'Then why be so timorous in the face of the Nubians? Surely they are the least of the many foes you have faced? Why fear them?'

Cato felt his pulse quicken. The confrontation had taken a dangerous turn once again. His commander had all but accused him of cowardice. If they had been facing each other in private, Cato could have confronted the accusation directly, but he was aware of the tension that now gripped the officers surrounding him and the legate. If he rounded on the man now, then Aurelius would be forced to apologise to him or dismiss him. An apology would damage his authority irreparably, so the legate would have no choice but to get rid of Cato and send him back to Alexandria. That would remove any opportunity for Cato to change his superior's mind with regard to his campaign plan. It would result in disaster, Cato was convinced of it. He knew that he must swallow his pride, for the sake of army, his friend Macro, and the fate of the province.

'I do not fear the Nubians, sir,' he responded evenly. 'I am merely offering you my professional opinion. Based upon my years of service to Rome.'

'And how many years is that, exactly?'

Cato felt furious with himself. He had walked into a trap of his own making. *Fool*, he cursed himself. 'Seven years, sir.'

'Seven,' Aurelius repeated with a half-smile. 'I served ten years in the ranks before being promoted to centurion. Then another twelve years acquiring the seniority necessary to become first spear and finally camp prefect. I rather think that I have all the experience necessary to command the army as I see fit. Seven years.' He shook his head and then swept his arm round, gesturing to all the other officers. 'I wonder, is there another man here with *less* experience than you, Tribune? Well?'

There was no response from the officers and the legate turned back to Cato with a triumphant expression. 'I think that places your advice in the appropriate context . . . wouldn't you agree?'

Cato did not reply. Anything he said now would damn him either way. He was conscious of the other men watching him closely, waiting for his response. He cleared his throat. 'I have given you my advice, sir. That is my professional duty. The command of the army is yours. It is up to you to give the orders for the campaign.'

'That's right. The decision is made and the time for consultation or dissent is over. Is that clear?'

'Yes, sir. Perfectly.'

'Then I expect you, and every one of my officers, to obey my orders without question from now on.'

Cato nodded.

The legate was still for a moment and then nodded. 'Very well then. You will all receive your instructions once the headquarters staff at Karnak have them ready. In the meantime ensure that your men are ready to advance the moment I give the word.'

The officers nodded and were waiting to be dismissed when a cavalry auxiliary entered the room and strode up to the prefect of the Alexandrian mounted cohort and quickly reported to him. The other officers looked on curiously as the prefect questioned the man and then dismissed him.

'Something to tell us?' asked Aurelius.

'Yes, sir. It seems that some of the defenders managed to escape us, sir. One of my squadrons was surprised last night. They were part of the perimeter we established round the temple. They were killed where they slept. One of the sentries was still alive when they were discovered this morning. Before he died he said that one of the men who attacked them was in Roman uniform and used the night's password to get close enough to surprise the sentries.'

'How did he get hold of the password?' asked Macro.

Junius pursed his lips. 'Perhaps he overheard some of our men use it around the temple.'

The cavalry prefect nodded. 'It's possible. Anyway, the attackers must have been the mounted men we saw at first light. I sent two of my squadrons to pursue them. They made off towards the north, into the hills. I've just heard that they've been caught in a dead end. We have them.'

Macro turned to Cato and muttered, 'That could be Ajax, I suppose.'

'More than likely.' Cato nodded. 'By the gods, that man is like a ghost. A bloody ghost.'

'How far away are they?' Aurelius asked the cavalry prefect.

'No more than four miles, sir. My men are watching them. The leading squadron had the worst of the first encounter. The officer in charge has asked for reinforcements before he tries again.'

Cato stepped forward to intervene. 'Excuse me, sir, but it's possible that Ajax is with them. He could have escaped with what's left of his band of rebels.'

'So?'

'Centurion Macro and I were tasked with tracking Ajax down. I request permission to take charge of his capture, sir.'

Aurelius considered for a moment. 'No. I will take command since I am here. Might as well complete the work I've started. I'll take the auxiliary horse and the archers, since they will be remaining on this side of the Nile in any case. The rest of the men can return to Karnak. However, I shan't deprive you of the pleasure of being in at the kill, Tribune. Nor you, Centurion Macro.'

'Thank you, sir,' Cato responded with forced politeness.

'Then let's not waste a moment longer.' The legate clapped his hands together. 'It's time to put an end to this rebel, Ajax. To arms!'

CHAPTER THIRTY

Cato and Macro were sitting in the shade of a rock. The horses of the auxiliary cavalry cohort were clustered together in whatever shelter they could find, while their riders sat on the ground, their cloaks propped up on sticks to provide some cover from the afternoon sun. They were waiting for the archers, together with Aurelius and his staff, to catch up before they attempted to attack Ajax and his men. Two squadrons had been sent to find another route to the top of the plateau that overlooked the gorge to make certain that none of the enemy would escape.

Even in the shade Cato felt the sapping burden of the sun's glare. The air caught in the defile was stifling and made worse by the pale rocks which reflected the harsh light. So much so that Cato found himself having to squint when he looked round at the rocky slopes rising up on either side.

'It's a hellish place,' Macro muttered sourly as he dabbed at his brow with his neck cloth. His mood was made worse by the failure of his men to locate the body of Ajax back in the temple. It was clear that the gladiator had escaped with the other horsemen trapped further up the gorge. 'Never been so bloody hot in my life. It's like the heat is sucking the bloody life out of me.'

He turned towards Hamedes who was squatting close by, arms wrapped round his knees and his head bowed. 'What did you say this place was again?'

There was no reply from the priest so Macro picked up a small stone and tossed it at him. The stone struck Hamedes on the arm and dropped by his side. The priest stirred wearily and looked round. 'Sorry, sir. What was that?'

'I asked you about this gorge,' said Macro. 'Earlier you said it was filled with tombs.'

Hamedes nodded. 'The tombs of the old kings, and their high priests.'

'Have you been here before then?'

'Some days ago, when I visited the temples on the west bank.'

'I remember,' said Macro. 'Thought it was a bloody silly time to go sightseeing. Anyway, about these tombs. What can you tell us? If they're anything like the temples that crop up all over the place, then they'll be quite a sight, I should think.'

'No, sir,' Hamedes replied. 'There's hardly anything to see, at least from the outside. Just holes in the rocks, for the most part. They look more like cave openings than anything else.'

'Caves?' Macro snorted. 'You expect me to believe your lot stuffed their kings into holes in the ground when they died? Bollocks. They slapped them in the heart of those pyramids we passed near Memphis. Told me that yourself.'

'Some of them, sir. Many of the others were buried here, together with their riches.'

'Riches?' Macro's eyes lit up.

Hamedes nodded. 'All the accoutrements they would need to take with them into the afterlife, but fashioned in gold and decorated with jewels. Of course, the tombs have been raided by thieves over the years. Picked clean.'

'Oh.' Macro's expression turned to one of sullen disappointment.

'What are the tombs like?' asked Cato. 'How easily could they be defended?'

'Defended?' Hamedes pursed his lips. 'They are just tunnels, sir. Cut into the rocks. There are scores of them. Some of them are little more than caves at the end of short tunnels. Others were cut deep into the cliffs with columned chambers. I took a torch into a handful of them and went as far as I dared. Ajax's men might try and hide in them, as a last resort.'

'Hmmm.' Cato took a sip from his canteen as he considered the priest's description. He tried to put himself in Ajax's position. The gladiator and his men had a limited supply of water. If they abandoned their horses and tried to climb out of the gorge, they would be faced by a long march across the plateau then down to the desert before they could attempt to cut back towards the Nile. Even if they managed to evade the Roman forces on this side of the Nile, it was likely the heat and thirst would kill them long before they got to safety. On the other hand, if they hid deep inside one of the tombs, they would be sheltered from the sun and could survive for days before they were forced to emerge. If they timed it to come out at night, they might be able to slip past any soldiers still in the area looking for them. The more he thought about it, the more likely it seemed to Cato that his enemy would make use of the tombs.

'If they do try to hide, it could take quite a while to find the right tomb, and even then we'd have to winkle them out. I doubt the prospect of spending that long hunting them down is going to appeal to the legate now that he's set his heart on putting a quick end to the Nubians.'

Macro looked up. 'You don't think he'll abandon the hunt? Not now, when we've got the last of them trapped, and Ajax with them, like as not?'

'You heard Aurelius. He wants the army to march as soon as possible. He won't want to waste time hunting down a handful of fugitives.'

'I'll not let Ajax get away again,' Macro responded. 'Not this time. I don't care how long it takes. I'll search every bloody one of those tombs until I dig the bastard out.'

Cato fully shared his friend's desire to put paid to the rebel. However, there was no question of Aurelius giving them permission to spend several days searching for him. He turned to the priest and regarded him thoughtfully. This might also be the opportunity to resolve something that had been troubling him since he had first heard of Ajax's escape a few hours earlier.

'Hamedes.'

'Sir?'

'I have a job for you. I need someone to go forward and spy out the enemy's positions. If they go to ground when we attack, then I must know which tomb they are hiding in. Since you know the place, you're the obvious choice.'

'Yes, sir.'

'You'll need to make an indirect approach.' Cato looked up at the crags and rocky outcrops that formed the sides of the gorge. 'It'll be hard going, and dangerous if you are spotted. Will you volunteer?'

Hamedes nodded at once. 'Yes, sir. I have as much of a debt to settle with Ajax as you do.'

'Of course.' Cato half smiled. 'I had little doubt you would agree.' He turned to Macro. 'Centurion, I want you to go with him.'

Macro raised his eyebrows. 'Me?'

'Two pairs of eyes are better than one. Hamedes knows the ground. You know how best to use it. Go with him and report back to me as soon as you have discovered which tomb the enemy are using. It'll be hot work. You can both leave your armour behind. Just take your swords.'

Macro opened his mouth to protest, then puffed his cheeks and nodded. 'As you command.'

Once the two men had struggled out of their chain-mail armour and rebuckled their sword belts over their tunics, Cato sent Hamedes to fetch some spare canteens from the nearest cavalry squadron. While the priest strode away, Cato addressed Macro in an undertone. 'I'd have gone myself, but for my shoulder.'

'I know.'

'Be careful, Macro. Don't take any risks . . . Keep an eye on Hamedes.'

The last remark caught Macro by surprise and he turned towards Cato with a puzzled expression. 'What?'

Cato glanced at the priest as he was explaining his

orders to the decurion of the nearest cavalry squadron. He faced Macro again. 'I'm not sure how far I trust him any more.'

'Hamedes?' Macro shook his head. 'What the hell are you talking about? He's served us as loyally as any soldier these last months. Besides, you know his story. Hamedes wants revenge just as we do.'

'That's his story,' Cato replied quietly.

Macro let out a sharp, exasperated breath. 'You mind telling me what's brought this on?'

Hamedes had secured two spare canteens and was striding back towards them.

'I can't explain now. Just do as I say. Go with him, find out what you can about Ajax's position, and watch Hamedes closely. I may be jumping at shadows. I don't know, but just watch him.'

'As you wish. But I'm telling you, Hamedes is all right. I feel it in my bones. He's no traitor.'

Macro stilled his tongue as the priest approached and handed him one of the canteens. Macro nodded his thanks and slung the strap over his shoulder, adjusted his sword belt and then looked at Hamedes. 'Ready?'

'Yes, sir.'

'Then let's be off.' Macro surveyed the sides of the gorge and then saw a small cut in an outcrop that seemed to offer a steep climb up to higher ground. 'That way.'

He was about to set off when the sound of hoofbeats echoed up the gorge. A moment later the legate and his staff officers appeared, cantering up the track. They reined in in front of Cato and the others in a cloud of dust and dismounted. Aurelius handed his reins to one of his orderlies and paced over to the three men who stood to attention.

'The archers are half a mile behind me,' Aurelius announced. 'We shall put this business to an end before the hour is up.'

'I'm not so certain, sir,' Cato replied, and explained his intention to send the two men forward to reconnoitre. The legate dismissed it with a brusque shake of the head.

'Out of the question. There's no time for it.'

'But sir, the moment we advance in force, the enemy will go into hiding. If we don't know which tomb they use for cover, it could take us days to find them. Better to spend an hour or so now than risk that, surely?'

Aurelius was perspiring freely from his ride up through the baking heat of the gorge and like most of his officers he had had little sleep for some days.

'You presume too much, Tribune Cato. I told you earlier, I am in command of the mopping up. Not you. You have no right to issue orders for our men to hold position while you send these two forward on some pointless spying mission.'

'Sir, I gave the order while we waited for you to reach the gorge. I did it because you wished to save time. You made it very clear that we must end this part of the operation as quickly as possible and march against Prince Talmis. Your priorities were very much in my mind when I gave the order.'

Aurelius sucked in a calming breath and frowned. Cato could see him struggling with the prospect of concurring with his subordinate's judgement while at the same time retaining his authority. At length the legate nodded curtly.

'Very well, we'll scout their position. But not Macro. It was remiss of you to involve one of my most valuable and experienced officers in such a risky venture. When the time comes to face the Nubians, I shall need Macro at the head of the First Cohort.'

'Sir, it's precisely because of his experience that I chose Macro.'

'Then you must choose another. Better still, I will find the man.' He turned to his staff officers. 'I need a volunteer to scout ahead.'

Tribune Junius took a step forward. 'I request the honour.'

'Done! Brave lad.' Aurelius turned back to Cato. 'Far better to give a fresh soldier the chance to win his spurs than lay additional burdens on the shoulders of those who have already proved themselves. See? That's how a good commander does the job . . . Tribune Junius!'

'Sir?'

'Remove your armour and go with this man.' He gestured towards Hamedes. 'He will explain the details as you go.'

'Yes, sir.'

The legate looked up. 'There are perhaps four hours of light left. I shall give you two hours to return. That is when I shall give the order to storm the valley.'

For over an hour the two men climbed higher into the rocks that towered above the gorge. They proceeded cautiously as they worked their way towards the small valley at the end of the track, taking care not to dislodge any large stone that might start a landslide and give away their position. Tribune Junius led the way, occasionally turning to Hamedes to ask for general directions. Above them the sun edged towards the jagged summits at the end of the valley and the heat wrapped itself around them like a burning vice so that every breath felt laboured and even the occasional waft of air was warm and cloying. Soon their linen tunics were saturated with sweat and stuck to their skin.

Then, as they crested a ridge that sloped down sharply towards the track, Junius froze and quickly eased himself down against the rock.

'What is it, sir?' Hamedes asked in a hushed voice.

'I see 'em,' Junius whispered, frantically gesturing for the priest to join him.

Hamedes shuffled forward and peered over the rocks, down into the valley. There was a large outcrop above the final bend of the track and four men in black robes sat amongst the boulders, keeping watch. A short distance beyond, the track gave out on to an open space where the horses were hobbled. Dotted around the cliffs were several openings of various sizes. Two men, with shields slung over their backs and armed with lances, appeared from behind some rocks further along and strode towards the horses.

Junius and Hamedes watched for a moment longer, then the tribune gestured towards an outcrop a hundred paces further into the valley. 'Come on.'

The two crossed the ridge as stealthily as possible, all the time watching the lookouts below for any sign that they had been detected. However, the Arabs' attention was firmly fixed on the track and they never once looked up the cliff above them. The two climbed along the rock cautiously, testing every handhold and step as they went. It was exhausting work and by the time they had reached the outcrop they were forced to stop and recover their strength. They took some water from their canteens, and then crept forward on to a flat slab sticking out at a right angle from the cliff. The drop on the far side was sheer and Hamedes felt a twinge of dizziness as he looked straight down into the valley. The two enemy soldiers had reached the horses and sat close by in the shade, foreshortened into heads and limbs from the point of view of those spying on them. There was no sign of anyone else and no clue as to where the rest of the men were concealed.

Junius scratched his jaw anxiously. 'We have to get closer. Somewhere we can see the entrances of the tombs more easily.'

His companion gazed down the cliff and then pointed towards another outcrop where the valley divided, a spur heading off into the rocks to the north. 'There, sir. That should do.'

Junius followed the direction indicated, thought a moment and then nodded. 'Right.'

They were making their way down the cliff when another figure emerged below them, striding towards the horses. Junius opened his mouth to say something then paused and turned to Hamedes.

'Recognise him?'

Hamedes squinted a moment to be sure and then nodded. 'Ajax.'

The gladiator stopped when he had a clear view of the horses and the lookouts in the rocks beyond. He cupped his hands to his mouth and called out, 'Any sign of movement?'

One of the Arabs turned and called back in accented Greek, 'Nothing, sir.'

Ajax was still for a moment, thinking, then he called again. 'They're coming. Sooner rather than later. Be sure to sound the alarm and then make every arrow count.'

The Arab waved his hand in acknowledgement and turned back to keep watch on the track. Ajax made his way over to the men waiting with the horses. There was a muted exchange before the gladiator turned away and returned the way he had come. As he departed, the two rebels approached the horses. The first man took the reins and patted the horse's flank soothingly while his companion went round to the other side, drew his sword and cut the animal's throat. It jerked back with a high-pitched whinny that was cut short by a strangled gurgle as the blood coursed from the wound and splattered the dust and gravel between its hoofs. It stood still for an instant and then its legs trembled and gave way and the animal collapsed. The pair moved on to the next horse, which stamped its hoofs but could not move far thanks to the length of rope hobbling it. The smell of blood and the terrified whinny of the first horse made the others afraid and skittish, and the rebels' bloody task proceeded with difficulty.

'Why do that?' Hamedes asked.

'It's obvious. Ajax has no need of the horses any more. He doesn't want them to fall back into Roman hands. Hello? Where's he got to?'

Ajax had disappeared round a huge boulder dividing the main course of the small valley and the spur. They waited a moment but there was no further sign of him. The tribune drummed his fingers on the rock in front of him and then turned to Hamedes.

'Wait here. I'm going forward for a closer look. We have to know where he's gone.'

Hamedes nodded.

'Make sure you stay out of sight,' Junius continued softly, though there was an anxious edge to his voice. 'Give me until the sun reaches the top of those rocks, then if I haven't returned, get back to the column and report to the legate. Understood?'

'Yes, sir.'

Junius edged forward, creeping through the jumbled rock on hands and knees, until he was lost from sight. Hamedes stared after him for a while, but saw no more sign of the tribune. Below, the two men killed the last of the horses and then retreated back to the shade, leaving the bodies amid dark stains and pools of blood where the flies and other small insects soon found them and began to feed. Hamedes glanced once more in the direction that Junius had taken and then cautiously made his way further down the slope towards the men.

CHAPTER THIRTY-ONE

'Are you quite certain?' the legate asked Hamedes directly.

'Yes, sir.' The priest nodded. 'I saw them enter the tomb. Ajax and some of his men.'

'What about you?' Aurelius turned towards Tribune Junius. 'Can you confirm this?'

Junius shook his head. 'I went in a different direction, sir. Beyond the place where the priest says he saw this tomb. I went to the end of the track that led off from the main valley. I must have missed it,' he confessed with a hint of shame in his voice. 'Just as well that the priest picked up on it, sir, or we'd never have located them.'

'All the same, good work. Both of you!' The legate smiled at Hamedes. 'I shall see that you are rewarded when the campaign is over.'

Hamedes shook his head and responded with quiet intensity, 'Revenge is its own reward, sir.'

Cato intervened. 'Can you describe the location of this tomb?'

'Of course, sir.' Hamedes squatted down beside the track where a small mound of gritty sand had collected in a hollow. Smoothing it out, he drew a basic map of the terrain with his finger as he explained. 'Here is the final bend in the track. Beyond that is the valley. There are many tombs dotted about the cliffs, but I saw no one enter or leave any of them. Just here are several large boulders. The track mentioned by the tribune branches off from the main valley and climbs up into the cliffs. About a quarter of a mile along it there is a steep path leading up to the base of the cliff. There is an opening cut into the rock there and steps leading down to a tomb entrance. It is easily missed, sir. I am not surprised the tribune passed by it without seeing anything. It was only because I saw Ajax and two of his men emerge from the steps that I discovered its location.'

'And you are certain you can find it again?' asked Cato.

'Yes, sir.'

'How many of his men did you see?'

Hamedes thought for a moment. 'Six Arabs, all told, and four big men, like Ajax, gladiators probably. There may have been more that I missed.'

The legate snorted with derision. 'Ten men, or thereabouts. It seems I have brought a mallet to crack a walnut. Very well, now that we know where they are we can move up and take them.' He glanced up at the sky. The valley was already in shadow. 'We have an hour or so before nightfall. I'll lead the attack. We'll take torches into the tomb and hunt them down. Two cavalry squadrons should suffice, and a half century of archers to pick off their lookouts. Tribune Junius will lead the rest of the men back to camp.'

Junius bowed his head. 'Yes, sir.'

Aurelius clapped his hands together. 'Let's be about our business then, gentlemen!'

It was dark by the time the contingent reached the entrance to the tomb that Hamedes had identified. The Arabs had only briefly delayed their entrance into the valley, hitting two of the auxiliary archers before they were pinned down by a steady rain of arrows while a second party of archers worked up to higher ground from where the Arabs could be easily targeted and swiftly disposed of. Aurelius led the column past the empty tombs in the main part of the valley where the horses were left in the charge of one of the cavalry squadrons. Then the priest guided them along the winding track, past a handful of other openings and then up the short climb to the steps cut down into the rock. As they approached, the Romans saw a figure just inside the entrance to the tomb. He shouted a warning to his comrades before scurrying down the tunnel that led deep beneath the cliff. The leading section of auxiliaries made a rush down the steps before Macro bellowed at them to come back.

'What the hell do you think you're doing? It's pitch black down there. You go flying into the tunnel and the first man that falls will break his bloody neck, and the rest of you will trip over him and go the same way. Get a fire going and make up some torches.' He turned to Cato with a disgusted look. 'Idiots.'

'Quite right.' The legate nodded as he peered into the dark tunnel. 'We'll need illumination. Plenty of it.'

The last of the daylight faded in the heavens as the soldiers gathered some dry branches of vegetation that clung to cracks in the rock. One of the archers produced a tinderbox and struck his flints until he managed to coax a tiny flame on to the thin slivers of charred linen in the box. The fire quickly took once the flame was presented to the kindling and soon the cliff above the entrance was aglow with the light from the flames that crackled up from the fire burning a short distance from the mouth of the tomb.

'Twenty men should suffice,' Aurelius decided. 'And I'll take a section of archers. If the tunnels are straight, they should be able to get a few shots off if they get the chance. Make sure we have plenty of torches, Macro.'

'Yes, sir.' He gestured to the tightly bound bundles of dry twigs and brush piled to one side. 'I've already seen to that.'

'Good man.' Aurelius nodded approvingly, his gaze fixed on the entrance to the tomb. Macro realised that the legate was rapidly losing his enthusiasm to lead the party now that he found himself staring into the dark hole, wherein lurked a small group of desperate and deadly fugitives.

'I'll lead the men, if you like, sir,' Macro suggested quietly. 'No need for you to come.'

The legate tore his gaze away from the tomb and frowned at Macro. 'Certainly not. A legate should share the same dangers as his men. Otherwise he is not fit to command them.'

'Yes, sir. Shall we begin then?'

'Yes . . . Yes, of course.' Aurelius strode across to the bundle of torches and picked one up. He lowered it into the fire and let it catch light, then stood by the steps leading down to the tomb entrance. Macro lit another torch and detailed two of the archers to go first, one with an arrow notched, the other holding a torch. Macro was about to follow them when Cato paced over to pick up a torch.

'You'd better stay here, sir,' Macro said firmly.

Cato shook his head. 'I'm coming.'

'Not with that arm in a sling. The first stretch of the tunnel looks steep. We'll need to keep a hand spare to stop stumbling. You'll only get in the way, sir. Be more of a hindrance than a help.' Macro meant it in a kindly fashion but Cato shot him a sour look.

'Thanks. But if you think I'm prepared to sit by while you go up against Ajax, then you're mad.'

'The centurion's right,' Aurelius interrupted. 'You'll stay here with the rest of the men until it's over. That's an order.'

Cato's lips pressed together in a thin line for a moment before he responded through clenched teeth. 'Yes, sir.'

He backed away and sat on a rock that overlooked the cut steps. He watched sullenly as the archers entered the tomb, then Macro descended the stairs, followed by Hamedes. Cato cleared his throat and called down.

'Take care, Macro . . . Watch your back.'

Macro looked up at him briefly and grinned, then he passed out of sight. The legate followed Hamedes into the tomb, then came the rest of the auxiliaries and archers, several of them carrying lit torches. The last man, bearing a coil of rope over his shoulder, entered the tunnel and the bright glow of his torch wavered and faded and then there was only the faint scrape of iron-nailed boots on the floor of the tunnel and echoed comments which gradually faded away. Cato sat still for a moment, uneasy with the burden of his fears and suspicions. Then he glanced irritably down at his arm in the sling and slowly eased it free and attempted to flex it. At once there was a red-hot shooting pain through his shoulder joint and he groaned and stilled his arm. When the pain had receded, he eased the sling back on and looked down at the pitch-black entrance to the tunnel. Whatever happened in the tomb, there was nothing he could do about it now. Without Cato being aware of it, his left foot began to twitch in an agitated rhythm as he settled back on his rock and waited for Macro and the others to return.

The passage was wide enough for two men to walk abreast, but the incline was steep and Macro found that he had to step cautiously down the pitted rock surface to avoid slipping. By the wavering and flaring light of his torch and the one ahead of him held by the archer, he could see that the walls of the tunnel were painted with detailed depictions of the native gods and kings. Sometimes the kings, wearing the combined crowns of the upper and lower Nile realms, were making offerings to the gods. In other images they were leading their armies to war. The images were interspersed with the incomprehensible but strangely beautiful script of the ancients that Macro had grown used to seeing on the religious buildings that dotted the province. The air in the tunnel was warm and damp-smelling and the further they went down into the rock, the more the walls and roof seemed to close in about him. It was an illusion, he told himself. He had never liked enclosed spaces and the fact that Ajax and his men lay in wait ahead only added to the burden of apprehension that settled on Macro.

They had gone at least a hundred paces when the floor of the tunnel evened out slightly and made the going easier. Macro glanced back to make sure that the others were not too bunched up, and then gave the order for the party to halt. The echoing footsteps slowly died away and the tunnel fell silent.

'What is it?' Aurelius whispered. 'Why have you stopped?'

'To listen, sir.' Macro touched his finger to his lips and then cocked his head to one side and stood still, straining his ears to detect any sound of movement from ahead above the rasp of his own breathing. At first there was nothing, then a faint rustling and soft whispers that made the hair rise up at the back of Macro's neck. He eased himself forward, past the archer holding his bow ready. The lead man held his torch out in front of him and was staring intently down the tunnel. The gently wavering hue cast by the still torch lit up the way ahead for a good twenty paces. Then, just as it faded into the darkness, there was a black outline as the tunnel gave out on to a wider space.

'Seen anything moving down there?' Macro whispered.

'I thought so, sir.'

'Thought so?' Macro growled. 'You did, or you didn't. Which?'

The archer swallowed. 'I–I did, sir. Sure of it.'

Macro nodded, and shuffled back past the second

archer. 'Be ready to shoot the moment you see any of 'em.'

As he returned to his original place in the line, Macro passed on the order to draw swords and make ready, then he hissed at the leading archer to continue down the tunnel. The line of men moved cautiously towards the opening. The glimmer of the torch revealed that their path continued downwards but there was darkness where the chamber opened out with a pit on either side. As Macro emerged into the space, he raised his torch and looked round. The builders of the tomb had cut out a cube, roughly forty feet in each dimension, through which a ramp-like walkway passed at an angle. The precision of the angles and dimensions appeared eerily perfect. On either side of the ramp there was a drop of about twenty feet, and by the light of the torch Macro could make out the spoil and rubbish that had been abandoned in the tomb by successive robbers and the curious who had dared to explore the darkened tunnel over the centuries.

'Watch it!' the leading man cried out as he ducked. An arrow whirred over his head and struck the next man in the right arm. He cried out and let go of the arrow string and his shaft skittered across the ramp. He staggered back, and the men behind him instinctively ducked down or moved aside as they anticipated another arrow.

'Watch it, you fool!' Aurelius's voice cried out behind Macro. As he turned, there was a scrabbling of boots and a desperate shout of panic.

He glimpsed the legate teetering on the edge of the ramp, arms flailing, his torch flaring madly, then he fell into the pit, the flames of the tumbling torch illuminating his swift descent, broken by a heavy thud that cut off his cry.

'Shit!' Macro snarled, as he braced his feet and looked over the edge of the ramp. By the light of the torch guttering close to the legate, Macro saw Aurelius lying spreadeagled on his back. His mouth was open in a soundless scream and his eyes blinked rapidly as blood, dark as pitch, spread out behind his head.

Another arrow shot up the tunnel, narrowly missing the two archers before it bounced off Macro's shield at an upward angle and clattered off the wall of the chamber. Macro quickly stepped past the wounded archer and lowered his shield to provide cover from the next arrow. A moment later there was a loud crack, amplified by the surrounding rock, as a second arrow struck Macro's shield squarely and punched through the layers of leather and wood as it lodged. He grabbed the torch from the leading archer. 'Get behind my shield and start shooting back!'

The man nodded and hurriedly plucked an arrow from his quiver, strung it, drew back and then bobbed up just long enough to release the shaft down the tunnel.

'Keep that up!' Macro ordered, and then turned to look up the ramp. The wounded archer was shuffling back along the line of men who had pressed themselves to the ground, and where the ramp entered the tunnel, they hugged the walls. Hamedes was crouched down a short distance behind Macro.

'What happened to the legate?' asked Macro.

'I don't know, sir. He was just ahead of me, then stumbled and must have lost his footing.'

'Right, well, we have to get him out.' Macro raised his

voice and called back up the line. 'Pass the rope forward!'

There was a brief delay, during which another three arrows came flying up from the depths of the tomb, two striking Macro's shield while the third whipped past and splintered against the rock just beside the tunnel leading up to the tomb's entrance. Then the coil of rope appeared, passed from man to man until Hamedes took hold of it. Macro had already seen that there was nothing to tie the end to and he pointed back up the tunnel. 'Find an anchor man to tie it round his waist and then have four more on the rope to take the strain.'

'Yes, sir. Let me go down and get the legate.'

'No. You take my shield. I'll do it,' Macro decided.

Hamedes came forward, squeezing between the archer and Macro, and took hold of the handle. Macro grasped his shoulder as he gave him his orders. 'Move forward, nice and slow, like. No more than ten paces into the next section of tunnel. The archer goes with you. Keep harassing whoever it is that's down there taking pot shots. Clear?'

Hamedes and the archer nodded.

'Then get on with it.'

As soon as the rope was ready Macro tied a loop in the end and put his boot in. He eased himself over the edge, clinging to the rope with both hands as his men took the strain and began to lower him into the pit. As soon as his boot touched the ground, Macro let go and scrambled across the rubble to the legate. Aurelius's eyes had closed and his breathing was swift and shallow. Macro carefully examined his body and felt a swelling around the legate's leg and the misshapen bend to his left arm. The back of his head was drenched in blood and felt pulpy. Aurelius let out a long deep groan and Macro withdrew his hands.

'You're in a bad way, old son.' Macro shook his head sadly. 'Best get you out of here quickly.' He pulled the rope over, called for some slack and then fastened it around the legate's chest, under his arms.

'Pull him up, nice and gently!'

The rope creaked under the burden as Macro guided the legate's body into the air. Halfway up he began to tremble wildly and let out a series of breathless grunts. Then he reached the ramp and the auxiliaries pulled him up the tunnel and returned the end of the rope to Macro. When he had climbed back up, Macro took a deep breath and gave his orders. 'Get the legate and the wounded man out of the tomb. Tribune Cato can have them taken straight back to the main camp. Meanwhile, we'll settle our business here.'

Macro made his way into the tunnel and rejoined Hamedes. The archer was squatting down beside the priest, making no attempt to shoot down the tunnel.

'What the hell have you stopped for?' Macro demanded.

'There's been nothing coming the other way for a while now, sir,' the archer explained.

'Fair enough,' Macro relented. 'Let's push on. Hamedes, you take charge of the torch, keep it as high as you can.'

With Macro holding the shield to the front, and the torch held up and to the side, while the archer fitted another arrow, the three men continued slowly down the tunnel, followed by the rest of the small force. Soon, Macro could discern another chamber ahead of them. This time, the space was illuminated as the defenders had lit some torches of their own. Another arrow whipped up the tunnel towards them, going to the side where it ricocheted off the wall. Macro kept moving. Now he could clearly hear voices ahead of them. He continued forward, to the threshold of the new chamber, and by the light of a torch left burning on the ground he could see that it was larger than the one they had passed through earlier but had a solid floor with square columns running down its length, also cut from the rock.

There was no sign of the defenders. Macro waited for the rest of his men to join him and prepare to charge into the chamber as soon as he gave the order. A movement by one of the columns to his left drew Macro's eye just as the man loosed an arrow. It struck the wall close to Macro's head and he felt a chip of stone cut into his chin.

He snarled, turning towards the man.

Macro roared as he rushed down the length of the chamber towards the enemy who hurriedly prepared his next arrow. He just had time to raise the bow, draw the string and release the arrow before Macro reached him. The arrow zipped past Macro's ear, and then he smashed his shield into his opponent, sending him flying back. He hit the floor with a solid thud. Macro looked quickly from side to side, but there was no movement except for the auxiliary soldiers spilling out into the chamber. By the light of the torches Macro saw that the man he had downed had a large stained dressing on his thigh. Near him, on the floor of the chamber, was a makeshift walking stick fashioned from a cavalry lance. He had recovered from the blow and was already reaching for his bow.

Macro stepped forward and kicked it away. The man reached for the dagger in his belt instead, drawing it and making a wild slash at Macro's leg. Macro parried the blow and stepped outside the range of the dagger.

'Drop it!'

The gladiator shuffled away until he reached the wall of the chamber and then he leaned back and held the dagger out, ready to strike again.

'I said drop it.'

'Fuck you, Roman!' the rebel spat. 'If you want it, come and get it!'

He held the knife up, daring Macro. With an impatient sigh, Macro stepped forward, parried the dagger low on his shield and then thrust his blade into the man's chest. He gasped under the impact, then slumped aside as Macro wrenched the blade free and turned away. 'Any more of them here?'

None of his men replied and Macro frowned as he sheathed his sword. 'Where the hell are they all? Where is Ajax?'

'Sir! Over here!'

Macro found one of his men pointing to a small opening on the far side of the chamber. There was a short slope down into yet another chamber. Macro squatted and cocked his head for a better look. There was no sign of any movement. He tried to listen but the footsteps of his men and their muttering filled the chamber.

'Stand still!' Macro bellowed.

As the last echo faded away, he listened again. There was no sound from the chamber. Nothing. Then he heard it, the faintest of sounds, like a dog panting in the distance.

'Ajax! . . . Ajax, you are trapped. I'll give you one chance to surrender, then we're coming for you and your men . . . Ajax, you hear me?'

There came no reply as he had expected and Macro listened again and then muttered, 'Damn.' He turned back to his men. 'I'm going down there. I'll call for you if I need help. If there's any trouble then you pile in and take no prisoners. Got it?'

Macro sheathed his sword and took one of the torches held by his men and inspected the passage more closely. It was steeper than the others they had descended, but no more than twenty feet in length. The floor of another chamber opened out beyond. Macro tested his boots at the top of the ramp but it was clear that he would not be able to keep his feet if he tried to walk down. Instead he crouched down, pushing his shield out at a shallow angle in front of him and held the torch aloft in his sword hand.

'Be careful, sir,' said Hamedes.

Macro smiled at him. 'Here I go.'

Macro shifted his weight and began to slide down the tunnel, his nailed boots scraping over the stone. The rush of air made the torch burn brighter, filling the narrow passage with a fiery glow. Then he entered the chamber and took half a step forward to establish his balance as he reached flat ground. He quickly turned from side to side, waving the torch in front of him. The chamber was much smaller than the one above, with just four columns. There was a crudely fashioned ladder, some discarded cloaks and waterskins lying on the ground but no sign of anyone, nor any sign of another opening in its walls.

Then he heard some scrabbling coming from the far corner of the chamber. Macro raised his torch towards it and saw a man sitting propped up against the wall. He wore only a loincloth and like his comrade in the chamber above he was wounded; he had a large dressing covering his stomach. He held a dagger in his hand but made no attempt to raise it towards Macro. The centurion cautiously approached him and the glow of the torch revealed the man's glistening skin and the sweat that dripped from his brow. His chest rose and fell in short jerks as he struggled to breathe. He shut his eyes for an instant and then blinked them open, trying to focus on Macro.

'Where are they?' Macro asked him. 'Where are Ajax and the others?'

'Gone,' the man rasped, and then licked his lips and smiled faintly as he repeated. 'Gone . . .'

'Where?' Macro asked harshly. 'They were in this cave. Where are they?'

The other man shook his head. 'Are you Centurion Macro?' The man struggled to get the words out.

'What if I am?'

'He – Ajax – told me to give you a message.' The man smiled weakly. 'He said to tell you that he's fucked you before, and now he's fucked you again, and he'll fuck you for as long as he lives.'

Macro stared at the dying man for a moment, his mind and heart filling with blind rage. The torch dropped from his hand and he snatched out his sword before he even realised that he had done so. With a cry of hatred and anger that tore at his throat, Macro raised the blade and smashed it down on the other man's head so brutally that skin, skull and brains exploded into one gory welter as the edge of his sword cleaved the man's skull from the top of his cranium right down to his jaw. Macro yanked his sword free and raised it to strike again, his lips curled back in a savage snarl, but the man was quite dead.

Macro's sword hung, poised over the body, blood dripping from its edge. He breathed in and out through his nose, his nostrils flaring. Slowly reason returned to him and he backed away from the body. He took one look round the cave in the hope of seeing something, some clue, that would reveal the presence of Ajax, but there was nothing. Macro turned back to the entrance to the chamber and called up to Hamedes.

'Lower me the rope. It's all over. We're done here.'

'And Ajax?'

'Ajax?' Macro shook his head. 'Not here. It's like he just vanished . . .'

CHAPTER THIRTY-TWO

'Will he live?' asked Cato.

The surgeon did not answer immediately but sat still on his stool beside the legate's bed and considered his patient. Outside, dawn was breaking and the bucinas were rousing the men in the camp at Karnak. Macro and Cato stood to one side of the surgeon, sand and dust griming their faces. They had returned from the far bank, with the two Roman casualties, during the early hours. Aurelius had been carried down to the river on a stretcher fashioned from two cavalry lances and some cloaks. As soon as the boat crossed to the landing platform, the legate was rushed up to the infirmary while the archer went to have his wounded arm cleaned and dressed.

It took an hour for the surgeon to set the legate's broken limbs as well as he could and then splint them. The head wound was a more complicated affair and the blood had to be carefully washed away before the wound could be cleaned and examined. Aurelius lay on his side, his body tightly packed with bolsters so that he did not move. His breathing was ragged and Cato could see that the back of his head was badly misshapen beneath a thin linen dressing through which the blood was slowly seeping.

'Live?' The surgeon looked up from his patient. 'I doubt it. He's lost a lot of blood, and some brain matter. It came away when I was removing the skull fragments. I've put in a brass plate and sewn the scalp up. However, I don't hold out much hope. Anyway, even if he does survive, his brain is damaged beyond repair. He would be condemned to spend the rest of his days as a simpleton. Death would be a mercy for him now.'

Cato nodded. 'I see. Then I'd be obliged if you would write up your conclusions and have them entered in the legion's log book.'

The surgeon stood up and faced Cato. 'Sir, I have a hospital full of wounded men following the actions of the previous two days. I have to devote my attention to them before I can deal with any reports.'

'I understand,' Cato replied gently. 'However, you must do as I say. The legate, though alive, is no longer capable of performing his duties. Therefore authority over the legion, and the rest of the army, passes to the next officer in the chain of command.'

'Namely you, sir.'

'Precisely. There must be no doubt that I have followed the correct protocols in assuming command. I cannot afford to have my authority challenged. For the sake of the men.'

'And to cover your back, in the event that the campaign does not end well for Rome, no doubt.'

'You can think what you like. But I need your statement entered into the records.' Cato spoke firmly. 'At once, if you don't mind.'

The surgeon hesitated. 'And if I do mind?'

'Then at once in any case. That is an order.'

'Yes, sir.'

Cato turned to Macro. 'Centurion, come. We need to talk.'

He turned and walked from the room set aside for the legate's treatment. Macro followed him, falling into step with Cato as they emerged from the hospital. They made their way across the temple complex towards the southern entrance and the headquarters beyond.

'That's a pretty bold step,' said Macro. 'I'm not sure the governor is going to be happy that you've assumed command of the army. It's all that stands between Prince Talmis and the lower Nile.'

'The governor is far from the centre of operations,' Cato responded. 'He is in no position to judge what course of action should be taken. In any case, the latest reports we have are that the Nubians are no more than a day's march from here. What would you have me do? Send a request to him asking for advice on how we should proceed, and then sit on my arse and wait for his response? By then we'll have been overrun and Prince Talmis would be well on his way to Memphis and the delta region. It'd be a bloody disaster, and you know it.'

'Of course I do.' Macro smiled. 'But then I'm not the one taking control of the army. If nothing else, it proves that you've got balls of solid iron, my friend.'

'Oh?' Cato turned to him. 'Don't think for a moment that I'm the only one who is sticking his neck out. I might be taking on the command of this army, but my first act is going to be to make you my camp prefect. So you'd better hope we come out of this covered in glory because the alternative won't smell nearly so sweet.'

'The thing that is puzzling me is how the hell Ajax could have got away from us,' Macro fumed as he settled on one of the comfortable stools in the legate's quarters. 'We had the right tomb. His men had been in there and he had left two of his injured behind. We didn't miss any side passages or openings. So he must have got out before we closed the trap.'

'Obviously.'

'But then how did he get out of the valley? He couldn't have climbed out, not without being seen, and he couldn't have got by us.'

Cato was silent for a moment. 'He didn't. We got past him.'

Macro frowned. 'What are you talking about?'

'Think it through, Macro. As soon as we knew which tomb he was in we made straight for it. Marched right into the valley and turned up that side track towards the tomb you searched. So what do you think happened?'

Macro thought a moment and took a sharp breath. 'It couldn't be that simple, surely?'

Cato shrugged. 'How else could he have escaped? He must have heard us march by. By the gods, I wouldn't be surprised if he had been bold enough to watch us from one of those tombs at the entrance to the valley. As soon as we passed out of sight, he and his men emerged, crept back down the track towards the Nile and made their escape.'

'He could be anywhere by now,' Macro reflected.

'That's right.'

Macro shook his head in wonder. 'Ajax has to be the

most cunning bastard we've ever had to deal with, aside from that little shit Narcissus back in Rome. He must have known we'd try to work out his hiding place, then he let us see just enough to convince our scouts before switching his men to another tomb. Clever.'

'Yes, clever. Or perhaps there's another reason he got away from us.'

'You mean luck? He just happened to switch tombs at just the right moment? Unlikely.'

'Extremely unlikely.' Cato folded his hands together and leaned over the legate's table to concentrate his full attention on Macro. 'I'm talking about something else, Macro. I'm saying that I think Ajax was warned. He was told that we had sent scouts to find his hiding place. That's why he changed it and was able to trick us.'

'Warned? Who by?'

Cato did not reply. He was quiet for a moment as his tired mind put his thoughts together. At length he leaned back and addressed his friend in an even tone. 'Don't you think that Ajax has had a rather extraordinary run of good fortune since we've been pursuing him across Egypt?'

'Good fortune?' Macro pursed his lips. 'What do you mean, exactly?'

'Let's start with recent events. Ajax's escape from the temple. You remember the cavalry prefect's report about the massacre of one of his patrols. He said that the attackers had used a password to get close. So, how did they get the password?'

'Might they not have overheard someone using it? Like Junius said.'

'They might, but the men are pretty good at talking

only as loudly as they must when making challenges. Even so, the man who gave the password was in Roman kit.'

'I suppose they could have stripped one of the bodies of the men we lost in the first assault.'

Cato nodded. 'That's what I thought. So I checked with one of your optios before we left the temple to head for the valley of the tombs. All the bodies were accounted for, and so was their kit.'

Macro stared shrewdly at his comrade. 'This isn't something that's only just occurred to you, is it?'

'I had my suspicions. Then when we got to the valley, there was the business with the wrong tomb being identified, and then the legate falling from the ramp.'

Macro shook his head. 'That was an accident.'

'You saw it happen?'

Macro was exhausted and had to concentrate hard to remember the details of what had happened in the tomb. 'We were on the ramp . . . An arrow was shot at us. I heard a cry . . . Turned and saw the legate falling. Yes, it was an accident.'

'Tell me, who was standing closest to the legate when it occurred?'

'Hamedes was there,' Macro replied, and then he stared intently at Cato.

'Hamedes.' Cato nodded. 'Precisely.'

Macro was silent for a moment as he took the accusation in. 'Are you saying he's a traitor?'

'That implies that he has betrayed us. I think he never was on our side in the first place. Think about it, Macro. What is his story? He was the only survivor of Ajax's raid on his temple.'

'Yes, but he was spared by Ajax to let others know who was responsible. Just like he left other survivors.'

'True,' Cato responded. 'Which is why we were predisposed to believe him.'

Macro shook his head. 'This is too far-fetched, Cato. If there is a traitor out there, it isn't Hamedes. I know the lad well enough. He's been straight with us. Why, he's faced every danger we have. These other things you mention are just coincidences.'

'Like the cobra in our tent? Ever wondered where that came from? Did you notice that Hamedes had a large kitbag when he boarded the barge in Cairo? It was a lot smaller when he disembarked. Then there were the fragments of a broken jar close to the tent. I wonder what the jar had contained, and where it came from? Just more coincidences? Tell me, have you never had any grounds to doubt him?'

Macro thought back over the time he had known the young priest. He recalled the raid on Ajax's base and the fire in the lookout tower that had given away their presence to the rebels. Hamedes could have lit the fire easily enough while the rest of them were preoccupied. The seeds of suspicion that Cato had planted were readily watered by Macro's recollection of that event.

There was a knock on the door frame and an optio stepped into the room.

Cato looked up at him. 'Yes?'

'I've brought the priest to you, sir. As ordered.'

Cato glanced at Macro. 'Let's see what Hamedes has to say for himself. Send him in, and stay with us.'

'Yes, sir.' The optio beckoned round the door frame.

405

'All right, gypo, this way. Smartly now!'

Hamedes entered the room, wearing a tunic. He looked dazed, as if he had just been woken. He smiled as he saw Macro and Cato. 'How can I help you, sirs?'

Cato stared at him without any expression and sat back in his chair. 'You can tell me what your real name is, for a start.'

Hamedes' smile faded. 'Sorry? What did you say, sir?'

'You heard me. I want to know your real name.'

Hamedes opened his mouth, closed it and looked helplessly at Macro. 'I don't understand.'

Cato puffed irritably. 'Let's try another tack. How long have you known Ajax? Did you join his rebellion in Crete, or did he recruit you from amongst the slaves of the ships he has raided since then?'

Hamedes swallowed anxiously. 'Sir, I am a humble priest. I have every reason to hate Ajax as much as you do. He butchered my brother priests and looted our sacred temple. I am Hamedes. You have to believe me, sir . . . please. I swear to you, on all that I hold holy, I am no spy. Believe me.'

Cato smiled coldly at him. 'By the gods, you would make a fine actor. No doubt that is why Ajax picked you for the task. Turns out to have been a good choice. After all, it was you who saved him from the temple, and later the tomb. And it was you who pushed the legate into the pit.'

'No!' Hamedes shook his head. 'I didn't do that. It was an accident. Centurion, you were there. You saw him fall.'

'I saw him fall,' Macro agreed quietly. 'But he could have been pushed.'

Hamedes looked at him with a horrified expression. 'You think *I* did it?'

'I . . . I don't know.' Macro shook his head slowly. 'Fuck, I really don't know.'

'Well, I do,' said Cato. 'There's more than enough evidence that points the finger of guilt at this man. After Ajax's escape from the temple, we know that someone in the army has been helping him. It was the escape from the tomb that confirmed my suspicions. This is our spy.' Cato paused. 'And there is only one punishment fit for a spy.'

Hamedes' eyes widened in terror. 'None of this is true! I'm innocent. By the gods, I swear it!'

Cato ignored him and turned his attention to the optio. 'Take him away.'

'What will you do to him?' asked Macro.

'We'll have him crucified at dawn, then send his head to the enemy. If Ajax has found his way back to the side of Prince Talmis, it will let him know what fate he and his men have awaiting them.'

The optio strode forward and grasped Hamedes by the arm. 'Come on, lad.'

Hamedes stood his ground, and the optio yanked him round harshly and steered him towards the door and out into the corridor.

'You're making a mistake!' Hamedes wailed. 'I'm not a spy. I'm innocent!'

Macro and Cato heard the sounds of a scuffle as the optio dragged him away. Then there was a shout.

'Oi, you bastard! Stop!'

Macro sprang up from his chair and ran to the door. Along the colonnade he saw Hamedes sprinting towards the exit. The optio had been knocked to the floor, but he recovered quickly, and drew his dagger as he rose to his feet. With a well-practised hand he flicked the dagger over so that he held the blade, then took quick aim, drew his arm back and threw the small blade as hard as he could after the fleeing figure. Macro saw the blade spin through the air before it struck Hamedes hard, just below his neck. His legs instantly collapsed under him and he fell, rolled over once like a child's doll and then lay still.

'What's happened?' Cato asked as he emerged behind Macro. 'Oh . . .'

The optio trotted forward and bent over the body. He placed a boot on Hamedes' head and pulled his knife free. He looked up at the two officers. 'He's done for, sir.'

Cato nodded.

Macro cleared his throat and muttered, 'I suppose it was a better end for him than the one he deserved. We were lucky, sir. If you hadn't exposed him now there's no telling how much more damage he would have done to our side.' Macro frowned and then admitted, 'I never suspected him . . . Never.'

CHAPTER THIRTY-THREE

Cato waited until the last of the officers had settled down on the benches set out in the courtyard of the priests' quarters. Macro stood a short distance to Cato's right, erect, boots apart, solid as a bull. The officers watched Cato expectantly, then he stood up and cleared his throat.

'Acting Legate Aurelius died of his injuries just after midday. I had already assumed command since he was incapacitated, attested to by the legion's surgeon. However, that is all academic now. As your new commander I have already given fresh orders for the prosecution of the campaign against the Nubians. There will be no division of the army. All forces will concentrate here, at Diospolis Magna, and then the army will march on the Nubians and give battle at the earliest opportunity.' Cato looked round at the officers. 'Any questions, gentlemen?'

The brevity of his address left most of his officers surprised. It took a moment before one of the older centurions, whom Cato recognised as being amongst the cronies of the late Aurelius, stood up. Centurion Aescher stared coolly at Cato and then gave him an insincere smile.

'Sir, I think I speak for most here when I say that the

loss of the acting legate is keenly felt. It comes as a hard blow on top of the death of the previous legate and the discovery of the spy that you unwittingly brought into our camp.'

Cato tried not to register his surprise and annoyance that word of Hamedes' treachery had spread through the legion already. The officer continued.

'One might be forgiven for thinking the Jackals have been cursed. Both previous commanders were men of immense experience in the service. Both knew the legion and its men well. Therefore, sir, you will understand me when I say that it is in the best interests of the legion, this army and Rome if we send a request to the governor in Alexandria to appoint a new, permanent, commander of the legion. It is in no way a judgement on your competence, sir. Rather, it is a reflection of the troubled state of the men's morale. They would prefer to be led by a man with the requisite experience and seniority,' the centurion concluded and resumed his seat.

'Thank you,' said Cato. 'Is there anyone else who wishes to speak?'

He looked round, but the officers kept their silence as they waited for him to respond to the centurion's remarks. Cato nodded. 'Very well, then. Your comments are noted. Now, hear my words.' Cato stared round the room. 'There will be no request. There is no time to refer the matter to the governor. I have assumed command legally and I will not tolerate any attempt to question my authority. The situation is too serious for playing games, gentlemen. The province is in great danger. We must deal with the threat swiftly and decisively. You may make all the protests you like once the Nubians have been defeated.'

The centurion rose again. 'Sir, might I ask what was wrong with the original plan? Legate Aurelius—'

'Acting Legate Aurelius,' Macro interrupted. 'Rather, Former Acting Legate Aurelius.'

The centurion shot Macro a hostile look before he continued. 'The previous commander's plan seemed sound enough to me. Your plan seems to be rather less subtle and far less likely to result in the trapping and destruction of the Nubians . . . sir.'

'Really?' Cato responded flatly. 'Forgive me, but I thought it was a common maxim of military strategy not to divide a weaker force in the face of a stronger one. Or do you do things differently here in Egypt?'

The sarcastic note of the last comment was not lost on the centurion and his companions. Cato ignored the brief chorus of mutters and continued. 'Aurelius's plan would have led to disaster. Our forces would each be defeated in turn and then Prince Talmis would be free to rampage across the province until such time as the Emperor could assemble an army large enough to drive the Nubians out. Meanwhile, the damage to wheat production and the destruction of the cities along the Nile would take many years to recover from. The same fate would await Egypt if we just sit on our arses and wait for a new commander to be sent to us. The only course of action that stands any chance of saving the army and the province is to strike at the enemy at once, with every man we can scrape together.' Cato paused and looked over the faces of the officers, men he needed to make his own if he was to have any chance of success. He moderated his tone when he spoke again.

'I do not need to explain myself to you, gentlemen. I have acted within the regulations laid down by the imperial army bureau, in the name of Emperor Claudius. That should suffice under normal conditions. I accept that our situation is somewhat irregular, but then when is war ever a neat and tidy affair? Until recent days the Twenty-Second Legion has been a garrison unit. The only action many of you and your men have seen is a minor skirmish as part of some police action or some punitive raid against brigands. Frankly, compared to the other legions that Centurion Macro and I have had the honour of serving with, the Jackals are second-rate. To be sure, the men are trained and exercised according to regulations, but they lack combat experience. That is the only true test of a soldier's value. It is a hard-won attribute. Now, some of the men have had the chance to prove themselves in the assault on the temple and they did well enough, but most of the men, and officers, are still to be tested. Including you, Centurion Aescher. I do not say this out of any desire to undermine you, but as a statement of fact. The other fact that cannot be disputed is that both Centurion Macro and I have had considerable campaign and battle experience. If anything, you should feel reassured that we will be leading you into battle. I cannot think of a more courageous example than Centurion Macro to inspire the men who follow him.'

Macro stirred uneasily at his friend's words then fixed his face in a stern expression and stood stock still.

'The Jackals have the potential to be fine soldiers,' Cato

continued. 'And our victory over the Nubians will give them a chance to win a battle honour for their eagle standard. But I will not lie to you about the scale of the challenge facing us. You must understand, and get your men to understand, that there are only two paths ahead of us when we march out to face the enemy – one leads to victory, the other to certain death. Now that I and Centurion Macro are in command, your chances have improved. The rest is up to you. Forget the past. Forget your plans for the future. Think only of killing your enemy. That is all that matters. It's a simple enough philosophy, gentlemen, and it has worked well enough for Centurion Macro and me over the years we have served together. Isn't that so?'

'Yes, sir!' Macro nodded.

Cato took a deep breath and looked round at his officers, seeing some spark of determination in their expressions. That was good, he reflected. Some of his words had struck home. He had done what he could to instil the right state of mind in his officers and stiffen their resolve in the face of the great test to come. 'The army marches from Karnak at first light tomorrow. You have the rest of the day to prepare your men, equipment and supplies. Dismissed!'

The officers stood up and began to make their way out of the courtyard, many of them conversing in low voices. Macro stood still until the last of them had left and then let his shoulders droop a little as he exhaled in a long, weary sigh.

'What do you think?' asked Cato.

'Oh, you were on fine form, lad. I have to say that I've heard the victory or death routine more than once before.

So have you. It's an old line but, so help me, it still stirs the blood.'

'Hmmm. I meant what do you think about our officers?'

Macro jerked his thumb towards the entrance to the courtyard. 'That lot? Not the best I've ever come across, and possibly not the worst.'

'That doesn't sound very encouraging.'

'Oh, they'll fight when the time comes.' Macro shrugged nonchalantly. 'After all, what choice have they got?'

'None, as it happens. I had the report from one of the patrols just before the briefing began. The Nubian army is still camped a day's march to the south. It has been for the last two days. It seems that Prince Talmis is challenging us to come out and face him.'

'Or we could wait for him here and hold him off.'

'No. If we do that, he'll surround us, bide his time and starve us into surrender. Either way, he has the advantage.'

Macro looked at his younger friend and could see the exhaustion marked in his face, and the bloodshot eyes. Cato had removed the sling before the officers had arrived and now supported his left arm with his spare hand. Macro felt a stab of paternal concern for Cato. 'Look here, there's nothing to be done now. The officers will make the preparations and I'll keep watch over them to make sure they do a good job. You should rest. Let that arm recover. We're going to need you in good shape tomorrow. Can't afford to have tiredness cloud your thinking. Not with all our lives at stake.'

Cato stared at him and smiled. 'Thank you. If there's time, I'll rest. But first I have to think about how we're going to win this campaign. Fine words are one thing, but they never won a battle. And after that business with Hamedes I can understand why they might question my judgement.'

'Bollocks. Hamedes was a spy. Spies are supposed to be good at winning trust. In any case, he didn't fool you in the end. You saw through him, and put a stop to his treachery,' Macro concluded bitterly.

Cato looked at him and saw that his friend was struggling to hide his true feelings. 'His betrayal hit you hard, didn't it?'

'Yes . . . I liked the lad. I thought he showed real guts in going into that valley to find Ajax's lair. Now I know it was all a sham. That bastard fooled me good and proper.'

Cato felt the need to offer his friend some crumb of comfort. 'For what it's worth, I think he admired you, despite being your enemy.'

'Even if that's true, what does it matter? Hamedes was Ajax's man. If I'd known, then I'd have killed him with my bare hands, without hesitation. I feel a bit of a fool, Cato. That's all there is to it. Good riddance.'

'Yes, of course.' Cato nodded, and knew it would be best to drop the subject. 'Macro, I need your help. I fear that we're in for the hardest battle we have ever fought.'

The first rays of the rising sun were angling across the low hills to the east as the Romans marched out of the camp at Karnak. The auxiliary cavalry led the way, its squadrons stretched out across the army to screen its advance. The main column was led by an auxiliary infantry cohort. Then came the legionaries, weighted down by their armour and the kit fixed to their marching yokes. Their helmets hung from brass hooks on their belts and the men wore light cotton headscarves to shield them from the glare of the coming day, and soak up the sweat from their scalps.

Long shadows were cast across the dust kicked up by preceding columns and from a short distance away, where Cato and Macro rode at the head of the small group of staff officers, the men appeared as dim figures amid the orange haze of dust. Behind the legion came the baggage train, together with the carts carrying the legion's complement of bolt throwers. There were rations for seven days and if the Nubians chose to fall back for any reason, Cato knew that he could only afford to pursue them a short distance. Prince Talmis would be certain to strip the land of supplies ahead of the Romans.

Tribune Junius edged his mount forward until it drew alongside the new commander of the army. He was silent for a moment and then coughed.

'What is it, Tribune?' asked Cato.

'Sir, I was wondering what your plans are for the coming battle.'

'To defeat the enemy.'

'Yes, of course, sir. Goes without saying.'

Macro turned to look at the tribune with a wry expression. 'So what more is there to say?'

Junius was not prepared to give in so easily and continued to address Cato. 'With respect, sir, I am now the senior tribune of the legion. In the event that anything happens to you and Centurion Macro, then the command will fall to me. I should know your intentions, sir. For the good of the army.'

Cato appraised him. It could only have been a few months since Junius was appointed a junior tribune and he was already bearing far greater responsibilities than his peers in other legions across the Empire. Such were the exigencies of war, Cato mused. It was true that Junius was third in the chain of command, in theory, yet although the centurions had accepted his own assumption of the legate's role, Cato doubted they would tolerate having to obey this callow youth, who had as much military experience as a raw recruit. Cato shook his head.

'You'll know my intentions in good time, Tribune. As for the prospect of having the command of the army foisted on you, I advise you to be careful what you wish for. You know how the saying goes?'

'Yes, sir. But I need to be ready, if misfortune should strike you and Macro.'

'Misfortune? That's a nice euphemism.' Cato chuckled drily. 'Learn the trade as fully as you can, Junius. Listen to the veterans and profit from their experience. Then you can think about command. For now, this is on-the-job training for you. That's all. You are not ready. If I fall, Macro takes over. If he falls, then it must be another man, not you. Despite regulations.'

'Oh . . .' A look of bitter disappointment clouded the tribune's face. 'I only want to serve Rome, sir. As devoutly as I can.'

'Devoutly?' Macro chuckled. 'This is the army, lad, not a religious cult. There's far more to it than rituals, ceremonies and mumbo-jumbo. We don't play at what we do. It's life and death for us and that means we have to be sure that the men are commanded by those who know what they're doing. See?'

Junius glared at Macro for a moment and then swallowed and nodded. With a curt nod of the head to his two superiors he halted his horse and fell back amongst the rest of the party of horsemen.

'Keen, isn't he?' Cato smiled. 'Reminds me of myself when I joined up.'

'Oh no, you were much more of a drip than him.'

Cato's eyes narrowed. 'Drip?'

'Come on, you know you were. Thin streak of piss, and clumsy with it. Yet you ponced in and thought you could command men in the field just because you'd read up on military history.' Macro smiled fondly at the memory. 'The army was the making of you, and you know it.'

Cato glanced round to make sure that the other officers were out of earshot of this rather frank appraisal of his early days in the service of Rome, and then turned back to Macro.

'It is true I might not have been ideal material for the Second Legion . . . but I learned quickly enough. Of course, I was lucky to have a fine mentor.'

'True,' Macro agreed, dispensing with false modesty.

Cato jerked his head back towards the others. 'Given time Junius will work out as well as I did. Better, in fact, given his senatorial background. Perhaps we should be careful how we speak to him,' Cato mused. 'One day he is sure to outrank us and then he might not be forgiving for past slights.'

'If today's little exchange still weighs on his mind years

from now then, frankly, he doesn't deserve to rise to senior rank. I've seen generals come and go, Cato, and the small-minded ones never lasted long in post. That's one of the advantages of having an Emperor, I guess.' Macro scratched his ear. 'Claudius can dismiss any man who's not up to the job. He can afford to choose the best. The Emperor doesn't have to worry about appeasing political factions and dancing to their tune all the time.'

'Now who's being green?' Cato laughed. 'You really think emperors are above politics? Why do you think the biggest armies are always entrusted to close relatives of the imperial family? And why do emperors watch their other generals like hawks? That's why we were sent out to the eastern Empire in the first place, to keep an eye on Governor Longinus in Syria. Politics doesn't stop at the camp gate. Emperor Claudius knows that better than most of his predecessors. The army handed him the throne and he's rewarded them with handsome donatives ever since to make sure they know he hasn't forgotten it. Politics . . .' Cato sighed. 'It's what we must wade through all our lives.'

'Like a sewer, then,' Macro concluded with a grin, and Cato responded in kind. They rode on in silence for a moment before Cato spoke again.

'Junius will turn out all right, I think.'

'I hope so.'

'You doubt him?'

Macro pursed his lips briefly. 'I don't know. He's just a little too keen to please. He's trying too hard to prove himself. That can be dangerous – to him, and the men he may command one day.'

'Assuming he lives long enough,' Cato replied quietly. 'Surviving the next few days may well prove something of a challenge.'

The army halted an hour before noon and the men fell out and set down their packs before seeking whatever shade they could find. Those without had to make do with shelters made from their cloaks propped up on the end of their javelins. The men rested through the hottest part of the day while the ground around them baked.

Cato and his officers were resting in the shade of a plantation of date palms when a lone cavalryman came galloping down the road into the column, leaving a fine haze of dust in his wake. The few soldiers still on the road backed away and then watched him briefly, wondering what his hurry could signify. The rider reined in and slipped off the back of his horse and ran up to the optio in command of the headquarters guard to make his report. The optio waved him through and a moment later he stood stiffly in front of Cato, chest heaving from his exertions.

'Beg to report, sir, the Nubian army has been sighted.'

The other officers stirred and rose to their feet as Cato asked, 'Where?'

The cavalryman quickly estimated. 'Just over eight miles from here, sir.'

'Are they on the march?'

'Yes, sir. The Nubians are advancing towards us.'

'Eight miles?' Macro muttered. 'Close enough if you intend to give battle today, sir.'

'Not today.' Cato looked round at the landscape. A short distance beyond the date palms stretched an expanse of arable land, less than a mile in width from the river to a line of barren hills stretching off into the desert. He pointed it out to Macro and the others. 'That is where we'll make our stand. The ground is pliable enough to make a marching camp. Macro, give the orders at once. I want our men behind field defences before the Nubians arrive.'

'Yes, sir.' Macro saluted and trotted off to find the senior surveyor and his assistants. Shortly after, they galloped off, trailing a string of mules laden with marking posts and surveying kit.

Cato watched them briefly and then turned to his staff officers. 'Get the men back on their feet. I want them ready to make camp the moment Macro's men have marked the perimeter.'

The haze smearing the horizon between the river and the desert marked the approach of the Nubian host long before the first of its men came in sight of the Roman camp. The legionaries were still constructing the palisade and the watchtowers as the first Nubian patrols appeared, small groups of men mounted on camels who stopped short of the Roman picquets and waited for the rest of the army to catch up. As the sun dipped towards the western horizon, it bathed the landscape in a lurid red, and picked out the armour, weapons and banners of the enemy glinting at the base of the dust cloud that slowly advanced towards the Roman position. The soldiers doubled their efforts to complete the defences in time. In addition to the ditch and rampart, they had dug lines of small pits with angled wooden stakes at the bottom in front of the camp. At each corner of the wall a platform of palm logs packed down with earth had been raised to serve as mounts for the bolt throwers.

When the main defences were completed, Cato gave the order for the patrols to pull back and the auxiliary cavalrymen turned away from the enemy and rode back into the camp, and then the gates were sealed. The army was formed up, in case Prince Talmis decided to attack as soon as he reached the Roman defences. The men and their officers stood and waited as the enemy host came on. The main Nubian column began to divide into three and soon the breadth of land between the Nile and the hills presented an unbroken line of enemy infantry, interspersed with columns of mounted warriors, on horses and camels.

As he stood in one of the watchtowers, Cato sensed the anxiety in his soldiers watching from the palisade. The men of the Twenty-Second and the auxiliaries had never faced such a threat before and few of them had ever fought in a battle. He just hoped that their training and discipline would be enough to ensure that they stood their ground when the time came to face the Nubians in battle.

'An impressive sight,' said Macro, at his side. 'But numbers aren't everything, eh?'

Cato did not reply as he scrutinised the dense ranks of the enemy. For the most part they appeared to be lightly armed, but there were several formations of soldiers who marched well and carried large oval shields and were equipped with an assortment of helmets and armour. There were also large formations of men carrying bundles of javelins. Few of the Nubians seemed to be armed with bows and Cato took some small comfort from that. There was a distant blare of horns and the Nubian army halted. Above them the haze slowly wafted to one side on the evening breeze blowing across the Nile.

'What do you think they'll do now, sir?' asked Junius. 'Will they attack?'

'I doubt it, Tribune,' Cato replied. 'We're in a strong position and any attack would cost Prince Talmis dearly. Despite their number, few of his men are trained soldiers. If his first assault fails, and he suffers heavy casualties, it will hit the spirits of his men hard.'

Macro pointed. 'There. We'll know what the Nubians intend soon enough.'

Cato and Junius turned to see a party of horsemen riding out from the Nubian army, straight down the dusty road that ran along the bank of the Nile. They came on unhurriedly, crossing the open ground between the two waiting armies.

'I don't want them getting too good a view of our defences,' Cato decided. 'Macro, have a cavalry squadron brought forward. We'll ride out and meet them.'

'Yes, sir.' Macro strode across to the ladder and clambered down from the tower. Cato continued watching the approaching riders for a moment and then descended to join his friend who was holding a spare horse ready. Cato swung himself up and settled into the saddle between the two sets of saddle horns and took up the reins, biting back on the pain in his shoulder.

'Let's see what they want.'

The legionaries on the gate facing the enemy scrambled to open it as Cato and his escort trotted forward and a moment later they passed out of the camp and rode down the track that had been trampled through a crop of wheat that led to the road. There they reined in and the escort formed a line behind the two officers, ready to charge forward if Cato gave them the order. The Nubians were only a few hundred paces away and came on at the same measured pace. There were eight of them, beneath a standard depicting a lion, its mouth agape in a silent roar. The leader, swathed in shimmering black silk and a head-piece wrapped round a conical helmet and covering all but his eyes, rode slightly ahead of the rest of his men. He slowed his pace to a gentle walk as he approached Cato and then tugged his reins when he was no more than ten paces away. His dark eyes regarded the Romans for a moment and then he reached up a hand and pulled the cloth away from his face.

'I wish to speak to the Roman general,' he said in Greek. 'Legate Aurelius.'

'Aurelius is dead. I am the commander of the army,' Cato responded.

'You?' For a moment the Nubian hesitated, then shrugged. 'Whether or not that is true, it makes no difference to what I have to say. So hear me, Roman. I am Talmis, Prince of Nubia, lion of the desert and com-mander of the army you see before you.' He swept his arm out to indicate the massed ranks stretching across the landscape. 'I have brooked Roman interference in our lands for too long. The time for retribution is at hand. I will not sheath my sword until my honour is satisfied, or it has tasted the blood of many Romans.'

Macro coughed and gestured casually towards the

Prince's scabbard and the jewelled handle of his weapon. 'If that is the, uh, sword in question, then it's only fair to point out that it is already sheathed.'

'Macro,' Cato muttered through clenched teeth. 'Be quiet!'

The Prince eased his mount forward, its legs high-stepping as he edged it close to Macro and glared into the centurion's face. Macro raised his eyebrows quizzically.

'Is this your pet comedian, Legate? I shall look forward to seeing how he laughs when I have my men disembowel him.'

'Centurion Macro is inclined to speak his mind more than is good for him,' Cato responded evenly. 'However, he does not speak for Rome. I do. What is it that you wish to say to me, Prince?'

Talmis stared at Macro a moment longer then sniffed with contempt and turned to Cato.

'I come to offer my terms for peace. Rome will cede all of the land south of Ombos to Nubia. In addition, I want half of this year's harvest from the province. And ten talents of gold.' His eyes narrowed shrewdly. 'The Roman measure of talents. Not Egyptian. These terms are not negotiable. If you refuse, then I will continue my advance along the Nile, sacking your cities and burning your crops as I go. Even as far as Alexandria.'

Macro laughed. 'I doubt that Rome would permit that. You come within a hundred miles of Alexandria and the Emperor will send enough legions to the region to obliterate you and your army.'

Prince Talmis shrugged. 'Nubia is a big land, Roman. Big enough for me to continue retreating until your legions die of exhaustion, or thirst. Rome does not frighten me. Well?'

'Your terms are unacceptable,' Cato said simply. 'The negotiations are over.'

He pulled on his reins and turned his horse away and began to walk it back towards the camp. His escort followed suit, with wary looks over their shoulders. At first Prince Talmis was silent, fists clenched in rage. Then he stabbed a finger towards the backs of the Roman horsemen.

'So be it! Within days the vultures will be picking your bones clean!' He snatched at his reins, forcing his horse round sharply, then he spurred it back towards his army, his robes flapping like the wings of a crow while his followers struggled to keep up.

Macro watched him briefly and then edged his mount closer to Cato. 'That was pretty blunt. What are you thinking?'

Cato spoke with a resigned air. 'What else could I say? I have no authority to accept his terms. Even if I did, the Emperor could never afford to. So we will have our battle.'

'When?'

'Tomorrow. At dawn.'

Prince Talmis and his senior officers had completed their plans for the disposition of the Nubian army and were feasting on heavily spiced mutton when their meal was interrupted. The captain of the Prince's bodyguard, a large scarred warrior, eased aside the tent flap and entered. Four of his men followed, either side of a tall figure in a ragged tunic and scale armour vest. His skin and hair were matted with sweat and dust and it took the Prince a moment to recognise him.

'Ajax . . .'

The other officers stopped eating as they turned to look at the gladiator. Their conversation faltered and an uneasy silence filled the tent. Prince Talmis wiped the grease from his fingers on the hem of his robe and leaned back from the polished silver tray from which he had been dining. He stroked his jaw in contemplation as he stared at Ajax.

'Is this the man who claimed that he would be a valuable ally in the war against Rome, I wonder?' he asked with cold sarcasm. 'From the look of you it would appear that you have seen some hard fighting. Is that so?'

'Yes, Highness.' Ajax bowed his head.

'I take it you had the worst of it.'

'Yes.'

'I see. Then tell me, have you achieved what I asked of you?'

Ajax, weary as he was, stood stiffly at full height, dominating the bodyguards who stood around him. 'My men have killed and wounded many of the Romans, as you wished, Highness. We took one of their forts, slaughtered its garrison and burned it to the ground.'

'And what of our casualties?'

Ajax hesitated briefly before replying. 'I regret to say that I and a few of my followers are all that survive. The rest are lost.'

Prince Talmis's eyes widened, and his officers exchanged anxious glances, waiting for him to give vent to his anger. The Prince's lips twitched. 'Lost? Explain.'

'After the fort was destroyed the Romans sent a force across the Nile to deal with my column, Highness. We held the bank for as long as we could before falling back on a temple that I had ordered the men to fortify. There we made our stand.'

'Not you apparently.'

'I had done as much as I could. My death would not have affected the outcome. My life, on the other hand, guarantees that I will continue to be a threat to the Romans. Which is to the benefit of us all, Your Highness.'

'How did you escape?'

'My spy arranged to save me and a handful of others.'

Talmis nodded slowly and was silent for a moment before he responded. 'So, you have cost me five hundred men. Is this what you meant by being of use to me? You, your men and your spy have failed me,' he concluded in a tone of contempt.

'We have killed many Romans, Highness. And I succeeded in holding back their advance for two days. As you wished.'

'That is so. But I do not consider the loss of five hundred of my men a success. In any case, I have the enemy where I want them now so your usefulness to me has been played out, gladiator.'

Ajax's eyes narrowed and he replied in a low, even tone. 'What do you mean by that, Your Highness?'

'The Romans will be crushed tomorrow so I will have no more need of you. If you had been one of my officers I would have had your head by now for the unnecessary loss of a considerable number of my men.'

'In order to fulfil your orders the loss was unavoidable, Highness.'

'I wonder.'

'And I am not one of your officers,' Ajax went on. 'I am Ajax, commander of the slave revolt on Crete. While I live Rome trembles,' Ajax blustered. 'If you kill me, you only serve the interests of Rome.'

'Perhaps,' Talmis conceded. 'However, your execution will provide a valuable example to the rest of my men of the price of failing me.'

'But I have not failed you.'

'I disagree. It is possible that your death will suit my purposes better than your continued service.'

Ajax glared at the Prince. 'You called me an ally.'

'A prince has no allies. He has only servants and enemies. It is up to him how to use his servants.'

The gladiator spat on the ground in contempt. At once the captain of the guard turned and struck him on the side of the head. Then he stood, fist clenched, daring the gladiator to defy the Prince again. Ajax shook his head to clear the dizziness caused by the blow. He looked at the Prince and spoke in a low voice. 'You are making a mistake, Highness. Kill me, and you kill the hope of all those slaves who wait to rise up against Rome.'

'Be silent, gladiator!' the Prince commanded. 'One more word and your life is forfeit.' He pressed his lips together in a cruel, thin line as he stared at Ajax. The other men in the tent dared not move as they waited for their master to continue. At length the Prince raised a finger and pointed at the gladiator. 'Your fate is mine to decide. It may be true that I have more to gain by keeping you alive and letting you spread your poison through the Emperor's domains. I will think on it. For now, you are my prisoner. I need to ponder on your fate.' He clicked his fingers at the captain of his bodyguard. 'Take this slave away. Place him under close guard, somewhere safe. He is not to be harmed. Nor is he to escape. If he does, you will answer for it with your life. Go.'

The captain of the bodyguard bowed deeply and gestured to his men to escort Ajax from the tent. Then he followed, still bowing as he backed out and then slipped the flap across the entrance.

Prince Talmis glanced round at his officers. None was prepared to meet his eye. They sat still and silent. He smiled with cold satisfaction at their obeisance and then reached for his wine goblet.

'Gentlemen, a toast!' He raised his goblet, and immediately the other men scrambled for theirs and held them ready.

'Death to Rome!' Talmis called out.

His officers echoed his toast in a loud bellow and outside, those soldiers who heard the toast smiled as they turned to stare at the campfires of the Roman camp, dwarfed by the flares from the Nubian army sprawling across the dark landscape.

CHAPTER THIRTY-FOUR

In the hour before dawn Cato sent out the auxiliary cavalry to attack the enemy outposts to divert their attention while the rest of the Roman army filed out of the marching camp. By the wan light of the stars they passed through the defence lines to take up their positions across the strip of open land a short distance beyond where the gap between the hills and the dense growth of palms and reeds along the riverbank was narrowest. Less than a mile beyond, the enemy's campfires were dying down and dotted the dark landscape in a blanket of flickering red sparks.

The centre of the Roman line was held by Macro's First Cohort, standing four ranks deep. On either side and slightly behind the centre were the two auxiliary infantry cohorts, then further back two more legionary cohorts. Behind the shallow crescent, bulging out towards the enemy, the archers stood in a loose line, ready to fire over the ranks of their comrades when the battle began. A single cohort of legionaries stood in reserve, and the remaining six stood in dense columns at each end of the crescent, as if to protect the army's flanks from attack. The bolt throwers had been carted forward to form two batteries covering the ground in front of each wing of cavalry.

Once the infantry were in position, Cato gave the order for the recall of the two cavalry cohorts and they formed up on the flanks. In the normal loose hit and run of cavalry skirmishing they would have been heavily disadvantaged by the enemy's overwhelming number of horsemen and camel riders. However, they were under strict orders not to charge but to hold their ground and protect the flanks of the Roman line.

As the first faint wash of lighter sky appeared over the dark mass of the hills to the east, Cato rode forward to take up his position behind the First Cohort. Macro had already dismounted and sent his horse to the rear. Cato recognised his stocky form standing a short distance to one side of the cohort's standard. Macro turned at the sound of hoofbeats and raised a hand in greeting.

'Are your men ready, Centurion?' Cato called out, loud enough for others to hear.

'Champing at the bit, sir,' Macro replied lightly. 'Keen as anything to get stuck in!'

'Good! By the end of the day, every standard in the legion is going to have won a decoration!' Cato reined in and swung his leg over the saddle and dismounted, handing the reins to Junius. He patted Macro on the shoulder and muttered, 'A word with you.'

When they were beyond earshot, Cato spoke softly. 'Everything depends on the First Cohort holding its ground today, and the rest the legion timing its move precisely. You understand?'

Macro turned towards him, just able to make out the strained expression on the younger man's face in the gloom. Cato had briefed him thoroughly on the battle plan the night before, along with the rest of the officers, and once more in person before they had marched out of the camp. Any irritation that Macro might have felt about being reminded of his duty yet again vanished as he recognised the anxiety that was consuming his friend. Macro slowed to a halt and faced his superior. 'Sir, I know what I have to do. So do the men. Don't let that concern you. The plan is in place. All that is left now is to wait for the enemy.'

'And when the Nubians come?'

'The men will do their duty. This is what they have trained for. When the fighting starts, that will be what governs their actions.'

Cato stared back. Despite Macro's reassurance he could not assuage his fears over the coming battle. He was not afraid for himself. No, he corrected himself, there was always the dread of a crippling wound and a long drawn-out death amid the carnage of the battlefield. Or, worse, mutilation and survival that would leave him an object of pity and ridicule. That prospect always haunted him before a battle and Cato had made himself charge forward with his comrades, or stand his ground, in spite of it, for the simple reason that he feared shame more than anything. That had always been a burden of his close friendship with Macro, he recognised; he never wanted to betray the confidence that Macro placed in him. Now that he was responsible for the lives of thousands, the burden had increased. Macro and all the other men looked to him, Cato, to lead them to victory, or die at their side.

Cato did not consider himself a brave individual. He could already feel the unsettled flutters in the pit of his stomach and the cold sweat pricking out down his spine. He wondered why he had not become used to it after so many years of fighting. What was it in him that preyed on his mind, thrusting forward terrifying images from past battles as well as imagined scenes of dreadful vividness? For Cato it seemed that there were two sides of his being locked in a perpetual struggle. The Cato he wanted to be – courageous, bold and respected, unburdened by self-doubt – and that other, truer, version – fearful, anxious and agonisingly sensitive to the view other people had of him. The latter could only ever act out the role of the former, winning the applause of the moment, before withdrawing into the shabby robes of his real nature. The thought sickened him and it was only when Macro cleared his throat and spoke again that his attention was redirected.

'This plan of yours . . .'

'Yes?'

'Seems a bit unorthodox. Mind me asking how you came to think it up?'

'It's not my idea,' Cato admitted. 'I remember something I read in Livius.'

'The historian?'

'That's right.'

Macro raised a hand and rubbed his brow. 'You, er, think that we are refighting another battle, then? Something from history. Which you've got out of a book.'

'More or less. A similar situation in many respects. An outnumbered army taking on and crushing the enemy,' Cato explained. 'I expect you've heard of the battle of Cannae?'

'Yes, thank you,' Macro replied patiently. 'But it didn't work out terribly well for our lads, as I recall.'

Before Cato could respond, there was a flat blast of a horn away to the south. The sound was picked up by other horns and soon the first of the enemy's drums added to the din. A thin blue light filtered through the air and the faintest of mists hung across the Nile like a silk veil.

Macro regarded the stirring Nubian host for a moment and then muttered, 'Now we shall see if Prince Talmis will give battle on our terms.' He shot a quick glance at Cato. 'Let's hope that Livius was never on *his* reading list, eh?'

Cato did not reply but stood erect, staring out over his men towards the enemy camp. It did not take long to discern the dense blocks of men and horses massing opposite the Roman line. As the sound of their horns, cymbals and drums rose even higher, the Nubian army began to emerge from their camp, blotting out the sight of the campfires they were leaving in their wake.

'It seems they are going to take the bait,' said Cato with a relieved nod. 'The first round to us then. I'd better return to my command post.' He turned and smiled at Macro. 'Don't worry, I won't remind you of the plan again.'

'As if I could forget.' Macro tapped his helmet. 'The skull might be as thick as oak but the brain still works.'

They clasped each other's forearms and then Cato strode swiftly back towards his horse and climbed into the saddle. He waved a hand at Macro and urged his mount into a trot as he headed back towards the small cluster of officers sitting in their saddles to one side of the reserve cohort. Macro watched him a moment, then went through the familiar routine of checking each strap and buckle of his armour and weapons. Satisfied that all was well, he handed his vine cane to one of the medical orderlies who was passing by with a bag stuffed with linen strips to dress wounds.

'Look after that for me,' he growled. 'I'll want it back after the battle. Any harm comes to it and I'll use what's left of it to break your back.'

The orderly took the vine cane reluctantly and continued on his way, holding the stick out to one side as if it might bite him. Macro grinned briefly at the sight and then took a deep breath and strode across to the optio in the First Cohort's colour party who was minding his shield. Macro grasped the handle and lifted it. He eased his way between two of the centuries and strode out some ten paces in front of the Roman line. He stared ahead, his gaze slowly sweeping round as he took in the enemy battle line trudging towards them. The dust kicked up by the Nubians was already smudging the air above them. Macro turned his back on them and examined the men of the First Cohort. They were all picked men, the best of the legion, and they would be the first of the infantry to come into contact with the enemy. Macro drew a deep breath and addressed them.

'It is about now that some of you may be rethinking your decision to pursue a military career.'

The comment brought forth some tense smiles from the men he could see most clearly in the pale light. A few even laughed. But there were some, he noted, whose expressions remained frozen.

'For those men, I promise that I will consider your application for a discharge as soon as I am off duty. In fairness, I should tell you that by the end of the day, with your first major battle under your belt, and a jug of wine in your bellies, and the spoils of war in your knapsacks, you will be feeling like bloody heroes, and the very idea of getting a discharge will be the last thing on your mind!' Macro paused. 'You chose to join the Jackals. The legion has given you the best training any soldier can get. You have the best kit of any army, and now, thank the gods, you have finally got a chance to put everything you have learned into practice. Relish the moment, men! This is the great test of your lives. Today you find out what it means to be a legionary and take your place in the ranks of the finest brotherhood of warriors in the entire world!' Macro jabbed his thumb towards the enemy. 'That lot think they're going to have us for breakfast. They know they outnumber us and they think that all their horns and drums are going to make us shake at the knees.' Macro sneered. He paused briefly, and hardened his tone. 'I will tell you now, there is nothing more dangerous than a Roman army sword, and a trained man who knows how to use it.' He drew his blade and raised it aloft. 'So let 'em know who they are up against. Let them know who crafts their doom. Let them know so that the few who survive and run from the battlefield when the day is out will spread the word about the men who destroyed them today! Up the Jackals!' Macro bellowed, punching his sword up. 'Up the Jackals!'

The men took up the cry, most with genuine enthusiasm and the remainder following their lead, until they, too, were caught up in the shouted chorus and their pulses quickened with the excitement of the moment.

The cheering spread to the rest of the legion, and then the auxiliary cohorts who had been attached to the Twenty-Second added their voices. The cry of the Roman army challenged the horns, drums, cymbals and wailed ululations of the host marching across the level ground to meet them. Macro turned to look at the Nubians briefly and then strode back through the ranks to rejoin the colour party.

Cato glanced towards his friend and found some faint reassurance in the knowledge that Macro could be trusted to inspire the men he led to follow his example. It was vital that the First Cohort did not break under the weight of the enemy attack. Victory depended upon the timing of the decisive manoeuvre. Not just victory, Cato mused, but their very survival and the survival of the province of Egypt. The horizon to Cato's left was now a bright hazy orange as the sun prepared to make its entrance and announce the birth of another day. For many men on both sides, it would be their last, and Cato felt an icy ripple flow across his scalp, and prayed that it was not a premonition of his own death. The image of Julia momentarily filled his mind and he felt a heated desire for her such as he had not experienced since the last time he touched her flesh.

'Sir!' a voice called and Cato turned to see the most junior of the tribunes pointing towards the enemy now less than a quarter of a mile away. 'They should be in range of the bolt throwers. Should I give the order to let them try a shot, sir?'

Cato was about to reprimand the youth for his presumption, but then saw that he had spoken the truth. One unit of camel riders, armed with javelins, had edged ahead of the rest of the Nubian army and was making for the cavalry on the left of the Roman line. Cato quickly estimated the range and then nodded to the tribune. 'Very well, have the commander of the battery fire ranging shots before he looses any volleys. No sense in wasting ammunition.'

The tribune saluted and spurred his horse into a gallop as he rode across to the battery commander, an auxiliary centurion whom Cato had chosen to command the bolt throwers on that flank. Shortly afterwards there was a dull crack as a bolt thrower's arms snapped forward against their restraints. Although full daylight was still some way off, Cato could easily follow the trajectory of the missile as it shot towards the enemy in a shallow arc and then landed with a puff of dust and grit just in front of the leading camels, causing one to stop dead in its tracks. The battery commander bellowed an order to the rest of his crews and they cranked back the torsion arms and placed the iron-tipped shafts into the channel that ran up the central bed of the weapon. When all were ready, the centurion raised his arm and called out. 'On my word, prepare to shoot!'

His men stood still, one at each weapon, holding the lever that would release the grip on the torsion rope. The centurion waited until he was certain the leading ranks of Nubians had ridden over the place where the first bolt had plunged into the ground. Cato was gripped with impatience as the centurion kept his arm aloft and continued to let the enemy draw closer.

'Get on with it, man,' he whispered harshly.

'Release!' the centurion suddenly bellowed, sweeping his arm down. The cracks of the bolt throwers sounded almost together, like the snapping of a fistful of sticks. Thirty small shafts whirred towards the camel rider unit, some five or six hundred strong, Cato calculated. The centurion had timed his order well and not a single shot fell short as the cruel iron heads of the missiles tore through the sandy hides of the camels and the robes of their riders. The stricken animals collapsed in heaps as their spindly-looking legs gave way and those behind them were forced to swerve aside, into the flanks of their companions, disrupting their move against the waiting Romans. For a moment their advance stalled, and then as the Romans reloaded their weapons, the Arabs worked round their casualties and continued on. The second volley shot out from behind the Roman lines and struck home, killing and wounding several more. Some of the riders proved a little wary of leading the charge and lagged behind, no doubt hoping to avoid the further attention of the artillery crews. The third and fourth volleys stopped the enemy dead, and they stood in some confusion as the bolts landed amongst them, and then the fifth volley broke their will. The commander of the unit turned aside and rode off towards the flank, beckoning his men to follow him.

A cheer rose up from the Roman ranks and some of the men punched their javelins and swords into the air. It was a pitiful achievement in terms of the scale of the coming battle, Cato realised, but he indulged his men just the same. It was good for their morale, and wounded the enemy's spirits. But even as the warm flow of satisfaction filled his heart, Cato saw a new, far greater threat. The dust on the flanks of the enemy line was thickening and then he saw the masses of horsemen surging forward, quickening their pace into a trot as they rode towards the cavalry cohorts on each side of the Roman infantry. This would be the first real test of the day, Cato knew. If his men failed to hold back the Nubians then the enemy would be able to surround the legion and the auxiliaries and fall on their rear. In that event, Cato and his men would be cut to pieces. He flicked his reins and gestured to his staff officers to follow him as he rode across the rear of the line towards the commander of the Syrian cavalry cohort on the left flank.

Prefect Herophilus nodded a greeting as his commander rode up.

'Your men will be in action soon.' Cato pointed to the dark line of riders approaching, the rumble of their hoofs clearly audible above the ongoing cacophony of Nubian instruments. 'Are they ready to do their duty?'

It was a rhetorical question, but it gave the prefect the chance to speak up for his men.

'My boys will be as steady as a rock, sir. You can depend on us.'

'I know it. If you don't mind, I will join your command for the present, and see for myself how your men fight.'

Herophilus bowed his head. 'My pleasure, sir.'

Both officers turned to watch the enemy. Cato struggled to make sense of their numbers due to the dust that engulfed those a short distance behind the leading ranks.

'There must be thousands of them,' said one of Herophilus's decurions.

'Quiet there!' the prefect snapped at him.

The enemy closed to within half a mile and Cato heard the clack–clack–clack of the bolt throwers as the crews prepared to shoot up the Nubian cavalry. Some of the auxiliary horsemen, distracted by the spectacle of the enemy force, allowed their mounts to move out of position until Herophilus cupped a hand to his mouth and bellowed, 'Keep the bloody line there! Decurions! Take the name of any man who can't control his horse!'

The sound of drumming hoofs filled the air and now Cato could feel the vibration through the ground beneath his mount. To his right he heard the officer in charge of the archers order his men to make ready. Then there was a brief stillness over the left flank of the Roman army as they stood their ground and waited for the action to begin. In that moment the sun finally crested the hills to the east and its rays poured over the battlefield, bathing polished armour and weapons in a fiery glitter.

The warm glow was suddenly pierced by the shadowy dashes of the missiles as they were unleashed from the bolt throwers and an instant later the crack of the torsion arms carried to Cato's ears. He watched the fall of shot and saw a rider plucked off his horse and hurled to the ground. More riders went down, together with horses, but they were quickly swallowed up by the waves of Nubian cavalry surging forward. More bolts slammed into the charging mass, and then the archers added their weight to the bombardment, their arrows angling higher into the sky before plunging down. Scores of Nubians were struck down, and yet it seemed to make little difference to their numbers or break the pace of their charge.

Cato drew his sword and his officers followed suit.

Herophilus slipped his left arm through the straps of his shield and took up the reins as he shouted orders to his men, his voice shrill with the strain of being heard above the deafening pounding of hoofs. 'Close up! Shields to the front! Make ready your spears and prepare to receive the charge!'

There was a shimmer as the long line of spear tips swept down towards the Nubians. The auxiliary horsemen drew their shields in close, covering as much of their bodies as possible. Beneath them some horses stirred nervously until steadied by a press of the thighs or a calming word. The enemy riders had closed to within a hundred paces now and Cato could see individual details. The riders' mounts were all at full stretch. Their formation had lost cohesion due to the speed of the charge and the loss of those who had been shot down by the archers and bolt throwers. They were still shooting, keeping the range long enough to avoid any danger to their own side, while lashing down on the Nubians at the rear of the charge.

'Here they come!' Herophilus shouted, his eyes wide.

An instant later the first of the enemy reached the Roman line. Their horses shied at the line of mounted men and the deadly points of their spears, and the impact of the charge broke as the melee spread along the line. The prefect and his officers dug their heels in and forced their way amongst the men to join the fight, the cohort's standard bearer following on, keeping the standard raised high for all his comrades to see. Cato edged his mount forward, to just behind the second rank of Roman horsemen. Beyond was a savage sea of gleaming blades, thrashing limbs, the dagger-like ears of horses and wild tossing manes, all accompanied by the harsh clatter and thud of weapons and the cries of rage and pain and whinnies of terrified and stricken cavalry mounts.

'We'll not hold back that host,' said Junius. 'We can't.'

'We must,' Cato replied simply. 'Or die.'

But even as he spoke, more and more of the enemy were pressing forward, forcing the Roman line back.

'Follow me!' Cato commanded, urging his horse forward. He pressed into the melee, knee to knee with the men on either side. They glanced at him in surprise before focusing again on the enemy. Cato raised his sword and gripped the reins tightly in his left hand. He was conscious of not having a shield but it was too late for that. He was committed to the fight and must stay with the men or look a coward if he drew back. To his right he was aware of Junius struggling to stay with him, but another rider intervened and the tribune was forced away and could not safeguard Cato's side.

A gap opened up between two auxiliaries directly ahead and Cato edged his mount into the space, fixing his gaze on the nearest of the Nubians, a lean figure with an ebony face split by brilliant white as he bared his teeth. He spotted Cato and urged his horse forward, raising a heavy curved blade overhead. Cato punched his arm up to block the blow and it glanced away, thudding into the shield of the auxiliary to Cato's right. The man swung round in his saddle and, with an overhand grip, thrust his spear at the Nubian, striking him in the chest. The folds of the robes he wore, together with whatever armour he had beneath, kept the spear point out of his flesh, but the impact drove him back all the same, almost toppling him from his saddle. Cato took advantage of the moment of imbalance and slashed at his sword arm, cutting into his elbow joint. The sword hand spasmed, releasing its grip, and the heavy weapon tumbled down between the flanks of the horses and out of sight. The Nubian howled with agony as he recovered his seat and hauled on the reins, trying to turn his horse away. He succeeded in bringing the beast side on, where it was trapped between the battle lines and left the man exposed to the second spear thrust which pierced his side, under his armpit, and went in deep. A rush of blood accompanied the spear as the auxiliary yanked it free, and the Nubian swayed a moment before falling amid the dust and stamping hoofs.

Cato took the chance to glance round and saw Junius dispatch an enemy with a savage cut to the head. Elsewhere the line had stopped giving ground and the better armour of the Romans meant that they were getting the best of the individual duels. Nor was the enemy pushing forward any more. They had been fought to a halt and as Cato saw, they were giving ground. The reason for this was clear enough. Over the heads of the men in front of him, Cato could see Roman arrows plunging down into the tight press of bodies behind. The Nubians there were anxiously doing their best to shield their bodies with the small round hide shields that most of them carried, but they were poor protection against the barbed iron points. Several men and horses were hit at a time, the wounded animals rearing as the pain of their injuries made them panic and impossible to control.

'Push them back!' Cato roared, edging his mount

forward, pressing up against the riderless horse and forcing it aside. A Nubian passed in front of him, out of sword reach, and Cato stabbed his mount in the rump instead. The horse let out a shrill cry and kicked back, narrowly missing Cato's leg, but striking the flank of his mount so hard that Cato heard a rib snap beneath the glossy hide. Abruptly both animals reared up, the Nubian thrown back into Cato's side as he threw his weight forward and clung on tightly to the reins to stay in his saddle. The Nubian's flailing hand caught Cato's tunic above his knee and the fingers clenched. Cato felt himself shift to the side and the terrifying prospect of falling to the ground and being trampled seized him. He cursed the man through gritted teeth and then swung his sword arm over and tried to cut at the hand. But the gap was too cramped to get a swing and the edge pressed into the flesh and did not cut through. Cato desperately started a savage sawing movement in the space that he had and the Nubian howled and a moment later was forced to release his grip and fell beneath Cato's horse where his panicked cry was brutally cut short.

Looking up, Cato saw through the haze of dust that the rearmost ranks of the Nubian cavalry were falling back, away from the arrows that rained down mercilessly. The fear swiftly spread through the enemy and as the last of them turned their mounts and galloped off, Cato looked down the battle line. The auxiliaries stared after the Nubians in silence for a moment, too stupefied by the blood rushing through their veins to realise that they had beaten the enemy off. Then Prefect Herophilus thrust his bloodied blade up and let out a roar of triumph, instantly taken up by the rest of his men as they watched the enemy flee. Bodies of men and horses, many still living, lay scattered across the ground amid the angled shafts of arrows.

As the cheers began to die away, Cato was aware of the sound of fighting from the other flank where the enemy had made another attack in an effort to break the Roman cavalry. Cato squinted to make out the details. It seemed that the Alexandrian cavalry unit was holding its own well enough and on the left flank, the archers and bolt throwers were taking their deadly toll.

Cato sheathed his sword and walked his horse over to Herophilus. 'Well done! That's fine work by your men. Get them re-formed and ready for the next charge.'

'Yes, sir!'

Cato beckoned to Junius and the others and then trotted back towards the centre of the line. He made a quick estimate of the cohort's losses. No more than a tenth of the cavalry had been lost in the first struggle but the Nubians would surely make another charge. Each time they did, the cohort's strength would be whittled down. The Nubian army must be broken before such attrition broke the Roman cavalry.

The small party of officers made their way across the rear of the Roman line and returned to the centre. Macro looked back and nodded a relieved acknowledgement that Cato was still alive, then turned to face the front. Over the helmets of the First Cohort, Cato could see the main bulk of the enemy army advancing straight at them, no more than half a mile away, dense blocks of infantry, with the most heavily armoured making up the centre of the line under the banner of Prince Talmis. Cato wondered if

Ajax was there amongst them, with the last of his followers from Crete. For an instant he fervently hoped that fate would give him, or Macro, the chance to face the gladiator one last time to settle the consuming hatred that had brought all three men to this battlefield on the fringe of the Empire.

He thrust thoughts of Ajax aside and turned to one of his orderlies. 'Tell the commanders of both bolt-thrower batteries to target the enemy infantry as soon as they come within range. The same order to the archers. Go.'

The officer nodded and wheeled his mount around and galloped off. Cato turned his attention back to the Nubians. It was impossible to gauge their number through the haze of dust rising up a short distance behind the leading ranks. If this was Prince Talmis's main blow, then there could be more than twenty thousand men tramping across the level ground towards the Roman line, three men to each of Cato's. The sheer weight of numbers would be certain to drive the small army back, which was what Cato had allowed for, indeed counted on, in his plan.

The steady rhythm of the enemy's drums and the clash of cymbals and blare of horns swelled in volume as the host advanced. Once the centurions were satisfied that the lines of their men were dressed as smartly as possible, they took up their places at the right of their commands and waited in silence. The Nubians were now close enough for Cato to make out their officers shouting encouragement and waving their men on with their gleaming swords. There was a moment when Cato felt tempted to say something, some word of comfort to the men around him, but he realised it would only betray the anxiety that bound his stomach in a vice-like knot. Far better to remain silent and seem calm and imperturbable in the face of an approaching sea of enemies.

On both sides the crews of the bolt throwers began to ratchet back the torsion arms with a sharp metallic clatter. Then the heavy, iron-tipped shafts, as long as a man's arm, were loaded on to the weapons and there was a brief pause before the order bellowed out, 'Loose!'

The brief chorus of cracks drowned out the enemy instruments as a veil of missiles seemed to waft up and over the intervening ground before disappearing in amongst the Nubian foot soldiers. Cato well knew the damage that such a volley could wreak amongst dense formations of men and yet the enemy came on without any sign of hesitation, or diminution of their battle cries. It was as if the host had simply absorbed the missiles rather than lost scores of men, pierced through and hurled back against their comrades by the force of the impact. A second volley arced towards the enemy, and this time the bolts struck some of the leading men, tearing through two or three at a time. Then the dead and wounded were lost from sight as their companions stepped round or over them and continued the advance.

At just over two hundred paces the Roman archers loosed their first arrows, with a sound like a rush of wind through the leaves of some great tree. The arrows lifted high into the air and then dashed down amid the enemy, and still they came on at an unbroken pace, hefting their shields round and grasping their weapons firmly as they closed on the waiting Romans.

'Front rank!' Macro called out. 'Prepare javelins!'

The first line of legionaries raised their javelins in an overhand grip, shifting side on to the Nubians as they took two steps forward and waited for Macro's order to hurl their weapons.

Just within a hundred paces of the Roman line the Nubians shuffled to a halt. They continued to yell their cries and taunts, and waved their weapons to challenge their foe.

'What are they waiting for?' asked one of the tribunes. 'Why don't they charge?'

Cato knew why, well enough, and drew a deep breath. 'Stand by to receive missiles!'

CHAPTER THIRTY-FIVE

As the order was hurriedly repeated down the line, a mix of slinghot and arrows began to rise up over the head of the front ranks of Nubians. They were shooting blind, Cato realised with a small measure of relief. Even so, some of their missiles were bound to strike home. He turned to his officers. 'Better dismount, gentlemen. Take what cover you can find.'

As he dropped down from his saddle, Cato gestured for one of the command post orderlies to bring him a shield and he swiftly raised it up as the first of the enemy slingshot began to whip down, smacking into the sandy ground. All around, the arrows and slingshot clattered off the shields of the legionaries. A handful of arrows pierced the leather covers and lodged in the layers of laminated wood, while other missiles succeeded in striking home. Close by, Cato saw an optio's head snap back as he caught a deflection off the top of his shield. The slingshot shattered his skull and the man fell to the ground and lay still. More men were struck, the majority wounded, but some killed outright, amid the ranks of the legion. Macro's cohort, being the largest and nearest to the enemy, took the brunt of the damage. Keeping a watchful eye out for any missiles, Cato was gratified by the sight of the men closing ranks wherever one of their comrades was struck down.

The exchange of missiles from both sides continued unabated for what seemed far longer than it actually was. Cato wondered how much his men could take before their ranks were thinned out enough for the enemy to break through on their first charge. Already, over a hundred of his men were down, he estimated, with more being hit all the while. And then the enemy's barrage slackened and died away as they began to expend their ammunition. Several horns blasted out and the Nubians let out a bloodthirsty roar at the signal, and then surged forward in a charge over the final strip of sand separating them from the Romans.

'Javelins!' Macro called out and the front rank rose up from behind their shields and drew their throwing arms back. The fleetest of the Nubians was already within range of the lightest javelins. Macro snatched a breath and cried out, 'Release!'

The legionaries hurled their right arms forward and the javelins leaped from their hands. Although the javelins had the least range of the missiles the Romans used to whittle down their attackers, they were almost as lethal as the bolt throwers, and Macro watched with cool satisfaction as the first volley skewered many of the Nubians leading the charge. At once the men in the second line of legionaries handed a fresh javelin to their comrades and a follow-up volley landed amongst the enemy, the heavy shafts bursting through shields and flesh and bone with flat thuds. There was just time for a third release of javelins before the front ranks wrenched out their short swords, swiftly ordered their ranks and presented their shields to the enemy.

Macro took his place in the middle of the cohort, in the second rank, ready to enter the fight at the first opportunity. The Nubians, having suffered severe casualties in the final charge, were robbed of impetus as they struck the Roman line, arriving as individuals and small clusters of lightly armoured warriors. Years of hard training had prepared the legionaries for close combat and the Nubians were cut down from sword thrusts from the side as they attempted to duel the man directly in front of them. The advantage did not last long, as more and more of the enemy joined the fight. As the enemy warriors surged forward against the bowed line of shields, Macro could not see an end to them before those at the back merged into the dust kicked up by thousands of feet.

'Hold on, lads!' he called out at the top of his voice. 'Hold the line!'

The legionaries alternated between quick thrusts with their nimble short swords and punching their heavy rectangular shields forward. The heavy chain mail and scale armour and sturdy helmets gave them far greater protection than most of the men opposed to them. Prince Talmis had few regular soldiers, and aside from some eastern mercenaries and the Arabs, his army was mostly made up from tribesmen. They carried an assortment of spears, swords and clubs, and carried flimsy hide shields. Consequently, they died in droves as they came up against the men of the First Cohort and the auxiliaries on either side.

The soldier in front of Macro made a thrust and then howled in agony as he withdrew his arm. A sword blow had nearly severed his wrist and the useless fingers twitched and released the blade. Macro pushed past him as the legionary groaned and clutched his mutilated limb to his chest, blood spurting down the silvered scales of his armour. Macro crouched slightly, carrying his weight on the balls of his feet, ready to move swiftly. He held his shield up to protect his face and stared over the rim at his enemies as he held his sword poised.

A large warrior in a thick leather cuirass held a heavy curved sword in both hands above his head. His eyes met Macro's and he smiled savagely as he stretched his arms back to make a powerful blow. Then he slashed down. Macro saw that the blade would split his shield in two, and take his left arm with it. He sprang forward, inside the arc of the massive blade and slammed his shield into the man's chest and head. The Nubian's arms struck the rim of the shield and the sword leaped from his hands, embedding the point in the sand behind Macro. He punched his blade into the Nubian's side, ripped it out and thrust again before stepping back into the line of the First Cohort. The Nubian stumbled away and was lost amid swirling robes of two Arabs with spears who took his place in front of the centurion. They immediately jabbed at Macro but their weapons were easily blocked by the shield and Macro made no attempt to step forward and strike at them. Their futile blows thudded against the leather surface until the press of their comrades behind them forced them right up against the line of legionaries.

This was the kind of fighting which the legionaries' equipment had been designed for and at which the soldiers excelled, and all along the line the Nubians found themselves confronted by an unbroken wall of heavy shields behind which well-armoured men stood their ground, striking brutally into the ill-protected bodies packed together beyond the shields. Mortally wounded and injured Nubians fell before the Roman line, and the terrified cries of the still living were stifled as their comrades trampled over them to get at the legionaries. Most were driven on by courage, hatred of Rome and the prospect of looting the province. Others, even the cowards, had no choice as there was no way to escape the battle through the dense mass of bodies surging forward. Those far enough back to be subjected to the continued fall of Roman arrows could do nothing to avoid the deadly barbs, only pray to their gods for protection.

The Nubians were spared the danger of the bolt throwers as Cato had given the order for them to conserve ammunition rather than fire blind into the dust that obscured the view a short distance from the battle line. The crews were whipping their mule trains as the carts on which the bolt throwers were mounted were driven back to the second position Cato had chosen the previous evening.

Slowly the vast numbers of the enemy began to tell and the First Cohort was forced to give ground, step by step. Men were falling, caught by spear thrusts through gaps in the shield wall, or sometimes overwhelmed when one of the Nubians managed to wrench a shield aside long enough for one of his fellows to strike a blow at the legionary behind. Though the losses of the Nubians were far greater, Cato could see that the four-deep line with which the cohort had begun the battle was reduced to three men in most places. The bowed-out formation was steadily flattened, and then began to curve inwards as the more solid formations on either side of the First Cohort still managed to hold their ground. Out on the wings the cavalry cohorts were fighting off a second, half-hearted attack by the enemy horsemen. The battle was going to plan, Cato realised, and he promised a generous offering to Fortuna if luck continued to favour the side of Rome, as the battle entered the decisive phase. It all depended on Macro and the First Cohort, holding their formation as they gradually fell back.

'Sir?'

Cato turned to see an optio standing beside his horse. 'Yes?'

'Message from the Prefect Scyllus, sir. He begs to report that his archers are running out of arrows.'

'Very well. Tell the prefect to save what he has left and form his men up behind the reserves.'

'Yes, sir.' The optio saluted and turned to run back towards his unit.

As the rain of arrows stopped, the enemy drums beat with renewed energy and the horns blared out to offer encouragement to the Nubians. The pressure continued and the Roman centre was driven inwards as the enemy pushed forward, heedless of their own dead strewn across the battlefield beneath their feet. Prince Talmis's body of heavy infantry had pushed their way through the throng and now engaged the tiring men of the First Cohort. Well trained and equipped, they were able to fight the Romans on a more equal footing and more of Macro's men were cut down. The line was growing perilously thin as Cato watched. Yet he dare not give the order to spring the trap before he was certain the moment was right.

'Sir!' Junius shouted, thrusting his arm out. 'They're going to break through!'

Cato turned and saw the threat at once. A short distance to the right of Macro's centre a single rank of legionaries was struggling to hold back the enemy. They thrust their shields forward and their iron-nail shod boots scrabbled in the sand and grit as they desperately tried to stand their ground. But it was like holding back a flood with a line of sticks. One of the men slipped and went down on his knee. At once two Nubians thrust his shield back, knocking the legionary flat. He was run through with a spear even before he could prop himself back up on an elbow. More men pressed through the gap and turned on the Romans on either side.

'Shit,' Cato muttered. The crisis of the battle had been reached. A rising cheer of triumph swept through the nearest of the Nubians as they scented victory. There was one chance left, Cato realised, wheeling his horse round to face the men of the reserve cohort. The legionaries stood to, shields resting on the ground, javelins held to the side.

'The fate of the army is in your hands!' Cato called out to them as he drew his sword. 'You must save your comrades of the First Cohort and seal the gap in our line! For the Jackals!'

The centurions led their men in a throaty cheer that was unmistakably half-hearted. Cato could not afford the reserve to fail, and with the briefest of hesitations he swung his leg over the saddle and dropped to the ground. 'Follow me!'

Cato strode towards the Nubians pushing forward

through the First Cohort. The senior centurion of the reserves gave the order to advance at the trot and the legionaries came on, grim-faced, javelin points held high as they rumbled across the parched ground. Cato was still twenty paces ahead of them when he reached the gap. Several of the Nubians had stopped in their tracks as they saw the fresh formation closing on them. Choosing the nearest of them, a man with wild hair and armed with a club, Cato broke into a dead run, hunched forward and sword held out to the side, ready to strike. His left shoulder burned with pain from the blow he had received at the temple and Cato gritted his teeth as he swerved to avoid the clumsy blow of his foe, and thrust out his left palm into the man's face, snapping his head back and knocking him to the ground. He didn't pause to finish the man but turned aside to the next, a dark-robed Arab brandishing a spear. The point came up, stabbing at Cato's throat. He parried the shaft aside with his sword and then grabbed it with his spare hand. The Arab growled a curse as he tried to snatch it back. Cato thrust his sword high into the man's arm, and again, until the grip loosened. As they struggled, the rest of the reserve cohort came charging up, the front rank lowering the javelin tips and thrusting out at the enemy who had managed to spill through the gap in the First Cohort's line. They pressed past Cato on both sides, one of them stopping to slam his shield into the Arab and send him sprawling. A quick javelin thrust killed the man and the legionary ran on as Cato nodded his thanks.

The sudden arrival of four hundred men sealed the break in the line and steadied the hard-pressed legionaries of the First Cohort. Cato drew back from the fighting and returned to his horse. Junius stared at him as if Cato were mad for leading the charge, but he ignored the tribune and turned to survey the battlefield. The bulk of Prince Talmis's army had been drawn into the centre of the Roman line, as Cato had hoped it would be, making for where the Romans seemed weakest. On the flanks the main weight of the legion still stood in column, scarcely touched by the enemy missiles. The moment had come, Cato knew. He must attempt to close the trap now, while the centre of his line was still intact.

He nodded to Junius. 'Give the order.'

The tribune hesitated. 'Sir, I—'

'Give the order!'

The soldiers carrying the bucinas heard the command and did not wait for it to be relayed to them. They pursed their lips and raised their mouthpieces and blew. Three strident notes blasted out across the battlefield. The signal was repeated and before the last note died away the two columns of legionaries began to advance, fighting their way forward along the sides of the Nubian horde, out beyond the buckling line of the Roman units holding the centre. Beyond them the cavalry cohorts also advanced, in echelon as they covered the flanks of the Roman army.

At first the Nubians appeared to be unconcerned by the columns of legionaries extending around the edge of the host. Those in the centre were still convinced that victory was in their grasp; they fought like lions to break through the Roman line once again. Cato saw a silken banner rippling from side to side above the centre of the Nubian ranks and he realised that Prince Talmis had come forward in person to urge his troops to shatter the slender force that still held them back.

The flanking cohorts tramped forward until the last century had linked up with the main battle line. Then they stopped. A command was passed down the line and each cohort turned inward to face the sides of the massed warriors of the Nubian army. Another command echoed along each of the extended wings and the legionaries formed their shields into an unbroken wall. Then they advanced, pressing the enemy back before them and cutting down all those who came within reach of their short swords.

While the legionaries closed the trap, the auxiliary cavalry charged forward, cheering as loudly as they could as they made for the enemy horsemen still formed up some distance behind their infantry. If the enemy's nerve held, no amount of noise and raw courage would save the outnumbered auxiliaries from eventual defeat. Cato had calculated that their sacrifice would buy enough time for the rest of the Nubian army to be defeated. However, as he watched, the Nubian horsemen and the camel riders began to break away from their formations, individually at first, then in small groups, streaming away across the landscape to the south.

'Bloody hell,' Junius exclaimed bitterly. 'What do they think they're doing? The cowardly dogs!'

Cato nodded. Only a handful of the Nubians stood their ground and were quickly cut down by the mounted auxiliaries. The suddenness of their victory went to the heads of some of the Roman horsemen and they set off in pursuit before their officers could stop them. However, most began to trot back to form up on their standards, and they turned to form a line across the rear of the mass of Nubian infantry still attempting to overwhelm the centre of the Roman line.

But the tide of the battle had already turned. Those on the flanks, facing the fresh Roman legionaries, were ruthlessly forced back, pressing on their comrades caught in the middle. There was nowhere to escape, and soon no way to move as the fearful Nubians were caught in a vice between the advancing Roman lines. The beating of drums died away and so did the wild ululations and war cries, and as the Romans hacked their way into the Nubians, the first cries of panic and blind terror came from those who were so tightly pressed together that they could barely move and had no way of seeing or understanding the reason for the crush.

As the uncertainty and fear spread to the men still fighting against Macro's line, the Nubians began to back off, looking over their shoulders until they were out of reach of the swords and spears of the Romans, then turning and trying to force their way back through the trapped multitude. The legionaries and auxiliaries paused, breathing heavily and arms drooping from their exertions.

'What the fuck are you waiting for?' Macro's voice boomed out. 'Get after them! Kill 'em!'

Without waiting for his men, Macro roared incoherently and charged forward, stabbing and hacking at the men in front of him. The rest of the men saw that victory was at hand, and charged after him, slaughtering the enemy without any mercy or pity. The sand beneath the legionaries' boots was soon dark with blood and bodies fell so swiftly that the Romans were advancing over them to get at the enemy. The wailing and desperate cries of anguish from the Nubians rose into the hot air as the heat of the sun made itself felt and added to the torment of those still caught in the closing trap. Cato saw that the banner of Prince Talmis still rose above the sea of dark-skinned figures and he could just make out the tight ring of gleaming helmets as the Prince's bodyguards struggled to extract their master from the massacre.

'We should offer them terms,' said Junius and Cato glanced round to see the sickened expression on the tribune's face. 'Sir, we should offer them terms. This is a . . . bloodbath.'

Cato could understand his reaction, but there was nothing that could be done to end the slaughter. The Romans were outnumbered. If they paused in their deadly work, they would lose the initiative, and with it the battle. They had no choice but to keep on killing. Cato shook his head. 'This is war, Tribune. This is the face of battle, and you had best grow used to it.'

Some of the Nubians tried to surrender, throwing down their weapons and holding out their empty hands as they pleaded for their lives in their tongue. To no avail. They died alongside their comrades who fought on, hampered by the stifling press of men, which made it impossible for them to wield their weapons effectively.

For more than an hour it continued as the Roman cordon closed round those still trapped, Prince Talmis amongst them. The auxiliary cavalry had blocked their retreat and speared those who tried to get past them. Occasionally small groups of fugitives did manage to thrust past the horsemen, but the survivors were allowed to escape and the landscape to the south was dotted with figures running for their lives. As midday approached, the killing began to slacken as the Romans became too weary to continue the slaughter. Some of the Nubians took advantage of this and slipped between men who made no effort to stop them. Cato rode forward and his horse had to pick its way carefully over the bodies as it crossed the killing ground.

'Stand to! Centurions, call your men to their standards!'

He saw Macro, spattered and smeared with crimson, leaning on his shield, chest heaving as he gasped for breath. 'Centurion! Let the enemy pass. All except the Prince and his bodyguard. And the gladiators. They mustn't escape. Understand?'

Macro nodded, blinking away the sweat that dripped from his eyebrows. He pulled himself up and lifted his shield as he turned to address his men. 'Form ranks!'

The men of the First Cohort wearily trudged back to their standards and waited for orders. Cato felt a bitter weight in his heart as he saw that less than half of the men remained. The reserve cohort that had rushed to fill the gap had suffered a similar proportion of casualties. Macro waited until the last of his men was in position and then ordered them to advance on the standard of Prince Talmis. Cato's horse shied at the mounds of bodies that lay in his path and he dismounted and made his way to Macro's side.

'Well, the plan worked.' Macro smiled wearily. 'Never thought I'd see the day when I'd be grateful to Hannibal.'

'It's not quite over yet.' Cato nodded towards the knot of bodyguards gathered around the Prince's standard.

Macro shrugged. 'They're finished, one way or another. Surrender or die, Talmis is ours.'

The Romans opened their ranks to let the last of the lightly armed Nubians and Arabs flee, and then closed in around the bodyguards. They were big men, with scale armour and conical helmets. They carried oval shields and heavy spears and stood shoulder to shoulder as the Romans advanced on them.

Cato raised his arm as they came within twenty paces of the standard. 'Halt!'

His men shuffled to a stop, watching the enemy warily. Cato stepped forward and cleared his throat. 'Does Prince Talmis still live?'

'He does.' An imposing figure edged his way into the front line of the bodyguards. Talmis wore a black cuirass over black robes and his helmet and shoulders were covered with the hide of lion. His expression was cold and bitter as he stared out over the bodies heaped across the battlefield. The Prince's eyes fixed on Cato. 'What do you want with me, Legate? My surrender?'

'Yes.'

'So that I can be displayed in Rome, no doubt, as a prize of your Emperor.'

'That is for the Emperor to decide,' Cato responded. 'My offer to you is simple. You and your men surrender, or I will be forced to have you cut down where you stand.'

'I don't think I will surrender,' Talmis said slowly, and his dark lips twisted into a calculating smile. 'You will let me return to Nubia freely, Legate.'

Cato's brow furrowed. 'And why would I do that?'

'Because I have what you want. I have Ajax. I'll give him to you, in exchange for free passage back across the frontier to Nubia.'

Cato felt his heart quicken. 'Ajax is here? With you?'

'No. I have been keeping him safe while I decided what to do with a man who had failed to serve me well. His life for mine. That is the offer.'

Cato turned to Macro and for a moment there was a tense silence as their eyes met. Macro swallowed but managed to contain any display of feeling that might influence his friend's decision. There would be no question of avoiding the anger of the imperial palace if the Prince was allowed to walk free. And yet the Nubians had been crushed. It would be many years before they dared to defy Rome again. Ajax, on the other hand, would present a far more immediate threat to the Empire if he were allowed to escape from Egypt. He had already stirred up one rebellion that had nearly brought Rome to its knees. Who knew what else the gladiator was capable of? Besides, Ajax was the reason why they were here in the province in the first place. It was the search for Ajax that had consumed their lives for months now. There was an unanswerable need to finish the business that had tormented them both since the rebellion on Crete. Cato turned back to the Nubian Prince.

'Well?' Talmis raised his chin. 'What is your decision?'

CHAPTER THIRTY-SIX

It was late in that afternoon when Prince Talmis reined in at the head of the small column of riders, trotting down the bank of the Nile. Both he and his bodyguards had been disarmed and were escorted by Cato, Macro, Tribune Junius and a squadron of auxiliary cavalry. Talmis pointed across the river to a small island, two hundred paces across the river. Like most of the islands Cato had seen, it was low and fringed with reeds. However, at the upriver end there was a sizeable slab of rock upon which a shrine had been built, five columns by four. Clumps of date palms grew around the base of the rock and a small landing stage lay a short distance further along the island, beyond which there were only reeds. A skiff was moored to the landing stage, and a single figure could be seen at the entrance to the shrine, watching them.

'I have them under guard there, in the shrine,' said Talmis.

'Them?' Macro raised an eyebrow. 'How many men has Ajax left?'

'There is Ajax and one other, a man called Karim. The others I had put to death when the gladiator returned to my camp with his story of failure. I was saving him for

466

later – that is, if I could not get a good price for him from your Emperor.'

'I'm glad I'm not your ally,' Macro commented.

'Ajax was not an ally. He offered to serve me. He was supposed to distract you and not give battle. But he wanted nothing more than to kill Romans, no matter what the cost to those he led.' Prince Talmis turned to look at Macro and Cato. 'I am impressed that a man can hate you two as much as Ajax does.'

Macro pursed his lips. 'It cuts both ways, Nubian. We have our own reasons for returning his feeling in kind.'

'Truly?' Talmis swatted an insect away from his cheek. He gestured to Macro to continue.

'That's enough,' Cato interrupted. 'It'll be dark soon. I want to deal with Ajax before the day is out.' He turned to the Prince. 'How many of your men are there on the island?'

'Six of my best men. I will send their captain to them to explain the situation and recall the guards. Then the gladiator and his friend are yours. And you will free me and my men.'

'Only when I have Ajax,' Cato said firmly. 'Have your men bring the boat over. I'll go across with your captain and some of my troops to take charge of the captives. Your men can return first, then you are free to go.'

'I see.' Talmis nodded and looked at him with a calculating expression. 'Legate, do you think your victory has ended my ambitions to seize the upper Nile?'

'No. But it will take time for you to mass another army. By then Rome will have sent more troops to the province and bolstered the defences of the towns and forts along the Nile. You will have even less chance of success than you did this time.' Cato looked at him steadily. 'I don't think Rome will have much to worry about from the Nubian quarter for a while. You're a spent force. Ajax, on the other hand, is not. That is the reason why I am prepared to trade your life for his.'

A frown flitted across the Prince's face. 'Really? I think you underestimate me, Roman. We shall see about that, perhaps sooner than you think.' Prince Talmis turned to the captain of his bodyguards and there was a quick exchange before the captain dismounted and climbed down the bank to the edge of the water. He raised a small horn to his lips and blew four times. Two figures scurried down from the shrine, boarded the skiff and set off across the current.

Cato gestured to the commander of the cavalry escort to join him and then spoke quietly to the decurion. 'I don't trust the Prince. I want your two best men to come with me. Once we reach the island and have the prisoners, I'll give the signal for you to release the Prince and his men.'

'Yes, sir. And what'll the signal be?'

Cato thought briefly. 'I'll raise my sword and wave it from side to side. You'll see that well enough from here.'

'Yes, sir.'

Cato glanced at the Prince and his men. 'If they make any attempt to escape before the signal is given, kill the men. Take the Prince alive, if you can.'

Macro moved closer to Cato and muttered, 'What's to stop us killing him anyway? Once we have Ajax?'

Cato shook his head. 'Talmis poses little danger to

Rome. I think that this defeat will weaken him. He'll be busy keeping his followers in line as it is. If we kill him, we give the Nubians a grievance that will need to be avenged.'

Macro shrugged. 'If you say so. Frankly, one more dead Nubian suits me fine.'

Cato nodded to the decurion. 'You have your orders.'

The decurion turned in his saddle to call back down the line. 'Castor! Decius! Dismount and escort the legate!'

The two tough-looking men swung down from their saddles and handed the reins to their comrades before unhooking their shields and trotting forward to the two officers. Cato dismounted and gestured to them to follow him. 'You too, Macro. And you, Junius.'

He led the way down to join the Nubian captain as they waited for the skiff. The men in the small boat worked the oars hard as they fought the current. As they waited, Cato stepped aside from the others. 'Macro, over here.'

They moved out of earshot and Cato turned to his friend with a searching look. 'When we get hold of Ajax it is my intention to take him back to Rome alive. Do you understand?'

Macro was silent for a moment and his expression hardened as he replied through gritted teeth. 'After all that bastard's done? You haven't forgotten Crete, Cato. But then it wasn't you he held captive in that shitty cage. It was me, and Julia.'

'I know.'

'Bollocks. I say we kill him, dump his body in the Nile and be done with it.'

'Those were not our orders.'

'Orders?' Macro leaned closer, face to face with Cato. 'Fuck the orders . . . Fuck 'em. Fuck Sempronius, Narcissus, the Emperor. Fuck the lot of 'em. I don't care. Ajax owes me, and I want my revenge.' He paused and softened his tone as best he could. 'Cato, lad, I need revenge, and so do you, for Julia's sake.'

'I won't speak for her.'

Macro stabbed his finger at Cato's harness. 'She's going to be your wife. Do you think you can live with that precious conscience of yours, knowing what he did to her and yet letting him live an instant longer than necessary?'

'Ajax will die,' Cato replied firmly. 'He will be condemned by the Emperor and crucified. You know it.'

'Oh, he'll be condemned all right, but what if Claudius decides to send him to the arena? You know how good he is. If anyone can win over the mob, it'll be Ajax. Then what? Supposing Claudius spares him, as a sop to the mob? Even if he dies, he'll go out a hero. Either with a sword in his hand spitting defiance, or screaming his hatred of Rome from the cross. If he's crucified, he'll be a martyr, just like Spartacus before him.'

'Then we'll have to bridge that cross when, or if, we come to it.' Cato grasped his friend's arm. 'Macro. We have no choice. We have our orders and I will carry them out. And so will you. Give me your word on it, or I'll have no choice but to send you back to the camp.'

Macro's face flinched with the effort of containing the poisonous rage that Ajax had planted in his heart many months before. At length he sucked in a deep breath through his teeth. 'As you command . . . sir.'

'Thank you.' Cato bowed his head slightly in gratitude

before he glanced towards the river. 'The boat's here. Let's go.'

They returned to the others as the skiff reached the shore. One of the men hopped over the side with a splash and guided the bows in. The captain climbed aboard and settled in the stern before the others took their places; Macro and Cato opposite the captain, then the two auxiliaries and Junius on the small triangular deck at the front. The Nubian pushed the boat off and the man at the oars turned the craft and started to propel it back across the glassy expanse of river towards the landing stage on the island. One of the legionaries leaned out to look down at the water and the boat rolled slightly to that side.

'Sit back!' Macro snapped. 'Don't move again.'

'Sorry, sir.'

The skiff was heavily laden and awkward to move and the man at the oars had to work hard to keep on course. The sun was beginning to sink into a murky orange haze to the west and the dark forms of birds swooped low over the water, feeding off the insects. They were not the only animals feeding, Cato realised as the skiff approached the landing stage. There was a movement in the reeds away to the left and a long glistening snout protruded briefly through the slender green growths, then with a swirl of water and swish amongst the tops of the reeds, it was gone.

The skiff approached the landing stage, constructed from stone in the forgotten days when priests once came to the shrine to make offerings. Now the stone was worn with age and mottled with bird droppings. The man at the oars shouted over his shoulder to Junius, and then pointed to the rope loosely coiled beside the tribune. Junius nodded his understanding and took up the rope, reaching out to the iron ring that was fastened to the side of the stonework. A thrust of the oars brought it within reach and the tribune grasped it and pulled the boat in. As soon as he could he slipped the end of the rope through the ring and pulled it back, drawing the craft closer. Once the craft was securely moored, Junius clambered ashore and helped the others up. When they were all on firm ground, Macro turned to the Nubian captain.

'You speak Greek?'

'Little.'

'Then no tricks, understand?' Macro slapped his scabbard. 'Or else.'

The captain nodded and then led the way up a crumbling stone path lined with palm trees. It was only a short climb before they emerged close to the entrance to the shrine. Cato turned back and saw the distant figures watching them from the riverbank. Then he strode towards the entrance with the rest of the party, his heart beating swiftly as he anticipated the meeting with Ajax. At his side Macro's expression was grim and his lips pressed tightly together. The two auxiliaries followed Macro, and Cato and Junius took up the rear. The sentry at the gate saluted as he saw the captain and there was a brief exchange before the Nubian led the party inside the shrine.

The interior was enclosed in a ten-foot wall on which hieroglyphs had been deeply carved to let the shadows accentuate each character. Two figures sat with their backs to the far wall, watched by two men with spears, some fifteen feet away. Ajax looked up as the new arrivals stood in the entrance. For a moment his face was blank, then his keen gaze took in the weapons in the hands of the Romans and he smiled weakly.

'So, Prince Talmis has been defeated. I wondered. Now I am to be your victim instead of his.'

Cato stared at the gladiator, his mind seething with hatred and a constant refrain to remember his orders. There was something else he was dimly aware of at the same time: a vague sense of disappointment that the long hunt had come to an end.

'We go,' announced the captain.

'What?' Cato turned to him. The Nubian gestured to his men and pointed in the direction of the skiff. Cato nodded curtly.

The captain called to his men and they backed away from the prisoners and gathered their haversacks and joined their officer. Then, with a brief nod to Cato, the Nubian led his men out of the shrine. Cato heard the pad of boots fading away and then there was silence as the prisoners and the Romans gazed at each other.

Ajax broke the silence. 'What will you do with me?'

'Take you back to Rome,' Cato said tonelessly.

'I see. You will make a spectacle of my death? A warning to other slaves of the cost of defying Rome.'

'I imagine that's what the Emperor will want. Frankly, I don't care about that. Macro and I just want to see you pay for all the suffering you have caused.'

'And what of the suffering you caused me?'

Macro growled. 'Your father was a bloody pirate. He deserved his end. As you deserve yours.'

Ajax glanced past the two officers and a brief smile

flickered across his face. At once Cato felt an icy tremor course down his back. He turned to follow the direction of the gladiator's eyes. Behind him stood the two auxiliaries, spears grasped firmly as they watched the prisoners closely. Beyond them Junius had drawn his sword and was waving it from side to side. The signal for the release of Prince Talmis. Cato felt his anger rising. 'I didn't give the order to—'

Junius stepped forward and swung his sword into the back of the nearest auxiliary's neck, cutting through the spine. The man's mouth sagged open as he collapsed. The other man half turned and looked down at his stricken companion, too shocked to react fast enough to save his life. Junius stepped forward and stabbed him in the throat.

'What?' Cato stared at the tribune aghast. It was Macro who grasped the truth first. He tore out his sword and turned on Junius.

'Traitor!' he roared. 'He's the one!'

'Traitor?' Cato felt as if he had been struck numb. The image of Hamedes lying dead with a knife in his back leapt into his mind. He felt sick with the terrible knowledge of his mistake. 'No . . . Not Junius.'

The tribune grinned. 'I doubt you'll ever find the body of Junius. The jackals along the road from Memphis will have seen to that. That's where we caught him, on his way to join the legion.'

He threw his sword over Cato's head and ducked down to snatch up one of the auxiliary's spears. The sword thudded into the ground in front of Ajax and he snatched it up and sprang to his feet, as did the other prisoner. Ajax laughed harshly.

'My thanks, Canthus. You save me again.' Ajax pointed the sword at Cato. 'The legate is mine. Deal with the centurion.'

'Canthus?' Cato felt sick, but still had enough presence of mind to draw his sword. The young man lowered the tip of his spear and thrust at Macro. His action was fast and Macro only just had time to lurch to one side to avoid the weapon. At once his opponent feinted again as he tried to keep him off balance. But Macro had managed to drop into a balanced crouch and easily parried the blow aside. The two men watched each other closely.

A padding of feet caused Cato to turn, just as Ajax slashed out with his sword. The tip hissed through the air and Cato ducked. Thrusting his blade up, Cato stabbed at Ajax's side. It was a hurried stroke, yet the blade cut through his soiled tunic and gashed the muscly flesh over the gladiator's ribs. Ajax snarled ferociously and backed off a step. He reached round with his spare hand to touch the wound. Behind him Cato saw his companion, Karim, the swarthy lieutenant he recalled from the rebellion on Crete. The man was hurrying round the far wall of the shrine, towards Macro's back.

'Macro! Watch out!'

As Cato shouted the warning, Ajax lunged forward, slashing at Cato's face. He tried to scramble away, but the sword point cut high on his forehead and swept on down across his brow, nose and cheek. It felt as if he had been hit in the face by a red-hot hammer and his vision instantly blurred and a terrible, agonising pain seared across his consciousness, blotting out thought of anything else. Cato stumbled back and fell, his sword slipping from his fingers.

The impact drove the breath from his lungs and blood spilled into his eyes and blinded him.

Macro heard the warning, and saw Canthus's gaze flicker to his right. Macro pounced forward, hammering his sword down on the fingers of the hand nearest him. The blade cut through and the severed digits dropped from the spear shaft. Canthus howled with pain. Macro ran on, and with his full weight behind the punch, smashed his fist into Canthus's face. As Canthus staggered under the blow, Macro struck with his sword, a savage blow to the side of his head that split his skull with a wet crack. Before Canthus hit the ground, Macro turned on the spot, bracing his feet and holding his sword point out. Karim could not check his sprint in time to avoid the weapon. The point plunged through his chest, shattering his sternum, driving the air from his lungs in a hot blast into Macro's face. Even so the impetus of his charge drove his body on and both men crashed to the floor, the point of Macro's sword bursting out of the rebel's back. Karim glared down at the centurion as blood dripped from his open mouth. Both hands reached up, desperately feeling for the Roman's throat. Macro felt them begin to claw at his neck and heaved him aside, wrenching at the blade.

There was a sudden blur of movement from the other side of the shrine as Ajax charged towards him. Macro slashed out with his sword, aiming it at the gladiator's knee. But Ajax's reflexes had been finely honed in the arena and he leaped high to avoid the blow, over Macro and the body of Karim, and ran on another two paces before scrambling to a stop and turning to face the centurion. Macro rolled on to his feet and rose in a crouch, sword held out to the side, ready. Neither man moved for a moment; and their breathing, the fading gasps of Karim and the moans of Cato echoed softly off the ancient walls.

Ajax licked his lips. 'You should have killed me alongside my father.'

'Yes, I should,' Macro muttered. 'That was a mistake . . . which I intend to correct.'

He paced forward and swung at the gladiator. Ajax parried the blows and then counterattacked with a swift series of thrusts and cuts that tested Macro's swordsmanship and sharp reactions to the limit. Then he stepped back and they stared at each other in the failing light. The blood from Ajax's side was flowing freely and he could feel the warm trickle running down the outside of his thigh. He knew that he would begin to weaken soon. The telltale chill already pricked at his skin. Soon his vision would begin to blur. The veteran instructor who had trained Ajax years before had drilled into his students the danger signs associated with wounds. As soon as a man knew that he was weakening, he must strike, or soon be reduced to begging the mob for Mercy. Ajax launched another flurry of blows and the clash of blades echoed shrilly off the surrounding walls. Still he could find no way past the Roman's defences. He caught the cold look of satisfaction on Macro's face.

Macro saw the wound in the gladiator's side and the streak of blood on his leg. Evenly matched as they were, time was against Ajax. His loss of blood would steadily slow him down and in the end Macro would kill him. Revenge would be his.

477

Ajax nodded bitterly as he grasped the truth of his situation. 'You think you have won, Roman. Do you really think you will defeat me? Do you think I, Ajax, would permit that?' He sneered. 'While I live, the flame of rebellion will burn in the hearts of slaves everywhere. And I live as long as you have no proof that I am dead. By that measure, you are defeated today.'

Before Macro could grasp his meaning, Ajax turned and sprinted towards the entrance and ran out into the dusk.

'Shit!' Macro glanced at Cato, momentarily torn by the urge to help his friend. Then he turned and ran after Ajax. The gladiator ignored the path leading down to the landing stage and headed across the cracked paving stones in front of the shrine, down the smoothed boulders and into the long grass. Macro followed him, losing ground thanks to his shorter legs. The grass rustled and whipped at his legs as he ran after Ajax, already some fifty feet ahead of him and gaining more ground with every pace. Ahead Macro could see that the end of the island was close to the western bank, no more than fifty paces of open water. Ajax entered the reeds and his boots splashed into the shallow murky water. By the time Macro reached the reeds, Ajax was already waist deep, wading out into the Nile. He glanced back and smiled as he saw the gap he had opened up between himself and Macro. Then he was clear of the reeds and leaped forward, releasing his sword. He began to strike out into the current.

Macro stopped ankle deep in the water lapping at the reeds and slipped his sword belt over his head. His fingers clawed at the fastenings of his harness. As he heaved his harness over his head and threw it aside, he heard a loud rustle in the reeds a short distance away, then a splash as a heavy body entered the water. A dark shape surged out from the reeds and made across the water at an angle towards Ajax.

At the last moment, the gladiator turned and saw the crocodile's unblinking eyes, set in its ridged tough hide. He turned and looked at Macro. 'No! NO!'

Then his head snapped forwards. His arms came up flailing, trying to beat at the monster that gripped him in its powerful jaws with sharp, tearing teeth. There was a great commotion in the water as the crocodile came up and rolled over, its light-coloured belly glistening in the last light of the day. Then it was gone. The disturbed water rippled for a moment before the Nile flowed peacefully on into the gathering dusk.

Macro watched for a moment, to be sure that Ajax was gone. His body felt numb with shock at the death of his enemy. Then there was a terrible rage that welled up from the pit of his stomach, burning his heart as he gritted his teeth, mentally cursing the gods with every resource of anger at his disposal. To have pursued Ajax for so long, and so far, only for this. Macro's fists clenched tightly and he trembled.

'Fuck . . . Fuck! . . . FUCK!'

His words echoed faintly from the far bank and then there was silence. He slowly turned away from the Nile, picked up his armour and waded on to dry ground before hurrying back to the shrine to see to his friend, Cato.

EPILOGUE

Two months later Cato climbed the path up to the imperial villa perched on the cliff on the eastern end of the island of Caprae. They had taken passage on an imperial courier packet from Alexandria, and braved the rough autumn seas to cross the Mediterranean and sail up the west coast of Italy, making for the port of Ostia on the mouth of the Tiber. When they put in at the naval base of Puteoli they were told that Emperor Claudius and the imperial secretary, Narcissus, were wintering on Caprae. Accordingly, the captain of the packet reversed course and made for the small rocky island thrusting up from the sea just off the bay of Naples. Cato had left Macro in one of the inns of the small fishing village nestling beside the harbour.

As he climbed the path, passing through checkpoints manned by wary Praetorian Guards, Cato collected his thoughts so that he could deliver a clear report to the imperial secretary. The defeat of the Nubians and the death of Ajax had brought his mission in Egypt to an end. Once the Twenty-Second Legion had returned to its base in Memphis, Cato and Macro had quit the legion and returned to Alexandria. They travelled down the Nile on a barge, Cato resting under an awning as he recovered from his wound. The Jackals' surgeon had sewn the wound up and it had taken many days before the flesh had knitted together in a jagged scar stretching across his face.

In Alexandria the governor had listened, grim-faced, as the two officers reported on the outcome of the campaign, the grievous losses suffered by the Roman army and the ravaging of the province along the upper Nile. Petronius had been angry at Cato's decision to exchange Talmis for Ajax, especially as there was no body to put on public display. But he took no action against the acting legate. Petronius announced that Cato would have to answer for his decisions before officials back in Rome, and take his punishment there. The governor had hurriedly written a preliminary report and sent it ahead of Cato for delivery to Narcissus, the Emperor's closest adviser.

Throughout the voyage home, Cato's mood had become more and more despondent. He yearned to return to Julia's side. She was waiting for him at her father's house in Rome and he could picture her, vividly, as he imagined himself stepping across the threshold and into her arms. Such thoughts were immediately soured by her reaction to the scar that now crossed his brow and cheek.

His mind was also burdened by the grievous error of judgement he had made over Hamedes. His reasoning had been faulty and an innocent man had died. Macro had spoken little of the matter and offered rough reassurance that Cato's mistake was understandable amid the chaos and bloodshed of the campaign. Cato was far less forgiving of himself.

He approached the main gate of the imperial villa at the top of the track and told the duty optio his name and rank and explained his request to see Narcissus and make his report.

'Wait here, sir,' the optio instructed and unhurriedly climbed the stairs into the villa. A cold wind was blowing over the island and gathering clouds threatened rain. To the north the hillside tumbled steeply down to the cliffs overlooking the sea and Cato stared over the bay towards the distant headland of Puteoli. A hundred or so miles further along the coast lay Ostia, and a short ride into Rome, and Julia.

'Prefect!'

Cato turned and saw the Praetorian optio beckoning to him from the top of the stairs. The guards on the gate parted to admit him. Then, at the foot of the stairs, another guard raised a hand.

'Excuse me, sir. I take it you have handed your sword and any other weapons in to the port guards?'

'Yes.'

The guardsman nodded. 'Good. Then there's one last search before you proceed, sir. Please raise your arms and stand still.'

Cato did as he was instructed and the guardsman expertly frisked his cloak, tunic and ran his fingers around the inside of Cato's belt before he stood back. 'That's it, sir.'

Cato advanced and climbed the stairs to the waiting optio, who led him through a marble portico into the atrium of the villa. The space was dominated by a large shallow pool with a tessellated image of Neptune and shoals of fish decorating the bottom. On the far side a short colonnaded hall led out on to a terrace. Through large doors to the right, Cato could hear voices, laughing and talking light-heartedly. There was a smaller opening to the left, leading down to the quarters of the slaves and lesser officials.

'This way, sir.' The optio gestured to Cato, who followed him across the atrium and down the corridor on to the terrace. A wide expanse of pink-hued marble stretched out before them and ended abruptly fifty paces away. Potted plants and trellised walkways surrounded the terrace, which afforded spectacular views across the sea towards the mainland. Cato could understand why the island had been the favourite playground of the imperial family for so many years.

There was only one other man on the terrace and he sat on a bench with his back to Cato.

'There you are, sir.' The optio halted and indicated the seated figure. 'I'll see you back at the gate, sir. To log you out.' The optio saluted and turned and marched into the villa. Cato continued across the terrace. Narcissus's thin frame was wrapped in a plain red cloak and his dark hair was threaded with grey. He glanced back as he heard Cato's footsteps and offered a smile that lacked any real warmth.

'Cato, it is good to see you again, my boy. Sit down.' He gestured towards another bench, set at an angle to the one he was seated on. A small table stood in front of the benches and a thin wisp of vapour rose from a goblet of heated wine. There was only one cup, Cato noted. This was typical of Narcissus, Cato thought, a small trick to remind him of his subordination, and put him in his place.

Cato eased himself down on to the seat indicated and Narcissus looked him over for a moment before he spoke. 'You've been wounded recently. That's quite a scar.'

Cato shrugged.

'It's been a while since we have spoken,' Narcissus continued.

'Over two years. When you sent Macro and me to spy on the governor of Syria.'

'And you both made a good job of that, as well as playing a leading role in saving Palmyra from the Parthians. Since then, you've done sterling work in Crete, and Sempronius informed me that he had sent you to find the slave rebel, Ajax.' Narcissus reached inside his cloak and pulled out a scroll. 'And now the governor of Egypt, our good friend Petronius, reports that you have resolved the matter. Well done. However, he takes you to task for letting the Nubian Prince go.' Narcissus watched Cato closely. 'Would you care to explain why you did so?'

'It was my judgement that the gladiator presented the greater threat, taking the wider picture into consideration,' Cato said firmly.

'The wider picture.' Narcissus smiled faintly. 'It seems I was right about you. You have the brains to consider the strategic situation in making your decisions.' He tossed the report on the table dismissively. 'Petronius is a fool. Your judgement was sound, young man, though you have made an enemy of Petronius, and there will be plenty in Rome who will not appreciate the nuances of your dilemma. Be that as it may, rest assured I accept what you did as the appropriate course of action, though I will not say so in public, nor will there be any official recognition of your

achievement in hunting down that infernal gladiator.'
Narcissus smiled apologetically before he continued.
'Then there is the difficult matter of Senator Sempronius's
decision to appoint you to the rank of prefect. He did so
in the name of the Emperor, I understand. However, he
exceeded his authority. Of course there was something of
an emergency to deal with and both the Emperor and I
approve of the actions Sempronius undertook to put an
end to the slave revolt in Crete and send you and Macro
to hunt down the ringleaders.' Narcissus gestured towards
the report. 'Now the crisis has passed and the danger is
over. You have my thanks. You and your comrade,
Macro.'

Cato bowed his head slightly in acknowledgement.

'However,' Narcissus continued, 'such a rapid pro-
gression through the ranks is bound to raise a few eyebrows
and ruffle a few feathers, eh? Emperor Claudius is always
mindful of the need not to upset those in the military, some
of whom are not as loyal as they should be. The murder of
his predecessor is eloquent proof of that. Which means that
you present him with something of a difficulty.'

'What do you mean?'

Narcissus stared at him for a moment, and smiled.
'You're an intelligent fellow, Cato. I know I don't need
to spell it out for you, but since you would derive some
satisfaction from forcing me to be blunt then I will be.'

'That would be appreciated.'

'It would not be wise to confirm your promotion at
present, particularly since it is your intention to return to
Rome to wed that lovely daughter of Sempronius. Your
presence in the capital would cause jealousy. There are

plenty of other senators with protégés they are seeking to advance.'

Cato listened with an increasing sense of bitterness. This was his reward for the sacrifices made in the service of the Emperor and Rome. An expression of gratitude and, no doubt, demotion to the rank of centurion. With that would disappear his automatic elevation to the equestrian class. He could well imagine how reluctant Sempronius would be to permit his daughter to marry so far beneath her. It was true that the senator had offered some encouragement to their relationship after the siege of Palmyra, but that was a very different setting to the cut and thrust of Roman social and political life. Cato's demotion would be seen as a mark of official disfavour, even if he had the private gratitude of Narcissus and Emperor Claudius. All the plans that Cato had made for his future with Julia began to crumble in his mind. Cato cleared his throat.

'Have these protégés served Rome as well as I?'

'No, they haven't, but then Sempronius is not nearly as influential as the other senators. You see my difficulty. Trust me, I don't want to stand in the way of your promotion, and your future happiness.' He winked. 'But there are political realities that need to be addressed. That is the nature of my job. I would not be serving the Emperor well if I acted without regard for the wider picture.'

'So you will not be confirming my promotion.'

'Not for the present. Perhaps when you are a safe distance from Rome, and far from the public eye.'

'You mean that I cannot remain in Rome and take the promotion.'

Narcissus was silent for a moment, then nodded.

Cato let out a long, weary sigh. 'Very well, find me a posting, somewhere I won't embarrass you, and not so far from Rome, nor so uncomfortable, that Julia will not wish to come with me.'

Narcissus had arched his eyebrows as Cato spoke and now responded in a cold tone. 'You do not make demands of me, young man. Be clear about that. Were it not for your fine record I would punish you for speaking so bluntly. Now listen. I will confirm your promotion before the year is out, whether you are in Rome or stationed elsewhere in the Empire. I give you my word on that. And here is the reason.' Narcissus paused and looked round, as if to make sure they were not being overheard. Cato saw through the pretence at once. The security at the villa was so tight that no spy could possibly penetrate the ring of steel the Praetorian Guard formed round the Emperor's residence.

Even so, Narcissus lowered his voice.

'I have need of you and Macro. Urgent need. You recall the dealings we have had with that nest of traitors who call themselves the Liberators?'

Cato remembered them well. A shadowy conspiracy of aristocrats and their followers who wanted to do away with the line of emperors and return Rome to the days of the Republic when the senate exercised supreme power. He nodded to Narcissus.

'I remember.'

'Then know that they are active again. My spies have heard rumours of a fresh plot against the Emperor.'

'The Liberators intend to assassinate him?'

'I don't know the details, only that something is afoot.

There are few men I dare trust with the knowledge. That is why I am meeting you out here, alone. I need men I can trust to investigate this further. To penetrate the heart of the conspiracy.'

Cato thought it through and smiled bitterly. 'So that's it. Either we do this for you, or you will deny me my promotion.'

'Yes.'

'And what does Macro gain from this?'

'His pick of the legions when you both return to active service. That, or perhaps the command of an auxiliary cohort.'

'And what guarantee do we have that you will keep to your side of the deal if we take on this task?'

'You have my word.'

Cato nearly laughed out loud but restrained himself in time. There was nothing to be gained from insulting the imperial secretary. Equally, there was much to be lost if he failed to accept the task being offered to him. He looked Narcissus in the eye.

'I cannot give you my answer now. I must speak with Macro first.'

'Where is he?'

'Down in the port.'

'Very well. Then go now. I'll expect to see you back here before the end of the day. Any later and I will assume that you refuse the task, and I will be obliged to find a more loyal man to carry it out. A man more worthy of promotion, if you understand my meaning.'

'Perfectly.' Cato stood up abruptly. 'I'll take my leave of you.'

'For the moment.' Narcissus nodded. 'Don't be too long, Cato. I'll be here, waiting for you,' he added with a ring of certainty that stayed with Cato all the way across the terrace, out of the villa, and down the long path back into the port as he went to find Macro.

'He's a real low, shitty, slimy, crooked piece of work, our Narcissus.' Macro shook his head. 'One of these days I'm going to take him for a nice little walk down a quiet alley and do him in.'

'Come the day,' Cato replied with feeling. He lifted the cup that Macro had poured him and glanced round the small inn. A handful of off-duty Praetorians were playing dice on a table on the far side of the room, dimly lit by the handful of oil lamps hanging from the beams. Cato lowered his voice. 'What do you think?'

'About Narcissus's offer?' Macro shrugged. 'We accept. What else can we do? The bastard has us by the balls and he knows it. Besides, if it gets me back into a legion on a permanent posting then I'm game. You too if you have any sense. How else are you going to get that promotion to prefect confirmed? I tell you, Cato, I'd do anything to get back to regular soldiering. If it takes doing one more job for Narcissus, then I'll do it.'

Cato nodded thoughtfully. His friend was right. There was no choice in the matter. Not if he wanted to marry Julia. He would have to do the bidding of the imperial secretary in order to win his promotion and rise into the ranks of the equestrian class. Only then could he present himself to Senator Sempronius as a suitable husband for his daughter. Cato reached up with his spare hand and touched his scar. He felt a stab of anxiety in his heart as he wondered how she would react when she saw him again.

Macro noticed the gesture and could not help a light chuckle.

Cato frowned at him. 'What?'

'Trust me, lad.' Macro smiled as he picked up the wine jug and reached across the table to refill Cato's cup to the brim. 'The ladies love a good scar. Makes you look more like a real man, not one of the pampered dandies that strut around the forum in Rome. So, let's have a toast. Death to the Emperor's enemies, and here's to the rewards that are long overdue to us both.'

Cato nodded as he tapped his cup against Macro's. 'I'll drink to that, my friend.'

AUTHOR'S NOTE

The Roman province of Egypt was one of the most vital assets of the empire. Rome had been interested in Egypt long before Octavian (who later adopted the title of Augustus) annexed Egypt following the suicide of Cleopatra – the last of the dynasty established by Ptolemy subsequent to the carve-up of Alexander the Great's conquests. Thanks to the regular floods of the Nile, the production of wheat was prodigious. Better still, the kingdom stood at the crossroads of trade between the civilisations of the Mediterranean and the east. The wealth accrued from agriculture and trade made Alexandria the most prosperous and populous city in the world after Rome.

So it was only natural that successive emperors would jealously guard the jewel in the crown of Rome. Unlike other provinces, Egypt was the personal domain of the emperor, who appointed a prefect to govern the province in his name. Members of the senatorial class, and even those from the lower rank of the equestrians, were strictly prohibited from entering Egypt without the express permission of the emperor. Not that the febrile brew of ethnicities in Alexandria needed outside agents to provoke it into violence. One of the recurring features of the history of the province is the frequent outbreak of riots and street-fighting between the Greeks, Jews and Egyptians who inhabited Alexandria and vexed the patience of the Roman governors.

Roman rule of Egypt was based on one overriding purpose: to extract as much wealth from the province as possible. Consequently, the administrative system was run extremely efficiently to maximise tax income, and the people of Egypt were taxed to the hilt. Much of the burden rested on the middle class of the province – the traditional and easy target of tax officials then and now. As a consequence, the unlucky taxpayers eventually succumbed to debt, and the long term decline of Egypt began.

The native Egyptians had already resisted the earlier imposition of Greek culture by the Ptolemies, and the Romans never managed to persuade the natives to buy into the Roman way. Latin was the language of oppression and, outside of Alexandria and the largest cities and towns, life carried on pretty much as it had under the pharaohs. Even today, many of those living along the banks of the upper Nile still live in the same mud-brick houses as their forbears and harvest their crops by hand.

Aside from the heavy hand of their Roman masters, the local people also endured frequent raids and small invasions by Nubians and Ethiopians across the frontier south of modern Aswan. The Roman outposts either side of the narrow strip of inhabitable land on both sides of the Nile were easily overcome or circumvented, and plunder easy to come by. The legions of Rome were always stretched thinly around the thousands of miles of frontier that protected the empire. It was no different in Egypt. The three legions that Augustus had stationed there were soon reduced to two, one of which was dispersed to various postings across Egypt. The balance of troops available to the governor was made up of auxiliary cohorts. Under the close watch of the Emperor, the governor had to ensure that the wheat and tax continued to flow to Rome, while managing barely adequate forces to maintain order and defend the frontier – a truly unenviable job.

As ever, I have made sure that I walked the ground on which the novel is set. I can vouch for the discomfort of those marshes in the delta, and the searing heat of the upper Nile! The ancient ruins are also well worth a visit and I could not help but be in awe of the civilisation that had created such vast monuments long before an obscure settlement on the banks of the Tiber even came into existence. For readers who want to experience Egypt for themselves I would heartily recommend a trip to Luxor (Diospolis Magna). Many of the locations mentioned in the novel are still there and, with a little imagination, can be viewed just as Macro and Cato would have seen them.

The Gladiator

Simon Scarrow

'I really don't need this kind of competition' Bernard Cornwell

At the end of a harrowing campaign, centurions Macro and Cato are sailing for Rome. Their journey is interrupted off the coast of Crete where an earthquake strikes. The transport ship is severely damaged, and they are forced to limp to shore.

The province is in chaos. Worse, the slave population has taken the opportunity to revolt. Against a strong legion, the renegades would have little chance, but the garrison troops are of poor quality. As Roman men and weaponry fall to the enemy, the balance of power is in danger of switching.

Macro and Cato face a rebellion that could ignite an uprising across the Empire. Against them stands a powerful leader: Ajax. A gladiator who has fearlessly faced death daily, Ajax is driven by a desire for vengeance both political and personal. And he may represent a force too great for Rome to overcome . . .

Praise for Simon Scarrow's novels of the Roman Empire:

'It's *Spartacus* meets *Master and Commander* in this rip-roaring, thoroughly entertaining tale of swashbuckling adventure' *Scottish Daily Record*

'All the hallmarks of Bernard Cornwell at his best' *Oxford Times*

978 0 7553 2779 9

headline